Lady Georgiana Fullerton

The Life of Luisa de Carvajal

Lady Georgiana Fullerton

The Life of Luisa de Carvajal

ISBN/EAN: 9783337331023

Printed in Europe, USA, Canada, Australia, Japan

Cover: Foto ©Raphael Reischuk / pixelio.de

More available books at **www.hansebooks.com**

THE LIFE OF
LUISA DE CARVAJAL.

BY

LADY GEORGIANA FULLERTON.

LONDON:

BURNS AND OATES, PORTMAN STREET

AND PATERNOSTER ROW.

1873.

✠

THIS LIFE OF ONE
WHO WAS CONTENT TO LEAVE HOME AND COUNTRY
AND TO COURT MARTYRDOM
FOR THE SAKE OF MINISTERING
TO THE AFFLICTED CATHOLICS OF ENGLAND
IN THEIR DAY OF PERSECUTION,
IS DEDICATED
TO THE HEIRS OF THEIR NAME AND RELIGION,
WHO, UNDER GENTLER LAWS
AND IN MORE TOLERANT TIMES,
ARE STILL THE OBJECTS OF PREJUDICE AND CALUMNY,
AND WHO HAVE NEED
OF THE HIGHEST CHRISTIAN VIRTUE
NOT TO DEGENERATE FROM THE EXAMPLE
OF THEIR ANCESTORS,
AND TO MAINTAIN, AGAINST THE SEDUCTIONS OF THE
WORLD
AND THE SCOFFS OF INFIDELITY,
THE PURITY OF THE FAITH
WHICH IS THEIR NOBLEST INHERITANCE.

✠

PREFACE.

THE sufferings of English Catholics in the sixteenth and seventeenth centuries, and the detailed accounts of the persecutions they endured, are gradually coming to light. History kept a long and deceitful silence on the subject. Some years ago, well informed and highly educated persons, happening to look into Challoner's *Records of Missionary Priests*, would have been astonished at the contents, and at the number of touching and tragical incidents connected with the lives and deaths of the adherents of the ancient faith in our country. This, however, is no longer the case—not, at least, to the same degree. The recent publication of authentic private biographies, as well as of State papers, and the increasing willingness to give a hearing to testimony at variance with the old Protestant tradition, which has so long governed not only English literature, but English history, are beginning to take effect, and to rescue from oblivion the memories of our English martyrs and confessors.

The autobiography of Father Gerard, S.J., has revealed new evidence of the spiritual magnificence of an epoch of which we have hitherto known so little; names once strange to us are becoming familiar to our ears; an intimacy, such as exists between the living and the dead in all ages of the Church, when personal details are handed down which enable the former to make to themselves friends of the latter, more really present in their daily life, more closely united to their hearts, than many even of those they may be seeing every day, is beginning to establish itself between us and those saintly men to whom we owe so deep a debt of gratitude. Their very features are made known to us, thanks to the reproduction of portraits carefully preserved in religious houses. Sanctuaries are raised in their honour, and ardent hopes entertained that the Church ere long will place them on her altars.

Amidst that group of holy priests and devoted religious, of indefatigable missionaries and devout women, who kept alive the faith in England during those glorious and terrible days, one humble and gentle figure has remained yet more unnoticed than those of the fellow labourers and sufferers with whom her lot was cast. It is that of a delicate, high born, timid lady—timid by nature, valiant through grace—a foreign flower (as the writers of that day would have said),. transplanted in an English soil; the daughter of a wealthy and noble Spanish house, linked by no one tie with our country except that of a passionate desire,. growing at last into an irresistible vocation, to labour for the salvation of souls in England.

The name of Doña Luisa de Carvajal y Mendoza is all but unknown in the land where she spent nine years in the exercise of every spiritual and temporal work of mercy towards her persecuted brethren in the faith, and died a victim, if not a martyr, to her apostolic zeal. The time seems arrived to tell the story of her wonderful life of love, penance, and toil; to study its details, and see how grace overcame the weakness of nature, and by a providential training, prepared this chosen soul for the exercise of an extraordinary charity, leading her even in childhood to shadow forth, by a series of austerities and voluntary sufferings, the cross she was so bravely to carry in her maturer years. It was a strange vocation that brought a Spanish maiden, reared in all the grandeur and state befitting her rank, and keenly alive to the 'point of honour,' as her biographer calls it—the sensitive pride of a chivalrous race—to dwell in a wretched abode in the dark streets of London, to haunt its prisons with her gentle presence, to stand at the foot of its scaffolds, cheering the dying, and burying the dead, with the finger of scorn pointed at her, and the hootings of the rabble dogging her footsteps, to reach, at last, a dungeon, from whence she issued only to linger on a bed of sickness, and die amongst strangers, far away from the sunny land of her birth. Soon after her death, in 1614, the process of Luisa de Carvajal's canonization was set on foot at Rome; miracles wrought in favour of those who invoked her, the efficacy of her relics, and the heroic sanctity of her life and death, were abundantly attested, but for some unknown reason, the progress of the cause was not actively pursued, and since that time a sort of oblivion has been permitted to steal over the memory of this gentle saint.

The materials of the present biography are drawn from the Spanish work entitled, *Vida y virtudas de la venerable Virgen Doña Luisa de Carvajal y Mendoça, su jornada a Inglaterra, y sucessos en aquel reyno*, published at Madrid in 1632 by 'el licenciado Luis Munoz,' with a dedication to the King of Spain. A letter in the Appendix of this volume will show that Munoz derived the information which enabled him to draw a complete picture of this saintly woman, and to furnish so many details regarding her interior dispositions and her spirit of prayer, from the most authentic possible sources—her own secret memoirs, and the statements of her confessors.

G. F.

London, Feast of St. Ignatius, 1873.

CONTENTS.

PART THE FIRST.

PART THE SECOND.

Contents. XV

CHAPTER I.

Parentage, Birth, and Childhood of Doña Luisa.

THE parents of Doña Luisa de Carvajal y Mendoza belonged to the most ancient nobility of Spain. Her father, Don Francisco de Carvajal y Vargas, and her mother, Doña Maria de Mendoza y Pacheco, were not only descended from an illustrious line of ancestry, but were also connected by marriage with families of noble and even royal lineage. Their wealth was proportionate to their rank. They had large possessions in the rich province of Estremadura, and were held in general estimation. Their habitual place of residence was Xaraizejo, a town in the neighbourhood of Placentia and the seat of the bishop of that city. It was there in her ancestral home that was born the child whose Life, written in Spanish in 1632, is now for the first time presented to English readers.

Don Francisco is described by his daughter's biographer as a grave, pious, and studious nobleman, endowed with an excellent understanding and a more than ordinary amount of learning. He was especially proficient in the Greek and Latin languages, and in every respect an accomplished scholar. As to his wife, Maria de Mendoza, she seems to have been one of those women whom we should naturally expect to be blessed with saintly children, for her life was a daily example and lesson of all the Christian virtues ; modest, truthful, and

B

kind, even as a child; dignified and reserved, though sweet and gentle in manner, there seemed to be in her character a natural inclination towards goodness. Her extreme unworldliness led people to say that she would probably have been a nun if she had not married early in life. This was, however, a gratuitous supposition, for the perfect manner in which she fulfilled the duties of a Christian matron, gives no reason to infer that she had not found her true vocation. Be that as it may, her whole life was sanctified, especially during its closing years, by the continual exercise of charity, as well as by incessant prayer. Food was prepared every day in her house for the poor, and she went about with her children and her servants distributing meat and bread to those of her neighbours who were in need of assistance. If any of them were ill, whether dependents of her house or strangers, she used to slip out at dark, with a single attendant, to visit them, carrying with her a basket of biscuits and all sorts of delicacies and comforts requisite for sick persons.

The old spirit of Christian reverence for the poor was so deeply implanted in her heart that she loved to bring them into the palace on cold winter days to make them sit down on the velvet cushions of her saloon and warm their shivering limbs by the blazing fire of her hearth. There was, likewise, something touching in her reverential behaviour to priests. In both cases it was our Blessed Lord Whom she honoured in the persons of His representatives and servants. Whenever in the street she met a priest, whether she knew him or not, her head was humbly bowed down to salute him even if he was walking another way and did not notice her. In her oratory, which was the delight of her life, Doña Maria spent many hours every day. The Presence of our Lord on the altar was ever present to her mind. When she received tidings of joy or of sorrow her first impulse was always to hasten to the nearest church and fall on her knees before the Blessed Sacrament, whether to acknowledge God's mercies with heartfelt gratitude or to adore His blessed will in the hour of affliction.

It does not always happen that all the virtues of holy persons are particularly appreciated by their own immediate relatives. But, in the case of Doña Maria de Mendoza, those who lived habitually with her seem to have been fully sensible of her extraordinary goodness. Her only brother, the Marquis of Almaçan, who eventually became a father and a guide to his young niece, Doña Luisa, used often to tell her in after days that she owed her birth to the best woman that ever lived, and when she made progress in piety and virtue, he encouraged her by saying—'You will be the living image of your good mother.'

Doña Maria had five sons, only one of whom lived beyond childhood. She passionately wished for a daughter, and offered up ardent prayers for this object. She also asked those of many great servants of God, and had special recourse to St. Peter of Alcantara, that model of austere sanctity. He assured her that God would grant her petition, and in gratitude for the expected blessing she made a vow that if her daughter wished to be a nun she would give her to God to serve Him in a cloistered order. No doubt the offering was accepted, but in a different way from that which the pious mother contemplated. She could not foresee what a singular vocation was in store for the child she had so longed for. It would almost seem as if St. Peter of Alcantara's shadow had fallen on Doña Luisa's path ; himself a martyr of penance, it was perhaps his prayers and his example that led her to a love of suffering, felt and acted up to through a life which ended by a slow

martyrdom. Her first years, however, were spent in
happiness by her loving mother's side. Few details of
that period of her life are recorded; but as far as they
go they indicate strength of character and an early bias·
towards the heroic virtues she was one day to practise.
For instance, when only four years of age she met with
a severe accident; her forehead was cut open, and with
her face streaming with blood she walked up to her
mother as quietly as if nothing had happened, and
though the wound was so bad a one as to be considered
dangerous, neither before the surgeon came nor whilst
he was dressing it did she cry or complain, though
Doña Maria and everyone in the house were in consternation. The cut was so deep that she bore all her
life the white mark of it on her forehead.

Sometimes, even before the age of reason, virtuous
instincts are apparent in children which seem to presage
future sanctity; a singular reserve and modesty, for
instance, the meaning of which they can neither explain
or understand, but which comes to them as a direct
gift from God. This was the case to the highest degree
with little Doña Luisa. She could not bear the least
approach to familiarity even from her nearest relatives.
A marked respect for truth also characterized her very
early. When quite a little child she heard one of the
maids say to her mother, in reference to something she
had stated, 'Don't believe her; she is only a baby,
and may be telling stories.' The little thing drew herself
up, and said with great gravity, 'No; the baby never
tells stories.' And in fact she was never known to do so.

Another trait of character was her dislike to company.
In such a large house as her father's there was necessarily
a great concourse of visitors, and this did not please the
little lady. She used to say to her attendants, 'I think
my mother is very easygoing (*lhana*) to let so many

people come and see her; when I am big I shall not
let them pay me so many visits.' As to fine dresses
and ornaments, she could not abide the sight of them;
it was always a struggle between Doña Luisa and her
nurse when the latter wanted her to put on one of her
smart frocks. Doña Maria liked her to be sometimes
richly attired, and fine clothes were therefore provided
for these occasions, but she generally preferred to see
her child dressed in a little habit of St. Francis, which
had been made on purpose for her. She intended to
place her at the age of ten in a convent of that order,
with the hope that her heart would incline to the religious
life. In the meantime she had the happiness to see her
inherit all her own love of the poor. She was continually
asking for money to give them. The servants complained
of her constant requisitions for her dear beggars, but
Doña Maria only laughed, and always allowed her to
follow her charitable impulses. Often when she was put
into her soft warm bed, the little girl sighed bitterly over
the miseries of those who were shivering out of doors
without bed, house, or shelter. Her greatest pleasure
was to gather around her as many poor children of her
own age as she could, and, seated in the midst of this
ragged assembly, to distribute to them sugarplums and
other things to eat. If she could manage to be alone
with her little friends, she produced a box filled with her
own toys and playthings and gave them all away. Her
mother had made her a present of a small chest with a
silver padlock which was easily unfastened. In this box
she kept all the money her father gave her, every penny
of which went to the poor, especially to the poor prisoners,
for whom she had a special compassion. The servants
used sometimes to take away and hide some of her
money for the sake of watching the funny and charming
manner with which she puzzled over her little accounts,

when she missed what they had taken away. Even as a little child she was always anxious to screen others from reproach. If there was anything lost or broken in the house and her mother questioned her on the subject, she would not name the delinquent, but simply said, 'I do not remember having done it.' Her intelligence was remarkable. When Doña Maria and her housekeeper were closeted together talking over household affairs, she gave her opinion upon them with as much gravity as if she had been grown up. If sent away to her toys she soon returned and joined again in the conversation. Her mother used to laugh and say, 'Here comes Luisica to tell us what she thinks, and to put her little spoon into the dish.' A refined Spanish version, be it observed, of the English corresponding proverb.

There was an elderly duenna in Don Francisco's house, greatly respected by his wife and himself for her faithful services and many virtues. This Isabel Aillon, whose temper was not very gentle, was the only person who scolded Doña Luisa. She did not however dislike her on that account. On the contrary, because she saw how much her parents wished it, she always showed her great affection and tried in every way to please her.

But the most remarkable feature in the early years of this delicately nurtured little girl was her strong bias to a life of poverty and austerity. When hardly four years of age she tried to imitate the discalced friars, for whom she had a special love and veneration ; with this view her great object when out of doors was to get rid of her shoes. She used to pretend there were pebbles in them, and when once they were off she refused to put them on again. At home, in the coldest weather, if she was left alone, both shoes and stockings were discarded, and she walked about the room delighted at the sight of her little bare feet. If any one came in she contrived by bending down to hide them under her frock. Whenever she met a barefooted friar, she ran to kiss his feet, and upon being asked one day by one of her cousins who was a religious of some other order why she did not also kiss his feet, her answer was, 'The feet of the discalced are made of gold.'

The foregoing details relate to the first six years of Doña Luisa's life, and they are all that have reached us. But those of her confessors to whom she revealed most of the secrets of her conscience, affirm that our Lord manifested Himself to that holy little soul at an extraordinarily early age. In after days she used to speak with much feeling and tenderness of the way in which He had in the very morning of her life occupied her heart, so that since she had the use of reason it had been wholly devoted to Him. A child obtained by the prayers of a saint, and such a saint as St. Peter of Alcantara, one who at the age of six was so lovely, so engaging, and so pious, was a gift too precious to be long enjoyed on earth. Doña Maria must have often felt how frail was the tenure of her happiness. When people said she ought to moderate her passionate affection for her little girl, her answer was that her Luisica was not like other children, and deserved all the love she lavished upon her. Perhaps a fear that this treasure might be withdrawn sometimes crossed her mind. But it was not the child who was to be taken from the mother. God had a work for that child to do, one for which she was to be gradually prepared by an apprenticeship of suffering. With adoring parents by her side she would scarcely have gone through this severe schooling. A mother's love so full of tender worship might have stood between her and the fulfilment of her strange vocation. We can almost presume that it was in the plan of Divine Providence to sever that young heart so early claimed, so early given to Him, from the nearest and sweetest earthly ties.

The memory of those six happy years was all that was left to Doña Luisa of her childhood's happiness. A change in her father's position which suddenly removed him and his family from their native place, proved the signal for a still more important one in all their destinies—a most sad change, humanly speaking, for the young daughter of Maria de Mendoza, but the turning point, perhaps, in her spiritual life.

CHAPTER II.

Doña Luisa spends four years in the Royal Palace at Madrid.

KING PHILIP THE SECOND of Spain, a monarch whose character and acts it is difficult justly to appreciate, from the fact that they have been made by some writers the subject of exaggerated eulogiums and by others of passionate invectives, but who undeniably possessed considerable talents for government, was constantly on the look out for men of merit and ability equal to important administrative posts. He did not fail to discern the remarkable qualities of Don Francisco de Carvajal, and watched for an opportunity of turning them to account. Accordingly, in the year 1572, he named him chief magistrate or governor of the Corrigimiento of Leon. The sudden change from a mild climate like that of Placentia to a cold and mountainous region seriously affected the health of his little daughter. She was seized with an attack of quartan ague, at first not so violent but that she could sit up dressed on a little bed in her mother's room, but afterwards so severe that fears were entertained for her life. Doña Maria sat up night after night by her side, nursing her with unremitting devotion. The little girl gave proofs of extraordinary patience during this illness, especially on one occasion, when, the weather being intensely cold, a servant who was to sleep with her that night, in warming for herself part of the bed, severely burnt one of the legs of the little patient. Frightened at what she had done, and at the probable consequences of her carelessness, the girl hastily applied remedies, and implored the child not to scream or cry, as, if the accident were discovered, she would lose her place. With extraordinary self-command in one so young, Doña Luisa did not utter a sound, great as was the pain, and when, some time afterwards, her mother, happening herself to take off her stockings, saw the marks of the burns and questioned her about them, she could not be induced to say how the mischief had occurred.

Doña Maria was scarcely recovering from her anxiety about her daughter when she fell dangerously ill herself with a virulent disease called the spotted fever. She had caught it from a person she had nursed and laid out with her own hands—a work of mercy she had often performed before without injurious consequences. But now the moment had arrived when God chose to remove her from a world in which, during her short life of twenty-seven years, she had done much good and given holy examples. No details of her deathbed are on record, save the simple but significant fact that as she had lived so she died, having received with great piety the last sacraments and peacefully commending her soul to God. Don Francisco could not be prevailed upon to leave her side. He closed her eyes himself, and, awakened by this overwhelming sorrow to a deep sense of religion, he made up his mind to become a priest and lead a life of strict holiness. But ten days had not elapsed since his wife's death when he sickened with the same fever that had carried her off. He felt at once that his days were numbered, and prepared himself to appear before God. After making a general confession to the Superior of the Jesuits at Leon, he received the

Blessed Sacrament with an abundance of tears and great devotion, settled all his worldly affairs, and afterwards expired with sentiments that gave great hopes of his salvation to those who witnessed his end. As to Doña Luisa, thus left an orphan at little more than six years of age, it may well be said that when her father and mother left her the Lord took her under His care. If old enough to estimate at the time the extent of her loss, we may infer from what has been said of her early piety that she took refuge in that love which was to be henceforward her all in all.

Don Francisco bequeathed to his daughter a considerable fortune, and left directions that at ten years of age she should be placed in a convent, and remain there until old enough to choose herself her state of life, and in the meantime he wished her to be brought up in the house of his cousin, the Marquesa de Ladrada. In accordance with their father's will, Doña Luisa and her brothers, the eldest of whom was only ten years of age, were taken to Madrid, where their guardians resided. It so happened, however, that none of the anticipated arrangements were carried out. As soon as Doña Maria Chaçon, who was Doña Maria de Mendoza's aunt by her mother's side, heard of the orphaned condition of her little kinswoman she proposed to take charge of her. This lady, as governess to the young Prince Don Diego and lady of honour to the Infantas his sisters, held an important position at Court. Her son, Bernardo de Royas, Cardinal Archbishop of Toledo and Grand Inquisitor, was also high in favour with the King. It is therefore probable that the royal authority was exerted in her favour, and overruled any difficulties arising from Don Francisco's will. Indeed, had he been alive and able to decide the question, it is not likely that he would have rejected an offer which promised Doña Luisa the affectionate care of her mother's aunt, and as brilliant an education as he could have desired for her.

Doña Maria resided at that time with her royal charges in apartments belonging to Doña Juana of Portugal, which adjoined the convent of some discalced nuns. A door of communication existed between the two buildings, and Doña Luisa's little feet were often heard pattering along the cloisters, for she had several aunts and kinswomen in that monastery. But she remained under the immediate care of Isabel Aillon, even after her own admission into the palace. Her father on his deathbed had especially recommended her to this faithful, devoted, and severe duenna. He had warmly thanked Isabel for her care of his family, and proved his sense of it by committing to her charge the child of his love. Soon afterwards another attack of ague proved nearly fatal to Doña Luisa. On that occasion she said to her old friend that she would be very sorry to die so young, because then she could not make her will and leave her what she wished, but, nevertheless, she hoped she would pray for her soul and recommend her much to God, for she had been a very great sinner. She was then only about seven years of age, and her regard for this stern governess was the more remarkable that it proceeded from her knowledge of her sterling qualities and the regard her parents had felt for her, and not because she showed her any indulgence.

During her convalescence from this long illness, a sense of her orphaned condition, and grief at the loss of her parents, seemed to affect the little Doña Luisa more deeply than it had done before; she often stole into solitary corners and wept bitterly over their deaths. Not that she disliked her new home, or was insensible to Doña Maria's affection and kindness; she was much attached to her aunt, and very anxious to remain with her. As soon as her uncle, the Marquis of Almaçan,

who was then in Germany, heard of the deaths of his
sister and her husband, he hastened to write and request
that his young niece might be sent to his house in
Monteguado, to be brought up with his daughters, whom
he had left in Spain.

But Doña Maria Chaçon was not the least inclined
to part with her little kinswoman, of whom she was
passionately fond. Touched by her tears and sobs
when she was told of her uncle's letter, the kind old
lady caressed her tenderly and said, 'Do not grieve,
my child ; I will never consent to give you up.'

Doña Luisa continued to evince during her residence
in the royal palace the same good dispositions she had
manifested in her father's house, and to win all hearts by
her sweetness of temper and engaging qualities. She
always showed a spirit of tender compassion for the
sufferings of others. The severity with which criminals
were treated in Spain caused her great anguish. If she
caught sight of poor wretches whipped through the streets
for some offence, her tears flowed in abundance, and
with her eyes and hands lifted to heaven, she asked
how she could possibly help them. On one occasion
the punishment of a runaway slave affected her to such
a degree that she was made quite ill by it. Even to
hear the servant girls scolded gave her great pain. As
to the first bullfight she witnessed, it sent her right off
into a dead swoon. From that day, and to the end of
her life, this Spanish maiden abhorred that dreadful
national sport, which the author of her life describes
as an impious amusement which not only leads to the
shedding of blood, but sets at naught the Blood of
Christ, through the loss of many souls. He supports his
words by the authority of a saint. Luis Munoz goes on
to quote the eloquent expressions of St. Thomas of
Villanova, the great Archbishop of Valencia, preaching

on that subject on the feast of St. John the Baptist, a
day on which it was customary to hold these sanguinary
sports. 'How comes it to be tolerated in our Spain—
this brutal, this diabolical practice of bullfights? What,
I ask you, can be more brutal than to goad a beast to
kill a man? O horrid spectacle! O most cruel amusement! You look at a beast rushing on your fellow man,
on a fellow Christian! You see, not only his temporal
life, but his immortal soul exposed to imminent peril,
for generally speaking these men die in mortal sin. You
see this, and you take pleasure in it! How earnestly did
the Fathers of the Church, St. Chrysostom, St. Augustine,
St. Jerome, and others, strive to deliver the Church
from these atrocious pagan sports! They succeeded
in banishing them from every Christian land except
Spain. Spain alone retains this heathen practice, to
the ruin and destruction of numbers of souls; and
shall no voice be raised against it—will no one protest
against this enormity? Yes; though my words may
have no effect, I will be true to my conscience. I will
not endanger my soul and yours by a cowardly silence.
I here solemnly declare to you, in the name of Jesus
Christ, that you who do this thing, or who consent to it,
or who when it is in your power do not prohibit it, not
only sin mortally, but are homicides in the eyes of God,
and that on the Day of Judgment the blood of those
slain by the beasts will be required at your hands; and
as to you who are spectators on these occasions, you
are by no means secure from the danger of mortal sin.
I will not venture to assert you commit it, and yet
St. Augustine's words on that point are very strong.
He says, "Men go to the hunt," a sport similar in
its nature to bullfights, "and they enjoy the sight!
Alas for them, if they do not repent. They will see
the Lord Jesus Christ one day, and it will be a sad

one for them!" This does not seem to imply venial sin only in the spectators of these fights. O holy Baptist, behold how they celebrate—ah, rather, how they profane—your festival with their unholy sports!' Thus, Munoz adds, did that great theologian venture to condemn what no long established usage and no apparent toleration can reconcile with the maxims of the saints.

To return to our little saint, whose pious feelings as well as her compassionate nature led her to shrink from a diversion which has so long been a disgrace to her noble country, we find her as devoted to the poor in Madrid as in her native town. She had not so many opportunities of exercising her charity as in her mother's life time, but she never lost an opportunity of doing so. When the Brothers of Anton Martin, a religious confraternity that begged alms for the poor, came to the palace, she used to take from them the bag they carried with them, and, slinging it on her shoulder, went into all the ladies' rooms and the offices collecting alms for their clients. Her piety, likewise, increased with her years. Her governess taught her a great many prayers, which she repeated with as much fervour and recollection as if she actually saw our Blessed Lord standing before her. She eagerly seized every occasion of going to confession. When a priest came to the confessional in the oratory of the Infantas she would instantly run to get her veil. The Señora Aillon sometimes refused to give it her, there being no necessity, she said, to confess so often, but on that point the little lady would have her way; she covered her head with the skirt of her frock, slipped away to the chapel, and satisfied her devotion. One of the Jesuit Fathers was her habitual confessor, and from that time dated her lifelong devotion to the Society of Jesus.

The attention with which she listened to the conver-sations of grown-up people, when they related to important and interesting subjects, greatly helped to form her mind and to store her memory with useful information. Before she attained the age of ten the superiority of her intellect and her powers of observation attracted much notice. Whilst so many young persons would have acquired in a palace a taste for gaiety and splendour, and high ideas of the importance of wealth, rank, and earthly honours, the orphan daughter of Maria de Mendoza seemed to gain in the midst of luxury and pomp a daily increasing contempt of the world, a deeper devotion, a more shrinking modesty, and a greater esteem of poverty.

Doña Maria Chaçon was so struck with the promise of eminent virtue which she saw in Doña Luisa, that she said one day to her daughter, Madalena de Ragos, a nun in the royal convent of San Domingo, ' Mark well that little girl. A day will come when her relatives will have reason to be proud of her.'

The Infantas were very fond of Doña Luisa, and wanted her to be always with them. On the other hand, the little Prince Don Diego was equally anxious for her company, and this sometimes gave rise to disputes between them. She was in fact a general favourite with every one. There was not a lady in the palace who did not caress and make much of the orphan girl, who would have been glad indeed to remain at Madrid, especially as her governess earnestly wished it. But Providence ordained otherwise. After four years spent under the protection of her excellent aunt, Doña Maria Chaçon, the death of that lady brought about a sudden change in Doña Luisa's life, and removed her to a distant place and a new home.

CHAPTER III.

Doña Luisa's residence at Monteguado and Almaçan.

DONA LUISA was about eleven years of age when her aunt Doña Maria Chaçon died, leaving behind her the reputation of a great servant of God. In consequence of this event, her guardians considered that the moment was come to comply with the request of her uncle the Márquis of Almaçan, and to consign her to his care. With the consent of Don Bernardo de Royas, Doña Maria's son and executor, this proposal was soon carried into effect. The young girl, with her governess, under the escort of one of Don Bernardo's chaplains and another priest who was tutor to her brothers, and accompanied by several servants, travelled from Madrid to Monteguado, the home of her uncle, where she was received in his name by Pedro Gonçalez de Mendoza, and introduced to her two cousins, the marquis' young daughters, with whom she was to be educated. They all stayed there some months, during which time she learned to write, and spent her time in various occupations suitable to her age, remaining, however, under the special care of her own governess. We give that name to the good woman who had charge of her, because there is no English word that answers to that of *aya* and conveys an idea of the position held by such a person in a Spanish family of those days. Though not in one sense above the rank of a servant, her authority over the children was sometimes prolonged till

c

they were of an age to be married. Their education, apart
from the teaching they received from masters, was often
confided to the *aya*, and in Doña Luisa's case this seems
to have been particularly the case. Isabel Aillon was both
a virtuous and a clever woman; she had constantly before
her eyes Don Francisco de Carvajal's dying recommendations, and she made it a point of conscience to cultivate
to the utmost his daughter's good dispositions. The finest
diamond, she used to say, requires careful polishing. We
shall find that her ideas of polishing were somewhat stringent, but it would seem that the extreme severity which
might have had bad effects on a weaker, less truthful, or
less amiable character than Doña Luisa, served only to
perfect her in goodness, and to teach her patiently to
endure suffering.   Isabel Aillon watched her charge with
the most incessant care, taking heed of every little minute
detail that could conduce to habits of self-control, to
purity of mind, and reserve of manner.   She never
allowed her to be dressed or undressed by any one but
herself, taught her to compose herself to sleep with her
arms crossed devoutly on her breast, and to observe in
every gesture and every act the most scrupulous modesty.
She was equally careful as to her words, never suffering
her to use any expression bordering on freedom or levity,
or to swear in play as children often do.[1]   If in her
presence any one said or did anything in the least
improper she led her away and spoke to her in the
strongest way of the horror that such actions should
inspire.   Gentleness and courteousness both in speech
and in manners she also insisted upon, and was very
sharp in her reproofs of laziness; if Doña Luisa leant
back in her chair she was certain of a scolding, and to
be asked what more she would do when she was eighty

---

[1] This probably refers to such expressions as 'by Jove,' 'by Bacchus,'
or the like.

years of age. Gossiping was also strictly forbidden.
'Learn to hold your tongue,' the prudent governess
would say, 'and be the last to speak of anything that
goes on in the house.' As to books, she would never let
her read any that were not edifying. If it came to her
knowledge that romances or tales of chivalry were being
read aloud in any room where she was she would start
up as if the house were on fire, and leaving her work, fetch
her away and give her some holy book to read instead.
There were no virtuous sentiments she did not inculcate,
or pious habits she did not enforce on this child, whom
her whole object was to bring up in the most perfect
manner possible. She trained her to be very patient
with her companions, never to give hasty answers, however much provoked ; to be invariably attentive and
devout at Mass and in sacred places ; and kept up in
her heart the desire to serve God in the persons of the
poor. She often said that she would have to render an
account to God of Doña Luisa's education, and would
spare no effort to acquit her conscience. She appears
at any rate not to have spared the rod, for Luis Munoz
relates that black and blue marks on the little girl's neck
and arms often gave evidence of the severe manner in
which she was punished for the most trifling faults.

People complained of this as cruelty, and called the
aya 'that terrible woman;' they thought it too bad that
Doña Luisa should be so treated by one who after all
was only a servant. But her good sense, even at so early
an age, made her value the training she received at the
hands of this stern old friend. The only complaint she
was ever known to make was once when she was between
seven and eight years of age, being violently scolded for
some little carelessness, she lifted up her hands and eyes
to heaven and said, 'Aillon wants to eat me up alive.'
But she was tenderly attached to her governess, could

C 2

not endure to be separated from her, or to hear a single
word said against her.

From Monteguado, Doña Luisa went with her cousins
to Almaçan, to meet her uncle, the marquis, on his arrival
from Germany.   She received him with tears of joy.   It
was as if she foresaw all that he was to be to her from
that time forward.   From the first moment he also showed
his little niece great affection, and noticed several things
in her which gave him much pleasure, but he remained
then only a short time at home, having to hasten to Court
to give an account of his embassy.

Doña Luisa remained at Almaçan with her aunt and
her cousins, improving her time in different ways.   She
learned to write and to sum, and by the marchesa's
desire, studied also the rudiments of Latin.   In their
leisure hours, her young cousins and herself strolled in
the woods and fields, and along the beautiful banks of
the Douro.   The lovely scenery of that delightful place
was enlivened by a prodigous quantity of game, herds of
deer wandered about the shady glens, and hares, rabbits,
and birds of every sort started at every turn out of the
thickets and bushes or ran across the green paths of this
smiling wilderness.   But the favourite amusement of the
young ladies of the castle was to play at being nuns.
They contrived sundry imitations of choirs, grates, and
cells, and moreover regularly sang office.   In her intercourse with her cousins and other persons in the house,
Doña Luisa conducted herself with a prudence and
discretion beyond her years.   Though her aversion to
foolish words, light songs, and levity of manner, daily
increased, she knew how to show that dislike without
giving offence.   By degrees more and more of her
time was occupied in prayer, especially in fervent
meditations on the Passion of our Lord, which began
then to take a deep hold on her soul.   She persuaded

one of her cousins, a child of her own age, to join in these devotions.

It was on the feast of our Lady's Nativity, in the Church of St. Michael at Almaçan, that Doña Luisa made her first communion. She was then eleven years old. So intense was her appreciation of the divine gift she was about to receive that a sudden trembling came over her as she ascended the steps of the altar. The fear of the Lord seems to have filled her young heart even in child-hood. She was constantly musing on the thought of eternity and speaking of it to her cousins. 'If we could add to a thousand years, ten thousand more,' she used to say, 'we should not be nearer to the end, no not if we could heap millions on millions of years.'

Even in this, on the whole, happy home trials were not wanting to the orphan girl. The marchesa was 'an excellent woman—pious, kind hearted in the main, and very good to the poor. She always took her daughters and her niece to church with her on festivals and holy-days, not only to high mass and procession, but also to vespers and the singing of the *Salve Regina.* Daily mass they of course attended in the chapel of the castle. Whenever the Blessed Sacrament was carried to a sick person in the town of Almaçan, she accompanied It through the streets on foot, and did not come away until It was replaced in the tabernacle. On all the festivals she made it also a point to visit the sick in the hospitals and to take them presents of food and various little gifts.

Doña Luisa was always with her on these occasions. But with all her merits this good lady had a trying temper, and this being the case it is not very wonderful that she and her niece's *aya* could not get on together. She took a dislike to 'that terrible woman.' This was perhaps natural, but it was hard to visit on Doña Luisa the faults she found with her governess. Between them both the poor child must have had a difficult part to play. Her aunt often gave her cold looks and sharp words which she was not conscious of having deserved. But she bore all with perfect sweetness, was always respectful and submissive, never murmuring when reproved, never putting herself forward or speaking to her when she saw she was not in the humour for it, but always on the watch to fly at the first word to do her bidding. The marchesa was by no means insensible to this conduct on the part of her niece, and though often ungracious in her manner to her, would as often praise her very warmly to others.

Doña Luisa had also much to suffer from a person high in authority in the house, who took at that time a violent dislike to her. It rose at last to such a pitch that one day as she was coming out of her room, this woman not only abused but struck her several times. She stood still, looked at her in her little quiet way, and said, with a smile, 'Are you satisfied now that you have put me in a passion? What a fine thing you have done!' The aggressor, whose object it really had been to make her angry, stood confounded; she owned in after years that what had enraged her was to see that little girl always so good, so charming, so sensible, and every one loving and praising her.

The Marquis of Almaçan had to remain two years at Court. At the end of that time he was named Viceroy of Navarre, and sent for his family to join him at Pampeluna, the seat of his government. Doña Luisa was then thirteen years of age. As her uncle became from that time not only a second father to her, but also in a great measure her model and her guide in spiritual matters, it will not be amiss to give some account of his life and the qualities for which he was eminently distinguished. Allowing for some exaggeration in Luis Munoz's enthusiastic description of his virtues, there remains every reason to believe that Don Francisco Hurtado de Mendoza, Count of Monteguado, first Marquis of Almaçan, and son of Count Juan, commonly called the Saint, was a thoroughly Christian statesman, an honest, energetic, uncompromising man, whose religious principles governed all his actions, and regulated every detail of his public as well as his private life ; one who was not less successful in governing others because he governed himself, and did not rule a province the worse for the hours he spent in communion with his own Lord and Master. During the years that young men generally devote to frivolities he indefatigably pursued his studies, and preserved through life an ardent thirst for knowledge. His reputation as a theologian and a scholar caused him to be chosen at the age of thirty-three by King Philip the Prudent, as his admirers call him, to represent his Catholic Majesty at a provincial council at Salamanca. This post must have required zeal, learning, and discretion. Subsequently he went as his Ambassador to the Court of the German Emperor Maximilian, and remained there seven years, rendering important services to both sovereigns and promoting on every occasion the interests of religion. At his return he was made a privy councillor, and at the end of two years Viceroy of Navarre.

Luis Munoz says of him—' The Marquis of Almaçan's appearance was that of a prince, noble and dignified, and at the same time gentle, courteous, and kind. He had a most generous heart and forgiving disposition, which he showed towards enemies, from whom he had much to suffer. There was no labour he did not gladly undertake in order to reconcile persons at variance, often taking long journeys and sparing no efforts for that purpose. In the province which he governed so long and so well, he strove hard to suppress immorality and public scandals.

'His own palace offered the most edifying examples, and with the assistance of his excellent wife he promoted in every way the respect due to religion and the practice of good works. Whatever time he could spare from public business was devoted to prayer, to the study of the Holy Scriptures, the writings of the Fathers, and books of mystical theology. He spoke with great power and unction on spiritual subjects, especially on whatever related to the Person, history, and character of our Divine Lord. He not only understood but could converse fluently in Latin, and composed in that language, as well as in Spanish, some beautiful devotional poetry. His voice in singing was remarkably fine, and sometimes when alone with his children he sang with them the Psalms of King David, of whom he was in many respects a faithful imitator. Every day he spent some hours in his oratory, pouring forth his soul before God in ardent supplications and with so many tears that at one time there was danger of his eyesight being impaired. His penances were severe and frequent. On the eve of the days he went to communion it was his custom to fast rigorously, to watch half the night, and to discipline himself so severely that his shoulders often streamed with blood.

'To all good people he was a father, to priests and religious a constant friend, but above all others he loved and honoured the Jesuit Fathers. Doña Luisa imbibed from him that devotion to the Society of Jesus of which she gave so many proofs.'

It is not wonderful, judging from these details, that this Spanish nobleman's house should have proved a school of sanctity. His children grew up more than ordinarily holy. His only son, Don Francisco, followed in the footsteps of his father. When Viceroy of Catalonia he practised in secret the austerities of a monk, received holy communion every day, and was looked upon as a saint. The two daughters of the Marquis, Doña Luisa's companions in childhood, became models of virtue. The eldest, Isabel de Velasco, and her husband, the Marquis of Caracena, gave eminent examples of piety in the world, and Francesca, the youngest, lived and died a nun in the Convent of Discalced Carmelites at Madrid. 'But,' exclaims Luis Munoz, 'the chief jewel in the crown of that saintly and noble house was doubtless our Doña Luisa, the niece of the Marquis of Almaçan, or rather the chosen child of his heart. She grew up by his side like a choice plant cultivated by a skilful gardener. Through his direction and his teaching, the gifts with which nature and grace had endowed her expanded like flowers in a soil daily watered by the refreshing dews of heaven, and ended by producing the fruits of sanctity which her future life was to show forth.'

CHAPTER IV.

Doña Luisa's Girlhood and Youth.

IT was in Pampeluna—the old Spanish city, on whose ramparts, fifty-eight years before, St. Ignatius had fought against the French with the same courage and indomitable resolution with which he was afterwards to fight the battles of Christ, and where he received the wound which brought about his conversion and ultimately the foundation of the Society of Jesus—that in 1579 began the holy intimacy between the Viceroy of Navarre and his young niece, which was only to end with his life. Those two souls, to use a common expression, took to each other at once. Both felt what God had given each in the other, and entered on this friendship, he with the spirit of a father and a spiritual guide, and she with the submissive and tender feelings of a grateful child. The Marquis of Almaçan quickly discerned in Doña Luisa a capacity for more than ordinary virtue, a strength of will and an ardent desire of perfection which bade fair for future sanctity. He resolved to do his utmost to conduct and urge her along the road that leads to those sacred heights. He applied himself to this task with a keen insight into what she was capable of understanding, of enduring, and of achieving, and used exceptional means towards this end, which could only have succeeded with a soul of so rare a stamp. On her side, she conceived an unbounded love and veneration for her uncle. He

filled in her heart the place of her deceased parents, and
of her *aya*, whom she lost about this time, after having
been for seven years subjected to her severe rule. She
found no difficulty in obeying the marquis. Any little
defects in her conduct which he took notice of were
instantly corrected. Her faults were few and slight,
and after the age of fifteen they entirely disappeared.
Once when she was about thirteen, she and some other
children with whom she was playing took some sugarplums out of a box belonging to one of her cousins.
The culprits were detected and pleaded guilty. The
marquis turned to Doña Luisa and said, 'What had
become of your discretion,[1] my child, when you did
this?' This mild reproof cut her to the heart. She
shed torrents of tears, and to the end of her life accused
herself often in confession of this and a few other childish
offences, weeping bitterly over them, and considering
them as grievous sins. Her confessors have stated their
conviction that she was never guilty of a mortal sin, and,
as far as is possible for a fallen creature, that she kept
her baptismal innocence unstained by wilful sin or
deliberate imperfections.

Her extraordinary delicacy of conscience was preparing her for the reception of singular graces, the effects of
which soon became visible in her life. Charity to the
poor had been habitual, we might almost say instinctive,
with her from her earliest childhood, but she now began
to look upon it in a more religious light, not as the mere
gratification of natural feelings of compassion which find
delight in relieving suffering and giving pleasure, but as
the means by which Jesus Christ chooses that those who
love Him should testify that love. This thought was
constantly before her, and she felt an intense desire to

[1] The Spanish word *cordura* answers to the French word *sagesse*, and
has no exact counterpart in English.

give her Lord some great mark of affection. In this state of mind she opened one day the Life of St, Francis of Assisi, and found that he had bound himself by vow never to refuse what was asked of him 'for the love of God.' The intention of that vow only referred to alms-giving, but the Saint's young imitator resolved to make one which should extend to whatever any one asked her to do in the name and for the love of God. She accordingly went into her uncle's oratory, and kneeling down before the crucifix offered up that vow with great fervour and humility. It appears to have been done on the impulse of the moment. Her uncle never heard of it ; she does not appear to have previously consulted her confessor. It was probably one of those acts which, though imprudent in themselves, are sometimes blest on account of the simplicity of heart and pure intention which has prompted them. Generally speaking, vows made without due deliberation and the sanction of an experienced spiritual adviser are very dangerous to souls, and a fruitful source of mental trials and temptations. Even Doña Luisa suffered from doubts and scruples regarding the extent and exact fulfilment of hers. She was obliged to have recourse to her confessor to solve these difficulties. For instance, when on festival days she went to church with her aunt, a crowd of beggars at the door were sure to beg for alms 'for the love of God,' as was their wont. She responded to the cry as long as she had any money in her purse, but then came the question, did her vow oblige her to part with her gloves, her handkerchief, her fan, or anything else she carried with her? On one occasion she did give away a beautiful pair of perfumed gloves. Her confessor, however, decided that she was not to give anything but money on these occasions, and only carry with her the amount she could properly bestow in charity.

A vow which would have been intolerable and even injurious to ordinary persons, proved of great use to so perfect a soul. She observed it strictly to thè end of her life, and found it a stimulus to incessant activity and zeal. She owned to one of her confessors that she was often astonished at the end of the year to see how many things she had undertaken and accomplished under the pressure of the stringent obligation which like a secret spring governed her actions.

Until she was of age and could dispose of her own fortune, Doña Luisa's means of assisting the poor were very limited ; her allowance was always spent upon them, but it did not enable her to satisfy even a small part of the wants she was anxious to relieve. Necessity being the mother of invention—and it was indeed a necessity to her to multiply her alms—she had recourse to a plan which had the merit of combining abstinence with charity. This was to support one and subsequently two poor persons by depriving herself every day of a portion of her own sustenance. She dined at her uncle's table with all the family and a numerous household, and generally began her meal with a basin of broth, into which she kept throwing small pieces of bread and eating them slowly, whilst the platefuls which the servants brought her were dexterously made over to a page, whom she had taken into her confidence, and who was always on the watch to receive these surreptitious supplies, which he afterwards carried to her poor people. The marquis was delighted with these stratagems, but not so the house steward, who felt indignant at seeing the food prepared for the viceregal table making its way out of the palace to the homes of the poor. The two persons thus assisted by Doña Luisa were, the widow of a soldier who had been left penniless, and a very old bedridden priest who lived opposite the Viceroy's residence. It

was for him she set aside the most delicate morsels, and
nothing would have induced her to touch anything that
she thought would please him.   When the marquis left
Pampeluna, which he was frequently obliged to do, in
order to visit other parts of the province, he always took
care to give orders that his niece was to have all she
wanted for the aged priest.   The practice she had
adopted—the Spanish writer calls it *a devotion*—was
imitated by degrees by all the members of the family.
First her cousins, and then her aunt, who was always
zealous for every good work, begun to set apart each
day a share of their food for some poor person.   Even
the marquis' son, and his son-in-law later on, had each
their *pobre* to whom they sent a part of their dinner.

Another of the pleasures of these Christian ladies, as
Luis Munoz calls them, was to take out of the streets
ragged little children of four or five years of age, and
carry them up to the rooms of some of the aged
duennas, where there was always a number of petticoats
and jackets, made out of the winter cloaks of the family
after the lace and fringes were cut off.   They dressed
the children from head to foot and sent them back to their
delighted parents.   Doña Luisa now began to exercise
also the spiritual works of mercy, gently and prudently
giving advice to the numerous women employed in the
palace.   But her happiest days of all were the Sundays
and festivals when the marchesa paid her wonted visits
to the hospital; she continued at Pampeluna what she
had always done at Almaçan, going regularly through the
sick wards and distributing to the sick basketsful of fruit,
biscuits, and other delicacies.   Doña Luisa always brought
with her on these occasions her own little store of provisions, carefully collected during the week.   During one
Lent she secreted every day her share of the sugared
lemon peel which formed part of the collation, and on

Easter Sunday one of the pages saw her keeping a
little behind the marchesa and slipping these sweetmeats
into the hands of the patients. He described this when
he came home, to the great amusement of the household.

The pleasure she took in all these charities was intense.
She used to wonder at the goodness of God, Who pro-
mises to reward what seemed to her so natural, and often
exclaimed, 'O my God, everything I have belongs to
the poor, and I belong to Thee. Is it possible that in
return for the perishable things that I give Thee, Thou
wilt give me Thy love?'

Once when she was travelling in the middle of the
winter, a man with nothing on but a few rags came up to
her as she was about to get into her litter, and implored
her for the love of God to give him something to protect
him from the cold. She had no money, and nothing with
her but the clothes she had on, still it made her miserable
to see him shivering and to go away without assisting
him, especially as he had begged her to do so *for the
love of God.* Suddenly she bethought herself of the
story of St. Martin, who, under the same circumstances,
had cut his cloak into two parts, and given half of it to a
beggar. No sooner was this thought of than done. Doña
Luisa was the next moment hiding behind a door and
cutting off with her scissors the lower part of her French
mantle. She reappeared with this treasure in her hand
and gave it to the beggar. The weather was so very
severe that day that she caught a bad cold. If she tried
the house steward's patience by her behaviour at meals,
she must have driven the ladies' maids nearly mad by her
treatment of her wardrobe. But her uncle only laughed
when these sort of grievances were brought to his notice.
These were early specimens of that ardent charity which
was to go on increasing with her years. Her devotion
to prayer kept pace with her love of the poor, and united

her every day more closely to her Divine Lord. By her
uncle's desire she soon began to practise mental prayer.
He wished her to devote at least one hour a day to this
holy exercise. It was in the evening that she generally
went to his oratory for this purpose, and if she was not
exact at the appointed time he always sent for her. In
the midst of his many occupations he contrived to find
leisure to give her the points of her meditations, which
were chiefly on the Passion of our Lord, on death, sin,
judgment, and hell. He bade her not make too great
efforts of mind, or too many reflections, but to content
herself with dwelling as long as possible on any one
thought that moved her to the love or the fear of God,
and to seek nothing else as long as peace and light filled
her soul ; when dulness and dryness made it hard to pray,
or drowsiness came over her, then she was to humble
herself before God, calmly driving away distractions and
fighting against sleep.

One of her favourite devotions at that time was a
prayer on the seven bloodsheddings of our Lord which
her governess had taught her to say on her rosary—
probably a set of the Franciscan beads, which are composed of seven decades, for the Circumcision, the Agony
in the Garden, the scourging, the crowning with thorns,
the tearing off of the sacred vestments, the Crucifixion,
and the piercing with the lance. She used to come out of
the oratory after these devotions with a heart softened by
tears and glowing with love, disposed for heroic efforts
and great sacrifices. Then began in that chosen soul a
strange conflict which throws light on her subsequent
career. By nature she had the keenest possible sense of
what is called by her biographer the *punto d'onor*, the
point of honour, the high-spirited sensitiveness of her
race. She was conscious of the antiquity and nobility
of her family, and daily witnessed in what estimation it

was held and what homage was paid to her own high
descent and her illustrious connections.. Human infirmity
led her to take pleasure in that consciousness and that
homage. This was the almost imperceptible stain that
was beginning to mar the purity of her heart. This was
the danger against which she had all her life to struggle ;
this it is that explains much of her future history. If we
find any saint eminent in the practice of some particular
virtue it is hardly rash to conjecture that it is the very
grace which he had to struggle most to acquire. St. Francis
of Sales, for instance, the gentlest of men, was by nature
hot and passionate. Once when his brother was wondering over the perfect sweetness with which he had listened
to a torrent of abuse poured forth against him, he said,
'You don't know what was going on within whilst the
exterior was so calm.' The extremes of humiliation to
which the daughter of the Carvajals and the Mendozas
subjected herself through life probably took their rise in
the aristocratic pride which she struggled to the death to
crush and to subdue.

At fifteen or sixteen years of age she began to be
intimately united to our Lord in prayer and to receive
lights from Him which filled her with contempt for mere
earthly happiness. Her uncle's teaching pointed to a
higher state of life than he actually proposed to her
acceptance. She pondered over the details of the
Passion till there arose within her something of that
burning desire for sacrifice and suffering, which when
it reaches to its utmost height, imprints on the hands
and feet and side of some chosen saints the Sacred
Wounds of our crucified Lord, and stamps a bleeding
crown upon their brows. She longed to abandon all
for God, but she cared so little for the things of this
world, that nothing of the sort seemed to her worth the
name of a sacrifice. The cloister or the desert would

D

have been welcome to her soul as the fountain of pure
water to the thirsting hart. She felt with a strength of
conviction that was more like actual vision than faith,
that to give up every human joy for Christ is gain and
not loss, even in this world, and she had a vague yearning
for something painful and laborious beyond what she
yet could conceive. This haunted her to a degree that
she sometimes wished she could sell herself to be a
slave.

When about seventeen, her constant meditation was on
the torments of the martyrs. To die for her dear Lord
seemed to her so sweet. 'He gave His life for me,' she
used to exclaim, with unbounded tenderness. 'Oh, that
I could give mine for Him!' This thought took such
possession of her, that she was apt to fall into fits of profound abstraction, in which it seemed to her that she was
going through the pains of martyrdom, and she remained
unconscious of the lapse of time. This happened once
on St. Lawrence's day. She was standing in the evening
at an open window, meditating on the flames in the midst
of which the saint had rejoiced. Hours went by before
she awoke from this sort of trance. The chill night air
caused an illness which gave her uncle great anxiety.
Prayer became gradually so habitual to her, that in every
place, and at all times, she lifted up her heart to God.
Sometimes, with her uncle's permission, she went and sat
in the garden of the palace. A beautiful one it probably
was in that lovely country, which unites the bright
verdure of a northern clime with the brilliant colouring
of the south. There, with the snow-capped mountains
in front of her, and the thousand beauties of that sunny
land at her feet, this young girl often covered her face
with a handkerchief, to exclude the earthly light from
her eyes, and rise in spirit to the contemplation of an
ineffable brightness. When walking in the country with

her cousins, by the river side, or in the woods, she often went apart into the most shady and retired spots, and rising from the sight of created beauty to the Creator, she dwelt on the thought of the Incarnate Word, and recalled with deep emotion how, in the solitude of the olive grove, He prayed to His Heavenly Father. If she could not go out of sight of her companions, she walked up and down to hide that she was praying. But it was only occasionally that she joined her cousins in their walks and recreations. Her uncle encouraged her to spend much of her time alone in her oratory. It is evident that he thought her called to a different life from theirs, and treated her accordingly. He wished her to avoid all species of distractions, and kept her as much as possible apart from the duennas and maids of the house; not that they were not all modest and good women, but he was always afraid lest the sort of conversation that goes on between persons not always very careful of what they say should mar in the least degree the singular purity of her mind and diminish her love of solitude and prayer. He kept her as much as possible with himself. If he was going out for some hours he often proposed to her to spend the time of his absence in his oratory or in her own room, and to secure her from interruption locked her up and took away the key with him. She had been watched and guarded through her childhood like a delicate flower, and he was jealous to maintain her in the midst of a large family and household in comparative seclusion, cutting off in this manner the occasions of small sins and imperfections, which easily crop up wherever a number of persons living together are perpetually retailing news, uttering complaints, and wasting time in various ways.

Doña Luisa's cousins naturally enough did not understand their father's views on the subject, and could not

D 2

see why she should be treated differently from themselves. They did not know that each soul is a little separate kingdom which requires special government; that distractions positively useful to certain natures may be to others an obstacle to perfection, and recreations innocent in themselves may prove dangerous snares to one whom God has called to tread a path on which it would be rash and perilous for another to venture. Therefore when Doña Isabel and Doña Francesca had asked leave to take out Doña Luisa with them, and the marquis answered that she could not go, that she had something to do at home, which they knew to mean that she would remain all the time in the oratory, they complained and told her that they considered it very hard that she should spend her youth in such a strange and solitary manner. She never made any reply, but a smile was on her face which showed that she did not think herself to be pitied. 'My child,' her uncle used to say to her, 'the less you converse with creatures, the more intimate you will become with God's angels and His saints.' And already she had found it so.

CHAPTER V

Early austerities.

IF it be true that different modes of treatment suit different souls, if solitude and abstinence from the ordinary recreations of life develope in some of God's chosen ones a higher sanctity than the generality of Christians are destined to attain, the same may still more truly be said of the austerities which in all ages of the Church have been practised, not only with a view to that filling up of the Passion of Christ, which St. Paul speaks of, not only in a devout spirit of reparation for sins forgiven, and yet mourned over by the penitent heart, but as a means of resemblance to our Blessed Lord ; a drawing nearer to Him in the way He chose for Himself on earth; a discipline by which the soul is prepared to receive His divine communications and raised to a perfect control and mastership over the senses. An attraction to severe dealings with themselves in innocent beings who have hardly committed a wilful sin is generally a sign that God has set them apart to do some great work for Him. It shows itself early ; it generates a thirst for penance incomprehensible to those who have never watched the wonderful effect of suffering on the spiritual life of man. This is a subject most difficult to treat in the presence of a puzzled, irritated, and disgusted world. It is one of those secrets of the heart with which the stranger inter-meddleth not, a miracle of constant recurrence in the

Catholic Church—strength, energy, and superhuman power springing out of the most crushing course of self-inflicted pains and privations ; joys intense beyond all earthly joys, out of the depths of humiliations and self-sacrifice ; poverty, penance, and prayer doing their strange work amongst men who shudder at their names but bow before their might.

The Spanish girl whose character we are describing gave very early proofs of that spirit of mortification which so often goes hand in hand with great achievements. She lived in an age and in a country where austerities were practised with extraordinary fervour. This kind of devotion seems to have particularly harmonized with the ancient character of a nation which combined great nobility and generosity of soul with a sternness sometimes amounting to cruelty in some of their customs, whilst in holy persons it tended to an uncompromising warfare with the lower part of their nature. Even their romantic sentiments found expression in voluntary sufferings. It is related that many a gallant courtier took pleasure in subjecting himself to strange inflictions in order to touch the heart of his lady love. Punishments were also more rigorous, and children and servants treated with a severity which in our days would be looked upon as inhuman. This partly accounts for the latitude which was given to Doña Luisa to practise at an early age extraordinary bodily penances. Even at that time it is probable that no young girl in England would have been allowed to inflict such sufferings on her tender frame as the Marquis of Almaçan encouraged his niece to endure. It must also be borne in mind that hers was no common character, and that neither her uncle nor her confessors judged her by ordinary rules.

We have already seen her depriving herself of food in order to assist the poor. She rigorously observed all

the fasts of the Church long before she had attained
the age when it is binding to do so, and voluntarily
fasted on the eves of the feasts of saints to whom she had
special devotion.   Her aunt used to make private agree-
ments with her on that point, and nothing gave Doña
Luisa greater pleasure than these pious proposals.   But
this was not enough to satisfy her thirst for this sort of
penance ; she had recourse to a variety of plans in order
to mortify her appetite and escape observation.   Sometimes she carried morsels of food to her mouth and
returned them to her plate without tasting them, or else
concealed them in her napkin.   Having read of a saint
who always abstained on the days when she went to
communion, she felt inspired to do the same, and
persevered in this practice a long time in spite of the
difficulty she found in it.   The festivals on which she
always communicated were precisely the days on which
great banquets were held at the palace, and it was not
easy to conceal that she eat nothing but a little fruit,
cheese, or salad ; especially as her cousins were always
on the watch.   If she tried to make it appear that she
was following her taste in this choice of food, they would
laugh and say, 'What an extraordinary fancy this cousin of
ours has for bad things (*malas cosas*).'   After awhile her
uncle made her give up this practice that she might not
appear singular.   To make up for it she began to curtail
her hours of sleep.   To her evening meditation a morning
one was added, and at first she found it very hard to
keep awake, but it was her wont to conquer such difficulties by strong measures, and we find her plunging her
hands in the middle of winter into freezing water, or
baring her knees on the cold stones in order to get the
better of drowsiness.   Her soft bed was the object of
Doña Luisa's special dislike.   She began by removing
every night one of its three mattresses, the thinnest and

hardest of them, to a summer couch composed of straps of leather, and making that her bed. But this soon appeared to her much too comfortable. The mattress was often discarded and lifted back into its place only in time to be seen when any one entered the room. A chance came in her way which she did not neglect. Her uncle having asked her one day to pack up for him some valuable books which he was going to send away, she bethought herself of unsewing her mattress and stealing from it the greatest part of the wool, in order to fill up with it the interstices in the cases. This succeeded perfectly; no one found out the trick, and her mattress turned out, of course, as uncomfortable as she could wish.

It is needless to enter into all the details of the numerous penances which Doña Luisa practised at an age when the sting of a wasp or the prick of a pin would draw tears to the eyes of most young girls. Whatever means saints have employed to keep nature in subjection and give the spirit mastery over the body, she was familiar with. Hair shirts, iron girdles, disciplines even to blood, she used, not by fits and starts, but steadily and perseveringly, never intermitting her austerities except in severe illness. She found these penitential exercises a help to prayer, to spiritual joy, and to humility of heart. Her rapid progress in holiness no doubt proved to those who sanctioned them that she was walking in the way grace had marked out for her. When she was about sixteen or seventeen her uncle subjected her to a strange trial. Whether it was that he wished to test the reality of her desires for sufferings, of her readiness to bear all that she was constantly in her prayers offering to endure; whether he had heard her utter that wild saintly wish—if we may dare to join the two words together—that she could sell herself as a slave for love of her Lord, and

determined to show her what was involved in that
desire; or whether again he feared that some slight
mixture of self-complacency might result from her self-
inflicted penance, for some reason or other he gradually
prepared her to accept and to undergo one of the most
painful and humiliating ordeals that could possibly be
conceived. He often spoke to her of the dangers of
self-will, of the illusions which mislead those who act
on their own impulses, of the necessity for those who
aim at sanctity to crush entirely that pride which lies
at the bottom of some of our best actions, of the
immense value of sufferings meekly borne in union with
the Passion of our Lord, till her heart burned within
her, and she was ready for every sacrifice. Then he
told her what he expected her to submit to. She was
to agree to his giving full authority over her to two
duennas—women of virtue and piety, but not above the
rank of servants—to treat her as he should direct. She
was to accept at their hands any treatment they subjected
her to. However severe, however insulting, she was
never to resist or to answer them. Everything that
was done to her she was to look upon as a mark of
conformity to her Divine Lord. The rigorous penances
she had inflicted on herself were to be prescribed and
inflicted by them; in short, she was to be the slave
she had desired to be, and, moreover, the slave of
servants. She accepted and went through this strange
ordeal with a patience, with a sweetness, with a courage,
that seem almost superhuman. It may be that the marquis
was resolved to see how far the heroic patience of his
niece would go, and permitted the absolute cruelties
which were practised upon her during the time that
trial lasted, or, perhaps, as seems more natural and more
satisfactory to suppose, the two women to whom he
had committed this charge exceeded his instructions.

The narrative of her sufferings reads like the history of a martyr. At any hour or moment she was liable to be called away by one or other of her directresses and subjected to terrible penances, which she thanked them for inflicting, which she accepted without murmur or hesitation, and bore without giving any outward sign of the pain she endured. Anything less suitable for imitation, or more reprehensible in ordinary cases, can hardly be conceived than the mode of training his niece to sanctity which the Marquis of Almaçan adopted at that time. But when we read of the simultaneous growth of extraordinary graces in her soul, of the heavenly expression which shone in her face when she came out of the oratory where she had been scourged, reviled, and trodden under foot, of the intense joy that filled her heart during her prayers, of the spiritual sweetness of her communions, and, above all, of her increased desire to serve God in the most laborious and self-sacrificing ways, it is allowable to suppose, not only that her uncle's pure intention and ardent zeal for her perfection was blessed by our Lord, even when evinced in a strange, exceptional, and perhaps imprudent manner, but that Providence thus prepared her to become in after days the friend, the servant, and the companion of martyrs. Many years afterwards her friend, Mother Ines of the Assumption, Prioress of Villafranca, with whom she was on the most intimate terms, asked her what were her feelings whilst subjected to those singular trials. She replied—'Ines, I thought of our humble and obedient Jesus, and bore in mind the example of the holy monks of the desert, whom I earnestly desired to imitate, and especially that of the good Brother Acanius, whose master used to inflict upon him violent blows, which he bore, St. John Climacus says, with perfect patience ; and I had always before my eyes the image of our Blessed Lord and of the saints, and felt how far behind them I was in practising this virtue.'

For twelve years she had also to endure the hatred and spite of some persons who took a violent dislike to her—either because they were jealous of the affection and admiration she inspired, or because they thought the Viceroy was too partial to her. Insulting language, scornful looks, on one occasion violence that nearly endangered her life, Doña Luisa had to bear, in daily intercourse with persons who lived under the same roof with her, and who were encouraged by her unalterable patience to vent their animosity on all occasions when they could do so with impunity. Her confessor, who knew very well the height to which this kind of persecution had reached, asked her one day why she never spoke of it in confession. She answered that she was not conscious of having given any reason for it. 'But you must sometimes feel angry, or at any rate irritated, with these persons?' 'No,' she replied; 'I always think they may have some good intention in what they do—at any rate, they only act in this way by God's permission, and He permits it for the good of my soul.'

One of her relatives, who had often had occasion to observe the outrageous manner in which she was treated, the silence she observed on these occasions, or, if obliged to speak, the gentle answers she made, used to say that it was only a saint who could show such composure and sweetness under incessant provocation. This long-suffering and total absence of resentment of injuries, was always one of the distinguishing traits of Doña Luisa's character, or rather one of the chief graces bestowed upon her, for we have seen that her natural disposition was to be proud and sensitive.

There are different kinds of fortitude, and some people will think that it required more courage in the Marquis

of Almaçan's niece to conquer her fears out of obedience,
in the way we are going to relate, than to fast on bread
and water, take the discipline, or listen patiently to a
torrent of abuse.   The Viceroy and his family generally
went in the spring for change of air to a place in the
country about two leagues from Pampeluna.   The climate
was charming; the gardens and neighbouring scenery
beautiful.   There was no chapel or oratory in the house;
but a large room at the end of a long gallery was fitted
up for that purpose, and at night when everybody was
gone to bed Doña Luisa used to go there to pray.   One
evening the marquis and his sons were sitting at the
entrance of the gallery enjoying the fresh air, and she
was standing some way off leaning against the railing,
making her examination of conscience.   There was a
tall almond tree exactly opposite to her, and suddenly
she saw, or fancied she saw, alongside of it a shadowy
form as white as snow, with something luminous about
it.   A shudder ran through her frame; she began to
tremble, and hastily moved away.   It was customary
for all the members of the family before they retired
to rest to go up to the marquis and ask to kiss his hand.
When she did so that evening he instantly saw in her
face that something had occurred which agitated her,
and insisted on knowing what it was.   She tried to
elude his questions, but was at last obliged to confess
that she had been frightened, and in what way.   Upon
this her uncle desired her to go back to the same
spot and stand there exactly in the same position as
before.   She replied that this appearance had no doubt
been only the effect of her imagination, but that it had
terrified her so much that she could not get rid of the
impression, and was afraid of what she should feel if
she saw it again.   But this would not do.   He told
her she must be more brave, and go back again; that

it was mean to turn one's back before an enemy; and taking her by the arm he led her to the place.

Contrary to her usual habits of implicit obedience, she made some resistance, which only determined him the more to insist on her conquering her fears. Seeing he was quite resolved, and that there was no help for it, at last, in fear and trembling, she went. No sooner did she arrive again at the spot than she saw the same appearance. Her colour changed, and she nearly fell down. The marquis hastened to encourage her by crying out—'Don't be afraid, my child. I see exactly what you do.' They left the gallery. Doña Luisa spent some time in prayer, and recovered her tranquillity. Meanwhile the marquis had gone to bed, but not to sleep. He kept revolving in his mind what had taken place. It struck him that his niece had not gone as usual to the oratory, and with his passionate desire to see her always act in the most perfect manner, he resolved that she should not indulge in a cowardice which had thus interfered, and would unless conquered often interfere, with her evening devotions. So he rose, rang the bell, sent for Doña Luisa, and then ordered her without reply or hesitation to go alone to the oratory with a lighted candle in her hand, and to do penance there for half an hour. It cost her a violent effort to obey. The night was dark; a profound stillness reigned in the house, every one being fast asleep. The dense foliage and profound solitude outside increased as it were the silence within. She had to pass by the place where she had been so frightened. Her hair stood on end, but she courageously went on, keeping her eyes fixed on the ground. On reaching the oratory, she placed her hourglass in its usual place, and took the discipline for half an hour. A great peace and joy soon filled her soul, and at the end of the time she

returned through the gallery to her room without the
slightest fear or emotion. Having thus far succeeded
in his object, the marquis followed up this victory by
continually putting her courage to the trial. He attached
the greatest importance to this conquest over cowardice,
which he considered a serious impediment to spiritual
perfection. He therefore seized every opportunity of
sending her into solitary places. Sometimes he locked
her up in his private oratory, and left her there in the
dark for a long time. If detained by business, he was
apt to forget to let her out till late in the evening. Far
from complaining of these trials, Doña Luisa felt herself
the importance of surmounting weak and groundless
fears, and of her own accord tested her courage by
going to pray in the dark and in the very places most
likely to excite them. Her biographer adds that the
evil spirits were suffered to try her resolution by harassing her in a hundred ways, and to create all sorts of
obstacles to her devotions ; but in the midst of terrifying
noises and appearances, she used to remain perfectly
still and recollected, never shortening her prayers or
giving heed to these distractions.

CHAPTER VI.

In what manner Doña Luisa spent her time in her uncle's house.

LUISA was oftener in the marquis' room than anywhere else, especially during the first years she spent under his roof. As long as she was a child he used to keep her with him even whilst he was doing business and dictating despatches to his secretaries. She sat at his feet reading a pious book. She was hardly ever seen without one either in her hand or under her arm, and read them over and over again till she knew them almost by heart. When her uncle was at leisure he delighted in talking to her on religious subjects. His mind, to use the expression of one of his daughters, was a never failing fount of spiritual instruction, and his little companion listened to him with an eagerness that made him call her in jest *his listener*. After dinner, when some time had been spent in recreation, he was in the habit of saying, ' Come, children, and I will teach you the fear of the Lord,' and leading the way to his library, closely followed by Doña Luisa, he gathered his children round him and spent some time conversing with them about matters of faith, and explaining to them the mysteries of religion, especially on the festivals of the Church which commemorate sacred events. The pleasure he took in these conferences carried him away sometimes, and his young auditors dropped off one by one. When he and Doña Luisa were left alone, he smiled and said —'*Vos estis qui permansistis mecum in tentationibus meis.*'

Most days he read aloud to her some of the Bible or the writings of the Fathers, translating them as he went on into Spanish with wonderful fluency and ease. She thus became so good a scholar that at the age of fifteen she could understand the New Testament and other Latin books, and in time her assiduity and quickness enabled her to read without difficulty the works of the Fathers of the Church. Under the guidance of so excellent a master, she made rapid progress in spirituality and in learning. He called her his Esther ; but used to say that whereas that holy Queen, trained to piety by her uncle from her earliest years, became the bride of an earthly monarch, his beloved niece would be the spouse of Christ our King. Her tastes and her occupations were all in harmony with a religious vocation. When she was not reading or studying in her uncle's room, she generally employed herself in various kinds of church work, especially in making artificial flowers for the altar. The marquis' oratory, where she spent so many hours in prayer, was confided to her especial charge. It was her delight before every great festival to adorn it with wreaths and garlands, varying them according to the colours appointed for the different feasts of the Church. Her skill and ingenuity in the arrangement of these decorations pleased her uncle so much that he used to take his relatives into the oratory to admire the work of the little sacristan.

His love for his niece went on increasing as she advanced in age, and she returned it by the tenderest and most devoted affection. But though she was more attached to him than to any one else in the world, she knew even as a young girl how inferior were the claims of any creature on her heart to those of her Creator.

Whilst rejoicing in the wonderful gift of a love such as she felt and such as she was the object of during those years of holy and happy intimacy with her uncle, she never forgot that God had the right to the supreme devotion of her heart, and that all human affection was to be as nothing to her in comparison with that divine love which had so early possessed it. This may have been his merit as well as hers. For if there was danger of her taking pride in his constant commendations of her conduct, his marked preference for her society, and the confidence in her judgment which he showed on every possible occasion ; if she could not help seeing that although he was a very tender father, his own children were not so dear and precious to him as she was, on the other hand, she had opportunities no one else had of becoming acquainted with the profound humility, the perfect detachment and'the ardent devotion of a soul on fire with the love of God. The more he opened his heart to her, the more she felt her own raised above this world, and detached from everything earthly, however noble and good. Our Blessed Lord had given her very early this sense of the worthlessness of creatures in comparison with the Creator. The loss of her parents, and her successive separations from the objects of her youthful affections, had, perhaps, been the means of impressing upon her this feeling. She often repeated the words of the Psalmist—'It is good to confide in the Lord, rather than to have confidence in man. It is good to trust in the Lord, rather than to trust in princes.'

Though she had not made a vow of obedience, it would have been impossible for a religious to obey a superior more exactly than she did her uncle. His will was law to her, she never would do the least thing without his permission, not even drive or walk out with

E

her aunt or her cousins, or go down alone to the garden.
She was also very submissive to the marchesa, and it
required a great deal of tact and discretion to combine
this double obedience and keep clear of all difficulties,
for about some minor questions the marquis and his wife
did not always agree, and she was liable to receive
contradictory commands.

One of her favourite books was the treatise on obedience of St. John Climacus. She used to call it her
beloved companion, and practise to the letter the lessons
it contained, never arguing, or disputing, or hesitating as
to what she was ordered to do. In a preceding chapter
we have seen the extraordinary and severe trial to which
her obedience was put, and it was not less complete in
little things. It used to amuse the family to see the
simplicity with which she did everything she was told.
One day that she was standing near a brazier in which
there happened to be no fire, the marquis said to her in
jest—'Come away from there, Luisa; you will burn
your hands.' She hastily drew them back as if they
had been scorched. 'What are you doing?' he asked,
laughing at her. 'Why did you move?' 'Indeed, señor,'
she replied, 'when you said I should burn myself, I felt
as if I was scorched.' Once, when they were staying in
Madrid, she went as usual in the morning to kiss her
uncle's hand and take his orders for the day. He was
then President of the Council of Orders, and being
very busy at the moment, he said—'Go to the oratory,
my child, I will come there and tell you what to do.' It
so happened, however, that, engrossed by his occupations, and in a hurry to get to the palace, he completely
forgot to pass through the oratory. An important lawsuit
detained him in court till four o'clock in the afternoon,
and from six in the morning until that hour, Doña Luisa
remained waiting in the oratory, much to her aunt's

·disgust, who did not at all admire mortifications of
this sort, and declared they would kill her before her
time. The worst part of it was, that when the marquis
-came home, he scolded her, and said that as the door
was not locked, she should have come out, and not have
made every one uncomfortable. She received this reproof
with perfect humility and meekness, and did not utter a
word in her own defence.

The details of this period of Doña Luisa's life give a
curious insight into the character of the Marquis of
Almaçan, and a high idea of the sense and prudence
with which she acted in a somewhat peculiar position.
She was a child of eleven when she entered her uncle's
house. He had assumed the care of her education, and
at the same time that of her soul; and as far as was
possible had always acted as her director. The ardent
interest he took in her spiritual progress, his admiration
for her great gifts of mind and her rare piety, and his
passionate desire to see her become a great saint, led
him to treat her in some respects with extraordinary
severity, whilst at the same time he made her the object
·of a sort of worship. He seems to have been an ardent,
enthusiastic, and very pious man, but not a very prudent
one. It is easy to imagine that as she grew older, the
direction of a layman, however holy, could not have
been always satisfactory, though gratitude, affection, and
the sense of all she owed him even in a spiritual sense,
made her no doubt unwilling to break through long-
standing habits of confidence and submission, and
withdraw herself from his control. It is impossible not
to be struck with the wisdom of her conduct under the
circumstances. She knew that every one in the marquis'
house was esteemed in proportion to his or her piety, and
this gave her a great dread of an outward display of
fervour. She kept her austerities and her devotions as

E 2

secret as she could, and was ingenious in her expedients
to pass them off as the indulgence of peculiar tastes and
original fancies.   In the manifestations of conscience
which the marquis continued to expect from her when
she was grown up, she observed great reserve.   Of her
defects and failings she was willing enough to speak, but
was very silent as to her penances, her mortifications,
and the graces she received in prayer.   She had a
profound conviction that the less a person reveals these
sort of favours, the more they are likely to be multiplied,
and that the interior riches of the soul must far exceed
what can be known to others.   She answered briefly,
sincerely, and exactly, her uncle's questions, but without
entering into any details. Whatever practices of penance
or devotion he enjoined, she scrupulously performed ;
but she said nothing about them unless questioned on the
subject.   This seemed to her the best and safest course.
In his ardent enthusiasm, he would have liked to hear
her express fervour, accuse herself of being a grievous
sinner, detail the great things she would wish to do for
our Lord, and crave his permission to undertake extraordinary acts of penance and mortification.   But this
was never her way.   She exactly obeyed his commands,
but otherwise went on in her own way silently and
humbly.   She felt that there was something incongruous
—he being a secular, and she a person living in the
world—in unrestrained and excessive communication with
him in spiritual matters, and thought it right to speak
little, to do much, and to be always ready to obey.
What she always told him was, that he should consider
before God what would be most profitable to her soul,
for that she was disposed to abandon herself entirely to
the divine will.   Though the marquis may have sometimes been disappointed at what seemed a want of
sympathy on Doña Luisa's part, he fully appreciated the

good sense and prudence of her conduct in this as in other respects. He was never tired of praising her to the pious persons who visited him, especially to the Fathers of the Society of Jesus, with whom he was in constant communication. If she happened to come in when they were sitting with him, he used to say, 'Here comes a prudent virgin!' or, 'Here is one of the number of the prudent.' Once, when he was at recreation with her and his children, he began, half in jest and half in earnest, to sing to her the office of a saint ; she looking very grave and severe, yet now and then smiling as if he had been addressing some one else. Luis Munoz, when he relates this anecdote, wonders whether this 'was an announcement or a prophecy.'

CHAPTER VII.

Retirement from the world.

In her youth as well as in her childhood, Doña Luisa preserved not only the most perfect innocence of life, but so great a purity of mind that no bad thought seems ever to have tarnished her imagination. The devil, who was frequently tormenting her in other ways, was apparently not allowed to molest this chosen soul by temptations against the angelical virtue. She went through life with a childlike ignorance of evil, which in her case had no dangers, for an instinctive delicacy of character inspired her with as much reserve and caution as the most profound experience of the world could have done. If in her presence any one spoke in the slightest degree objectionably, she instantly turned away or left the room. Nobody could see her without being struck by the dignified modesty of her demeanour. In those she cared for most she did not suffer the least approach to familiarity. Even her tender love for her uncle was not demonstrative. Her biographer describes in a quaint manner the grave and reverential character of her affection for him. 'She used to look at the marquis,' he says, 'as people look at holy images.' As to other gentlemen, she did not give them as much as a glance or a thought unless they were persons from whose conversation she could derive spiritual benefit. It was a joke against

her that she could never tell whether people were handsome or ugly, or how they were dressed, though she
might have seen them but a few days before.

When she was about fifteen years of age, the marquis
would have liked her to marry, because he thought that
the world was greatly in need of virtue in the married
state, and that she would have proved a perfect model
of a Christian wife and mother. He sometimes spoke
to her in this sense. She listened quietly, smiling a little
and answering nothing. It seemed to her better not to
enter on a premature discussion of the subject, but rather
to treat it as a joke. But each time it was renewed, the
more strongly did she inwardly protest that nothing
should ever induce her to forego her resolution to live
and to die unmarried. She could not understand how
her uncle failed to see that the whole drift of the training
she had received from him, the high aims he had continually set before her, the mortifications, the penances,
the love of poverty, which he had taught her so highly
to esteem, and the words 'God alone,' which summed
up all his teachings, were not likely to end in a vocation
to the married state and a life in the world. A more
definite proposal was soon submitted to her acceptance ;
one of her cousins, a knight of Santiago, and the wealthy
lord of numerous vassals, wished to obtain her hand.
The marquis favoured his suit. When the subject was
mentioned to Doña Luisa, she smiled and shook her
head. Her uncle pressed for a positive answer. She
then expressed astonishment that he should think such
a thing possible, and when he went on to say that it was
a very desirable offer, and that he would like her to
accept it, her whole countenance changed, an indes-
cribable look of pain came over her face, she turned
pale, tears filled her eyes, and she begged him never
to speak of it again.

The marquis was struck with her manner. It was grave and earnest beyond her years, and he felt unable to urge her any further. Everything in her conduct at home and abroad was in keeping with her resolution. Her cousins were all very fond of Doña Luisa, and had the greatest respect for her; they never allowed themselves to say anything in her presence that could seriously offend or displease her, but sometimes they permitted themselves, especially on winter evenings, we are told, when they had nothing else to amuse them, to teaze her by jokes about her marriage—supposing, for instance, that she was engaged to such or such a gentleman, and drawing up imaginary contracts, in which various conditions were laid down, such as that she was always to spend six months of the year at her uncle's elbow, wherever he was, and the other six at her husband's palace, on the strict understanding that he should be absent all the time.

After a Viceroyalty of seven years, during which the Marquis of Almaçan had exercised a most beneficial influence over the province he governed and the people committed to his care, he returned to Madrid, leaving his wife, his daughters, and his niece at his ancestral house at Almaçan. Doña Luisa felt very keenly this separation from him who was to her at once a father and a spiritual guide. She found her only comfort in the pious use of her time, and an increase of her devotional exercises. Her uncle's house communicated with the parochial church of St. Michael by a private gallery, which architects had pronounced unsafe. She did not feel afraid of trusting her light weight on the dangerous flooring, and having obtained the key of a door in her aunt's apartments which opened upon this gallery, she used to go into the church at night and in the early mornings and spend long hours in adoration before the Blessed Sacrament. If any one had seen her slight figure emerge from the dark gallery which no footstep had trod for years, and in the church, lighted only by the solitary lamp before the tabernacle, remain entranced in prayer, silent and motionless like one of the marble images in their shrines, she might well have been taken for an angelic apparition. Those long communings of her soul with God during the months she spent at Almaçan, inflamed her desires to lead a completely spiritual life, and to embrace with the help of her Divine Lord the highest line of Christian perfection. Day by day she offered herself to Him whilst in His Sacred Presence, with an heroic resolution and generosity of heart which had no limits but His will. All the fervent aspirations of her childhood had deepened and expanded with the progress of time, and her contempt of the world increased in proportion with her knowledge of it. The devotions, the austerities, the sacrifices, of so many years had kindled in that ardent soul a burning thirst to find out how she could do something for God; simple words, which express the feelings of a soul whom our Lord calls to follow Him in the apostolic life in the world no less imperatively than He summons another to the desert or the cloister. She was now nearly twenty years of age, advancing in life, and it seemed to her that the time was arrived to consider seriously in what manner she should serve God with the exclusive devotion she desired.

This was no easy matter, for whilst on the one hand an overpowering attraction led her to forsake the world and despise everything earthly, she did not see any obvious way to this renunciation, for in spite of those aspirations she had no vocation for the religious life in a cloister. Our Lord seemed to close this path to her for no reason that she could discern, except that such was His blessed will.   More impetuous every day became the impulse to leave all for Him, more ardent the fire of love in her heart, more abundant the tears she shed.   Most anxiously she prayed for light on so important a subject, and many were the schemes, all embracing a life of perfection, which she turned over in her mind.   None of them, however, remained so steadily before her eyes as that which involved the closest resemblance she could imagine to the life of our Blessed Saviour on earth.   This idea took at last possession of her mind, to the exclusion of all others.   She could not recollect herself before God, nor glance even for a moment at the sacred image of our Lord, without feeling in her inmost soul a violent transport of love, and a vehement desire to walk in His footsteps even unto death.   Her biographer says that a *terrible* love of suffering was awakened in her soul by this constant contemplation of the Passion, and she began to consider how she could carry into effect these pressing desires for a life of poverty and humiliation.

It was evident that this would be impossible in her uncle's house.   Though she lived there amongst good and pious people, the habits of persons of the world, the love of finery, luxury, and esteem of worldly rank, which prevailed amongst them, would never have accorded with the kind of existence she had in view. The way of the Cross, as she understood it, could not be followed under the gilded roof of a palace, amidst the wealth, comforts, and dignity of a high position.   The plan she had conceived was to shut herself up in a small house with a few pious companions, and to live there in obscurity devoted to pious exercises, out of sight of the world and forgotten by every one.   Her idea was to make in this way an offering that should cost her more than any other sacrifice could have done.   What she proposed to renounce by this mode of life was what her biographer calls *honour*. Perhaps we might best express his meaning in English by the word ' consideration.' In order to estimate the heroic courage of her resolution, it is well to remember the times in which Doña Luisa lived, the character of the Spanish people, and her own natural disposition. When she deliberately made up her mind to endure every shame and disgrace to which it might please God to subject her, she made a far greater effort than it would have been to lay down her head on the block. At that epoch it was considered honourable as well as edifying to go into religion. There was no family, however noble, that would not have been flattered at counting amongst their sisters or their daughters a Carmelite nun or a Poor Clare. Heroic as was the act of a young maiden who forsook all the pleasures of the world and the joys of domestic life for the seclusion of the cloister and a life of constant prayer and close union with God, contempt and obloquy were not amongst the trials she had to bear. The case is now reversed. A vocation to penance and prayer meets with little sympathy and encouragement. Whilst many a godless man of the world will bestow warm praises on a Sister of Charity, the very idea of a contemplative nun inspires in all but sincere Catholics a feeling of pity bordering on contempt. Active orders amongst women had scarcely begun to exist in the sixteenth century, and the notion of the daughter of a noble house going about the streets dressed like a beggar, unattended by servants, and performing for herself and others menial offices, without the dignity attached to a religious profession, was intolerable to all but those—and they are the few in every age—who rose above worldly prejudices and took the Gospel at its word. And then if in addition we call to mind Doña Luisa's natural love of position and temporal splendour,

the way in which she had been taught to esteem, though
within Christian limits, the advantages of rank and high
station, and the precocious abilities she possessed for the
management of a large fortune, a characteristic which all
her friends had noticed in her, we shall have some idea
of the effort it involved to run counter to all these
feelings, and expose herself to the ridicule of her friends
and acquaintances.

So strong had been her susceptibility on that point,
the weak one in her character, that it had been difficult
to persuade her that this overweening estimation of
fortuitous advantages was inconsistent with Christian
perfection. When she had already renounced pleasures,
amusements, and comforts, and was winning signal graces
in prayer, she did not seem to profit by the instructions
of sermons and spiritual books on that subject. But now
a fierce struggle rose in her heart between this deeply
rooted passion and her ardent desires to embrace shame
and suffering for the love of our Lord. It seemed to
her at moments perfectly impossible to subject herself to
the humiliations of a life, not of religious austerity, but of
common vulgar poverty, which was what she felt sure
that God expected of her. This subtle pride fought
vigorously against the divine inspiration. It was firmly
lodged in a heart otherwise deeply humble. She would
willingly have kissed the feet of a beggar, performed acts
of the deepest humility, listened without reply to the
bitterest reproaches. But to be numbered amongst the
common herd, to forego all the distinctions which she
was entitled to as a high born lady—this was an effort
almost beyond her strength. But a steady contemplation
of the Cross of Christ, constant meditations on the shame
and humiliations of Calvary, at last got the better of these
risings of the natural heart, and kindled a love which
could refuse nothing to Him Who had first so loved His

creature. Full of these thoughts she wrote a letter to
the marquis, in which she begged him to recommend
her desires to God, and showed how strong and earnest
they already were, although, according to her usual habit,
she felt much more than she expressed.

Such was the fruit of Doña Luisa's residence at
Almaçan, and of those long nightly prayers before the
Blessed Sacrament in the old church attached to the
castle. She had no sooner formed her resolution than
a summons came to the marchesa to join her husband
in Madrid, where he had been appointed President of the
Council of Orders. Thither she removed, with all her
family and household. Doña Luisa arrived in that city,
'sighing for solitude rather than for a Court,' her biographer says. It was painful to her again to inhabit a
palace, and a sort of loathing took possession of her for
the very things which she had been in danger of caring
for too much. The remembrance of the hold they once
had upon her soul filled her with shame and regret, and
increased the aversion which she felt for them. Narrow
had been her escape. They had well nigh ruined her
desires of perfection, and inflicted on her soul wounds
which were healed, but still tender. No wonder that
she now abhorred the sight of them. That fierce conflict
which had ended in victory had left her more experienced,
more humble, more courageous, more full of love for our
Lord, in Whom she placed all her reliance, and by Whom
she trusted to see her hopes fulfilled and blessed. She
could find no rest but in Him. There was no one in
that city, whither she was returning as a stranger, to whom
she could open her heart, or speak of its earnest desires,
or receive comfort and consolation, in the great difficulty
in which she found herself; on the one hand feeling
intensely anxious to fulfil what she felt convinced was
God's will and her vocation, and on the other dismayed

at the almost insuparable difficulties in her way, seeing that she did not wish to enter a convent, and that the whole of her fortune was in the hands of trustees.

It would have seemed natural that she should have broached the subject to her uncle and discussed it with him; but great as were her affection and confidence in the marquis, she did not feel sure in what way he would take this disclosure. Sometimes they talked about poverty— in what it really consisted, on its merits and its advantages. He opposed her ideas, evidently for the sake of hearing her defend them, for he always seemed pleased with her answers. At last she could hold out no longer, and resolved to break through all restraints and leave her uncle's house. Great was the effort, for if, in the words of a martyr to his bride, she loved him far less than God, she did love him far more than herself. Summoning up all her resolution, she laid before him her intention, the way in which the Holy Spirit was leading her, the inspirations she received in prayer, and the irresistible might of the love which constrained her to follow them. The strangeness and novelty of her design took the marquis entirely by surprise. He set his face decidedly against it, and declared that it would be a disgrace to him if his niece left his house without his appointing for her an establishment suitable to her rank; that so extraordinary a step would be looked upon as madness; her youth, her beauty, and the state of her fortune making it very undesirable for her to live separated from her relatives, who would all exclaim against so extremely foolish a resolution. She would be cast off by all her family, who would feel indignant and ashamed at seeing her live in a way which would reflect disgrace upon them. If she did not wish to marry, then why on earth not become a nun? The right thing was, to choose one or the other of those states of life. He could

not admit that it was proper for a woman to remain free
and exposed to the risks and accidents of an unprotected
position in the world. She answered him as follows;
we give her own words—'Señor, I confess that it is my
own unworthiness that prevents my aspiring to so high
a state as the religious life. I wish with all my heart
that I was called to it, and I earnestly beg of our Blessed
Lord, if it be His will, to grant me that grace; but I
have never felt in myself anything that led me to think
that He would have me to be a nun.'

Many discussions took place between the marquis, his
niece, and many pious and learned persons. He used
sometimes impatiently to exclaim, 'How is it, Luisa, that
you can will and not will?' He evidently thought that
her reluctance to enter a convent proceeded from irreso-
lution. She tried to reflect on what he said, and thought
how blest and secure the life of a nun would be, but the
instant she began to take it into consideration, she felt
restless and miserable, whereas, when she reverted to her
first idea and left the future in God's hands, peace and
tranquillity returned, even though she had then, and
retained all through life, the deepest esteem and reverence for the conventual life. The upshot of their
discussions was, that the marquis gave her leave to alter
the fashion of her dress, to abandon worldly attire, and
to live in a retired part of his palace with three or four
attendants, spending her time in devout exercises, asking
God to give her light as to the future, and making as
it were an experiment of the life she wished to lead.
A year was spent in this way. She increased her prayers,
her mortifications, and her penances, but with a constant
sense that she was not where God was calling her, pining
for greater solitude and a total separation from earthly
ties. What she called solitude was not mere retirement
from the world and religious enclosure. She comprised

in that word an entire abandonment of what the world esteems and honours—exposure to the opprobrium, the loneliness, the ignominy of a life conformed to our Lord's suffering life, an open rupture with His enemies, a public profession of that enmity, the acceptance of every one's blame and contempt, the being as it were thrust out of the house into the streets, leaving behind her a world provoked and irritated at this open defiance of its customs and its laws.

This was her ideal, somewhat resembling the view of perfect happiness which the Saint of Assisi described to his brother Leo as they travelled in the snow across the plains of Umbria. She knew this call must be obeyed, and often said, with a painful presentiment, that our Lord would remove in His own way the obstacles to her vocation. This foreboding proved true. The Marquis of Almaçan died soon afterwards, full of years and merits. At that sad mement all Doña Luisa's deep love for him seemed to revive with tenfold force. She struggled with a grief which for the moment seemed almost overpowering, and mastered it with a strong effort. It seemed now as if the difficulties in her way had vanished, but it was not so. The marchesa, who had become more and more attached to her husband's niece, now looked upon her as a sort of bequest from him. The passionate affection he had borne Doña Luisa made her precious in the eyes of his broken hearted wife, and she could not endure the prospect of a separation. Not only did she absolutely forbid her departure, but declared that if she left her house she would follow her and force her entrance into her abode, wherever it was. With a heavy heart Doña Luisa submitted, in order not to add to the sorrows of one already so deeply afflicted, but she said to Ines, the companion we have already mentioned, and of whom we shall have often occasion to speak—'Ines, how my señora sets herself against my resolution! God grant that she may live many long years, as I earnestly wish her to do, but I have a conviction that our Lord will remove every obstacle between me and my vocation.' This foreboding was likewise fulfilled. The marquesa died six months after her husband, and then Don Gonzalo Chacon y Mendoza, brother of the deceased marquis and uncle of Doña Luisa, proposed to her, as she did not intend to be a nun, to share his retirement, he being a priest and not a man of the world. 'No, señor,' she replied; 'God calls me to something very different from living with my relatives.' This good man died shortly afterwards; and at twenty-four years of age she remained her own mistress. None of her relatives sought to control her actions, though they would all have wished her to remain with them, particularly her cousin, the young Marquis of Almaçan, of whose virtues and piety mention has been already made.

Some little further delay arose in the accomplishment of her project, in consequence of various negotiations about matters of business in which the interests of her brother Alonzo were involved as well as her own; this furnished a plausible reason for putting off the final step. As sometimes happens, she may have felt less keen to hurry it on when she was perfectly free to act on her own responsibility than when she had to fight the battle with others, or perhaps she was really persuaded that on account of her brother she was obliged to bring those arrangements to a conclusion before she entered on her new mode of life. Be that as it may, our Blessed Lord showed her in an unmistakeable manner that He was displeased at this want of immediate correspondence with grace, and compelled her in some sort to accomplish her design at once. She recognized that divine voice

F

speaking to her heart, adored that sacred will and that guiding hand, took up her cross firmly and resolutely, and leaving behind her wealth, position, comforts, relatives. and friends, in simple faith began to lead that life the details of which will be given in the following chapters. of this work.

CHAPTER VIII.

Doña Luisa's house in the Via de Toledo.

THE life which Doña Luisa embraced in her twenty-sixth year was far from being unprecedented either in the early centuries of the Church or in her own age and country. We read in ecclesiastical history and in the annals of the saints of a number of Christian maidens who consecrated themselves to a life of special devotion and virginal purity, not only within the walls of a cloister or in the solitude of a desert, but in the midst of crowded cities and under their father's roof. The writings of St. Jerome, St. Ambrose, St. Augustine, and other Fathers of the Church, make us familiar with the names of many holy women thus remaining with their families and managing their property, but at the same time aiming at the highest perfection, and following the evangelical counsels according to the rules given to them by those saintly men. They were not seen in public assemblies ; they did not go out without a proper escort ; they eschewed all vanity in dress ; they absented themselves from feasts and idle entertainments ; avoided all unnecessary conversation with persons of the world ; gave alms to the utmost of their power ; ministered to the sick and the afflicted ; and took a special care of orphans.

The first great model of this religious though uncloistered life was, no doubt, the Virgin Mother of our Lord. At Nazareth, at Cana and Bethany, or in her later years at Jerusalem and Ephesus, she presented the

F 2

most complete example of sanctity, of the highest consecration of soul and body to God in the midst of the
daily occupations and ordinary intercourse of social and
domestic life. This type of womanly perfection must
have been constantly before the eyes and in the mind of
the early Christians. Mothers no doubt looked upon the
Mother of God as their special patroness, and virgins and
widows found in her the ideal of the life they wished to
lead, before cloisters and convents had gathered together
holy souls in religious seclusion. St. Petronilla, St. Peter's
daughter, for instance, who made in the flower of her
youth a vow of perpetual chastity, and prayed to die
early, in order to leave the world with her soul as pure
as on the day of her consecration to Christ, must have
derived the desire and the spirit of that vow from what
since her earliest years she had seen and heard of the
Mother of Jesus. In the Court of a Roman Emperor,
St. Asella led a life of strict retirement, finding in her
little room in a palace as holy a solitude as the anchorites
sought in the deserts of Egypt. St. Jerome eloquently
describes the virtues of St. Eustochium, St. Paula's
daughter, who, treading under foot the pride of her
consular lineage, and despising the luxuries of the high
born Roman ladies, renounced marriage and bound
herself by vow to the observance of the evangelical
counsels ; and also of that other illustrious maiden,
Demetria, who on the very eve of her nuptials took off
the jewels and ornaments with which she had been
adorned, divested herself of her silk robes, and, clad in
a course homely garb, declared to her mother Proba and
her grandmother Juliana, two Christian widows devoted
to a life of holy poverty, her irrevocable resolution to
share their obscure labours and live and die a virgin.

No age has been without examples of similar con-
secrations. The tradition of such vocations is unbroken

in the Church, and she has always given them her sanction. In Doña Luisa's time, alongside of the wonderful examples of sanctity in the monasteries founded by St. Teresa, instances were to be found of single women leading lives of heroic virtue, and favoured with supernatural gifts in solitary or in obscure positions. Doña Sancha Carillo, the daughter of the lord of Guadalcazar, one of the first nobles of Andalusia, abandoned the world and retired into a small house adjoining her father's palace, where, under the direction of the great master of the spiritual life, John of Avila, she attained to an extraordinary degree of holiness.[1] At Valladolid a woman only twelve years older than Doña Luisa, and who long survived her, Marina de Escobar, lived in a little room in her father's house in such great sanctity, that nothing that we read of in the lives of canonized saints excels what the famous Jesuit writer Luis de la Puente has left on record regarding her singular holiness, and the marvellous graces she received from God. Yet this saintly woman never belonged to a religious order. She had earnestly wished at one time to become a Carmelite nun, but the weakness of her health having stood in the way of her admission, she does not seem to have made any subsequent efforts to change her mode of life, or to leave the room where she spent long years in

---

[1] We read in the Life of St. Peter of Alcantara, that when the three daughters of the great house of Chiaveses had been converted by his preaching, from a life of vanity and dissipation, and went to him with tears in their eyes to announce their intention of forsaking the world in order to become religious, he would not agree to their leaving their father's house. Foreseeing the wonderful good their example would do amongst the ladies of Placentia, if they remained there, he told them that their own house and the church were to be their convent. He gave them the habit of the third order of St. Francis ; and under his direction they made such progress in piety and virtue that they all died in the odour of sanctity. Maria de Mendoza, the mother of our Doña Luisa, may have known these holy women and spoken of them to her little daughter.

mystical converse with the Lord of saints and angels, where she was visited by celestial messengers, and favoured by heavenly revelations. From that little cell she exercized a strange influence over the world, converting sinners, reconciling enemies, advising kings, performing cures on the sick and infirm, and reading the future in many a wondrous vision. Miracles were wrought by her touch and afterwards vouchsafed at her tomb. Yet in the eyes of men she was not a nun, nothing but a poor woman leading an obscure existence in an ordinary condition of lowly poverty.

Doña Luisa's vocation was, in its measure, of this kind. She had very humble thoughts about herself and God's dealings with her soul, and was convinced that it was her own unworthiness which precluded her from becoming a religious. No doubt crossed her mind as to the life to which she was called, and her first care, as soon as she was able to fix the time for leaving her cousin's palace, was to find a small house in Madrid suitable for her purpose. It was necessary for her to reside in that city on account of her temporal affairs, and also in order to remain, as she had done for years, under the guidance of the Jesuit Fathers. After some consideration, she asked her cousin to let her a very small inconvenient tenement which belonged to him in the Via de Toledo, close to the College. The mean appearance of this building was in strict accordance with her wishes. On the appointed day she took possession of this her obscure abode, accompanied by three or four women who had belonged to her late uncle's household. They had shared her retirement in the palace and her devotional exercises during the last years of his life, and now expressed a desire to follow her to the poor home she had chosen. As soon as the door had closed upon them, Luisa seemed to breathe freely, like a person from

whom a heavy weight has been removed, and made
them a little speech, full of that dignified simplicity
which was one of her peculiar characteristics. These
were her words—

'I give thanks to God, my sisters, that after a troublesome navigation, attended with many difficulties, we
have entered this haven of peace, where, I trust, we shall
be safe from the dangers of the world. Again and again
I thank Him that He has brought about at last, in so
happy a manner, what I have anxiously desired for many
years. I acknowledge the goodness of God, His infinite
mercies, His innumerable blessings, and my own insufficiency to make any return for them, or to serve Him as I
would. I have always wished, and this also has been
one of His mercies, to correspond with His grace, and
not to repay with ingratitude so many signal favours.
The house of my good lord the marquis, and his affection for me as his niece, have been to me a prison and a
hard chain, a long and heavy cross. For ill did it become
the spouse of one Who was poor and lowly to live in the
pomp and luxury of a palace. My intention now is to
give myself up wholly to God, as far as my strength will
allow, and, by the help of His grace, to imitate His
life on earth, and follow His counsels of perfection.
Poverty, solitude, retirement, prayer, and penance, are
the treasure whence we draw the most perfect virtues. I
wish this poor house to be to me a strict cloister, in
which I may live as recollected as in the most austere
monastery. Up to this day you have always called me
señora. Henceforward I renounce that title. You will
call me nothing but Luisa. You are my companions;
you are my sisters; our love and our behaviour to each
other must be in accordance with that name. If we
belong to the same Spouse, if we go and receive Him as
equals side by side in church, why should we be separated

at our meals? We shall receive our food from Him Who holds all things in His hands. Faith does not fear hunger. Too many cares about sustenance are thorns in the side of faith. As to the solitude of this life, and the abandonment of my relations, to whom it will seem a strange one, fear it not. I promise you that God will take care of us if we devote ourselves to serve Him. I have no doubt that some of you think that what I undertake is too rigorous, but it falls short of what I owe to God. If with courage and good will you follow me in this life which I have chosen, I will help you as far as my feeble power will go. I trust that God in His infinite goodness will give us all His grace, so that after valiantly fighting during the brief space of this life, we may win crowns of everlasting glory in the world to come.'

No sooner, then, had Luisa taken possession of her little abode than she began to carry into effect her intention of leading a life of strict poverty. The first thing she did was to sell everything in her possession which had the slightest value, and to give away to the poor the sum thus obtained. Whatever could be turned into use for the altar she bestowed on churches, and at the end of a few days she sent to the hospital some plate which had been set aside for her use. The very modest wardrobe which had served her in her uncle's house was discarded as too costly, and replaced by coarse and plain clothes. She wore a coarse tunic of rough serge, with no other garment than a petticoat of the same texture, and over it a habit made of the cheapest possible stuff, without train or hanging sleeves. All her beautiful hair she cut off, and covered her head with a thick linen hood which hung over the face. Her shoes were of the heaviest description, and sometimes when she could do so unperceived she went barefooted. The furniture of the house was in keeping with her dress—the walls as bare as possible, only a few chairs in the parlour, no couches or cushions, no pictures except a few common prints, and in each room a rude cross made of pine wood.

The best bed she allowed herself, and it was the same with her companions, was a mattress stuffed with straw, and a bolster of a similar kind; sheets made of the coarsest hempen cloth, and a horse rug for a blanket. It was only when she began to suffer from numerous infirmities that she indulged herself with even this amount of comfort, if such it could be called. At first she used to sleep on bare planks. The parlour was furnished with plain shelves for their few books, wooden boxes which held their work, and common candlesticks such as the poorest people have in their houses. Two moveable seats were brought in when her confessor and his companion paid them a visit. She had herself neither desk, or cabinet, or coffer; a small wooden chest held her papers, and a similar one her scanty wardrobe. Their plates, knives, and forks, and all the little articles for daily use were made of the commonest materials. The oratory was fitted up with silken antipendia, and other ornaments were allowed, still it partook of the general poverty of the home, and nothing costly was admitted into it.

She arranged with her companions that each, herself included, should attend by turns to the household work, and for a week at a time act as the servant of the others. She insisted upon being the first to undertake this responsibility, but accustomed as she had always been to be waited upon, and totally without experience as to that kind of work, it may be easily imagined how difficult she found it to acquit herself of her various duties. In the first place she had to clean the house from top to bottom, down to the street door, then to wash the vegetables and the meat, to light the fire, make the *olla* for the dinner, lay the knives and forks, and clean them after the meals. Nothing could exceed her zeal and diligence, but her knowledge was not by any means equal to her activity. She was sadly puzzled about making the *olla*, and was obliged to go with the salt bag in her hand to one of her companions to inquire how much she was to put into the saucepan. Her cooking in those days must have been an admirable kind of mortification to her friends as well as herself. She was so anxious to practise obedience in the smallest as well as the greatest things, that in order to act continually on that principle she left her confessor no rest until he consented to name one of her former maids as her superior in temporal matters, so that she might, as far as these were concerned, submit in everything to her commands. He gave way to her importunities, and fixed upon the oldest of the party, a sedate austere person who had been the late marquesa's attendant. This good woman was exceedingly devout and zealous, and seems to have had high ideas of the duty of imposing penances on other people. Understanding that it was on purpose to practise mortification that the señora had subjected herself to her authority, she determined to second this desire to the utmost of her power. These Spanish duennas, judging by the specimens which Doña Luisa's life affords, were formidable disciplinarians, and this good lady began at once her office by doing nothing but scold, rebuke, and contradict the poor señora, finding fault with everything she did, and interrupting her at every moment to order her about here and there. If she ventured to speak, the duenna jumped up and cried—'What is all this about? What foolish things you are saying!' Luisa received these constant rebuffs with the most invariable sweetness, and when commanded by her servant to hold her tongue, kept silence as humbly as if an angel from heaven had spoken. Strict fasts and frequent abstinence were favourite devotions with this good lady, and in this respect also she exercised her sway over her mistress. The others were not placed under her obedience, so that she could not impose upon them all the privations she was so fond of. But as to the victim, bound by voluntary submission to this severe subjection, she often made her suffer severely from hunger, never giving her anything but a dish of herbs, seasoned by a very little bit of meat and a limited quantity of bread, and multiplying on every occasion fasts and abstinences. Ines, the dear friend and favourite companion of the señora, was indignant at this conduct. One day she gave vent to a burst of feeling on the subject. The good Luisa had been telling her that she found this practice of obedience very beneficial to her soul, and that she advised her to put herself under obedience to the same person, upon which Ines exclaimed—'No, señora, I dare not do so. She makes you die of hunger, and I cannot endure to see her torment you in so many ways.' 'Ah, my Ines,' Doña Luisa answered, 'the more I suffer, and sometimes I indeed almost cry from hunger, the more I feel that our Lord gives me grace to profit by it.'

She would not take any step to bring this state of things to an end. After two years the rigid monitress went into a convent, and the little society was delivered from her tyrannic rule.

Luisa had once been much struck with what the holy Abbot Pambo, one of the Fathers of the desert, said on his death bed on the subject of manual labour. He declared that ever since he had lived as a solitary no day had elapsed that he did not work with his own hands, thereby gaining his sustenance, instead of having recourse to the charity of others. She had always wished to conform her life as much as possible to that of those holy anchorites, and she resolved to earn likewise her own means of support. With this view, all the time that was not employed in religious duties was devoted by herself and her companions to working with their hands, chiefly in embroidering with gold. She thought this plan so conducive to spiritual improvement, that she used to recommend it strongly to all pious persons with whom she had anything to do : to prefer always, whenever it was possible, gaining their livelihood than depending on alms. She quoted in support of this opinion the example of the Apostle St. Paul, to whom she had a great devotion.

It was a hard life this lady had undertaken, she who had been brought up in such a different manner. It was harder to persevere in than to begin, but though she had still some severe conflicts to go through, her courage never flagged, and she pursued her course with unwearied energy. Ines, who seems to have followed her, at least at first, more from devoted affection than from an enthusiastic sympathy with her longings for poverty and humiliations, said to her one day—'To leave the world and enter a cloister, however strict and austere, is after all no such great effort. Every one respects nuns, and though they live on little they are sure of that little ; but it is really intolerable, señora, that you should be in such a state of poverty as actually to earn your own bread, or if you cannot do so to be obliged to beg. And then to expose yourself to the contempt of those who see you going along the streets to Mass, or to buy what poor food you do eat, in danger of being run over by the carriages and horses of your own relatives ; dressed in mean and shabby clothes, ill lodged, ill fed, and meanly attired, you have neither rest or comfort.' 'O Ines, how little you understand the spirit of this life, and that we do it for our Lord,' was Luisa's gentle reply to her friend's remonstrances.

The rule of life which she adopted was as strict as that of any religious. In winter and in summer she rose at three in the morning and spent three hours and a half in prayer. Then, with a face as sweet and calm as an angel's, she came out of her oratory, taking care to inquire before she went to church whether there was anything for her to do in the house. If such was the case, she accomplished whatever task was assigned to her with the greatest care and diligence, and when it was done went to the church of the Jesuit Fathers, where till eleven o'clock she prayed, heard Masses, and conferred with her confessor—briefly, however, and only as much as was necessary, for she measured everything she did, and never acted on mere impulse.

After dinner, which was at eleven o'clock, she spent an hour in recreation with her companions; afterwards they worked with their hands and conversed together on edifying subjects. Slight penances, such as are practised in religious communities were imposed whenever idle or vain words were introduced into the conversation. The señora was the first to accuse herself, and to give an example of humility in this respect, but it was difficult to find even the shadow of anything reprehensible in what she said. Heavier penalties were imposed for disobeying or murmuring. During part of the time allotted to work, silence was observed. At four o'clock, Luisa always read aloud some spiritual book, sometimes the Holy Scriptures, sometimes passages out of the writings of St. Bernard, St. Bonaventure, St. Augustine, and other Fathers of the Church. She selected whatever was best adapted for the instruction and guidance of the little society; and so great was her facility in translating Latin into Spanish, that no one could tell in what language was written the book she held in her hand. Her

explanations and comments on what she read were full
of clearness and unction. She remained with her companions till six, and then withdrew to the little oratory
for a hour of mental prayer. At seven, they supped
on eggs and vegetables, and then worked and conversed
again till nine, when they made their examination of
conscience, said the rosary and night prayers, and read
the points for the next morning's meditation. Luisa
went to bed at ten o'clock, and slept five hours. She
recited the divine office every day as long as her health
lasted. Year after year she observed this rule, never
losing a single moment of time, a point of perfection
to which she attached great importance. So great was
the recollection and reserve maintained in her abode,
that a devout gentleman who lived in the same street
and who had long had a pious curiosity to catch sight
of her, declared that he had passed before her house
more than once every day for many years and had
never seen any of the inmates either at the door or
at the window.

Few were the visitors admitted into that little house
of the Via de Toledo, and none for the purpose of idle
conversation. It was not in order to waste time in that
idle manner, Luisa used to say, that she had withdrawn
from the world. From four to five she received those
who came to her for counsel or consolation. These
were chiefly devout ladies who frequented the church
of the Society of Jesus. She spoke to them on these
occasions in the kindest and gentlest manner, and had
a singular gift for saying to each of those who consulted
her what was most suited to their state of mind and their
spiritual necessities.

Such was this lady's life, not for two or three, but for
all her remaining years. It was not, however, without
a violent struggle that she overcame that pride which

she had conquered before, but which the actual reality of humiliations foreseen and expected, but now for the first time experienced, reawakened in her soul. It is easy to endure insults, to welcome neglect, and bear mortifications in imagination. Few Christians when meditating on the Passion fail to have some transient desires for sufferings, but the revolt of nature at the first trial which puts those desires to the test too soon evinces their unreality. Luisa had fought and won her first battle with pride in her uncle's house when she deliberately planned and resolved to embrace a mode of life despised and ridiculed even by pious persons. But a harder one was in store for her when she actually found herself exposed to contempt, in need of some of the things which up to that time she had considered from habit as necessaries, and gradually forsaken and forgotten by friends and acquaintances. It is easier to leave the world than to be glad to be abandoned by it. As, in the first days of a great sorrow, excitement supports the soul by a fictitious strength, so in heroic sacrifices, there is at the outset a charm in the very magnitude of the effort, which disappears with novelty, and leaves the heart under the weight of monotony. But Luisa went through this phase of reaction, but her ardent love of our Lord carried her through it. The passionate desire for a close union with Him, which she believed could only exist when self was annihilated, gave her a kind of holy hatred for the enemies of her soul—pride, vanity, and sensitiveness. She met them in the true spirit of Christian warfare; went, as it were, into excesses on the opposite side in order to tread them under foot. To the last day of her life the pleasure she took in humiliations, if such a word can express the strange sweetness which saints find in suffering, was the result of a series of victories over the strongest passions of her soul.

CHAPTER IX.

How Doña Luisa observed the Evangelical Counsels.

THE three vows which form the basis of the religious life—those sacred engagements by which Christians bind themselves to the literal observance of the counsels of Christ, their Captain, as Spanish writers love to call Him—were made by Doña Luisa in the purest spirit of devotion, and observed with as much fervour and strictness as if she had been a Carmelite, or a Poor Clare. It is not precisely known at what age she made a vow of perpetual chastity. It probably was at a very early period of her life—at any rate, long before she retired from the world. The extraordinary purity of her life and of her soul, her dislike to the idea of marrying, and fixed resolution to consecrate herself entirely to God and renounce all earthly ties in order to live only for Him, have been already spoken of. No cloistered nun could observe the rules of modesty and reserve with a more careful circumspection. Although no shadow of temptation had ever crossed her path; though no thought had passed through her mind which could not have been revealed without a blush; yet she was as cautious and prudent as if she had been in constant danger of sin. Her very appearance awakened respect in all beholders. When, at a later period of life, she was often thrown amongst strangers, no one ever ventured to address to her a free or objectionable word. All her movements were measured and dignified. She performed the most ordinary actions with a calm composure that corresponded with that sense of the presence of God and attention to her guardian angel which never for a moment forsook her. The Queen, Doña Margarita, having heard of her virtues, felt a great desire to see her, and, by the express order of her confessor, Luisa obeyed the royal summons, and paid Her Majesty a visit. Whilst she was sitting with her, notice was suddenly given that the King was coming to the Queen's apartments. Luisa said nothing, but a slight blush and the expression of her countenance betrayed uneasiness. 'You remain here against your will,' the Queen said, with a smile. 'You are embarrassed at the thought of seeing the King.' 'Your Majesty will indeed do me a very great favour by sending me away,' Luisa replied; and taking the permission for granted, made her obeisance and hastily withdrew.

After she had spent two years in the little house of the Via di Toledo, the son of one of her relations, a nobleman of high position and character, bethought him of her beauty and many virtues, and expressed a great desire to marry her. A proposal to that effect was conveyed to Luisa. She was this time much more amused than annoyed at the unexpected offer. She could not help smiling, and said to her companions: 'I have been for two years the scandal and disgrace of my relatives, under the feet of their servants and horses, and here is one of them who wants to marry me !'

After having practised poverty of spirit ever since she could understand the meaning of the word, and led a life of actual poverty for some time, in the year 1593 Luisa made the following vow. We give it in full detail,

G

as it shows the minute care she took to place every circumstance of her life under that religious spirit which reigned in her heart—

To the greater glory of God our Lord, Who has mercifully given me the greatest possible desire to please Him in all things. I make with all my heart, in the presence of His Divine Majesty and in the hands of my Superior as His representative, a complete renunciation of all personal right and dominion over any money and any kind of property that can be considered as belonging to me, or that is to be spent for my vocation, or for my support ; without any exception whatever, it will always be subject to the direction, opinion, and counsel of my Superior. With his permission, I shall be able to use it, excluding all superfluities and vanities and mixing up of ruinous imperfection in its employment ; and with the same permission I shall be at liberty to recover debts, to receive the price of our work, and what out of kindness or charity may be given to me, and to hold and use it for the time being and in the way that my Superior will direct. The following expenses and things will be provided for out of what will be given to me as alms for those purposes. A moderate quantity of food in health or in sickness, varying according to the necessities of those states. The clothes I generally wear and am always to wear, without ever admitting into my dress anything contrary to a religious life, or that tends to a worldly style of dress. Bedding and furniture suitable to our mode of life, and other small articles of necessity requisite in health or in sickness. Medical attendance and remedies, and what it will be proper to spend for my companions, whether at home or elsewhere. Likewise decent and becoming ornaments for the oratory, and for Mass when it is said in our house ; reliquaries also, but not too costly, or with gold frames. Images and objects of devotion for the house, and instruments of penance and relics for myself, according to the orders of my Superior. Books such as are requisite for the consolation and spiritual instruction of my companions and myself; copy books, and the books which I shall translate for money, always excluding what is superfluous and unnecessary ; and if it is requisite to keep papers or other things under lock and key, I shall ask permission of my Superior, as also for any expenses in hiring or building anything I may require. In travelling, I will spend what is proper for the security and privacy of my companions and myself.

As to the vow and promise marked with a cross,[1] I shall be at liberty to do whatever may tend to its greater and more complete accomplishment, without any scruple of conscience, even if it seemed to go against my present vows ; so that with the leave and the blessing of my Superior, I shall be free to spend all the money I may require for it, even if it should have to pass through my own hands. As to all which I have said, and all matters of the same sort that may hereafter be in question, I will seek the direction of my Superior, and his permissions may be general or particular, or for whatever length of time he may see fit to grant them. If my Superior should be in some other place than myself, or absent on a journey, and without any fault or negligence of mine delays occur in writing or receiving answers, I shall be justified in acting in the manner which will seem to me most pleasing to our Lord.

If in the course of time there should be scruples in my mind, or doubts should arise concerning things not fully expressed in this vow, my Superior will have the power, at my petition and request, to decide as, in his conscience, he will deem most to the glory of our Lord and the good of my soul. All the vows of poverty, more or less strict, that I have hitherto made, and those which in any way concern my property, are dispensed and commuted by the contents of this paper, and I declare that if at any time I inherit property, or that any bequest is made to me, I shall be bound immediately to give it away to whatever pious work will seem to me most for the glory of God.

She kept this vow with great punctuality according to the spirit of the Gospel and the traditions of the primitive Church, taking every occasion of denying herself the smallest indulgences. A devout friend sent her once when she was ill a gift of sweet things and game, and

---

[1] This was a vow relating to martyrdom, which will be spoken of further on.

expected that in consideration of her sickness she would make use of these delicacies, but she learnt afterwards that every bit of her present had been instantly bestowed on the poor.

During the last years which she spent in Spain some of the pious great ladies of her acquaintance, who were devotedly attached to her, often came to seek her advice and converse with her on spiritual subjects. Sometimes they asked for a glass of water, and as the mugs in the house were too coarse and common to be presented to persons of such high rank, most of them amongst the highest ladies of the Court, Luisa for a great wonder bought a jar and plate of talavera, which proved by far the finest article in the house. One day out of fun they said to her, 'Señora, if two or three of us are with you at the same time, are we all to drink out of the same jar?' The Duchess of Medina de Rioseco, who was there with her daughters and other noble ladies, said, 'I shall send to my house for a service of porcelain, and it can remain here for our use.' A large supply arrived, and the duchess said it was not for Luisa but for herself and her daughters. Upon which Luisa smiled, as much as to say that she perfectly understood, and without a moment's delay she despatched the china to the infirmary of a neighbouring convent, and the glasses to the sacristy of the church.

Her love of obedience was equal to her love of poverty. There had never been a time in which, in some way or other, she did not practise that virtue. We have seen her submitted to the most severe trials of the kind. Her stern governess, and her loving uncle, successively employed themselves in fashioning her soul to a religious submission to the will of others and surrender of her own. In 1595, at the age of twenty-nine, she made the following vow—

Full of gratitude for the immense benefits that I have humbly received from our Lord, I offer Him and deliver up to Him that free will that it has pleased Him to give me, by a vow and promise which I make to His Divine Majesty, to obey as much as it will be possible to me the orders, mandates, and deliberate counsels of the person whom I shall choose to be, in His Name and in His place, my Superior and my guide, and I bind myself to do this on my side as much as possible, even should it happen that he did not agree to it.[2] I shall be bound to choose a Superior, either the same as I obeyed during the preceding year, or some other person present or absent, as will seem to me at the time most suitable for my soul. And if my Superior was to die in the course of the year, I would immediately fix on some one to replace him until, on the following Whit Sunday, I made another choice. And to obtain the blessing of God upon this election, for some time before the feast I will make humble supplications to our Lord, begging of Him that I, in choosing and obeying, and my Superior in guiding and governing me, should do His blessed will as perfectly as possible. And after having duly made choice of the most suitable person, without any human respect or self-willed inclination, I will accept him as my Superior in the presence of God, and from that moment respect him as if given to me by His Divine Majesty, as long as the time of his superiority lasts. The interruptions caused by his absence will be made up for by letters and similar means, and with such general or particular permissions as he may think fit to give ; and in case there occurred unavoidable delays in my sending him letters giving an account of myself and in receiving his answers, I should, in the meantime, conduct myself according to my knowledge of his will, and what my conscience would show me to be most for the service and good pleasure of our Lord.

[2] We have no information as to the person who was at this time Luisa's confessor and director ; but we may presume that it was one of the Jesuit Fathers, and the more so, as in drawing up the formula of this vow, she seems to expect some difficulty on the part of the priest whom she calls her superior to admit of this vowed obedience to him, a difficulty which would be quite in accordance with the practice and spirit of the Society.

And I declare that if in this vow and the obligations it involves there was anything that required elucidation, or there should arise in the course of time unforeseen doubts and difficulties concerning it, my Superior would have the power to solve them, by ordering whatever would seem to him best for the service of our Lord and the good of my soul, without changing anything herein clearly expressed. And as to the principal vows by which I am bound, as these papers testify, my Superior will never have the power, in virtue of this vow, to dispense me from them, nor oblige me to consent to this, nor to ask for any commutation or dispensation. I have been dispensed from all the vows I have made up to this time, and now henceforward I oblige myself to observe, to the greater glory of God, what is stated in this paper. All of which will be a help against the impediments and inconveniences which may arise in the course of time if one has one only and absolute Superior.

This vow was kept with the same zeal and care as the others. In proportion to the difficulty of the things she was commanded to do was her joy and eagerness in performing them. Her whole happiness was to consult her director and to follow his orders in every little detail. If he was absent she submitted to him by letter each doubt as it arose, and when she received his answers would take heed of everything he enjoined in order to execute it exactly. After so many years of experience and self-watchfulness she was as simply obedient as a little child, and there was nothing she did, however trifling, that was not regulated by submission to the will of her Superiors.

Sometimes, according to the spirit of the times, and to exercise her in the deepest humility, her Superior desired one of her companions to chastise her. She would kneel down and receive the discipline at her hands with the utmost devotion and submission. At other times they were ordered to try their former mistress by saying harsh and severe things to her; she always bore this with the most sweet and humble patience, and an intense joy, which shone in her countenance,

Pressed with an ardent desire of perfection, it was not long before she added to those three principal vows, one which may be termed their complement and crown—

+ 1595.

After having experienced not a few of the difficulties which are wont to oppose themselves to a progress in virtue, I have arrived at last at feeling a great ardour and the strongest desires to acquire it at the price of whatever trouble or effort it may cost me; and finding my courage increase every day, it seems to me that I may also increase the stringency of the obligations of my conscience, and I accordingly make the following vow :—Humbled by a profound sense of my nothingness, and in the sweet presence of Christ my Lord, considering what I owe Him and what I hope of His immense mercy, I have made a firm promise and vow always to do in everything what I shall consider to be most perfect in the divine sight, and to do it in the most perfect manner that will be possible to me. To avoid scruples and to make the meaning of this vow more simple, I divide it into two parts.

The first regards all those things that, from being trifling or momentary, do not require long and careful consideration, and I wish it to be understood that it will be enough for me to do them in whatever way will plainly and securely seem to me at the moment most in accordance with the perfection prescribed by my vow.

The second concerns matters of greater importance, in which I intend, if something presents itself, about which I remain in doubt as to what is the most perfect way of acting, to represent the case to my Superior and to follow his opinion, but to do this only so long as the state of doubt continues. I have never felt since I have made this vow that it bur-thened me in the least, or that it caused me disquietude or narrow scruples; on the contrary, I have always felt very glad to have made it, and a great desire to observe it to the best of my power.

Fourteen years after she hade made this vow, Luisa mentioned it to a Jesuit Father to whom she went to confession, and who was intimately acquainted with the state of her soul, and the delicacy of her conscience. This was no other than the great master of spiritual life, Luis de la Puente, the same who wrote the Life of the holy Marina de Escobar. He said no other proof was necessary of the sanctity of Luisa than that she should have made such a vow, and during so many years never wished to have it commuted, and found it a source of contentment and peace. In the observance of it not only did she avoid the slightest deliberate fault or imperfection, but she took the greatest pains to give to all her actions the highest attainable perfection. Those who had constant opportunities of watching her at every moment of her life, declared that neither in health or in sickness, nor under any circumstances, did they see her do, or hear her say, the least thing that could be considered wrong or even imperfect. Many times a day she used to lift up her heart to God and implore Him to take away her life rather than let her fall into any deliberate sin, however small. So great was the purity of her conscience that her confessors could hardly find matter for absolution in her confessions, and she had always to accuse herself of sins of her past life, and even those were not very grave. If, as must sometimes happen to the most holy persons, she did commit some little fault, she lifted up her eyes to our Lord and said, 'Do not You love me any more, my dear Redeemer? Why have You not granted me what I so earnestly desired? Your slave begs of You, my Lord, to take away her life, for she does not wish to live if it is to offend You. Henceforward I shall hate it if such is to be my fate.'

CHAPTER X

Luisa's spirit of penance.

IT was not to be expected that after having practised the utmost severities of penance from a very early age, and found that her love of God, her ardour for the salvation of souls, and the spiritual joy of her heart, increased in proportion to the tremendous austerities she performed, the holy soul which God had led in such extraordinary ways should have failed to devote herself in her retirement with still greater zeal than before to those heroic pleadings for others which saints have always been wont to combine with their voluntary sufferings. No instrument of penance seemed too sharp, no privations, no pain too keen, to one who lived in continual contemplation of a crucified, scourged, and dying God. It was a relief to her to suffer, to shed her blood in union with the blood that flowed in Gethsemani and Calvary, to carry on her aching limbs a weight similar to that which had pressed on Jesus' bruised frame, to pray that God's kingdom might come, His name be sanctified, and His will be done, not with her lips only, or even her tears, but with every pulse of her throbbing heart, and every wound of her lacerated body.

The thirst for suffering which is experienced by so many saints is a mysterious yearning, only comprehensible when considered in connection with the redemption of the world through unparalleled agonies. ' I fill up what is wanting in the sufferings of Christ.' Those startling words of St. Paul throw light on this page of the spiritual life. They explain the nails, the scourge, the cross, and the bitter draught held to the sacred lips, they account for the bloody disciplines, the iron chains, and the long fasts of the saints. The delicate girl whose history we are tracing shrank from none of these methods of subduing nature, till it became so completely subservient to the spirit, that a new and supernatural life sprang up within her, making her capable of the most heroic sacrifices. Not the least remarkable of her sufferings, that' which cost her the most, that which involved the longest exercise of patience and steady persevering endurance, was a tormenting lawsuit which she had to carry on for twelve years in order to recover her property, which since her father's death had remained in the hands of a trustee who refused to make it over to her. It is impossible to describe the delays, the disappointments, the trials, the false accusations, the extortionate pretensions she had to endure in the course of that long period of litigation. The difficulty of obtaining audiences, the bad faith with which she was treated, in consequence of the retirement in which she lived, as well as her detestation of lawsuits, her habits of solitude and prayer, all made her hate the circumstances of this trial. But she never once shrank from it. She was not to enjoy her fortune, she was not to profit by the recovery of her property; she was bound by her vow of poverty to give away at once every stiver of it. For the sake of the poor, for the interests of religion, in humble obedience to her superiors, she pursued the distasteful task, never discouraged or discontented by the slights she received or by the humiliations she went through. Ines, who shared those wearisome labours with her mistress, used sometimes to exclaim—

'Good heavens, señora, is it possible that for the sake of what you are never to possess or enjoy that you go and run under the horses' feet, and stand among servants in order to speak to the judges, looking all the time like death, and making yourself an object of derision to the world? Oh, do let us, for the love of God, leave it all alone, and let those who will have the enjoyment of it plead for its possession!' 'Do not you see, my Ines,' Luisa would answer, 'that I act under obedience, and how right it is that what I give to God should not cost me little? I wish the offering to be pure and complete, and to give my Lord not only my property, but the labour, and the trouble, and the suffering which I endure in recovering it.'

On all these trying occasions she preserved the same inward peace of heart and composure of manner as in the ordinary actions of her life. One of her advocates, an eminent lawyer, was wont to say that every time he had to confer with her on matters relating to her suit, he was struck by the excellence of her understanding and the calmness of her mind. He said he had never met with any one who united so much prudence with so much humility and modesty, and that all those who had any business to transact with her were always filled with respect and admiration for her mind and character. We must presume that she was divinely assisted in the course of this affair, for otherwise it would be difficult to imagine how a person living in poverty and obscurity, separated from her relatives, and without any of the interest which more or less influences decisions of this kind, should have brought it to a successful issue against powerful antagonists. However, one friend at last lent her his assistance, the Count de Miranda, President of Castille. He was an ardent lover of justice, and hastened the termination of her lawsuit. The use to

which she devoted the fortune thus painfully and labori-
ously recovered, will hereafter be seen.

In any life, however austere, some recreation is
necessary, some change of scene, some relaxation of
mind. Luisa's pleasures on Sundays and festivals were
her visits to the hospitals. She went through all the
wards of the women, giving them little presents, and
selecting the most disgusting and repulsive cases, in
order to distinguish them by special kindness, washing
and feeding them with her own hands, making their beds,
and gently caressing them. Her words, full of ardent
piety, and louder compassion, reached many a hardened
heart. When she spoke of our Lord it was with a
power and a tenderness that was almost irresistible.
Even over the depraved and abandoned creatures, the
scum of society, who came to die in these public
hospitals, she exercised a holy influence, which was
felt on their death beds. If any of them were dying she
remained by their side to the last, inspiring them with
feelings of contrition and hope, and smoothing their
passage to eternity. If in the streets she met some
poor, infirm, or sick being, she often brought her into
her house, seated her at her table, and treated her with
the greatest tenderness. Even poor degraded creatures
coming out of houses of shame were brought into that
home of spotless angelic purity, and if they showed a
desire to relinquish their disgraceful life nothing was
spared to withdraw them from scenes of temptation.
Once a woman was brought to her, diseased from head
to foot, and her soul more foul and miserable than her
body. She was full of pride as well as vice, and seemed
determined to fly in the face of God and of man.
Luisa took her in, made her take her meals with her,
dressed her wounds herself every day, and conquering
by an heroic effort the vehement repulsion which she

felt for this poor creature's past mode of life, actually walked in the streets of Madrid holding her by the hand and treating her as her equal.   This was too much, even for her companions.   They remonstrated—they could not endure to see this contact between their saintly mistress and so degraded a being.   They told her that the house was small, that it was intolerable to harbour in it such a wretch, that they would lose their reputation, especially if she were seen holding her by the hand.   But Luisa persisted, crushed in herself every feeling of aversion and repugnance towards the sinner, so that she might win her from her sin, and she had her way at last.   She had her reward.   The proud heart was softened ; fierce obstinacy gave way to sorrow and repentance.   The object of her care made a good general confession, and like so many others, was placed in safety and released from a life of shame by the charity of one who had bound herself by vow to tread in our Lord's footsteps *as nearly as possible.*

To all her severe penances, and privations of the most ordinary comforts of life, were soon added intense sufferings from ill-health and various painful infirmities, which often kept her for months together on her miserable couch, unable to move or almost to raise her hand.   The austerities she had practised since her childhood had probably impaired her strength, and the violent efforts she had to make in order to conquer pride and subdue in herself the risings of that passion affected her heart and made her subject to terrible palpitations.   Her sleep was constantly broken, sometimes for twenty nights running she never closed her eyes, and had at the same time to struggle with extraordinary feelings of depression and spiritual desolation.   Inwardly and outwardly her existence was a perpetual martyrdom, and she never allowed herself any indulgences in her sicknesses unless she was too ill to be conscious of what was done around her, or else when her confessor enjoined anything contrary to her ordinary habits. Once at Valladolid, where she followed the Court in order to carry on her suit, she had a violent fever, with so terrible a headache, that the Court physicians wondered how a person could exist under so great an agony. Indeed, at times her sufferings arrived at such a pitch, and her ardent yearnings after union with our Blessed Lord so overwhelming, that she would have expired had He not come to her assistance and filled her soul with such a flood of spiritual consolation, that she revived as by a miracle. The doctors were sometimes astonished at finding a person whom they had left apparently at the last extremity, after a few hours restored to health and activity. No trial, bodily or spiritual, seems to have been spared to this soul, whom God had chosen to purify like gold in the furnace. Often in her sleepless nights she watered her couch with tears, and exclaimed in the words of the Psalmist—'The sorrows of death have got hold of me and the terrors of hell have compassed me about.' Fears of the divine justice seized her at times, and apprehensiveness that she might be separated from God for eternity. At this thought a cold sweat covered her forehead and a fearful trembling shook her frame. In these hours of anguish her recourse was to lift up her voice, and cry to Him from the depths of her sorrow and humiliation. Passionate pleadings such as these would escape her lips—'Lord, because Thou art what Thou art, and through Thine immense goodness, I ask Thee, not for the joys of earth or heaven, not for deliverance from temporal or eternal sorrows, but this I implore with all the strength of my soul, that I may never be separated from Thee. Let me love Thee. Grant me this grace. Let me feel that Thou lookest upon me as one of Thy servants, and then shower upon me all the punishments that my sins deserve, all the sufferings with which it may please Thee to visit me.'

When she had poured forth her soul in this prayer, a great calm usually followed, a firm confidence that in the midst of these storms of anguish and temptation her Divine Lord was by her side and that He would never forsake her. In her infirmities, her illnesses, her mental trials, she never omitted the practice of penance or ceased to offer herself up to yet severer sufferings for the salvation of others. Enough has been said already to convey an idea of her extraordinary humility. Her opinion of herself was the lowest possible. She utterly despised the praises that people sometimes gave her for her good works and her piety. It seemed to her simply absurd that those who did not know the interior of her heart should pretend to form an opinion as to her merits. 'Correspondence with grace,' she was wont to say, 'was the only criterion of real virtue, and none but herself knew how she had fallen short of what she ought to have been after the many favours which had been granted to her. Like St. Francis of Assisi, she believed that no one else who had received such graces would have profited so little by them. Even in her early youth she seemed so insensible to praise that her uncle used to say she had a wall in her ears when her own merits were spoken of, and that there was no danger of making her vain, for the more she was reminded of what God had done for her the deeper was her self-abasement at seeing herself still as imperfect as she felt herself to be. She behaved to every one as if they were her superiors, and after she had left the house of her relatives it never happened to her to address the poorest or lowest creature in existence without speaking in the third person, which amongst Spaniards is a token of respect. She was sweetness itself in language and in manner. Though very reserved

and modest, there was a singular sweetness and gracious-
ness in her countenance and manner. Austere as was
her life, she never put on an air of gravity or severity.
Nothing ever induced her, after her retirement from the
world, to sit down at table with persons of rank, and
if, in the course of her troublesome lawsuit, she was
obliged to visit some grandees at the hour of the noonday
meal, and that they importuned her to take some refreshment, she eat something with the women servants, and
availed herself of that opportunity to speak to them
of religion and awaken good desires in their minds.
Amongst her own companions she always took the
lowest place, and never would allow them to show her
any marks of consideration. Sometimes, when she went
to hear Mass at the church of the Jesuits, she took with
her a cork mat. One of her attendants begged that she
would let her carry it. 'Oh, no, Sister,' she said ; 'if I
am obliged to have a mat to sit on, the least I can do is
to carry it myself.'

Once, in Valladolid, she was looking attentively at
some men who were working in the streets. 'What are
you thinking of, señora?' one of her companions asked.
'Of my own inferiority to those poor men,' she replied.
'I do not understand how that could be, either in
the eyes of the world or the eyes of God,' the other
answered. 'We are equals,' Luisa rejoined, 'in that we
are children of Adam, brought into the world in the same
manner and destined to go out of it in the same way ;
and in the spiritual order it is more than probable that
they will have a higher place in heaven than me.' Her
humility was founded not on ignorance of the gifts and
graces which God had bestowed upon her—these she
recognized with adoring gratitude—but on the deep
sense of their being gratuitous and undeserved mercies,
for each of which she would have to render a strict

account. Her self-abasement and fear of her Heavenly
Father increased, therefore, in proportion with her
progress in holiness. The more she advanced in perfection the more did the claims of our Blessed Lord press
on her soul with force and clearness almost overwhelming. The words of the Gospel—'From him to whom
much has been given much will be required,' seem to
have been ever sounding in her ears as a warning
stimulus, and an incentive to humility. When engaged
later on in England in heroic works of charity, she wrote
to one of her confessors who had asked her if she felt
tempted to vainglory—

I very much relished your warning against vainglory,
which comes naturally from so grave a person when placing
such elevated considerations before eyes which are so lowly
and so unworthy of them. However, the old grace is
preserved, increases, and is strengthened by the new
and continued motive of the love of my most sweet Lord ;
and others that I am always discovering in my most
unfaithful correspondence and my weakness are such, that
I am in greater danger of faintheartedness than vainglory.
Nor do I know how nor in what manner that which so
powerfully draws a soul out of herself, carries her towards
her Beloved, and transforms her so marvellously into Him,
can cause self-complacency ; for that soul so desires to make
Him the absolute master of her glory that, supposing the
glory were hers and not His, she could not tolerate that the
least particle should not be His.

CHAPTER XI.

Luisa's love of humiliations and zeal for souls.

ALWAYS engaged in fighting her most dangerous enemy, Luisa took every opportunity of acting contrary to the feelings of pride, or rather of esteem for rank and position, which had once reigned in her heart. Not content with performing the work of a drudge within her house, she sometimes issued from it with the basket of sweepings on her head, and emptied it into the middle of the broad Calle de Toledo. If any of her relatives or her acquaintances were passing at that moment, she did not draw back or turn away, but went straight on with her business, neither more slowly nor more quickly than if no one had been observing her. On one occasion some carriages were stopping the way, and she had to stand still till they moved on. One of the coachmen said to the other—'Look at that woman ; she is a cousin of your master's.' The other man took this as an insult, and cried—'She must be a mad woman.' The rabble in the streets often amused themselves by calling her names ; she listened to their insults with the same serenity of countenance as if they had been showering praises upon her. Vitoria Coloña, Duchess of Medina de Rioseco, one day driving through the Plaça de Valladolid, saw Luisa with a basket on her arm buying some vegetables at a stall. She stopped her carriage and said—'How can you, dear Luisa, mortify and humble yourself in this way?' 'Your excellency humbles and mortifies herself much more than I do,' Luisa replied, with a smile, 'by condescending to speak to me here.' The duchess tried to persuade her to get into her carriage, and to let her drive her home, but the offer was steadily refused. Another time, in Madrid, the Countess de la Puebla found her very far from her home, and insisted on conveying her to her house. Luisa was obliged to give way to her importunities, but she would not sit by her side· in the carriage, and ensconced herself in a corner at the bottom.

Once, also in Madrid, she was buying eatables in the Plaça, and standing in the mud, when her first cousin, the Marquis of Almaçan, rode by with a numerous retinue. He pretended not to see her, but his servants began to whisper to each other, and to wonder at seeing her in so mean a dress and occupied in so menial a manner. The companion she had with her was a little vexed at this, but Luisa went on making her purchases with the most perfect contentment and self-possession.

One day when she was very ill, her confessor sent her word that there was a dying person whom it was important she should visit, for the sake of her soul. As she literally could not stand, they brought her a portable chair, but she was quite shocked at going through the streets in such state, and insisted on riding a waterman's donkey. Her weakness was so great that one of her companions was obliged to support her or she would have fallen off, and not being used to riding she had great difficulty in keeping her seat. The boys laughed and pointed at her as she went along, but those who accompanied her declared that her face during that time was more like that of an angel than a mere woman.

She used to wear a coarse sort of tippet over her woollen dress, which she said was to keep herself warm.

H 2

In reality it was a constant occasion of mortification. People were always inclined to laugh when they saw it. They asked what she would sell it for, and gave it all sorts of nicknames. Another time when it was raining torrents and she wanted to go to Mass, she covered herself with an old rug and walked to church in that singular attire. A group of urchins who had taken shelter under a doorway, caught sight of this strange figure and ran after her crying, ' Mother witch, mother witch,' and other similar names. She did not show the slightest displeasure, but went on her way rejoicing at the victories she was gaining over her old enemy, the passion for esteem and honour. If at one time of her life she had had a full share of praise and consideration, the case was now reversed. Everything most contemptuous and disparaging was said about her. Some declared she was out of her mind, and ought to be shut up ; others that her relatives were more to blame than herself; that they ought never to have allowed an unmarried lady of noble birth to lead so mean and absurd a kind of life. These things were often repeated to her. She took no notice of them, and if they sometimes caused her pain, she offered it up, like her other sufferings, to Him for Whose sake she had renounced the world.

The severest struggle she had with herself was to become a beggar in the strict sense of the word. She had despoiled herself of everything she possessed in favour of the poor, and had acquired the right to solicit alms like the most necessitous amongst them. But actually to do this was a terrible effort. With the permission of her confessor, which she always asked on these occasions, she one day said to Ines, the sole deposity of her secret acts of charity or humiliation, 'Come with me, Ines ;' and hiding a bowl under her cloak, she led the way to the Church of San Francisco.

She was then living in Madrid. She reached the church a little while before the distribution of food. As usual, Luisa went into the church, adored our Lord on the altar, and then came and seated herself amidst the women who were waiting for alms. She seized the opportunity, as was her wont, of speaking to them of God and holy things in a way suited to their comprehension. When the religious from the adjoining convent appeared, bringing with them the food which out of their poverty they bestowed on the needy, a hungry and clamorous crowd pressed forward to receive it. Luisa advanced with the rest holding her bowl in her hands, and with great humility and composure said, ' Father, for the love of God, give me an alms.' Something in the sound of her voice struck the good Father, he looked at her attentively and said, 'You seem a respectable person, take this,' and he filled her bowl and gave her several bits of bread. She received what he bestowed upon her with great reverence, and went back into the church carrying it with her. She put down the bowl on a seat, and kneeling down with her hands clasped together she praised God for His great goodness. Her prayer lasted so long that Ines, who was afraid that the religious would come into church for vespers and find her in that position, began to call her mistress and to pull her by her gown. She was so absorbed in devotion that for some time it was impossible to make her attend; at last, by dint of efforts, her companion succeeded in rousing her. She quietly took up her bowl and her bread, and sitting on the steps outside the church, she and Ines enjoyed this rich repast, carefully putting by the bits that remained, for their evening meal, as people do who set aside food they have particularly relished. She did this several times both in Madrid and in Valladolid. On one occasion she had not brought a bowl with her; an old, blear-eyed woman by her side, seeing she had nothing in which to eat the soup that was being distributed, offered her the bowl she had just been using, cleaning it at the same time with a very dirty hand. The poor old beggar's appearance was so disgusting, that it was only by a violent effort over herself that Luisa could bring herself to accept the proffered kindness. Hardly anything could have cost her more, for she was extremely particular about clean-liness; but humility, the spirit of mortification, and the fear of wounding the poor old soul prevailed over her repugnance; she took the bowl, held it out to be filled, and seated amidst the beggars swallowed the soup which was poured into it.

In Madrid, she left off this practice because the religious found out who she was, and the poor knew her also and began to call her the poor saint. At Valladolid, a monk gave her one day a severe rebuff, and told her to go and look out for work or for a situation, instead of wandering about the streets. She received this reproof in the humblest manner, and with-drew in silence.

Whilst thus training herself to the practice of the most profound humility, Luisa was continually engaged in the most strenuous efforts for the conversion and sanctifica-tion of souls. No one, her biographer tells us, ever effected more in that way with as little noise or publicity. His expression is, that 'she seemed to do nothing, and she did wonders.' She never spoke of what she did, but she acted unremittingly. Without appearing to seek it, she exercised an extraordinary power over the hearts of others, maintaining them in the right path or recalling them to it as the case might be. She had a way of saying in a few words what was most likely to have an effect on those to whom she was speaking. A hint from her, a passing remark was sometimes enough to awaken repentance or revive good resolutions or excite to perfection persons whom she casually addressed. Her manner and her words were always gentle and kind. Nothing by force, everything by sweetness, was one of her favourite maxims. She used to say that our Lord's way of dealing with us was like that of a tender and wise father who manages his children with great suavity, not that of a galley-slave master who rules by blows and violence. Hers was the true spirit of an apostle. It was perfect misery to that ardent and loving soul to see our Lord offended and ungratefully treated by those for whom He had shed His Blood. Her prayers, her penances, and her sufferings were all offered up for that one object: that souls might be converted to Him. And no trouble, no sacrifice, was too much if an opportunity offered to draw away any one from sin. If she saw or heard somebody doing or saying something wrong, she would go to them and in a manner that was almost irresistible induce them to leave off offending God.

In her own house she did not overlook the least thing that was reprehensible, but she pointed out faults with such a tender charity that her remonstrances were more a pleasure than a mortification to those whom she reproved. She had a marvellous talent for inspiring courage in the practice of virtue and the exercises of penance. Of the joy which follows sacrifices, the intense happiness of a soul which has obtained a victory over self, the deep peace of a heart whose passions are subdued and whose will is lost in that of God, she spoke in a way which seemed to lift those under her care over the repugnances and difficulties of the heavenward path. If she knew that any persons were estranged or offended, she did not rest until they were appeased and reconciled to each other.

To all those capable of such teaching, she urgently recommended not to content themselves with keeping the commandments, but to aim at the observance of the evangelical counsels, and many persons by her advice entered into the most reformed religious orders, and proved by their devout and fervent lives how good had been the training they had received from her. Others, to whom so high a vocation was not given, learnt from her to practise mental prayer, and to lead lives of piety and self-denial. She took the greatest pains to instruct and advance in virtue poor people who could not read, and were ignorant of spiritual truths. The slaves and servants of the ladies who frequented her house were the objects of her constant solicitude. She spoke to them of their duties, and persuaded them to serve their mistresses faithfully for the love of God, and not out of fear or interest. Her talents, which were of no common order, her powers of speaking and of writing, were all devoted to one end. She had a singular gift for quieting and cheering souls distracted by scruples and temptations. By her words or by her letters, she often restored peace and tranquillity to disturbed and anxious hearts. Not a moment of this holy woman's time was wasted. She acted, she spoke, she thought, but with a view to the glory of God. Grace was given to her to perform actions which were quite out of the common order, and which none could venture upon safely without a special gift and a special inspiration. The peculiar characteristic of Luisa was the union of a delicate timid reserve with an undaunted fearlessness that never shrank from any difficulty or danger where God's interests were concerned. Pure as an angel, and as ignorant of evil as a child, she would go into the abodes of women of bad reputation, seat herself in the midst of them, and in terms of moving eloquence and imploring earnestness, entreat them to abandon their sinful lives, and turn with contrite hearts to God. She would lead them by the hand out of the house of iniquity, and dare the rage of those from whom she was rescuing them.

One of her relatives, a religious, had left his monastery and embarked in various worldly enterprizes, to the great grief of his holy kinswoman. She sent him repeated messages and warnings, and when he fell into difficulties, assisted him repeatedly—not, she said, because he was a nobleman, but because, being poor, he had a right to her alms. At last a violent fever seized him, and he became dangerously ill. She sent him a message imploring him to have mercy on his own soul, and make a general confession. He sent her word that he could not, that the power of speaking failed him. Upon which she went to her oratory, and on her knees, pleading with God for that soul, wrote him a letter which had more effect upon him than the message. The next day, after fervent prayers, she wrote again with still more pressing earnestness than the first time, and sent the letter by a priest of the Society of Jesus. The victory of grace was this time achieved. The dying man confessed his sins with great contrition, and after receiving the Viaticum, died in the habit of his order. Luisa's joy at this conversion was great, but even then she did not abandon the soul for which she had so fervently pleaded, turning to her companions, she said—'Now we must help him, for great are his sufferings in Purgatory.'

One of the persons who was employed in Luisa's lawsuit was well repaid for the trouble he took for her by the spiritual help and advice she gave him. She persuaded this man of the world to go to Communion once a week. During thirty years he persevered in the practice. If at times tepidity or discouragement tempted him to omit it, the thought of that servant of

God, who had been so anxious about his soul, strengthened him in those weak hours. She had also advised
him to moderate earthly desires, and restrain ambitious hopes. Her words sunk so deeply in his mind,
that he gave up many temporal advantages that he might
well have aspired to, and in the latter part of his life
thought of becoming a priest. His last years were
employed in writing the lives of some of the saints in the
Roman martyrology.

Doña Aldonça de Zuniga, daughter of the Count of
Miranda, President of Castille, attributed her vocation to the holy examples and instructions of Luisa.
Young, beautiful, and rich, sole daughter of her father's
house and heart, she chose evangelical poverty as her
portion, and was the first of the many highborn Spanish
maidens who entered the Convent of the Incarnation at
Madrid. Her life was worthy of a friend of Luisa's.
She was wise as well as holy, and gained many souls to
the Augustinian Reform, to which she was particularly
devoted.

CHAPTER XII.

Luisa's Devotion to the Blessed Sacrament.

FROM the time that in her eleventh year Luisa de Carvajal made her first communion in the parish church at Almaçan, and nearly fainted with emotion at the foot of the altar where she was about to receive Him Whom she had loved since her infancy, her devotion to the holy Sacrament of the Altar became every day more intense. She found in it the strength to lead so austere and penitent a life, and the graces which she was the means of imparting to so many souls. As long as she lived in her uncle's house, she found impediments to the practice of frequent communion, and an especial difficulty in approaching the sacraments on certain great festivals ; in the home of such pious persons as the Marquis of Almaçan and his wife, this seems surprising. The reason alleged by her biographer shows how even the most religious people are apt to give in to the objectionable habits of the times in which they live. Luis Munoz, writing as he does about seventeen years after Luisa's death, says that in palaces these festivals are wont to be celebrated rather by banquets and gaieties than in the devout spirit with which they were instituted.[1] It was the custom on those days to go to processions and functions, and come home very late to public breakfasts, at which she was obliged to be present. In order not to be deprived of her heavenly food, she had

[1] This probably refers to the feasts of patron saints, rather than the great festivals of the Church.

to fast until a late hour, and procure a Mass to be said at which she could communicate.

During her residence with her uncle she did not go to Communion more than once a week, which at that time was considered to be very often. After she left the world and adopted her peculiar mode of life, she was allowed by her confessor, a Jesuit Father, to communicate on Sundays and on Thursdays. She wished very much to have leave to do so on all the principal festivals, and that her two communions should always take place in the course of the week, though on different days, if any impediment had occurred on those given by her director. But she could not obtain this permission, not even in case of her having been confined to her bed by illness. This was a severe mortification. The ardent desire she had of the Blessed Sacrament made it a cruel suffering to be deprived of it. Her soul literally pined for the heavenly food and a daily union with her Lord. But she never hesitated to submit to her confessor, though many spiritual persons took upon themselves to advise her otherwise. She never would listen to their suggestions, and would rather have died than disobeyed. For four years at least after she had settled in her wretched little house she underwent this privation. At the end of that time her confessor left Madrid, and the priest that succeeded him took a different view of the question. He allowed her many extra communions, and after a time came to the conclusion that it would be well for her to communicate every day. Her life was a perfect one ; it was filled by a constant succession of holy exercises. There were no distractions in it or impediments of any kind.

At that time the Society discouraged its confessors from granting to their penitents permission to communicate every day. The Provincial appointed certain

Fathers well versed in spiritual matters to examine and judge of the virtue, the piety, the devout exercises, the recollection, the spirit of prayer, and, in short, the whole state of the soul, to whom there was question of granting that privilege, and none, however pious and good they were supposed to be, were exempted from this ordeal. Luisa went through it to the great edification and satisfaction of those who were appointed to examine her.

Speaking of the various opinions that exist in the Church relative to the degree of virtue requisite in those who daily receive Communion, the author of Luisa's life declares that he cannot resist quoting the description which John Rusbroch, a learned and eminent Carthusian deeply conversant with spirituality, gives in one of his works of the persons to whom that favour may be safely granted, and that he does so because a more exact portrait of the holy woman whose life he writes could not be given—

'Such persons (says Rusbroch) are recollected in the interior of their souls ; by the grace of God, and in a holy liberty of spirit they keep themselves constantly in the presence of God. So strong is their habitual recollection, that it governs and controls their hearts, their minds, their bodies and all their faculties. They make continual progress in self-mastery, and enjoy great internal peace. If temptations sometimes assail their souls, they are soon overcome, for evil passions cannot establish their dominion where nature is habitually mortified. They have much knowledge and light regarding our Lord Jesus Christ, both in His Divinity and His Sacred Humanity ; their minds being free from worldly thoughts and images, they are able to contemplate His holy mysteries in the interior of their souls, and their hearts, detached from the love of creatures, rise with an intense love to the Divine Creator, whilst their exterior actions are united every moment with the actions and the virtues of Jesus Christ. The more they know the more they love, and the more they love the more they taste the delights of Communion, and the more they taste the more they hunger and thirst after them, ever desiring, ever seeking, ever experiencing that with their whole heart and soul and spirit they truly love the Lord. These are the persons who, when they look upon their sins, their faults, and their imperfections, and how far they are from the perfection to which they aim, are discontented with themselves, and feel a holy fear of God, in Whose awful presence they stand in respectful adoration. Their good works are as nothing in their sight ; their sufferings, whether external or internal, they despise, entering into themselves in order there to find the Lord, going out of themselves to hold as nought their best actions. Those who understand these things, and who live in this way, may safely be permitted to communicate every day. Their life is composed of purity of conscience and freedom from any grave sin, wisdom in contemplation and in action, a true humility of heart, of spirit, and of conduct, and a perfect submission of their will to the will of God.' This is part of what the holy Carthusian required in those who daily approach the altar, and what Luis Munoz tells us was true to the life of Luisa.

The permission given to her to communicate daily was not absolute and general. She had to ask it day by day of her confessor, who was very particular on that point, and tried her by occasional refusals, which were as many severe mortifications, on account of the peculiar manner in which she felt the privation of Communion. A more frequent approach to the sacraments produced, as might have been expected in one who corresponded so carefully with the graces vouchsafed to her, an extra-

ordinary increase of holiness and piety. The weak parts
of her character were strengthened ; her .imperfections
disappeared more and more ; a clearer light was given
her to discern on every occasion God's will, what He
required of her soul, and a more absolute sense than
ever that to know Him and to love Him were the only
worthy objects of this earthly life.

Her preparations for Communion were most exact and
careful. In fact, the whole of her existence was passed
in preparation and in thanksgiving for that great gift.
Most days she went to confession, in order to clean her
soul from the least defilements, and then approached the
altar with a keen sense of her unworthiness, her nothingness, and an awe which increased instead of diminishing
as time went on. The frequency of her communions did
not affect, but rather heightened this feeling. As she
grew more united with her Lord, her consciousness of
the overwhelming majesty and astonishing condescension
of her Heavenly Guest became more keen, and her watch-
fulness over herself more exact. She counted the hours
between one Communion and another. Nothing but
actual impossibility to leave her bed could keep her
from church even in the severest weather, and before
she had leave to have Mass in her oratory, the fear of
this privation was the only reason that made her dread
being ill.

In a severe illness, during which she was so prostrated
as to be hardly able to speak or move, and seemed
scarcely to recognize any one, it was observed that she
always watched the clock, and after it had struck twelve
would take nothing, nor even rinse her mouth, for fear of
swallowing water and losing her Communion. These
ardent desires, this constant faith and constant craving
for the Divine Presence in her heart, were rewarded in a
singular, it might almost be said a miraculous, manner,

for when she obtained leave to have Mass and to go to Communion in her oratory, hopeless as it might seem beforehand, a priest always came to offer up the Holy Sacrifice in the little chapel where our Lord was so lovingly expected. Like her countrywoman, St. Teresa, Luisa would have braved any danger for the sake of Communion, and yet, with all this impassioned fervour, this enthusiastic devotion, this overpowering joy in the possession of our Lord, one word from her confessor was enough to stop her on her way to the altar. The same love which made her yearn for that sacred Presence in her heart made her unhesitatingly obedient to the voice which spoke in His name. The simple words, ' Do not. communicate to-day,' arrested at once those pious transports, and caused her an amount of suffering which only saints can appreciate. Her obedience was frequently put to the test. Her director knew that there was no other sacrifice which would cost her anything in comparison, and to increase in her that surrender of the will without which no sanctity is real, he often deprived her of Holy Communion for days together. Her body as well as her soul languished for lack of the heavenly sustenance, and she seemed so ill and exhausted that her companions were uneasy about her. Once when this happened one of them said—' Do go to Communion, señora.' Luisa raised her head, and answered with her quiet energy—' If every saint in heaven and on earth were to tell me to communicate, and my confessor forbad it, I would rather die than disobey.' Every day she asked the question, ' Shall I communicate ?' and if the answer was ' No,' she humbly bowed her head, spent the usual time in church, and performed all her daily duties with the same sweet and serene countenance as at other times. She never spoke of her trial, or allowed herself to think that she was treated with undue severity.

If her companions adverted to the subject she would only say—'Sisters, our business is to do God's will in everything, without stopping to discuss the commands we receive and the reasons why they are given.'

Luisa's biographer, at this point of her history, enters into an elaborate defence of the conduct of her confessors in having thus deprived her at times of Holy Communion, and of her prudence and virtue in submitting to their orders. He apprehends that some of his readers may argue that they had no right to subject her to the privation of so great a blessing and acknowledged means of grace, and that she not only might but ought to have disregarded their prohibitions, and communicated without their permission on the strength of the words of St. Paul, 'Let a man prove himself, and so let him eat of that bread and drink of the chalice.' But this, he goes on to say, was not that holy woman's opinion; she thought that the safest road she could follow was that of obedience, and she received abundant proofs that God rewarded her humble spirit of submission to those appointed to be her guides. Secular persons who wish to lead a life of close union with our Lord, and have not, like nuns, constant opportunities of having their will and their understanding brought into subjection, are often in danger of delusions, and it is incumbent on their directors to try the spirit which animates them, and judge by their humility and obedience whether what is out of the common way in their mode of life and their devotions is the genuine fruit of holy inspirations or only the result of a fanciful imagination or a self-willed love of notoriety. Sacraments are the means of acquiring virtue; and no doubt Luisa's confessors knew that when she accepted the most painful of sacrifices because it was required of her by those she looked upon as our Lord's representatives, this act of

I

obedience was more useful to her soul than uninterrupted communions.

It was her practice whenever she had received our Lord in her heart to spend a hour in prayer as motionless as a carved image, enjoying a happiness beyond what human language can express. It was only by pulling her by the arm or by the cloak that she could be recalled from that blissful trance. Once when she was praying in the church of the Jesuits at Madrid, the groom of the chambers of a great lady came to lay down a carpet where Luisa was kneeling. Ladies in those days, Luis Munoz satirically remarks, came to church, and did not, as in his time, make their palaces their parish churches. The zealous attendant ordered her several times to get out of the way, but though he pushed her, she remained immovable, upon which he lost his temper and struck her leg with the stick of the carpet he wanted to unroll. When her companion came out of a neighbouring confessional, Luisa told her of the pain she felt in her limb, but did not know what had caused it. During those hours of sacred converse and intimate union with God, she had so keen a sense of the Divine Presence within her that the suffering was almost equal to the joy. At all times she seemed to be filled with a mysterious pining to share in the anguish of our Lord's Passion. Her thoughts on spiritual subjects were often consigned to paper. Many of these outpourings of a soul on fire with the divine love exist. We will occasionally give some extracts from them. The following passage exhibits the craving for suffering just described.

+
J. H. S.

On Friday, the 12th of February, 1599, after I had communicated, and was inwardly contemplating the Person of the Incarnate Word of God, such as He looked when He

was ill treated by His enemies, His delicate head wounded
with sharp thorns, and His royal and incomparable hands
pierced by the nails, my soul seemed to cleave to Him by an
unspeakable love, as if He was thus really within me in that
state. I felt an incredible satisfaction, and an increased
desire, and an excessive though painless thirst, to be afflicted
and insulted, and a keen sense of what Christ had then
endured. A little book happened to be in my hand. It was
opened at the twenty-first chapter of St. Augustine's *Meditations*, in which he sweetly discourses of the happiness of
heaven. I glanced at the page, and I could see no charm
nor take any pleasure in that description. My soul was
constrained to turn from it and withdraw into itself, and
nothing could distract me from that inward contemplation.
A tender but mighty love had taken possession of my whole
will, which found therein full and entire satisfaction. It
only tormented me to think of all that heavenly glory and
felicity, and of anything that was not that which I was then
feeling, and it seemed as if I could not bear to have my soul
drawn away from that Divine and most sorrowful Presence,
and that I chose for my only and supreme glory to be trans-
formed into the likeness of that Divine Person, and myself
in the same state in which I saw Him, my soul nailed to the
Cross, pierced with the same thorns, and suffering as far as
possible the same pains ; and I could not fancy having, or
ever having had, any other joy than that inestimable and
close union with the Incarnate Word of God wounded and
despised for me, or any heaven or glory but that of suffering
His torments and His humiliations. I had a deep and
refined sense of the sufferings of Christ, which did not then
give me pain, but a feeling of ardent love that entirely
engrossed my heart and seemed to raise it to a higher
sphere.

After what has been said of her feelings about Communion, it is scarcely necessary to add that Luisa had a
special devotion to our Lord in the Blessed Sacrament.
The Spanish expression used is that she paid a continual
court to that Sacred Presence. By preference, she always
went to Communion and said her prayers before the

I 2

altar where It was, and expressed the happiness she felt there by saying that she did not care for heaven so long as she might remain before the Blessed Sacrament. On Holy Thursday she did not leave the church day or night whilst Christ our Lord was in the sepulchre. On the feast of Corpus Christi and whenever the Blessed Sacrament was exposed, she watched before It with enraptured devotion. In her walks through the streets she always entered every church on her way, and, falling down on her knees, repeated with the most profound reverence those words of the Psalms — *Omnis terra adoret te et psallat tibi.* If the church was locked it did not hinder her devotion. She prostrated herself on the outward steps, and paid homage to her Sovereign Lord, residing in an earthly tabernacle. She lost no opportunity of persuading others to adopt this practice, and to utter those words of praise with a deep feeling of love and awe.

It need scarcely be added that one so devoted to our Divine Lord was a devout daughter of His Blessed Mother. She evinced this in every possible manner, but chiefly by a continual endeavour to imitate her virtues. The little *casicas*, whether in Madrid or in Valladolid, where she sanctified every hour by prayer, labour, charity, and silence, presented perhaps as close a representation as can be conceived of the holy House of Nazareth. From the first dawn of reason Luisa had followed the example of her Mother in heaven, by consecrating her whole being to God, and as we shall see later on, she made her the inheritor of all her earthly substance. St. Mary Magdalene was her favourite saint. She loved her because she loved our Lord so much. Then, out of a strong attachment to the three theological virtues, she had a particular devotion to St. Louis of France, whose faith was so great that, when some persons were urging him to come to a church where they said that a miracle was taking place, and our Blessed Lord visible in the Host, he said, 'Let those go who have ever doubted that our Lord is there;' to the patriarchs of the Old Law, whose expectation of the Redeemer's coming exemplified hope; and to St. Augustine, whom she looked upon as the type of charity. His writings were her delight, especially his meditations on the Holy Scriptures. St. Chrysostom also she venerated, because he has spoken so well of the love of our Lord and of mental prayer. Saints who had once been great sinners she had a special attraction for, as is often seen in peculiarly pure souls; but, above all, for those who had endured great persecutions for the sake of religion. This gave her an extraordinary attachment to St. Ignatius of Loyola, the 'captain of that glorious Society, which conquers the world by suffering and endurance.' She exulted in those persecutions, which then as now make it the chosen portion of Christ's army. St. Catharine of Siena she venerated especially, on account of the ardent apostolic spirit which would have made her wish, if it could have been permitted, to put on the habit of a Friar preacher, and go about the world converting souls to God. This desire naturally found an echo in the heart of one who was one day to sacrifice everything for the sake of winning back to the Church some of her deceived and estranged children.

We have now to speak of Luisa's spirit of prayer, and the long hours she spent in communion with God. In modern biographies, details such as these regarding the interior life of saints, or persons whom we may suppose to have been saints, are reserved for the concluding chapters of their lives, and form, as it were, an appendix to their history rather than a part of it. Luisa's biographer follows a different plan, and it may be well to adhere

to it; for the more we become acquainted with the tone
of her mind and the character of her piety, the better
we can appreciate the resolution we shall see her take,
which, extraordinary as it was, especially at the time
in which she lived, was evidently not the result either
of a violent enthusiasm or a love of notoriety and excitement, but a strong, calm, deliberate carrying out of the
object she had proposed to herself from her youth
upward, that is, to imitate our Lord as closely as possible. We find through the whole of her life this one
unvarying principle of action; no abrupt changes, no
intermitting fits of fervour and tepidity—a perpetual
thought of God, a constant sense of His presence, a
rigorous adoption of what, at any rate, appeared to her
the line of conduct most in accordance with the evangelical counsels, an extraordinary one, no doubt, and
framed on the model of the most austere sanctity, but
consistent, firm, and calm. Her piety had gone on
steadily increasing from her earliest years, like a river
that deepens and widens as it advances, and the graces
she received in prayer were no doubt very great, but she
preserved a constant silence regarding them. God alone
knew the secret of what passed between her soul and
Him, and she did not even dwell in her own mind on
those extraordinary favours of which others would have
thought so much. Her whole study was how to promote
the divine glory and the salvation of souls; self was the
last subject of her reflections. Whilst she lived, little
was known of her interior life, for it was only to her
confessors, and that only when desired to do so, that
she spoke of the spiritual favours vouchsafed to her;
to no other creature did she speak of them. It was
God's concern, not hers. It all came from Him. She
had no right to deal with such graces as if they were
her own.

When any friends tried to make her break through this reserve, the expression of her countenance showed that they were infringing on what she held too sacred for human converse. No one could speak of our Blessed Lord more admirably than she did, but it was always with great recollection, and a fear of displeasing Him by unguarded expressions. After her death, the following account of what she aimed at in prayer was found amongst her papers—

JESUS. MARY.

I do not wish to proceed further without saying that I do not remember ever in my life aspiring to sensible devotion and tenderness in prayer, or taking notice of anything of the sort. What I desired was essential virtue, and to acquire a pure and strong love of God, and that my soul should be in that state which would please Him ; and I was too much occupied by this to have time or to care much for anything else. I paid very little attention to what I read about revelations, for I was occupied with what referred more directly to the mortification of self and of the senses, and detachment from creatures, and I liked conversations and books which treated of such subjects. On that I took my stand. Not only did I read and listen to the reading of such works without ever being tired of them, but I tried, as it were, to print their contents on my soul, just as if they were written in a book, and preserved them in my memory, so as to have them at hand at every step, and I have never taken pleasure in any other kind of reading or thinking. It was distasteful to me, and fatigued my mind. Our Lord no doubt permitted this in order to make me conscious of its bad effect on my soul.

Luisa's prayer was not discursive, and was for the most part without sensible sweetness. It was continual. She prayed all day, and the greatest part of the night. Her hands were actively employed in work, but it cost her an effort to apply herself to any occupations, however good in themselves, which drew her mind away from positive communion with God—such as writing on devotional subjects, or drawing up accounts of her examinations of conscience, so as to compare one week with another, and thank God for all His mercies. She was for so many hours alone in her room, that her companions, anxious to know how she spent the time, made holes in the door through which they could watch her. Whenever they thus indulged their curiosity, she was always seen in the same position, her head raised, and her eyes uplifted with a beautiful expression. Her hands were clasped, her body motionless, her spirit rapt in prayer. They had to knock over and over again before she heard them. Whenever she left her oratory, or anywhere rose from her knees, she used to say—'Come with me, my Lord;' or, 'Do not let me go without Thee.'

It once happened to her to kneel down on a winter night to make her examination of conscience in a gallery, where the morning sun found her still on her knees in the same attitude, absorbed in devotion, and utterly unconscious of the lapse of time. Sometimes, in the middle of a meal, she became suddenly rapt in prayer. When her companions roused her, and asked her what she was waiting for, she waked as from a dream, and perceiving she was at dinner, turned it off by exclaiming, 'What an abstracted fool I am!'

During all the time that her lawsuit lasted, she was often obliged to attend the sittings of the court. If released for a few minutes from the business of the moment, she bent down her eyes, or closed them, if she could do it without attracting attention, and was instantly plunged into devout contemplation, as undisturbed and as recollected as if she had been a hundred miles from the city. The instant she was wanted, with perfect composure of manner and clearness of mind, she was ready to give all the requisite answers, and astonished the lawyers, on both sides by her accurate memory, excellent understanding, and unfailing presence of mind. Indeed, she herself wondered, just as if she had been watching somebody else, at the way she could pass from the most harassing discussions to high contemplation as easily as a person shuts up one book and opens another.

Some of the most extraordinary supernatural favours vouchsafed to the greatest saints seem to have been granted from time to time to this holy servant of God. The mysteries of the Life and Passion of our Lord were continually present to her mind and stamped on her heart. For days together she was unable to distract her attention from these lively inward representations of the Divine Saviour, whether in the crib or on the Cross, in the arms of holy Simeon, or in prayer on the mountain and the olive grove. For the space of several months, whenever she began to pray there appeared to her a vision of our Lady and the Infant Jesus. Like St. Antony of Padua, St. Stanislaus Kostka, and other saints, she felt that the Blessed Virgin, condescending to her ardent love, placed in her arms the Divine Child, and suffered her to clasp Him to her heart in a mystical embrace. The scenes of the Passion were even more frequently enacted, as it were, in her soul; and with her accustomed simplicity, she used to say to her dear Saviour—'O my Lord, if You vouchsafe to me so holy a society, and so great a favour, how can I leave You to attend to other things?' She also enjoyed at one moment a privilege similar to the one granted to St. Frances of Rome, in the sensible consciousness of the presence of a guardian angel protecting her against the attacks of an evil spirit.

But all these visions and these ecstasies never for a moment held comparison, in Luisa's estimation, with the virtues which it was her constant aim to acquire. To avoid not only sin, but the slightest faults, and to obey out of love for Christ, Who has said, 'He that loves Me will keep My commandments,' was the one study of her life. The following passage is extracted from her writings—

I have now received a new mercy from Thee, my God. One which I had been a long time praying for, and till now had not obtained. That is, so strong a desire and will not to offend Thee, I do not say venially, but in the least, the slightest possible matter, that I would avoid it even at the cost of my life, for now I feel that I had much rather die than wilfully displease Thee in the smallest matter. And not only would I exchange my life against such a possibility, but I wish to pray every hour, as I do several times every day, that rather than suffer me in any way deliberately to offend Thee in the slightest manner, Thou shouldst let me die, even though it were by lightning or the dagger of an assassin. I had been asking Thee a long time to feel this, and the understanding, aware of the weakness of the will, impelled it forward, but with effort and difficulty. But now, my Lord, the way is so smoothed that the difficulty no longer exists. From my earliest years I was dreadfully afraid of committing mortal sin, and for many years I would sooner have died in any kind of manner than remain in any respect in disgrace with Thee, and so I asked, and for a good while past have had sufficient light to see, that not only death, but all the torments of hell, are a less evil than to offend God in the least thing.

Two conflicting virtues, if such an expression may be used, filled the heart which our Lord was gradually preparing for a strange labour of love. On the one hand, a passionate desire to suffer every kind of torment, and death itself, for His sake, and on the other, perfect conformity to His will, which subdued and restrained these vehement longings. This state of soul was in itself a keen suffering, and one which few could understand and compassionate. It belonged to the highest degree of that love of the Cross which 'to them who perish,' St. Paul says, 'is foolishness, but to those that are to be saved, the power of God,' and essentially so to the chosen ones who are in any way called to labour for the salvation of others. Yes, to them first comes the yearning and the suffering, then the special inspiration, then the decisive summons, and at last the power of God—the mysterious power to accomplish what men have been calling a wild dream, but which He brings to pass in His own day and hour. That day and that hour were at hand for Luisa de Carvajal.

We find in her writings, for since her earliest childhood she had used her pen, frequent traces of the yearnings above described. In one of her sonnets she bursts forth in admiration of the martyr's sacrifice, and exclaims with poetic fervour—

> Esposas dulces ! lazo deseado !
> Ausentes trances ! hora vitoriosa
> Infamia felicissima y gloriosa
> Holocausto en mil llamas abrasado ![2]

And elsewhere these lines, written in a time of desolation and breathing the spirit of a strong soul—

> Bravo mar, en qual mi alma engolfada
> Con tormento camina dura y fuerte
> Hasta el puerto y rivera deseada.[3]

When we look back at the holy Spanish women of the sixteenth and seventeenth centuries, we cannot but be struck with the energy, the courage, and we might add

---

[2] Sweet fetters ! desired bonds !
Distant struggles ! victorious hour !
Most happy and glorious infamy !
Holocaust consumed amidst a thousand flames !

[3] Tempestuous sea, in which my soul is engulphed,
And advances amidst torments hard and fierce
Towards the haven and wished for shore.

the mental power, which Catholicism imparted to their lives and characters.   Its influence was felt in every fibre of their being : in their virtues, their studies, and their aims.   When in any one of them piety and natural gifts were combined, the strong will to achieve great things was seldom wanting.   And how should it be otherwise?   Does not energy spring from faith?   Can there be sacrifice where there is no hope, heroism without charity?   Can the atmosphere of doubt, the vain striving after a resting-place for mind and heart, the ever seeking and never arriving at the knowledge of truth which constitutes the mental state of so many in our days, produce aught but effete efforts and feebler results?   Is it not the first condition for willing strongly to be able, with a firm footing and an uplifted eye, to look up to heaven and say, 'I know in Whom and in what I have believed?'

PART THE SECOND.

CHAPTER I.

Luisa's Vocation.

WE have seen, in the first part of this work, the way in which it pleased God to lead Luisa de Carvajal, step by step, to a high degree of perfection, the graces which were granted even in childhood to that chosen soul, and which went on increasing as life advanced. Throughout the years which she spent in her uncle's house, and afterwards when she retired into the obscure abode where she practised poverty in its most rigorous form, the characteristic of her devotion appears to have always been the love and the desire of suffering. We might almost suppose that she had taken for her model St. Peter of Alcantara, whose name and whose image must have been familiar to her from infancy. For Placentia, near which her family resided, was one of the principal scenes of his labours, and as has been already said, it was to his prayers that her pious mother always attributed the accomplishment of her intense desire to have a daughter who would prove a great servant of God. To that child she must have often related the details of the saint's life, its superhuman austerities, its almost terrific sanctity. He had gone about the world like a living crucifix, converting souls, at times by the mere aspect of a face and form, which recalled the Passion of Christ more forcibly than the most eloquent words could have done. In its measure and its sphere her life resembled that of the great Franciscan saint. In her seventeenth year, she began to draw from long meditations on the Passion and sufferings of Christ an ardent desire for martyrdom, a passionate wish to die for the defence of that One, Holy, Catholic, and Apostolic Church which calls forth, on the one hand, an affection and an enthusiasm, and on the other, a hatred, which no earthly object has ever inspired. Cherished as a mother, and honoured as a queen, by generation after generation of faithful children, whom the world hates because they love her, she has been assailed for eighteen centuries with a virulence proportionate to the sense of her indomitable power.

The young Spanish maiden, on her knees before the crucifix, weak and powerless as she was, felt in her strong and fervent heart one of those impulses which often evince or decide a vocation. Across her mind, like a lightning flash, shot the name of England— England, where Catholics were suffering and dying, and scenes enacted closely resembling the acts of the martyrs in the early ages of Christianity. She could not conceive a greater joy than to go to that distant land, and by her life or by her death confirm the faith of her afflicted brethren. She mentioned to no one this thought, not even to her uncle or her confessor, lest they should think her mad. It was with God alone she spake of it, in the secret of her heart, and during long hours of prayer at the foot of the cross, where these kind of follies meet with mercy and more than mercy, at the hands of Him Who died for love of men. The only outward vent her feelings found was sometimes in conversation with her cousins, when she would descant on the glory of the martyrs, and the happiness of dying for Christ. But though twenty years elapsed before that desire was carried into effect, it never for a moment left

her. Whether it was ever to have a practical result she
did not know, but felt sure that if it was pleasing to God
He would, however improbable it seemed, open the way
to its fulfilment. Soon after the first idea of offering
herself to God for England had dawned in Luisa's mind,
she happened to read a letter written by Don Juan de
Mendoza, the Spanish Ambassador in London, in which
he gave a detailed account of the martyrdom of Father
Edmund Campion, and others who had lately suffered
death with heroic constancy for the Catholic faith. This
added fuel to the flame burning in her heart. If she
could not die on the scaffold like these glorious martyrs,
she might at least one day minister to some of their
brethren, who might at any moment be called upon to
tread in their steps. When she was about twenty-one
years of age, and residing at Pampeluna at the viceregal
palace, she determined to open her mind on the subject
to a person whom, together with most of the holiest
persons in Spain at that time, she believed to be a great
saint. This was a certain Maria de la Visitacion, a
Portuguese nun, who turned out a melancholy instance
of the way in which a designing person may for a time
delude even wise and good people. Luisa imparted to
her by letter the intense longing she felt to go to
England, and evince her gratitude to our Blessed Lord,
Who had been so good to her, by living in a country
where the violent persecutions against Catholics afforded
opportunities of dying, or at any rate suffering in His
cause. She begged her to think this over in prayer, and
to tell her if she thought this desire came from God, and
as she knew her to be in correspondence with Fray Luis
de Granada, one of the holiest men and most learned
theologians in Spain, she added a request that she would
send him her letter and consult him upon it. At the
same time she wrote herself to that great master of

J

spiritual life, and humbly asked him to give her his opinion on the question which Sister Maria de la Visitacion would submit to him.

For some reason or other, the latter took no notice of Luisa's letter, and did not send it to Fray Luis. He wrote to her that the communication she alluded to never having reached him, he did not know what was the question she wished him to answer. Luisa seems to have made no further effort to continue the correspondence. Perhaps she looked on this disappointment as an indication that it was not God's will that, at that time at least, she should entertain any positive hopes on the subject, or seek for light on the future, when to act was, for the present, obviously impossible. As far as the Portuguese nun was concerned, it was fortunate that she should have had no intimate communications with such a person, or received advice from her. Luis Munoz does not inform us of the reasons which prevented her, after her uncle's death, from seeking to carry out her cherished project, but it is clear that she never for a moment abandoned it. During the years she spent in the way described in the foregoing chapters, both at Madrid and at Valladolid, her prayers, her penances, her acts of heroic charity, appear to have all been offered up for the English Catholics and the reconversion of their country. Her whole manner of life was a preparation for the hardships of what was ever before her eyes—*La jornada de Inglaterra.* She used to hold cheap her instruments of penance, and exclaim, 'It is not these light chains I want; it is the heavy irons of the English martyrs!' In the close retirement of her poor abode, she sighed for the prisons where confessors of the Faith were languishing in destitution. If blood flowed from her limbs under the penitential scourge, she longed to shed every drop of her life blood on the scaffolds of London.

In 1595, or the ensuing year, a little book fell into her hands which stirred her soul to its inmost depths. This was the narrative of the life and death of the Jesuit Father Henry Walpole, who after having been nine times tortured was executed at York, on the 7th of May, 1595. It is more than probable that she had seen and conversed with that indefatigable missionary at the time that he resided at the Seminary at Valladolid, and learnt from him many details concerning the condition of English Catholics ; but whether she had been personally acquainted with him or not, it was with impassioned enthusiasm that she pored over the pages of this small volume. She used to carry it everywhere about with her, and to fall asleep with it in her hand. From that moment, what had been so long a hope and a desire became a constant intense yearning, which seemed to consume her whole existence. Extreme weakness of health, and frequent severe illnesses, vainly opposed apparently insuperable obstacles to this irresistible vocation. By day and by night it seemed as if God was calling her to the far off land which she so often visited in thought. Once, after feeling her heart pierced whilst in prayer by a sharp but sweet and peaceful pain, urging her powerfully on to accomplish what she saw no means of compassing, and yet could not and would not forego, she made, to ease that suffering, the following vow.

JESUS. 1598.

Feeling an impetuous desire to give up my life for the love of my Lord Jesus Christ, and to walk in His dear footsteps and unite my heart, pierced by a wound which nothing else will relieve, with His wounded Heart, I make this vow.

I, Luisa de Carvajal, with the most firm purpose, bind myself closely by vow to God our Lord to seek occasions of martyrdom in whatever way it may be lawful and not

J 2

contrary to His will to do so. And that I will never turn my
back or withdraw from or avoid such occasions, and that
whenever so happy an opportunity presents itself I will
readily and joyfully embrace it. The making of this vow
has filled me with joy, still happier shall I be if it is possible
to execute what I purpose, and in the meantime I console
myself by wishing that miserable as I am, the adorable will
of God may be perfectly accomplished by and in me.

This was of course with a view to England—the
thought of it was never absent from her a moment—
she seldom conversed with any one without speaking
of the English martyrs, their glorious and, in her eyes,
blessed fate. This was so well known, that though she
very seldom received visits, even from priests, her confessor never failed to take to see her any English Father
of the Society or priest from the English Seminary that
happened to be within reach. She never tired of hearing
them speak of the sufferings of their Catholic fellow
countrymen. And the more harrowing were these details
the more ardently she longed to be amongst them to
share their miseries and assist them in their needs. Her
companions were so well aware of this being her weak,
or rather her strong, point, that when she was very ill,
and so prostrated that nothing seemed to rouse her,
they would begin to talk of the persecutions in England
and the English martyrs. They knew that the word
England, breathed in her ear, acted upon her as a spell.
It was like the sound of the clarion to a dying soldier.
Her countenance instantly lighted up, her attention
was aroused, and her whole soul concentrated on that
favourite subject. The fire that had smouldered so
long burst forth at last, and she disclosed her wishes
to her confessor and other learned and holy persons
of her acquaintance. They all praised her zeal and
fervour, but at the same time did not attach much

importance to what she said, treating it rather as a
devout fancy than a real project. This indeed was
natural enough, considering how strange and unprecedented was the step she proposed to take, and the
variety of obstacles it was certain to meet with. Here,
they urged, was a person suffering from continual infirmities and frequent severe illnesses; a single woman
who had lived for years in close retirement, actually
contemplating the possibility of taking a journey through
foreign countries, passing through crowded cities, travelling along highways or yet more dangerous byways,
exposed to all sorts of accidents and dangers, and
across stormy seas, to a distant kingdom in a remote
region, which closed its doors to the Catholic religion
in so unrelenting a manner that the apostolic men who
laboured to propagate it had to do so at the cost of
unspeakable labours and at the price of their lives.
What would become of a weak and delicate lady in
the midst of these furious enemies of her religion, and
especially a Spanish lady, whose nation was particularly
obnoxious to the English on account of its devotion to
the Catholic faith? Moreover, the affairs of her lawsuit required her attendance at the courts of law; to
go away, under the circumstances, was to ensure its
loss. Pious desires are not always meant to be carried
out; they may proceed from the enemy of souls who
feigns to propose some higher perfection in order to
draw us away from the good we are actually doing.
The design in question could hardly be reconciled with
sound reason, which should temper even holy aspirations
and restrain them within the limits of prudence and
moderation, the necessary concomitants of all virtuous
actions. She was bound to follow the advice of wise
counsellors, few of which, if any, would recommend her
to pursue so extraordinary a project. In the meantime

she would do well to place the matter before God in prayer, and offer up all her spiritual exercises with the view of obtaining light as to her vocation.

Such was the general tenour of the answers she received. They were in accordance with those generally made by prudent directors when those under their care consult them on any line of conduct out of the ordinary course of Christian perfection. Such a thought may be a direct inspiration from God—if so, no discouragement will stop its accomplishment. It will only test the faith, the sincerity, and the humilty of the soul to which it has been vouchsafed. It applies the touchstone which detects the nature of such schemes. If it is imaginative fancy or vanity, not grace, that has originated it, the cold words of a prudent adviser will dissolve at once the illusion or will call forth a resentful annoyance that leaves no doubt as to the character of the supposed inspiration.

Luisa's desire, on the contrary, stood the test not only of those discouraging replies, but also of the interior opposition which arose in her own mind against so difficult an undertaking. Whether from the natural weakness of human nature, or that the enemy of souls waged war against a resolution which tended to their salvation, every objection which at that time others placed before her, rose with double force in her own mind, and depicted to her the hopelessness of the attempt with almost overwhelming force. This, however, was never the case when she prayed. The dark clouds then dispersed, light shone on her soul, all was serene and calm. She felt neither fear or impatience, nothing but the desire that God's will should be fulfilled and His glory promoted, together with an intimate conviction that if her project was agreeable to Him, He would enable her to carry it out. 'In quietness and confidence shall be thy strength,' seems to have been her motto

during those early days. Nothing would have induced
her to act without the sanction of her spiritual guides,
and with patient perseverance she continued to place the
subject anew before them, and to consult other enlight-
ened persons. She had often received in prayer, as was
afterwards known, many indications of God's will, which
did not allow her to doubt of her vocation. But her
humility shrank from disclosing them; she preferred to
wait and leave the matter in His hands, rather than to
impart to others those supernatural favours. But she
always assured the holy persons she conferred with, that
it was her firm conviction that it was the divine will
that she should go to England; that so strong a desire
in one so weak and helpless as herself could only
proceed from Him Who uses the most miserable instruments to achieve His own purpose.

By degrees her confessors and others began to look
upon the subject in a new light. It struck them that
she was in many ways singularly well fitted for such a
vocation; that she possessed gifts and capacities corresponding with the work in view; and it became a question
with them whether, after all, there was not something
real in this strange and persistent desire, whether it was
not, after all, the result of a holy inspiration. They
weighed in the balance against its many difficulties and
objections, Luisa's great sanctity, her good sense, her
humility, the perfect conformity of her life with the spirit
of the Church, the many years during which she had
persevered in the belief that our Lord required of her
this sacrifice, and after long and careful deliberation,
those who had been most opposed to it at the outset,
and amongst them men of great holiness and learning
belonging to various religious orders, came to the conclusion that it would be rash to disregard the marks of a
true vocation in the project submitted to them; that it

might after all be for the good of religion, and that she should undertake this difficult enterprize—one, indeed, far surpassing the strength and capacity of an ordinary person, but not above the courage they discerned in her soul. Though her bodily weakness was great, energy might supply the place of physical strength, and enable her to carry through the generous enterprize. The animating effect of her ardent faith and charity, the sympathy she would show to the afflicted Catholics, would no doubt tend to confirm them in the steadfast practice of religion, whilst her life and conduct would set before their eyes a singular example of Christian perfection. The more they thought of it, the more it struck them that England might indeed be the field in which she was called to work. One of the persons she consulted at that time was the famous Jesuit, Father Luis de la Puente. After several conferences with her, he said that if on the one hand he did not venture to advise her to go to London, far less did he dare to dissuade her from it. The undertaking was beyond her natural strength, but none could say what supernatural aid might enable her to accomplish.

What chiefly influenced the decisions of Luisa's directors in favour of her unprecedented vocation, was the fact that, notwithstanding her hatred of the world, her love of retirement, her devotion to all spiritual exercises, and a docility which had never failed to show itself under the most trying circumstances, and to the most trying persons, she had never had the least attraction for the cloister. For some mysterious reason which she could not herself have explained, an insuperable obstacle had always seemed to stand between her and the conventual life. Whereas no shadow of change had ever passed over the one desire of her soul, to go where she should be exposed to suffer and die for the Catholic faith. At last the assent which she had waited for so long was given. The word was spoken, and nothing now remained but to prepare for her departure, and the final leave she was about to take of all she had ever known and loved.

No sooner was her mind made up, than two circumstances occurred which singularly favoured her project, by removing some of the principal difficulties in its way. The first was the treaty of peace between England and Spain, which was signed after Queen Elizabeth's death between King James I. and King Philip III. The second was the speed with which her lawsuit advanced, which up to that time had been slowly dragging along its weary length. Through the exertions of the Conde de Miranda, President of Castille, it was brought at last to a happy conclusion, and ceased to be an obstacle in her way.

No sooner was the verdict given in her favour, than she proceeded, according to her vow of poverty, to divest herself of every portion of her recovered property. She had long intended to devote it to the formation of an English Jesuit Noviceship in Belgium—a work which she considered most important to the interests of religion. By her will, dated Valladolid, December 22nd, 1604, she left twenty thousand ducats for this foundation, and during her lifetime made over all the income proceeding from this capital to trustees appointed for this purpose. At first she had yielded to persuasion, and reserved two hundred ducats a year for her own wants, but no sooner had this clause been inserted in the document, than she drew her pen across it, and resolved to observe her vow of poverty to the letter ; and if it proved harder to do so in a foreign country, far from friends and relations who in any urgent need at home would have assisted her, then it was all the more in the spirit of the apostolate she embraced. The translation of her will, part of which has been given in the Rev. Father Morris' work, *The Condition of Catholics under James I.*, will be found in the Appendix to this volume.

Before two years had elapsed, her intentions were carried out. In 1606, Father Persons obtained possession of a large house in Louvain, which had been inhabited by the Knights of Malta, and thus came to be called St. John's. It stood on a high ground commanding the city; below was a walled garden, and on the slope of the hill pleasant walks amongst the vines which were ranged in terraces, and the whole, though within the walls of a town, as quiet and calm as befitted a religious house. The first novice received at St. John's was Father Thomas Garnet, the nephew of the Provincial. He must have passed quickly from the peaceful home of his religious life to the English mission, and from thence to the scaffold, for we find that in 1608 he was martyred at Tyburn. Luisa lived to see numerous martyrs and confessors emerging from the saintly house she had founded, and shedding their blood on the soil she was watering with her tears. In 1598, there were in England nineteen Jesuits in all, of whom one was a lay-brother, and two others were not priests. In 1620, fourteen years after the Novitiate was begun, there were scattered throughout the country one hundred and nine Jesuits, and there were as many more English Jesuits on the Continent, the majority of whom were studying for the priesthood. We may hence infer the importance of the work which secured to successive generations the ministrations of those heroic men who, amidst incredible dangers, and in the fear of death—and what a death !— kept supplying the place of their slain brethren, first in the secret sanctuaries of the English mission, and when their turn came, in the prisons and on the scaffold.

CHAPTER II.

Luisa leaves Spain for England.

As a prelude to her departure, Luisa had a severe illness, in which she suffered much pain, and which left her with a cold on the chest, a bad preparation for the journey she was about to take in the very midst of the winter. But before leaving Spain, she had to make a sacrifice to which no other sacrifice could be compared; one which it had never entered her mind to expect. For thirteen years the most intimate friendship had existed between her and Ines, one of the companions who had shared her seclusion in her uncle's palace, and followed her to the poor abode whither she retired after his death. Both at Madrid and at Valladolid, they had always lived together. Their feelings, their tastes, and their devotions were alike. Ines was tenderly—indeed, passionately—attached to one who was at once her mistress, her friend, and her model. She tried in everything to imitate her; studied all her words and actions, and made it her object in life to work with and for her. In her severe and frequent illnesses, Luisa had no other nurse than Ines. By day and by night she never left her side. It had always been considered by them as a matter of course that if she went to England, Ines was to accompany her. Everything had been arranged, and even the necessary equipments for the journey provided with that view. It was the one only human support and consolation Luisa

could look forward to in that approaching separation
from every other earthly tie. Their mutual attachment
and confidence was so great, that it had never occurred
to Ines to inquire if her mistress meant to take her, or to
the mistress to ask if her friend could follow her. And
so matters stood until a few days before the one fixed for
their departure. They both went to the church they
habitually frequented, and confessed to Father Lorenzo
de la Puente. Luisa had finished her confession, and
retired to pray in another part of the church. Ines
stayed a long time in the confessional, and when she left
it, Father de la Puente came straight up to the place
where her mistress was kneeling, and said—'Ines is not
to go to England.' He attested afterwards, that Luisa
looked up, and answered, without a change of countenance, without the least emotion or displeasure, 'Very
well, Father. Let all be arranged accordingly.'

In the conference which had taken place between Ines
and her director, the latter had ascertained beyond a
doubt that she was going to share the risks of Luisa's
enterprize solely out of strong human affection for her,
and not only without any vocation for the course she was
following, but moreover with a decided vocation of her
own, which she was resisting, to a cloistered and contemplative life. He did not think it right that so heroic
an enterprize. should be undertaken on merely human
grounds, or dangers incurred where grace might be
wanting to meet them. It was but one more occasion
for Luisa to test her own abandonment of all earthly
considerations, and the trial proved how genuine was
her sacrifice. She never uttered a word of complaint
or even regret, and before her departure made all the
necessary arrangements for the entrance of her friend
into the Convent of the Incarnation. The sanctity which
that friend attained in the fulfilment of her vocation was

at once a confirmation of the prudence of Father de la Puente's decision and a reward to Luisa for the generous courage with which she made this last and greatest sacrifice. She. would not accept any of the pressing offers of her former companions to accompany her. She felt convinced that only a special call and a special grace could enable a person to bear the spiritual and temporal privations of such a change. A chaplain whose services she secured for the journey, a man and his wife who were returning to England, strangers to her, but persons of piety and good character, and two men-servants recommended by the Fathers of the English College, formed her escort for the journey.

Before her departure she wrote the two following letters. The first is addressed to her brother, Don Alonzo de Carvajal, a nobleman of high character and good abilities, in great favour with King Philip III. of Spain, and employed by him in several important ways.

JESUS. MARY.

The strict obligation binding upon us all to do that which in our own case we think will be most pleasing to God, accounts for the step I am taking, for I have no doubt that it is in this way that our Lord chooses to make me entirely His, and I desire, with His powerful help, to correspond to the utmost with His grace, having no other aim in end than the accomplishment of His divine will in any position or manner that it may please Him to appoint, whether high or low, great or small, honourable or despised, public or secret, hoping that His gracious mercy will never be denied me, and that no created thing, present or future, will be able to separate me from the love of Jesus Christ our Lord, in Whose sovereign hands I place my unworthy heart, as in its happy refuge. I implore of His Divine Majesty, that I may also see your heart and that of my sister, and the dearly loved little ones, Ana and Francesco, enriched and happy in the same blessed manner. I shall rejoice if I can help you

before the throne of His greatness, who can do nothing for
you in earthly ways. God knows how happy I should be to see
you all, but I am happier still to have this sacrifice to offer
up for you, until it shall please Him that we should meet
again.   I ask your mother, and your grandfather and grandmother, to pray for me, and you, brother mine, to remember
what you owe to God, and think only of pleasing Him in a
way that will make up for past negligences ; and during my
absence, act with that true Christianity and wisdom which I
pray God may never fall short of what His greater glory
demands.   In the meantime, may you be as united to Him
as I always desire and pray.

LUISA DE CARVAJAL.

Valladolid, January 13th, 1605.

The following day she wrote to Father Ojeda, S.J.,
the Rector of the College of the Society at Madrid,
who had been for many years her confessor and her
director.

JESUS. MARY.

A strong inspiration, a persistent, efficacious, and carefully
examined vocation, has brought me, señor, from step to step,
to the point of breaking through every impediment, and
resolving to go hence with one only end and desire, the
accomplishment of God's will.   That I am doing His will, I
feel assured, and I know also that I am acting in accordance
with yours, and secure on such solid foundations, I abandon
all concern about the future, only attending to what I have
now to do, and devoting all my strength to that one object
which I set above all hopes of glory, or fear of suffering, or
life itself.   It seems to me that His Divine Majesty gives me
a calm and fearless heart, and so great a freedom from
ambitious or dazzling thoughts, that I should only be too
happy to die for His sake in a hut on the roadside, or in any
other obscure and lowly manner.

All my affairs have been brought to a favourable termination, though I am not yet actually in possession of my
fortune, but I have an inward feeling that keeps urging me
not to delay my departure a single day beyond what is

necessary. Your Reverence knows that my property is, like its owner, devoted to the Society of Jesus during my life as well as after my death. It is offered to it by one poor in effect, but rich in goodwill and affection. I trust that your Reverence's charity will not suffer you to forget before the Divine Majesty of God your most humble servant, who asks your prayers in the name of His love. Most sincerely do I beg of our Lord to keep you in all the spiritual happiness I desire for you.

LUISA DE CARVAJAL.

Valladolid, January 14th, 1605.

A few days afterwards, without uttering a single expression of sorrow or regret, or shedding a single tear, and as if she was doing the simplest thing in the world, Luisa took a final leave of her beloved Spain, leaving behind her a number of friends of all ages and ranks, and breaking through natural and spiritual ties of every sort. She bade farewell to the magnificent churches of her native land which had been for years like the homes of her soul, to all the magnificence of Catholic worship, to the convent, the doors of which had closed on her beloved Ines, to the devout Spanish people who even in our own days cannot be seduced from the Church by infidel Governments and iniquitous laws, to all the associations of childhood and the outward beauty of religion, which to one of her race and her character must have been almost a condition of existence. She was thirty-nine years of age, midway through life, old enough to measure the blessings she was foregoing and the trials she was encountering, and without the least expectation of ever returning to her native country.

It was on the 27th of January that this extraordinary journey was begun. She took with her only money enough to carry her to England. The President of Castille, her great friend, made her every offer of assistance. She would accept nothing but her passport and

some letters of introduction.   The Duchess of Infantado,
another of her friends, after vainly imploring her with
tears to give up her intention, wanted to provide all
sorts of conveniences, she called them necessaries, for
her journey.   The only thing she accepted was a mule
to ride on.   Her biographer tells us that the roads were
very bad, the weather very severe, and that it took her
three days to cross the mountains of Biscay.   Easy
travelling has never been the boast of Luisa's native
country, and in her days, if we take a contemporary
description, we shall form some idea of its hardships.
The following passage is taken from a letter of the
Rev. John Sandford, dated London, March 6th, 1610,
and is addressed to Sir Thomas Edmondes.   This
gentleman was about to accompany to Spain Sir John
Digby, who was going there as Ambassador, and begins
by lamenting his destination and declaring that 'he has
always been crossed in what he most desired, and taken
from that wherein he most delighted.'   And he goes
on to say—

My opinion of Spain, as also my affection towards it, is
the same that ever it hath been.   I hear Catholics lately
come from thence to speak much good of that country, but
when I read Clenard's epistle of his journey thither I am
apt to believe the contrary : who, having been a public
reader at Louvain, as he passed through Biscay, having
broken a little drinking glass, he was fain to drink water
like Diogenes in his hand because all the village was not
able to lend him another.   Near Valladolid he could hardly
get a faggot of nine branches to warm him in a sharp
weather.   His supper at nights was indeed *cæna dubia*, not
as the Latins meant it, a plentiful one which made the
guests doubt where to feed, but *quod incertum erat an
cogeretur jejunare.*   His *olla* was a poor deal of bacon
which he was fain to buy by ounces.   His stomach roaring
for want of victuals, he was forced to betake himself to roast
onions.   His inn could not afford him either bed or straw,

but having hired three blackamoors, he slept by hanging on their shoulders or by being stayed up by them. I first read this narrative with delight, but now having to make trial of it with fear and horror, the rather for their sakes amongst us who having been used to much tenderness will find it strange after a tedious and dangerous passage by sea to be entertained in this kingdom of Cabal, a land of mountains and deserts. I am told for certain that my Spanish jennet must be a Biscayan mule who will fling as if with her heels she would hit him that rideth her on her back.

So far Mr. Sandford, as the writers of that time would say. Luis Munoz does not tell us whether Luisa's mule kicked in the way above described, but he does say that between Valladolid and Paris there was no hardship from snow, wind, rain, frost, ruts, precipices, and other dangers incident to a journey, and that in winter time, which she did not undergo. The days seemed interminably long, and yet she was always frightened at the speed with which they rode. For two hours they were once in the utmost danger of being drowned. The horses and mules could not make their way across a river, or turn back to the shore. At last some boatmen saw them wave a handkerchief as a signal of distress, and came to their assistance.

Luisa had indeed not been used to the tenderness to which Mr. Sandford's companions had been accustomed, and her ideas of substantial suppers must have greatly differed from his. So on the whole, perhaps, her journey was less trying than he feared his would be, and, moreover, he had not the same consolations which she enjoyed in these her last days in a Catholic land. If the food and the beds were of the worst description, the little band of pilgrims had the comfort of hearing Mass every morning. Each day Luisa went to Communion, and found a recompense for all the hardships of the way in the spiritual joy which had never before so abundantly

K

filled her soul.   Singing and making melody in her
heart to the Lord, she went along like the youth in
Longfellow's poem,

> Who bore through snow and ice,
> A banner with that strange device,
> Excelsior.

Starting at early morn and stopping at nightfall, the
whole party rode side by side without interruption or
disorder.   Rough and poor were often the places where
they found shelter for the night.   They had provided
themselves with padlocks, as a precaution against possible dangers in solitary inns, but the chief protection
they looked to was the guidance of their guardian angels,
and the divine aid of Him Whom they doubtless invoked
in the beautiful words of the Catholic wayfarer's prayer,
' Be unto us, O Lord, a tower of strength from the face
of the enemy.   Let not the enemy prevail against us, or
the son of iniquity approach to hurt us.   Be Thou our
support in our setting out, our solace on the way, our
shadow in the heat, our covering in the rain and cold,
the chariot of our weariness, the fortress of our adversity,
our staff in the ways of slipperiness, and our harbour in
shipwreck, that under Thy guidance we may reach in
safety the object of our journey, and finally the haven of
our eternal salvation.'

Luisa seldom indulged on the way even a pious
curiosity, and visited none of the remarkable edifices
which attract the attention of travellers, except the
Cathedral of Burgos, where she went to venerate a
famous crucifix, and 'the principal church of Paris,'
which must mean Nôtre Dame.   In the latter city she
also visited the professed house of the Jesuit Fathers,
and spent a week at the convent of the Discalced
Carmelites, having been forcibly compelled to prolong
her stay in the French capital.   She probably found

acquaintances amongst the little Spanish band of St. Teresa's daughters, whom the Abbé Pierre de Bérulle, at the head of a regular French embassy, had carried away some years before, almost by force, from their religious homes to France. Not that the holy Anne of Jesus and her companions had a will of their own in the matter—they were ready to go wherever obedience sent them, but the Carmelite Fathers, their Superiors, resisted almost to the death parting with these six pearls of great price, whom the future Cardinal, armed with a Papal brief, and supported by the Catholic King, had ruthlessly selected for the accomplishment of the work which he and the saintly Madame Acarie had so long toiled to effect, the establishment in Paris of the great Carmelite Order, reformed by St. Teresa.

Those who have visited the house in the Rue d'Enfer, Faubourg St. Jacques, that same house to which Madame Acarie conducted the Spanish nuns on their arrival, where Anne of Jesus intoned, on entering, the Psalm *Laudate Dominum omnes gentes*, a pious impulse which grew into a precedent and rule for future foundations, and where, during the late siege of Paris and the reign of the Commune, the Carmelites of our own days remained to pray, to suffer, and offer up their lives for the salvation of a maddened people—can picture to themselves the arrival of the little band of travellers from Spain, in 1605, and the welcome they must have received in the French home of their holy countrywomen; how Madame Acarie must have hastened to salute and embrace Luisa de Carvajal, and talk over with her the projects and the hopes that were taking her to England. It was a subject on which they must have sympathized. The exiled English priests in France had not any more devoted friend than Madame Acarie. She was personally acquainted with many of them, and took the deepest interest in the

K 2

sufferings of the English Catholics. No one could better understand such an act of self-devotion as Luisa was performing. In the midst of the perfect fulfilment of her duties as a wife and mother, she overflowed with apostolic zeal, and kindled a spirit of ardent faith and self-sacrificing devotion in all who conversed with her. We can almost fancy we see Luisa's face lighting up at the words which, we are told, were so often on Madame Acarie's lips—

Trop avare à qui Dieu ne suffit.

The Spanish Carmelites and the holy traveller had all bidden an eternal farewell to Spain. Never again were they to look on the deep blue southern sky and the orange groves of their native land. Heavy crosses were in store for all these voluntary exiles, but they had in their souls the joy with which a stranger intermeddles not, and they were on their way to the heavenly home to which martyrdom is the shortest road. This, no doubt, they all felt as they looked on Luisa's pale, almost unearthly face, and heard her speak of her hopes and aspirations. Perhaps, they almost envied her, and thought her nearer than was the case to their fulfilment.

From Paris the little travelling party proceeded to Rouen, instead of going through Brussels, which would have been the easiest way. Luisa wished to avoid the necessity of an interview with the Infanta Isabel, with whom she was a great favourite. Nothing would have suited her less than to visit a Court, and renew acquaintance there with the royal friends of her youth. Generally speaking, she and her companions were treated with much respect in France. She was supposed to be a nun on her way to found a monastery, as the Discalced Carmelites had lately been doing. But sometimes they had to pass through places where the Calvinists were numerous, and there might have been danger of their

being insulted, especially as she could never be persuaded to hide the outward evidences of her faith.
Through the most hostile neighbourhoods she rode with a
large rosary and a crucifix hanging to it outside her cloak,
and a missal in her hand. It is to be hoped that her
chaplain and her escort had the same dauntless spirit as
herself, and did not feel like poor Abbondio in the
Promessi Sposi, that saints are very dangerous people to
have to do with, and that you never know into what
scrapes they may lead you.

At St. Omer she remained a month, in the house of a
cousin of Father Persons, entirely devoted to recollection
and prayer. Her confessor wished her to stay there
until he had received an answer he expected from Rome.
It seems that the Fathers of the Society in England, on
account of her high rank, her well-known name and
connections, as well as the weakness of her health, her
ignorance of the language and want of knowledge of the
country, rather apprehended her arrival. However, Luis
Munoz tells us that when Father Garnet, the Provincial,
and the other Fathers were informed how holy and
how prudent she was (prudent was, perhaps, hardly the
word we should have expected her biographer to use,
after his own account of her manner of riding through
the Huguenot villages), they withdrew their opposition,
and sent a confidential person to St. Omer to arrange
about her passage and accompany her to England, without
which she might have been exposed to serious risk and
inconvenience.

Thus safely escorted, she went down the river in a
small boat, and on reaching the sea engaged a vessel for
her party, so that there was no one on board but the
owners, who were people of a very good sort, a French
child, and two poor English boys, who begged her to
take them on board out of charity. She had an extra-

ordinary aversion to sailing, from the experience she had had of it in crossing rivers and arms of the sea in her journey through France, and it was with no small effort she embarked on the stormy British Channel. The wind became violent and the sea very high, soon after they left the shore, and the vessel was driven towards the coast of Holland. This added another kind of danger to the passage. The Dutch ships were cruising about in those seas, and on the watch for French ships. At last the moon shone out in the midst of the dark clouds, the wind changed, and two hours and a half afterwards they arrived at Dover.

Luisa was the first of the passengers who went on deck. As she was preparing to jump on shore, and looking where to set her foot, so as not to sink in the deep sand, she saw a youth of apparently fourteen or fifteen years of age, standing before her, and offering her his assistance. His fair complexion, his bright smile, and remarkable beauty, gave him the appearance of a heavenly vision. She leant on his arm for an instant, and landed without difficulty. But when, after looking back to see if her companions were following, she turned to thank him, the boy had disappeared, and she found that none of the others had noticed that any one was standing on the shore. Luis Munoz hints his belief that this youth was an angel in disguise, welcoming her to the land of her exile. Without venturing to deny it, we could easily imagine that after nights and days in a dark cabin, tossing about on the rough waves, and in a moment of such highwrought excitement as that of first setting foot on the English shore, Luisa might have taken for a celestial apparition a fair blooming boy, an English Catholic perhaps, who on his side would have been as much struck at the sight of the veiled form of the pale, dark-eyed lady emerging from the vessel with her crucifix on her breast, and her rosary hanging round her neck, as she could have been at his bright aspect. After smiling a welcome to her, he might have deemed it safer to withdraw. Before turning from the spot where she had landed, Luisa knelt down on the sand, and with hands and eyes upraised, poured forth ardent thanksgivings for the attainment of her lifelong desire.

At this point of her biography, it will be well, perhaps, to prepare our readers, who may be looking forward to the narrative of her residence in England as the most interesting portion of this work, for the disappointment that must be felt at the absence of names, whether of persons or places, which is inevitable in a Spanish book published only twenty-seven years after Luisa de Carvajal's arrival in England, and eighteen after her death, at a time when the persecution against Catholics was raging, and every indication as to the names of houses or persons she frequented, might have led to fatal, or at least, disastrous consequences. This prudent and necessary reserve considerably diminishes the value of a biography which would have been, otherwise, extraordinarily interesting ; but even with this drawback, it contains new and striking details of the state of England at the beginning of the seventeenth century, and of the aspect which it presented to the eyes of a foreign Catholic. The fragments of Luisa's letters embodied in the narrative, make us regret that a more considerable portion of her correspondence has not been preserved. We are often left to conjecture, where we would fain know what were her thoughts and impressions. At any rate, the forthcoming pages give a picture of her life in London, which will be found worth notice in an historical as well as a religious point of view.

CHAPTER III.

Arrival in England.

NOT a single word is to be found in the Spanish Life of Luisa regarding her first impressions of England as she travelled for two days on horseback, from Dover to a house in the country belonging to a Catholic family, which, judging from a circumstance subsequently mentioned, must have been at about a day's distance from London by road, and near to the river. A ride through Kent in the first days of May could hardly have failed, if the weather was at all favourable, to have inspired her with admiration. The beauty of the country must have been at its full height. Every field and grove clad in fresh green ; every bank and copse carpeted with flowers ; every village with its Maypole, adorned with gay streamers, and its houses decked with hawthorn branches. She fell in, no doubt, with many a party of gay morrice dancers, set again in fashion by King James in defiance of the Puritans, who anathematized such sports, not, perhaps, without reason. The figures of Robin Hood, Little John, Friar Tuck, Maid Marian, and the rest of the motley group, including the Hobby Horse and Dragon, would naturally astonish the eyes of foreigners ; but we can also imagine that the boys and girls wearing garland in honour of the day, or footing it round the Maypole, 'new with glee and merriment,' would, on their side, glance with surprise at the sober and solemn travelling party, headed by a veiled lady dressed in black, and must have wondered if it too formed part of a pageant. An ancient ballad says—

The spring in all its gladness
Doth laugh at winter's sadness.

The aspect of merry England on that 1st and 2nd of May 1606, as far as nature and youth are concerned, probably justified that metaphor; but as Luisa rode through the smiling hamlets, and looked at the daisied meadows and laughing children gathering flowers, did not her eyes fill with tears at the thought that those children were estranged from their Mother the Church, and those flowers no longer plucked for our Lady's shrines? As she passed the ivied towers of the old grey parish churches, did not her heart ache at the consciousness that our Lord, Who once dwelt within those hallowed walls, was banished from those altars, where so many generations of Catholics had knelt to receive the Bread of Life, or to adore, day by day, His Sacramental Presence? 'Breathes there a man with soul so dead,' we may ask in the poet's words, who, if he is a child of the Church, does not even now suffer on his return from foreign travel, when this thought presents itself to his mind? There is always a strange thrill of joy in the heart at the sight of our native land after a long absence. The eye rests with grateful pleasure on the wooded parks, the cottage gardens, the heathy commons, the ancestral homes of England; but a sudden chill damps that joy when we feel that we can no longer salute as we pass them the high cathedral of some distant city, or the little chapel on the road side; when we miss the consciousness that sheds such a brightness over the surface of Catholic lands, that our Lord is present in the green valley and on the mountain

top, the Word made Flesh and dwelling amongst us in the
humblest as in the loftiest shrine. And if this is the
case with us, what must it have been to that ardent
soul to whom faith was life itself? How dull and
cold the landscape looked to her, even in its spring
beauty, when no altar was in sight? Like St. Mary
Magdalene, she must have longed to cry out, 'They have
taken away my Lord, and I know not where they have
laid Him.' Now, thank God, though the sanctuaries
built by our Catholic forefathers are still shut to Him
and to us, we can note, as we travel to and fro in our
country, many a dwelling-place raised of late years by
devoted hearts for His reception. Day by day they
multiply, and the spiritual desert begins to blossom like
the rose; but at the time when Luisa landed in England
it was only in the most secret recesses and hidden
corners that the Blessed Sacrament was reserved, and
she must have looked on the smiling valleys and the
woody hills of Kent as the thirsty traveller in the
desert at the sandy plain, where no green oasis meets
his eyes.

An oasis, however, was in store for her. On the
second day of her journey she reached a place where
the Fathers of the Society had secured for her a most
hospitable reception. Luis Munoz describes it as 'a
devout house, full of religious consolations.' Its Catholic
owners had lived there for three years perfectly unmo-
lested. Their chapel (he says) was adorned with pictures
and images, and enriched with many relics. Several
Masses were said in it every day, and accompanied by
beautiful vocal and instrumental music. After dinner
and supper, sacred airs were likewise played to recreate
the mind and raise it to heavenly thoughts. There was
a beautiful garden before the house, in which they spent
a little time every day, but taking care to keep them-

selves as quiet and retired as possible. Luisa remained a month in this happy abode. What was the name of the place and who it belonged to can only be conjectured. It may have been Scotney Castle, which stood on the borders of Kent and Sussex. Father Blount's escape from the old seat of the Darrells took place in 1598, and the family having been heavily fined at that time, were perhaps left in peace during the ensuing years. Lady Lovel's house is also named in a list of the abodes of Jesuits in England, and it was likewise in Kent. Whatever was the Catholic house where the Spanish lady was received on her first landing in a country which she knew to be the scene of such cruel persecutions, it must have been a strange surprise to find herself in so peaceful a retreat, surrounded by pious persons of her own faith, under the same roof with several priests, and a chapel adorned not only with all the requisites, but all the luxuries, so to speak, of Catholic worship ; the country, too, more beautiful, the sky more fair, no doubt than she had been led to expect. We can fancy her wrapped in her black veil, kneeling for hours in that secret chapel, and asking herself if she had indeed reached England, the land of sacrilege and bloodshed, or walking on a spring morning in a pleached alley, saying her beads, within hearing of the harmonious sounds of holy music floating in the balmy air, and wondering if that was the dark, cold, gloomy climate, which Spaniards never spoke of without a shudder. She was for some days ill and confined to her bed at this place of quiet rest and sacred privileges ; and it was well that her strength was in some measure restored before the beautiful dream was rudely dispelled.

One night, after she had been at this place about a month, a secret warning was given to the master of this hospitable mansion, that he had been denounced as a harbourer of priests, and that the pursuivants would invade his house on the morrow. In consequence of this information, measures were immediately taken to hide all traces of Catholic worship, and a general dispersion took place. Some persons went to London by the river, others passed into the adjoining counties, or hid themselves in the neighbourhood. Luisa had to rise and dress in a great hurry, and to travel to London in a coach with some of the ladies of the family. They arrived at a poor obscure little house in the city. Her companions had to go on further the next day; but before their departure they took her to the house of a Catholic lady, where Mass was always said. She stayed there a few days, and had some difficulty in finding a place of abode where she could be secure of this blessing. At last she succeeded in this, and by a singular mercy, amidst frequent changes and great inconveniences, she was always able to hear Mass every day and receive Holy Communion. It would appear that the Catholics were somewhat ungracious to her at first. Luis Munoz says that during the first months she was in London she resided at some of their principal houses; but adds that, according to the custom of the country, she had to pay all the expenses of moving from one to another, even when her hostesses were ladies of the highest rank and position. His Spanish ideas of hospitality were evidently shocked at the conduct of these English grandees. Her desire was to retire into a quiet part of the city, unknown even to the Spanish Ambassador, or any of her country people, in order to devote herself to the study of the English language, as a necessary means of carrying out the object which had brought her to England. But the discovery of the Gunpowder Plot and the storm which ensued defeated her calculations and overthrew her plans.

It would be useless to recapitulate here the details of the horrible persecution, the maddening oppression and the refinements of cruelty, which drove a few men wild with despair to plan the sudden destruction of a King and of a Parliament which were heaping upon Catholics the direst sufferings, and imperilling the souls of their children by the prohibition of Catholic worship and education. The sight of continual outrages, perpetrated under the name of law, worked like madness in their minds, and oblivious of the divine command not to do evil that good may come, they deemed it justifiable to use any means, however terrible, to deliver their brethren from a King who publicly drank 'damnation to the Papists'—one whose mother had died on the scaffold consoled and strengthened in her mortal agony by the Catholic Faith—and from lawgivers who placed them and their co-religionists beyond the pale of the law,[1] tortured and slew their priests, seduced their children from the Faith, insulted and imprisoned their wives, invaded their homes, ruined their fortunes, confiscated their lands, and trod their rights under foot, and that for no other offence than worshipping God as every Christian had worshipped Him for fifteen hundred years. No wonder that, yielding to human passion, they conceived the thought of swiftly

---

[1] The following extract from the letter of a Protestant gentleman of that day then residing in London illustrates this point. Sir Edward Hoby writes to Sir Thomas Esmondes—'My Lord Salisbury showed a paper of the King's own hand, under the name of "His Meditations,"(!) which seemed so to concur with the heads of both the Houses that you would have said an Act of Parliament, the form only wanting. To give your lordship some taste of the heads, of some among many of which there is now no doubt but the law will ensue—"All recusants, convict and not communicating, shall stand in the case of excommunicate persons, whereby they are clean out of the King's protection, subject to many dangers, and, upon any injury offered, not able to plead in any of the King's courts. The King to choose whether he will take £20 a month or two parts of their living. All women incapable of their dowers or jointures." '

and suddenly destroying the destroyers, forgetting Who has said, 'Vengeance is Mine, and I will repay.' If extenuating circumstances can ever be pleaded for a great crime, the Gunpowder Plot may claim the benefit. It ranks in history by the side of Guillaume Tell's arrow and Charlotte Corday's dagger. Who shall dare to say that it exceeded the sin of the rulers who provoked it, or that the maddened victim does not deserve more mercy than the cold-blooded tyrant and ruthless oppressor? Be that as it may, they sinned, and they suffered, and all the Catholics of England suffered redoubled persecution through their guilty act. Fear made their enemies savage. The most sanguinary laws were passed, and all the fury of popular passion let loose against them.

Such was the moment in which Luisa de Carvajal found herself in London, in the midst of Protestants exasperated against everything Catholic, and Catholics terrified at the consequences of the fatal 5th of November. She was staying at that moment with a lady whose alarm was so great that she told her she could no longer afford her the shelter of her roof. Various reports were in circulation concerning the origin of the Gunpowder Plot, and Spain was falsely accused of having encouraged its perpetration. The solitary invalid shut up in her little room, poring all day over grammars and dictionaries, was deemed a dangerous inmate from the fact of her being Spanish, and in consequence urged to take her departure. It happened most fortunately that, a few months before, Don Pedro de Zuniga, a nobleman nearly related to some of Luisa's greatest friends, had come to England as the Catholic King's Ambassador, and had brought with him as his chaplain Fray Juan de San Augustin, a man remarkable for learning and literary talents, and still more for holiness and wisdom. He subsequently became Cardinal

Archbishop of Toledo and preacher to the Spanish monarch. Luisa's friends wrote to Don Pedro that she was in England, a fact which greatly astonished him, for she had never gone near the Embassy, or made herself known to any of the Spanish residents in London. But when she found herself under the necessity of living alone in a hired house or lodging—for she saw that the Catholics were all afraid of receiving her—she thought it would be well to try and secure one near the Embassy, on account of the protection it would afford her in case of need, and, above all, for the sake of hearing Mass in the Ambassador's chapel. She wrote therefore to Fray Juan, and then had an interview with him, in which she asked his help to find a small house which would answer this double purpose. No sooner did Don Pedro de Zuniga find out where she was than he hastened to invite her to take up her abode in his house. He assured her that at that moment her life would be in danger anywhere else, and with the utmost kindness insisted on her accepting his offer. His conduct towards her seems to have been that of a brother rather than of a kinsman.

Compelled to avail herself of his hospitality, she found the very solitude she had been sighing for where it might have been least expected. Fray Juan gave up to her some rooms he had hitherto occupied. They looked on a garden, and were cut off from the rest of the house. There, with two pious English girls, she spent nearly a year in as great a seclusion as she could 'desire, and practising the same exercises of devotion and penance as in Spain. We are told that even then she used to go out and visit the priests and other Catholics in prison and those she knew in different parts of the town, consoling and encouraging them to the best of her power. We may conclude, though no express mention

is made of it, that one of the first martyrs she must
have thus assisted was the Rev. Henry Garnet, Provincial of the English Jesuits. He had been the first to
encourage her devotion and to welcome her to England.
She had not been there a year before he was arrested,
thrown into prison, cruelly racked, and then condemned
to death.   On the 6th of May, 1606, just at the time
when, in the previous year, she was staying at the
country house in Kent, enjoying a transient, and, as
regarded Catholics, a deceitful glimpse of happiness in
an English home, the execution of Father Garnet took
place at St. Paul's Churchyard. We are not told if she
was one of the vast multitude assembled to behold
him ascend the scaffold, with so serene and bright an
aspect that the railings of the mob were instinctively
hushed ; whether she heard the words he spoke that
day on the finding of the Cross—'the Cross in which
it was given him in that hour to share'—or watched
him bowing down on his breast his venerable head and
saying, *Adoramus te Christi et benedicimus tibi, quia per
sanctam Crucem Tuam redemisti mundum*, and then, with
a short invocation to the Queen of Martyrs, resigning
his soul to God, with so heavenly an expression that,
when his head was held up by the executioners, his
very enemies could not cheer as usual, and the awe-
struck crowd dispersed in silence.   If not present at
that awful moment, doubtless she went often to contemplate those revered features, now glorified with the
halo of martyrdom, during the twenty days that they
remained fixed on London Bridge, 'retaining the same
lively colour they had in life, which drew all London
to the spectacle.' We would fain know if she ministered
also to the sufferings of the heroic Lay-brother, Owen,
commonly called Little John, the architect of half the
hiding places for priests throughout England, who, shortly

after his Superior's death, was so cruelly racked in prison that he died soon after he was taken off the torture.

As to this early part of her life in England few particulars are given. Luis Munoz says in general terms that her extreme sensibility, of which we have seen proofs in her earlier years, made her keenly sensible to the sufferings she witnessed amongst those whom she so ardently sympathized with, and still more acutely did she grieve at the immorality and vices produced by the absence of faith and the deteriorating effects of the so-called Reformation. London seemed to her like a dry land without water, a desert without spiritual refreshment, and, like most great cities, a sink of iniquity, with no counteracting influence to check its progress.

There was one circumstance connected with the sufferings of Catholics which she had not been prepared for and which cut her to the heart. Besides the endless troubles which beset them during life, their enemies found means of embittering even death itself. To many of them there was joy in the thought of sacrificing it for the sake of their religion. But the wicked cunning of those who stamped their adherence to the faith of their fathers with the name of treason, and put it about that they died, not because they were Catholics, but for rebellion and conspiracy, robbed them in some degree of that consolation. It was at any rate a snare to those over whom human respect and natural feelings still exercised some power—those to whom reputation was dearer than existence, and Luisa, whose weak point, as we have seen, was an overweening attachment to chivalrous ideas of honour, which she had imbibed from infancy, and which were like a second nature to a high-born Spaniard, discovered with grief and indignation this new and painful feature in the English

L

persecutions. It cut her to the heart. Luis Munoz says 'she could hardly have suffered more if she had been a captive amongst the Turks. Sometimes her courage almost gave way, though nothing betrayed her anguish. The iron entered into her soul not so much at the sight of the sufferings of her brethren in the faith as at the malicious calumnies heaped upon them. During the first few months she was in London she shed torrents of tears, though her countenance was always calm and serene. As one who navigates in troubled waters grasps firmly the oar in his hand, so she clung fast to the protection of our Blessed Lady, the comforter of the afflicted.' Sometimes she pictured to herself the life of a nun in Spain, the peace and beauty of an Augustinian monastery, the silence of the cloisters, the loveliness of the gardens, the sacred music of the choir, the undisturbed communion with God, the sweet sanctity of kindred souls all devoted to His service ; and then, looking around, she saw nothing but fears and dangers and animosities enough to discourage the bravest spirit. She felt at times an almost overpowering dread of the future, but speedily rousing herself, exclaimed, like St. Martin, 'My God, I do not refuse to live and to work.' The struggle was long and sharp. Sometimes she would for a moment doubt if it was really God's will that England should be for her not merely a halting place in the journey of life but the abiding scene of her earthly pilgrimage. It was not that her desire for sufferings had changed, but a faintness came over her at the sight of difficulties which she had apparently under estimated, and her humility made her despair of doing any real good in the face of such immense obstacles.

At other moments, when grace shone with its full light on her soul, and divine love communicated to her heart

its burning ardour, strength and consolation were poured
into it; her fate then seemed to her a blessed one.
Created for no other purpose than for the greater glory
of God, she was surrounded with the means of advancing
it by daily acts of sacrifice and self-renunciation. But
these hours of fervour would again be succeeded by fits
of discouragement, against which she had often to fight
hard in the solitude of her chamber and the absence of
all external sympathy. The greatest of her trials was the
difficulty she found in learning the English language. It
seemed at first almost insuperable, and opposed a bar
to all communication with those she most desired to
converse with and to win over to the faith. But she
persevered, and after a year's incessant labour and
study arrived at speaking it with facility and writing
it correctly.

When she had acquired this power she became anxious
to leave the Embassy and to take a lodging of her own.
The necessary restraints imposed by her residence in
Don Pedro's house interfered with the exercise of her
charity towards the poor Catholics, and she was impatient
to begin the work for which she had been so earnestly
qualifying herself. But the good Ambassador would not
hear of her leaving the shelter of his roof. He anticipated
serious dangers for her anywhere else. But, well aware
that to speak to Luisa of danger would very little
influence her, he dwelt much less on the fear of her
being insulted and assaulted in the streets, and her
house possibly mobbed, than on what he assured
her would be certain to happen if she was arrested,
and that was that the Government would insist on her
being sent out of the country. He reminded her of
her favourite saying that she wished to go to heaven,
not through Spain, but through martyrdom, and so
judiciously used that argument that he persuaded her

L 2

to remain some months longer in his house. The persecution was in the meantime raging more violently than ever. Laws still more cruel and oppressive were added to the penal code against recusants, and nothing reached her ears but reports of banishments, deaths, threatened wars with Continental powers, and startling rumours which gained credit for awhile till their falsehood was evinced. The closest retirement, the most obscure position, did not suffice to protect a person professing the ancient faith, and whichever way the Catholics looked there seemed for them no earthly hope. The very air seemed to ring with blasphemies against the Church and insults to the Holy Father and all that they held sacred. Maliciously or erroneously, reports were constantly spread that the King had died by the hand of a traitor. The Council was hastily assembled, the gates of the streets closed, and proclamations made that his Majesty was still alive. There was no peace, no repose, for those whose lives and fortunes depended on the breath of popular fury.

Seeing that this state of things was likely to be prolonged, several persons of weight and influence, and amongst them the chaplain of the Ambassador, Fray Juan de San Augustin, who sometimes used to confess Luisa, began to think that there was no use in her remaining in England, as on the one hand there was no prospect of her actually being put to death for her religion, the penal laws being only applicable to the subjects of the Kings of England, and as, if she gave offence by speaking openly in behalf of Catholicism and endeavouring to persuade people to be reconciled to the Church, they would only forcibly expel her from the kingdom, or insist upon the Ambassador sending her away; or, on the other hand, if she was to spend her days in solitude and prayer it would be far better to do so in tranquillity at home than in the midst of the ceaseless troubles and agitations of England. And as to the good her example and her influence might do, it would be far greater in her own country where she was known and loved, than in London where she had so few friends and acquaintances. With regard to teaching Catholic truth to the English and converting them to the Church, there was no opening or opportunity for anything of the sort, and she was only wasting her time by remaining in England. Luisa admitted the strength of these arguments. All she could urge against the conclusion to which they pointed was, that whenever she laid the subject before God in prayer, her mind was so vividly impressed with the conviction that it was His will she should stay where she was that it seemed impossible to her in the face of it to return to Spain.

Fray Augustin persevered in his opinion and often pressed it upon her. She saw that reason was on his side, and tried hard to conform herself to his wishes, even going so far as to tell him that she thought of taking the habit of the Sisters of St. Augustine in the monastery which her great friend, Mother Maria Anne of St. Joseph, had recently founded in Flanders, after establishing in Spain a number of communities noted for their fervour and strict spirit of observance. Humanly speaking, this prospect must have been to Luisa like an opening vision of Paradise. To join this beloved friend of her youth, to live under her gentle rule in a quiet convent in a Catholic country, cooperating in her work of zeal and helping her to train in the religious life young and ardent souls overflowing with love and fervour, was a prospect so sweet, so bright, so full of holy joy, so singularly in contrast with the sad lonely life she was leading in London, to the perpetual heart-ache, constant spiritual privations, the gloom, the savage hatred of her religion,

which compassed her on every side, that it seemed like
a ray of light shining into a prison and speaking of the
fields and sparkling waters beyond its dark walls.   But it
would not do ; it was in vain that she tried to think that
others were right and that she was wrong.   As soon as
she knelt down to pray, the bright vision plainly showed
itself to be a temptation, and the voice of God said to her
heart, ' Tarry here in the land of exile until I call thee to
thy heavenly home.'

By degrees, Fray Augustin came round to her way
of thinking.   As he grew better acquainted with her soul
and knew more of the. great graces she received in
prayer, it began to strike him that the continual progress
she was making in sanctity, precisely by means of the
sufferings she endured from the sight and sound of the outrages lavished on what she loved most in the world—the
Catholic Church—and of the cruel wrongs of her children,
did appear a token that it was God's will and not her
own that she was following with so strange a persistency ;
that she might after all be of use to many a soul amongst
those whose miseries she felt so keenly.   He prayed and
said Masses to obtain light on this subject, and finally
remained as firmly convinced as herself that her vocation
was not an illusion, but an inspiration of the Holy Spirit,
and that in return for her desire to shed her blood for
the sake of Christ, a long and equally meritorious martyrdom was vouchsafed to her.   She also wrote to consult
some other learned and holy persons as to the vow she
had made, and the question how far her actual inability
to perform what she had intended and the absence of
danger to herself from living in London affected its
fulfilment.   She made up her mind to place their answers
in the hands of her confessor, and then abide by his
decision.   In the meantime, with more ardour than ever,
she sought for grace and light in prayer.   ' And our

Lord,' her biographer says, 'manifested Himself to her
soul many a time saying, "Fear not, here am I." And
then she would cry out, "O Lord, there will be obstacles
and so it will be well for me to turn back and fly."
And the same divine voice said to her, "Have you yet
encountered them? Have you not seen when they have
threatened to arise how easily and powerfully they have
been removed? Look back on your natural condition,
and what you have already experienced, and learn Who
it is Who was able to bring you and Who is able to keep
you here. To your hands is committed the care of your
own perfection. Leave all else in Mine."' These sacred
teachings stamped on her soul gave her a supernatural
courage to overcome all fear and resist the constant
efforts made to induce her to return to Spain.

Amongst those she consulted were Father Bartolomeo
Perez, of the Society of Jesus, assistant for Spain in
Rome, and Father Persons, rector of the College and
prefect of the English mission. They were both of
opinion that she should persevere in what she had
undertaken and employ the talents God had bestowed
upon her in the service of His Church in England.
Much had been given to her and much would be
required of her. She was bound to correspond generously
with the grace she had so abundantly received. Father
Perez moreover informed her that his Holiness, Paul V.,
having heard of her going to England, expressed the
strongest approval of her piety and courage, and sent
her word to continue as she had began. This letter
put an end to all doubts and hesitations on her own
part and that of her confessor. The highest sanction
was afforded to her resolution, and from that time
forward it never wavered even in the face of the most
urgent persuasions. Besides the opinions of these two
Fathers and the message of the Sovereign Pontiff, she

had the consolation of hearing from Father Creswell, S.J.,
what Don Juan de Ribero, Patriarch and Archbishop of
Valencia, a most holy and zealous prelate, wrote to him
on this subject.   These are his words—

Your Reverence's letters always give me consolation, but
the one I received a short time ago, and in which you inform
me of the arrival in England of Doña Luisa de Mendoza, most
especially filled me with joy.   I thanked our Lord with all
the strength in my power for the graces He has bestowed on
that lady.   It affects me to think of this rare example of
what His blessed hand can do to strengthen weakness, and
confound by feeble instruments the fury of His greatest
enemies.   Our Lord knows how I wish I had deserved to
be the chaplain of this lady, and that I should esteem that
privilege more highly than the greatest honours and dignities
of earth.   I think she knows me by name, as I was very
intimate with and devoted to the Marquis of Almaçan, in
whose house she was brought up, and so I conclude she
must have often heard me spoken of.   You Reverence will
do me a great kindness by giving her a message from me
to say that we shall constantly recommend her to God, and
to beg her to pray for my needs, which are very great.   The
gentleman who consulted me some days ago showed me a
letter from our Ambassador, in which he says that he apprehends great danger for Doña Luisa, and that the people
in England are too obstinate to be converted.   Following
St. Athanasius' principle, I felt inclined to advise her to
return, but now that I have read what you say, I dare not
give any other counsel than that of the Apostle St. John—
*Unctionem quam accepistis ab eo, maneat in vobis.   Et non
necesse habetis ut aliquis doceat vos: sed sicut unctio ejus
docet vos de omnibus, et verum est, et non est mendacium.
Et sicut docuit vos, manete in eo.*

CHAPTER IV.

Luisa's life in London.

THE testimony of the Fathers of the Society of Jesus is
adduced by Luisa's biographer in support of his assertion
that her presence in London greatly encouraged the
English Catholics to bear up against their troubles, and
in some cases to profess their faith more openly, and at
the peril of their lives, than they had hitherto done.
The insults they were continually subjected to, the fear
of losing their property and all chance of distinction
and advancement in life, caused a number of persons,
thoroughly Catholic at heart, to 'conform to the times,'
as it was called, and for the sake of peace and temporal
advantages, to profess the religion by law established.
The example of a lady of high rank and ancient
lineage, beloved and looked up to in her own country,
not only by the learned and devout, but by persons
of royal birth and exalted position, naturally produced
a great effect on Catholics of this description. They
were struck with the fact of her voluntarily exchanging
home, friends, and the full and free exercise of her
religion, for the restraints and miseries attendant upon
it in England. Her ardent devotion to the Church
reawakened in many hearts the courage to declare
themselves her children. A Jesuit Father wrote at the
time—' It would seem as if this lady had been sent here
for the express purpose of shaming our want of courage.

The example she sets us by her bold profession of the Catholic faith, and her desires of martyrdom, are a rebuke to our timidity.'

The first extract we meet with from Luisa's own letters, gives an amusing idea of her estimation of England as a place of residence, and the impossibility of any sacrifice exceeding that of exchanging Spain for 'an intolerable country,' where her expectations of going through an earthly Purgatory had not been disappointed. And then she adds—'Sometimes, when I urge the Catholics here to be bold, and 'not to stagger in the profession of their faith, they say that it is very easy for me to talk, who am not exposed to the same dangers and loss of fortune as they are. To that I reply—"Just consider whether your King can ever reduce you to a life of greater poverty than I am leading, and should it even come to that, you would be consoled by the love of your country, which is the strongest feeling a person can have. You would still be surrounded by your relatives and friends. And, moreover, you were not born in Spain, and do not know what it is to exchange it for England. Nothing can go beyond that !"'

The following account is given of a characteristic scene which occurred during the first months of Luisa's residence in London. Luis Munoz mentions that at the time of the general destruction of crosses consequent on the so-called Reformation, a very beautiful cross had been spared, partly on account of its exquisite workmanship, and partly because it adorned one of the most ancient edifices in London. This memorial of our Lord's Passion in the midst of the heretical city, this emblem of the ancient faith, was one of Luisa's few joys, and the object of her special devotion. As often as she passed that way, she paid public homage to the sign of our redemption, before which no head had been bowed, and no knee bent, for many a long year. One day in particular, she knelt down at the foot of this monument of England's Catholic days, and prayed with as much fervour and recollection as if she had been alone in her room, totally heedless of the cries of the mob, who shouted that she was a Papist, and threatened to stone her on the spot. She would have asked nothing better. One man cried out—'Ah, the arch-Papist! she asks a blessing from the cross! The gallows is what she will get!' Others vociferated that she should be dragged to prison. Insults, if not stones, were levelled at her from every side. Quite unmoved, she finished her prayer, and whenever the opportunity occurred, failed not to perform this act of devotion. When she saw in the shop windows odious representations and caricatures of the Pope, she used to buy them, and as she walked away, tore them into pieces, and trod them under foot, saying, as well as she could in English—'What strange people they must be, who like to draw such wicked pictures!' Her boldness generally took the bystanders by surprise. They stood looking on in silent wonder, till some one raised the cry that she was a Papist, and then all hooted and reviled her. But after awhile, her confessor told her to abstain from these open demonstrations of her faith, as they might defeat the object she had in view, and impede greater good. It was a sacrifice of her feelings to comply with this order, but the principle of obedience was paramount in this faithful child of the Church, and she yielded the point at once.

Her residence at the Embassy had one most happy and important result. As Luis Munoz says—'Love is a great schemer.' She enjoyed there the blessing of daily Mass and Communion, and the thought that those mercies were vouchsafed, like the rain that fell on

Gideon's fleece, to her and a few others, whilst outside
the walls of that house there was an almost universal
dearth of those means of grace, often filled her with
grateful but sad emotion. But she could not remain
satisfied without the privilege of spending, as she had
been wont to do in Spain, whole hours of the day and
night before the Blessed Sacrament, joining her prayers
with those of the angels who kept watch before the
tabernacle. It seemed to her 'that there could be no
reasonable objection to the reservation of the adorable
Sacrament in the Ambassador's chapel, and to His
Divine Majesty enjoying the immunity of the Catholic
King's own residence, in a city where for so many
centuries innumerable temples had been honoured by
His presence.' The pious Don Pedro de Zuniga, and
Fray Augustin, to whom she expressed this thought,
were quite disposed to carry out her wishes. Their own
devotion inclined them to it, and reverence and affection
for their holy countrywoman would have prompted them
to acquiesce in any proposal of hers had it been even
less congenial to their own feelings. No sooner was
their consent obtained, than Luisa and her two English
companions set to work to ornament the chapel for the
reception of the heavenly Guest. They made it as
beautiful and devotional as they could; a lamp burned
continually in the little sanctuary, and from the heart of
Christ's devoted servant, all on fire with divine love, rose
the incense of incessant prayer. After so long a privation, to be able to find at all times our Lord on the
altar, was a joy that made up for all past and present
sufferings. The English Catholics were singularly edified
and struck with this installation of the Blessed Sacrament in so becoming a manner and so secure a
place. Since Elizabeth's accession, it had never been,
comparatively speaking, so openly honoured, or so acces-

sible to their devotion. This must have been in itself a conclusive proof to Luisa that she had not come in vain to England. Divine love not only schemes, but is restless in its covetousness. She pined to see the great blessing of our Lord's perpetual presence on the altar extended to other parts of London, and she endeavoured to persuade the Ambassadors of other Catholic powers to imitate the example of Don Pedro de Zuniga. The energy of her character, and something particularly engaging in her manners, gave her great influence with good people. The wife of the Ambassador from the Low Countries, a pious lady of high birth, took a great fancy to the recluse at the Spanish Embassy, and used often to visit her. Whenever she pressed her in return to come to her house, Luisa used to say, that to pay visits was not in accordance with her mode of life. Moreover, that being weak in health, she could with difficulty walk as far as from one Embassy to the other, and never went in a carriage unless absolutely compelled to do so. 'But,' she added, 'if the Blessed Sacrament was reserved in your chapel, then I would gladly make the effort of going on foot, as on a pilgrimage, to your part of London, in order to visit our Blessed Lord on the altar.'

These two pious ladies, by dint of perseverance, obtained what they desired, and many a time Luisa crossed London on foot, to adore Him Who was the life and light of her soul. Some time afterwards, to her great joy, the French and Venetian Ambassadors followed the example of their colleagues. She speaks of this in a letter written at a subsequent period to her cousin, the Marquesa de Caracena, dated April 17, 1611.

The Ambassador has had in his chapel this year a beautiful sepulchre, and we have had one [1] more remarkable for its devout appearance than its size, but very pretty and nicely

---

[1] At that time Luisa had removed into a small house of her own.

arranged. This must not be mentioned on any account, not even to Spaniards, for it would cause us a hundred new difficulties. We have also got a Paschal candle, for the houses of Catholics are the Catholic churches of England, but scarcely any one ventures to keep the Blessed Sacrament except for a short time, and in places which happen to be, for some reason or other, more secure than the rest. I persuaded Don Pedro de Zuniga to have It reserved in his chapel, and the French and Venetian Ambassadors have followed his example.

There is some difficulty from the omission of dates, precisely to give the periods of Luisa's movements, or the exact time to which various circumstances in her life relate. Luis Munoz says that she took up her residence at the Embassy soon after the Gunpowder Plot, and remained there a year, lodged, fed, protected, and befriended by Don Pedro's kindness. During that time she had often to endure the sneering remarks of ill disposed persons amongst her own countrymen and others, who laughed at what they said her famous journey to England had ended in, that is, leading a useless life amongst her own people. She did not trouble herself in the least at these unkind comments on her conduct, but continued humbly to obey her confessor, and to abstain from acts which would have been far more congenial to her feelings than the acceptance of a hospitality which shielded her from dangers and inconveniences. If she had been less submissive, it is probable that the Blessed Sacrament would not have been placed in the chapels of the four Embassies, or a blessing rested on her subsequent labours. Inaction seems often imposed for awhile on ardent natures as a preparatory trial, before work is granted and blest.

When the violent excitement produced by the Gunpowder Plot had subsided, Luisa expressed her desire to leave Don Pedro's house, as we have said, for one of her own. The good Ambassador heard it with dismay. As she would not remain at the Embassy, he implored her to return to Spain, declaring that anywhere than in his house she would run terrible risks, and that she should be contented with having sown good seed in London, which would hereafter bear fruit. Fray Augustin told her, with tears in his eyes, that she was going into the lion's den. The household of the Ambassador tried to frighten her, by assurances that they would not be allowed to admit her into the chapel, or even to see and speak with her, because one of the articles of the recent peace was that Spaniards were not to interfere in the religious affairs of the country, and it was apprehended that she would certainly mix herself up with them when once left to her own devices. For her part she had no fears, for nothing in the shape of persecution would have come amiss to her. Now that the actual necessity for it had ceased, the peaceful retirement, where she lived like a solitary in the desert, did not satisfy the yearnings of her soul, or advance the apostolate she had always had in view. As a woman and a foreigner, many opportunities were open to her from which English Catholics were debarred. She was not afraid of the future, and kept herself ready to profit by those occasions as Providence threw them in her way. Her reliance on God was so complete, that she never doubted each day's bringing with it its appointed work or suffering. Hitherto, shelter and sustenance and Mass and Holy Communion had never failed her. She had the feeling, as she wrote to her friends, of being at once the most helpless and the best cared for person in the world, the most unprotected of creatures and yet the most secure.

She had, indeed, barely the means of hiring a house, and providing it with what was absolutely requisite.

Still, she succeeded in establishing herself and her companions in a very small one, close to the Embassy. Of this abode, and of her neighbours, her biographer gives an unflattering account. He describes it as dark and confined, in a court or yard, shut in by a gate, which, he says, was the case with most of the London streets.

Poor as she was [he adds], she found it necessary, on account of the character of the neighbourhood, to spend a good deal in making it fast and secure, seeing that she was surrounded on every side by violent heretics. But if she could protect herself by bars and bolts against assaults, there were no means of shutting out the sounds which reached her, even in her sleeping room. She was often kept awake all night by the shouts and outcries of persons fighting, drinking, and gambling under her very windows, as also by the noise made in throwing down on the pavement huge joints of meat, which they roasted on a spit, and this most especially on Fridays, as if in scorn of the abstinence which Catholics observe in memory of the Passion of our Lord. They seemed to choose that day most specially for the indulgence of their coarse appetites. In inns and hostelries, and in private habitations as well, they have roast and boiled meat served up on Fridays, and make no difference even between Good Friday and all other days in the year. Nay, the great English nobles seem to make a point of choosing the day on which our Lord was crucified to give great banquets, at which every variety of food is served up. It seemed more like living amongst Jews and Turks than Christians. The favourite way this people have of showing their piety, is to manifest on all occasions a virulent hatred of the Catholic Church. They despise the ancient and holy custom of keeping Lent, one of the most primitive practices of Christians; and the corruption of morals which reigns in their country gains every day : increasing evidence of the fruits of the new gospel set forth by the infamous apostate, Henry VIII.

There was a time when, in speaking of the pretended Reformation, its leaders, its character, and its results, a Catholic thought it necessary sometimes to restrain his pen, for fear of giving offence to earnest and conscientious Protestants, or at any rate, in quoting the foregoing passage from a Spanish author, would have felt called upon to support his statements by those of contemporary English authors, Protestant as well as Catholic. But now such scruples have become unnecessary, and such precautions superfluous. Nothing that the Spanish Licenciado says can exceed on these points the sentiments expressed by some of the Ritualist members of the Church of England, in language sometimes more violent than we should like to use. This, at any rate, relieves us from the obligation of apologizing for Luis Munoz's expressions.

The plague was beginning to rage in London, and the closeness and bad air from which Luisa suffered in her obscure abode was particularly irksome at such a time ; but she forgot all these miseries during the hours spent in Don Pedro's chapel, hearing Mass, receiving the Lord of Glory in her heart, and lingering in prayer before His solitary altar. This was her strength and consolation when in that heretical city, like the Jews by the river of Babylon, she thought of her dear native Spain with its thousands of altars, where a thousand times each day the Holy Sacrifice was offered and God worshipped in a Catholic manner. Nothing is mentioned in this part of her Life concerning the first year she spent in a house of her own, beyond the fact that a severe illness confined her for some time to her bed. But further on an account is given of an interview she had with the Rev. Robert Drury, of the Society of Jesus, previously to his martyrdom, and as he was put to death on the 6th of February, 1607, it is clear that it refers to this period ; we therefore insert it here.

The clear-sighted faith of Luisa and her knowledge of spirituality, acquired not only by study and reading,

M

but by constant intercourse with the holiest and most learned theologians of Spain, came into special use at a time when doubts arose in the minds of some of the most earnest priests in England with regard to the lawfulness of taking the oath of allegiance set forth by the Government for the express purpose of ensnaring the consciences of Catholics. It became the occasion of a fierce renewal of persecution. The prisons were filled with servants of God of every age and sex, and the difficulties of carrying on Catholic worship and the administration of the sacraments were so great, that some wavered on the subject of this insidious oath, and questioned whether, in the face of such terrible evils, it might not be admissible to take it.

Luisa never for an instant doubted as to the nature of this oath, even before the Papal brief had made the matter clear, and she never failed to exhort earnestly all those she could influence to make a firm stand against it. The Rev. Robert Drury, who had studied for five years at the Seminary at Valladolid, and then for twelve years laboured in the English mission, was arrested in the year 1607, and was offered his life and liberty if he would subscribe to this oath.

He was not inclined to do so on his own account, but it did not appear clear to him that seculars might not be justified in doing so under the stringent circumstances in which they were placed and the threatened total ruin of their fortunes, providing it was with the intention of obeying the King in all temporal matters, and detesting all renunciation of the Pope's spiritual authority. Having been known to express this opinion, it was easy for others to urge upon him that life was more precious than liberty or goods, and, his own being offered to him on those terms, that what he had approved of for laymen he might do himself without sin. The

Protestant clergymen pressed him hard on that point, for they knew that his example would greatly influence others. Luisa went to see him in his prison, and spent two whole days discussing the point with him, and urging that, after the Pope's declaration, it was impossible that a Catholic could take the oath without committing a mortal sin. The following passage in the Spanish Life seems to indicate that it was her arguments which convinced Father Drury on this momentous point—

The holy priest, who, on no pretext, however pious, would transgress the commands of the Sovereign Pontiff, made up his mind not to take the oath, and clearly expressed his opinion against any Catholic taking it ; and having done so, applied himself to prepare for death. What passed during those two days between the martyr and her who was sent to strengthen him in that conflict, God, Who was alone present, knows. He expressed great gratitude to His Divine Majesty and also to Doña Luisa, who writes thus on the subject to a friend in Spain—' He showed me more affection than ever when I went to visit him, and I tried by every means I could to cheer and confirm his courage, so that he should not suffer himself to be overcome by the vehement persuasions wherewith they endeavoured to induce him to subscribe the said oath of allegiance, set forth a year ago by the Parliament. The so-called Bishop of London, before whom he appeared, knows by this time his prisoner's happiness, and can cry out, " These are those whom we had one while in derision, and who are counted amongst the sons of God." '

The arch-persecutor to whom Luisa alludes had, a short time before, been suddenly called to appear at the judgment-seat of God. The unjust judge had soon 'followed his victim, and the thought of the lives and ends of these two men would naturally suggest to her mind a probable contrast as to their eternal fate.

We read in Challoner's records—' Early one morning the holy Robert Drury was carried to the place of his martyrdom. He went thither with so radiant an expression of countenance that, being naturally handsome, his beauty was more like that of an angel than that of a man, and looked like an anticipation of the glory to which he was hastening.' Luisa kissed his chains with many tears, and there was no merit in that act, she said—probably meaning that human sorrow had a share in the feelings with which she witnessed the death of one she had so long revered and loved. She acted towards him the part of the beloved disciple, for with his dying breath he commended his mother to her care. And faithfully she fulfilled the charge; for she took her home with her that day, and did not part with her until she had amply provided for her maintenance and comfort.

Luisa continued to devote a great deal of her time during this period, not only to the study of English, and to all sorts of works of charity in the prisons, but also to the perusal of books treating of controversy. Even before leaving Spain she had qualified herself for the task of defending and advocating her religion by a diligent study of theology, and especially of the doctrines of the Church most attacked by heretics. One of her favourite spiritual books was the *Summary of Christian Doctrine*, by Luis de Granada. Every day she read a portion of this treatise, and it was seldom out of her hand. She used to say that it thoroughly taught a Catholic what he was to know, to believe, and to do; and that if he possessed that work and the Lives of the Saints he could dispense with other books. Her knowledge of the truths of religion, of the grounds of Christian and Catholic faith, and of the science of the saints in all its branches, was united to a singular talent for explaining and elucidating points of doctrine, and a great readiness in answering objections and detecting fallacies in argument. These gifts, so uncommon in a woman, had raised her highly in the esteem of persons of weight and learning in Spain. People who conversed with her about religion used to say that she spoke like an apostle and a saint rather than a lady nursed in pomp and splendour.

Some years before her departure she secretly purchased the Latin works of St. Augustine, St. Thomas Aquinas, and other Fathers of the Church, for the express purposes of storing her mind with refutations of modern heresies, and detecting the misstatements of Protestants with regard to the early centuries of the Church. Her friends were surprised to see her, who would hardly buy the merest trifle for her house without an absolute necessity, spending money in books. She did not give her reasons for this expenditure, but devoted every moment she could spare from her spiritual and charitable duties to the attentive study of controversy. In England she gave herself with increasing ardour to this pursuit, carefully reading English as well as Latin works on both sides of the question, and particularly preparing answers to the difficulties which Protestants draw from Scripture. Her intimate acquaintance with the Bible enabled her to refute them successfully. She never lost an opportunity of consulting theologians as to the meaning of controverted passages, and daily added to her stores of knowledge. To this preparation she added fervent prayer, penance, watching and fasting, and the constant mortification of self-will.

In the spring of 1608 she must have witnessed the martyrdoms of George Gervase, a secular priest, executed at Tyburn in April, and of Thomas Garnet, S.J., who suffered likewise in June of the same year. He was the firstfruits of the Novitiate of Louvain—the first of the many who were trained within its walls to live and die on the English mission. Luisa's heart was no doubt deeply affected by the heroic death of one to whom she was bound by a spiritual tie, as the foundress of the religious home where he had learnt the lessons which in those days seldom led but to one end.   The details of his last moments are so fully given in Challoner's records, that it is useless to repeat them here.   He died with the words of our Blessed Lord on his lips—' Father, forgive them, for they know not what they do.'   Luis Munoz says—' They showed him so much courtesy as to let him die before they tore open his breast and plucked out his heart.'   He was nearly related to the Rev. Henry Garnet, who had been executed one year before.   Luisa wrote home accounts of these holy deaths, and we can only regret that her biographer gives us the substance of her letters—not the letters themselves.   Some time after Garnet's martyrdom—in the month of May of that year —we find her carrying out a bold measure of contro-versial aggression against the heretics of *Chepsaid* (Cheapside), 'the principal street of London.'   The pages which relate this *successo* shall be literally trans-lated from the Spanish.

CHAPTER V.

Luisa in prison.

'ONE day in May, Doña Luisa went with Aña and some
of her other companions to the street called Chepsaid,
which is the principal one in London.   It is inhabited
by a number of rich merchants, the greatest part of them
Puritans, plunged in error and obstinate beyond measure
in their heresy.   A fiery kind of people, who become
violently excited when they talk of religion.   She entered
a shop to buy an altar cloth, and happened to ask the
youth who was showing her the linen whether a young
girl who was standing by him was his sister.   He replied,
"She is my sister in Christ."   This pious way of speaking
led her to inquire if he was a Catholic.   " A Catholic ! "
he exclaimed.   " No ; God forbid ! "

'"His Divine Majesty forbid that you should not be
one," Doña Luisa rejoined, "for it is of the utmost
consequence for your salvation." And starting from that
point she began to speak with great animation about
religion to the young men and women around her who
assembled to listen, while others came in from the
neighbouring shops.   Finding she was a Catholic, they
asked her questions about Mass, confession, and Holy
Orders, but mostly about the Pope.   She said he was
the Head of the Church, that his predecessors held the
keys of St. Peter, and had handed them down to him.
She asserted the claims of the Roman Catholic Church,

and the necessity of belonging to it in order to be saved. For two hours she spoke on these points, and told those she was addressing that she much regretted that her imperfect knowledge of their language prevented her being able fully to show them the falsehoods with which they had been deluded with regard to the Catholic religion, and the necessity of embracing it if they wished to save their souls. They assured her that she spoke English very well, that they understood her perfectly, and that she had quite the accent of an English person. Some of her hearers took great pleasure in listening to her, others were enraged at her boldness. She was running some danger of her life, or at least of being arrested and thrown into prison, but no fears could deter her from trying to open their eyes to the truth.

'One of the shopkeepers told her that their King was much too wise to order them to follow a religion that was not the true one. Both the schismatics and the Catholics think it very dangerous to speak against the King or his Council. The prudent Doña Luisa, wishing to get out of this difficulty without disguising the truth, said that there was no necessity to speak of the King, who had never known his Catholic father, and from infancy had been separated from his Catholic mother and brought up among Puritans. She added that he had a much better title to the crown than the late Queen Elizabeth. They exclaimed at this, for the King was not at all beloved, and asked what she meant, and why he was a more legitimate sovereign than his predecessor. "Because he is the great-great-nephew of Henry VIII.," she answered, "whereas Queen Elizabeth was born during the lifetime of that King's legitimate wife, Queen Catharine of Aragon."

'Then they begun again to argue about religion. One of the disputants gave the name of traitor to a holy

Benedictine monk who had been lately hung, drawn, and quartered, and borne his sufferings with exemplary patience. "What crime was he condemned for?" Doña Luisa asked; "what had he done?" "He was a Popish priest and would not give up his religion," they said. "Oh, if that was the case," she rejoined, "it is nothing to wonder at. The Catholic Church calls such persons martyrs." And then again the religious discussion was renewed.

'There was one man in particular who eagerly kept it up, and addressed her a number of questions. At last the mistress of the shop grew tired, and declared that it was a shame to let this Papist talk on as she was doing; that for her part she did not think she was a woman, but a Romish priest in disguise going about to convert people to his religion. She became violently excited, and threatened to detain her till a constable was fetched, who would take her before a magistrate. It was getting dark, and the crowd beginning to disperse, so Doña Luisa took leave of them, and begged that they would take in good part all she had said, as it was out of charity and for the sake of their souls she had spoken to them as she had done. As she walked away they stood looking after her in great astonishment, not knowing at all what to make of this strange lady. Ever since that day the shopkeepers of Cheapside spoke of her as that desperate Papist against whom they were to be on their guard, for that she was determined to convert them to her religion.

'About a fortnight afterwards, one Saturday evening during the octave of Corpus Christi, Doña Luisa went into the same street to make some little purchases for her household. The strict economy she was obliged to observe forced her to attend herself to these details. Whilst thus occupied she became conscious that three men were watching her movements, evidently for the purpose of ascertaining if she spoke of religion in the shops she went into. Their aspect was so hostile that she called a good old Catholic servant, her usual escort on these occasions, and desired him to conduct home at once one of her companions, a young girl called Faith, whom she had recently received into her house, while the others, who were older, remained with her. In the meantime the three spies had sent for a constable and posted him at the end of the street. As she came out of a shop they accosted her, and said that she must go before a Justice of the Peace, as they are called. These persons exhibited no warrant for her apprehension, which they ought to have done, especially in the case of a foreigner. She took it very quietly, thinking it a good thing for her soul to suffer this insult patiently, and also wishing to avoid making them angry and creating a tumult in the street. She said that she was ready to go where they wished. And one of the principal and most respectable shopkeepers, seeing how gently she spoke, came forward, and desiring the constable to stand off, with great civility conducted her himself to the house of the judge. He was a grave looking man, of about sixty years of age. They found him seated before his house, in a sort of hall with a projecting roof, with a scrivener by his side. This was the place where he transacted business. From six to nine o'clock at night he detained Doña Luisa there whilst he examined witnesses, who did not agree in what they stated, but mentioned nothing more than what had been previously said. She was then asked what was her name and her country, and what had brought her to England. She was determined, at whatever cost it might be, to answer the exact truth, so she said that her name was " Luisa de Carvajal," that she was a Spaniard, and lived near Don Pedro de

Zuniga's house and heard Mass in his chapel, that she had come to England to follow the example of many saints and holy persons, who had voluntarily abandoned their native land, relatives, and friends, to live in a foreign country poor and unknown for the love of our Lord. The judge did not seem at all to understand this language. He and the scrivener looked at each other and laughed. Then he asked her what faith she professed, and if she had any disciples, and whether it was true that she had said that the Pope was the Head of the Catholic Church, and that the Roman Catholic religion was the only true one. She answered, "Yes, that she had said so." "Did she mean," he asked, "to persist in that opinion?" "Certainly," she replied, and that she was ready to die in support of it. Then he began to blaspheme about the Pope, and said that if what she believed was true, then she must mean that people could not be saved in the religion of the English people. She replied that she had not expressly said so, but that no doubt she had intimated as much by maintaining that the Catholic religion is the only appointed means for the salvation of souls, and that all other religions are erroneous. He looked hard at her for some minutes, and then exclaimed—"You are indeed a proper sort of woman to live in England, and to be going about from shop to shop talking of such things!" and did not she know that in Spain they would kill English people who spoke against their faith, and was it not fair they should act in the same way towards Spaniards?

'She paused a little, finding some difficulty in answering this question in English. She did not know how to explain the difference between the two cases so as to make the judge understand her, and wished much at that moment that she could have spoken in her native tongue. He then proceeded to question her about her companions—how many she had, who had introduced them to her, whether they went to Mass, and such like inquiries. She refused to answer any questions which concerned others. "Would she like as well to have Protestant attendants as Catholics?" he asked. "No; not if she could have Catholics," she replied. He then taxed her with having said that Mr. George Gervase (el Maestro Chiaves) had died a martyr. "And so he did," she answered. "He died for no other cause than the Catholic religion." "If that had been the case you would have been right," the justice retorted; "but he died because he was a madman." Then he said, "Why did you affirm that the late Queen had not the same legitimate right to the crown as his present Majesty?" "Because he is the legitimate descendant of King Henry VIII.'s sister," she answered; "whereas Queen Elizabeth was born in the lifetime of his legitimate wife, Queen Catharine." "Who told you so?" he asked. She said that she had read it in the histories and annals of the times.

He answered that her knowledge was incorrect; that Queen Catharine was not King Henry's legitimate wife, and so her daughter, Queen Mary, had no right to the throne. She would have had much to say in reply to this, but by that time she had become weak and faint, which increased her difficulty in speaking English, and made her unable to carry on the argument. The judge then proceeded to examine her companions, whom he treated with a much greater amount of civility, no doubt because they were English. These heretics have an inordinate esteem and admiration for their own country, and an equally great hatred and animosity against Spain. Besides being a foreigner, it told against Doña Luisa that she was dressed in mean attire. Her old black dress, patched and mended in several places, and the shabby hood she wore on her head, gave her the appearance of a poor woman. This was just what she liked, and it pleased her to see that they treated her attendants much more respectfully than herself. She had been afraid that they would all have been searched in order to discover if they had crosses and rosaries, but nothing of the sort occurred. The English girls did not answer as directly to the point as Doña Luisa had done, and the judge began to give her credit for truthfulness, and said he looked to her for information, for that she seemed to be a women not given to lying. Still he got very angry with her because she defended them, and put herself forward to speak in their behalf. The wife and daughters of the judge kept all the time going in and out of the room. A number of persons had in the meantime gathered round the door of the house. Those who had procured her arrest excited the populace of these two or three great streets, full of shops and offices, declaring that she was a Roman Catholic priest dressed as a woman, and going about London in that disguise to persuade people to embrace his religion. There were at the least two hundred of them struggling to enter into the audience-room.

'The justice went out to speak to them, and tried to send them away, but without success. As there were three prisoners they said they must be all priests, and most likely monks. He told Doña Luisa that if he was to send her at that moment through the streets to prison that the mob would tear them in pieces. She said she was sure he had too much charity to do so. The doors were locked, and a great noise went on outside. At nine o'clock the justice went to his supper, leaving his prisoners locked up in a chamber adjoining his office, in charge of his secretary and a constable. The night was damp and cold. They were kept there till half past eleven o'clock at night, waiting till the frantic crowd should disperse. Doña Luisa and her companions spent that time praying that God would inspire them to say something to their keepers about our holy faith which would have an effect upon their hearts; and in the excess of her weakness, for she had never quite recovered from the illness she had had before leaving Spain, Doña Luisa still found strength to speak to them very forcibly and earnestly about religion. A most incorrigible Papist she must have appeared to the constable and the scrivener. At last the justice came back, and said that he hoped she would be sent out of the kingdom, but that in the meantime she was to go to prison. She begged him not to send them to the prison he mentioned because it was a very noisy one, full of riotous men, and in the worst part of the city. Nobody in it was imprisoned on account of religion. The justice laughed rudely at this with the scrivener, and told her she was so ugly, so badly dressed, and such a figure, that she need not be afraid of any one taking the trouble to look at her. They were then given in charge to the persons in whose custody they had been at the office, and marched off to prison. The streets were very muddy, and the rain falling in torrents. About twenty persons from the neighbourhood followed them. The scrivener whispered to the gaoler that he should treat them well, which however he did not do, though not so badly as Doña Luisa had wished; for she was not loaded with chains like our Lord, although imprisoned for His sake. He took them up to the top of the building, and locked them up in a small room. There were in the same passage a number of prisoners in separate cells.

'The old Catholic servant, who had followed his mistress there, was not satisfied with the bars and bolts, but chose to afford her a living protection also, and for that purpose remained all night lying on the floor across the door of the cell where she was confined. It was very narrow, and almost all the space in it was taken up by a wretched bed on which they had all to lie down. Being greatly in want of food, the English girls asked the gaoler to let them have a little bread and beer. He said he had none, which made them laugh. They were anxious, however, about some books and papers they had at home, and this apprehension kept them all night awake. If the house were searched, which appeared probable, nothing but a miraculous interposition of Providence could prevent their being discovered. Doña Luisa asked the gaoler to move them the next day into the part of the prison where he said his wife and daughters lived. Money smoothes away difficulties, and either out of kindness or for the sake of his own interest, he came on the following morning at ten o'clock and conducted them to a decent room far from the other prisoners, but close, dark, and noisy. His wife kept her provisions in the cupboard of that chamber, and was continually going in and out.

'Doña Luisa's first care was how to arrange that Holy Communion should be brought to her, but neither on that day, which was a Sunday, or on the Monday was it possible; on the Tuesday and the Wednesday a priest came in disguise to her room, carrying with him the Blessed Sacrament in a small silver case. She and her attendants had made such friends with the gaoler and his family that they offered no opposition and stayed away whilst they went to confession and communion. Our Blessed Lord did not abandon them in their imprisonment, and in return they did their best to advance His interests during their captivity. To all the heretics who came to see them, to the officers and servants of the prison and also to their wives and daughters, they spoke much about religion, remembering the words of St. Paul, that he was an ambassador in a chain. One of the gaolers whispered to her one day—"If you want to go to the devil, follow our religion; but if to Almighty God, stick to your own." He was a schismatic, that is a Catholic at heart, though professing to be a Protestant.

'Her internal joy was great during those days. She rejoiced intensely at being in prison on account of having publicly borne witness to her faith, and would have been only too happy to go from it to the scaffold. She did not say like Isaac, "Here is the wood and the fire, but where is the holocaust?" On the contrary, the cry of her soul was, "Here is the victim, where are the wood and the fire?" But on the other hand she wished to be released on account of the young girls she was training to the religious life; and also because her scanty resources could not sustain the heavy expense of the hire of a private room. Yet it was impossible, if not for her own sake for that of her companions, to submit to be crowded in the same apartment with thieves and women of bad character. If those who had her in their power had only chosen to send her at once to heaven, what a blessing she would have felt it! The inferior part of her soul recoiled from a return to her life in London. On first entering the prison she had been almost over-powered by the darkness of the room, the want of fresh air, and the vociferations of the prisoners on the other side of the yard. She missed her books, and felt for a moment depressed; but joy at suffering for Christ soon got the better of this weakness, and she willingly accepted the prospect of a long captivity, though any kind of death would have seemed to her preferable.

'On the third day after her arrest, Don Pedro de Zuniga despatched to her Fray Juan of San Augustin to tell her that she must not be surprised if he could not procure her immediate release. He did not think it advisable to take for the moment any step about it. She was not to be anxious about her board and lodging whilst in the prison, and arrange everything in the best way she could for her health and convenience—that he would be answerable for the expense, and to begin with he sent her a purse containing a hundred gold ducats. Doña Luisa begged Fray Juan to express all her gratitude to this generous friend, and to say that he need not provide for her future wants in prison, seeing that he was so near at hand, and, as she had already experienced, so charitably desirous of assisting her when there was occasion for it ; that she begged him not to endeavour to obtain her release unless it included also the liberation of the young persons who had been arrested with her ; that she had no doubt it was God's will that he should take no measures on the subject, and that she was quite content it should be so. She would not accept the purse, but said that if she was in want of money she would let him know. Fray Juan insisted on leaving her two hundred reals, which sufficed to pay the expences of their imprisonment, for on the following day they were released.

The King's Council, and one Robert Cecil in particular, happened to see the papers relating to her arrest at a moment when for political reasons the English Government was anxious to conciliate the Spanish Ambassador, and at ten o'clock on Wednesday night she and her companions were set at liberty and conducted at once to Don Pedro's house, whence she immediately went to her little home. Great was the joy of the two young girls who had remained there during her absence, at seeing her and her fellow prisoners. They had visited her at the prison, dressed in the clothes of two of

N

Don Pedro's washerwomen.   One of these young ladies belonged to one of the first families in the kingdom. 'This was the first time that Luisa fell into the hands of the heretics.   This occurrence by no means daunted her courage.   It only inspired her with the hope of renewing the encounter when she should have acquired more fluency in speaking English.'

Don Pedro de Zuniga, on the contrary, seems to have been, and we cannot much wonder at it, not a little dismayed at this first result of Luisa's zeal.   He had never contemplated the possibility of her being treated with so much indignity and thrown into a public prison, and his first impulse was to insist on her returning to Spain.   He urged that it would be highly imprudent for her to remain in that part of London, that she might meet with people who would recognize her, and run the risk of being murdered in some obscure street, or again dragged before a magistrate.   And being evidently and not unnaturally out of temper, he added, 'What will they say in Spain and Flanders of what has happened?   A person of so high a rank thrown into a low prison, full of miscreants, and for what?   For attempting to convert four or five shopmen, and with no result after all! and this wilful imprudence is to go by the name of suffering for the Faith!   And then, what was the use of keeping five or six young persons together, wearing a secular dress, which would not be thought at all proper in Spain for women professing to lead a religious life, which religious life the heretics cannot endure even to hear of?' Having scolded Luisa, the good Ambassador proceeded to scold her confessor, because he did not order her at once to leave London.

It was a bitter trial, like flakes of ice falling on her heart, we are told, to hear such severe words from one who had been so kind, and to whom she owed so much

·gratitude. On one occasion, he went so far as to tell her :that she might be the occasion of a rupture of the peace between England and Spain. It cost her great pain to appear to him obstinate, but looking on this question in a different point of view from his, and with an intimate conviction that she was where God willed her to be, and doing a work pleasing to Him, she could not and would not yield to his importunities, feeling persuaded that her heavenly Father, about Whose business she had come to a place from which every human feeling would have prompted her to fly, would ward off disastrous consequences to others from her boldness. Her four companions entirely shared her feelings, and there was a rivalry amongst them as to who should accompany her when she went out, and share the risks she might run. At the same time she seems to have so far yielded to the advice given her, as not to carry out the intention with which she had left the prison, of resuming public disputations as soon as her knowledge of English would allow her to do so with greater facility. Ardent and uncompromising as was her character, she never acted ·on impulse, or in the least degree against obedience. Her confessor probably insisted on a prudent line of conduct, and the following letter from Father Luis de la Puente, S.J., which she received in answer to one in which she had related to him the circumstances of her arrest and imprisonment, no doubt served to moderate what had been rash in her zeal.

Father Luis de la Puente to Doña Luisa de Carvajal.

The letter I have received from your charity gives me great consolation. I rejoice to find with how much courage God our Lord enables you to drink of His bitter but precious chalice—bitter indeed to the flesh, but sweet to the spirit, which remains united to Christ our only Good, in Whom all that is naturally bitter turns into sweetness. Let your charity

N 2

bear in mind that fervent Apostle whose belt a Prophet took, and binding with it his feet, announced to him, by the inspiration of the Holy Spirit, that he who owned that belt would be bound and imprisoned in Jerusalem, and how, when thus addressed, that courageous man, undismayed and nowise sorrowful, exclaimed, that he was not only ready to be bound, but to die, for the love of Jesus.   Imprisonment is a first step towards martyrdom, and those who love our Lord very much rejoice when they find themselves on the way to torments and death, whereby they can testify to the utmost their devotion to Him.   It appears to me, señora, that your fervour goes on increasing, and that what you suffer seems to you little in comparison with what you would wish to suffer. This is well ; but let it be a discreet fervour, for the heavenly Bridegroom, Who inspires His spouses with celestial affections and orders charity in their souls, wills that even in love there should be order, so that fervour may not be rash and violent.   Even as He hates tepidity which takes the name of prudence, so He hates indiscretion which calls itself fervour.   Blessed be His wisdom and His charity, which supplies for our defects, which inflames tepid hearts and makes them brave, and to the fervent imparts light and prudence.   A pure, holy, and simple intention in all we do to please God alone, can effect much.   His infinite mercy will not permit that those who have no other desire should be deceived by spirits of darkness suggesting cowardly fears, nor by the noonday devils which beguile us to excesses. May you always have that very pure intention to please God alone in all things, founded on the most profound humility and sense of nothingness as to any good that we can do ; and hope in your heavenly Father, Who will never abandon you until, from this valley of tears, you are translated to a paradise of delights.   As God has placed you in England, go on there advancing from virtue to virtue, till you arrive at seeing Him in the heavenly Jerusalem.   And if our Lord removes you thence to some other place, do not distress yourself. The place where He chooses you to be will be just as good for your spiritual advancement as the one where you are now.   Keep close, then, to your God.   Wherever He chooses you to be, there you will be in safety.   He Who did not abandon you when in prison will not abandon you, even if, like Himself on Calvary, you were to be crucified between two thieves. Do not, however, imagine yourself worthy of dying for Christ. It has been denied to many a fervent saint; but desire and strive to be worthy of such a grace. I think of you in a particular manner when I read the psalm in matins which you pointed out to me. Remember me in your holy prayers, and quietly and discreetly endeavour, not only to go to heaven yourself, but to draw there many others with you. I earnestly beg of our Lord to have you in His holy keeping.

LUIS DE LA PUENTE.

Valladolid, 1608.

CHAPTER VI.

Apostolic labours.

THE English Catholics, at the time we are writing of,. were eminent for their virtue and piety. The heat of persecution, like the furnace in which gold is refined, maintained the purity of their morals and the steadfastness of their faith; but owing to the secret manner in which they had to practise their religion, and the long intervals during which they had no opportunity of hearing sermons and instructions, together with the difficulty of procuring, and the danger of keeping in their homes, Catholic spiritual books, they were often deficient in the knowledge and practices of the interior life. To many such persons, Luisa was of infinite use. They were so sure of her discretion, that they were not afraid of letting her into their secrets. Her intimate acquaintance with the best spiritual writers, her constant intercourse in Spain with priests of the most eminent sanctity and learning, and the patient use she had made of their lessons since her earliest youth, enabled her to impart solid instruction to those she frequented. Her own example was in itself a constant incentive to higher perfection. Both in the house where she lived during the first year of her residence in London, and in the house which she afterwards hired near the Spanish Embassy,. she was at all times ready to give advice and instruction to those who came to her, as well as to assist them to, the utmost of her power in temporal matters. The Spanish Ambassador, at her special request, maintained in his house an aged English priest, for the express benefit of the London Catholics. She arranged secret interviews for them whenever the circumstances of the case required it, and thus secured to many the opportunity of approaching the sacraments without exposing themselves to danger.

At the time that she was staying in his house, Don Pedro had written to the King of Spain, Philip III., an account of the good she was doing in England, the zeal with which she laboured for the salvation of souls, and the services she rendered to the English Catholics. He had expressed his veneration for her extraordinary holiness, and mentioned her having given away all she possessed for the advancement of religion, so that she now lived on the work of her hands and the alms of the faithful. The King had always had a great regard for Luisa, and on hearing these details, he at once assigned her, out of his privy purse, a pension of three hundred reals a month, which he desired the Ambassador to pay her. This placed her, as she laughingly said, 'in riches and luxury.' We need scarcely say that the money came into her hands only to pass into those of the poor. She grudged herself every mouthful of food, and only thought of returning to God what He had sent her as fast as she received it.

This pension, and the large donations she received from her uncle, Don Bernardo, Cardinal Archbishop of Toledo, the Duchess of Medina de Rioseco, the Countess de Miranda, the Marquis of Caracena y Siete Iglesias, and Beatrice Ramirez de Mendoza, Countess of Castellar, whom Luis Munoz calls 'the Paula of that day,' gave her abundant means of assisting Catholics of all ranks in their various needs. With the exception of a very shabby garment made of black serge, and food just sufficient for her sustenance, she bought nothing for herself. So great were the miseries of those faithful children of the Church, that she often felt compelled to bestow upon them what she and her companions absolutely needed. They were quite of the same mind with her on that point, and never better pleased than when they found themselves without a single stiver, or a bit of food in the house. However, when it came to that, our Blessed Lord never failed to send them, by some means or other, what was necessary for their sustenance. This constant experience of His mercy encouraged her to be as profuse in her charities in England as in Spain, where she seldom had a real in her purse. Must we add that she had no scruple in winning the hearts of her English friends by little presents, particularly of Spanish gloves, which seem to have been in great request at that time in England,[1] for the Spanish Ambassador used to distribute them to the ladies of the Court? It must be borne in mind that she had to make her way with persons violently preju-diced against her country and her religion, and that when, as her biographer tells us, she ingratiated herself with persons of all ranks by making them small gifts,

---

[1] A passage occurs in Miss Strickland's *Life of Queen Anne of Denmark* which exhibits the character of Don Pedro de Zuniga in a very different light from that in which the writer of Luisa's Life represents him. It is a curious instance of the opposite description which can be given of the same persons by authors of different opinions and sympathies. 'The Spanish Ambassador (she writes) was, too, in attendance (at Woodstock Palace), and sad to say, was in far greater favour with Queen Anne and her ladies than the illustrious Sully, who had lately been on an especial embassy of congratulation from his master, Henry the Great. Even the highly gifted Arabella Stuart joined in preferring to Sully the Ambassador of Spain—a coxcomb of the first water, who distributed Spanish gloves to the ladies, and perfumed leather jerkins to the gentlemen of the Court.'

and showing them kindnesses, it was a harmless way of disarming the enmity which formed a barrier between her and them she wished to win over to her faith. She sometimes bought things in shops and from pedlars, even when she did not want them, for the sake of an opportunity of talking to people about religion. When, by dint of hard labour and painful practice, she had arrived at speaking English fluently, she was ever on the watch for occasions of this sort, going on the principle of the sower who scatters his seed where he hopes it may fructify and grow, but does not grudge if some of it falls on the hard road, the barren rock, or the thorny hedge, knowing that a shower of rain or a gleam of sunshine may, even in the most unlikely spots, and after a long lapse of time, cause it to spring up and bring forth fruit, even though he may never see or hear of it in this world.

At that time there were few persons who could venture to speak a word in behalf of the Catholic Church. The priests were obliged to conceal themselves, and for the sake of their own people could not expose themselves to an entire cessation of their ministrations amongst them, by addressing promiscuously an ignorant multitude, deluded by their rulers and the Protestant clergy into believing the most monstrous falsehoods about the faith of their fathers. She had nothing to risk, nothing to lose, by her bold attacks on that religion which, founded on private judgment, resists appeals to free discussion on the part of the Catholic Church. She had discovered how often returns to that Church had been brought about by a word casually uttered by a friend, a neighbour, or even a servant. It had fallen on the ear, sunk into the heart, and long, perhaps, lain dormant in the mind. Then, in an hour of grief and sorrow in some cases, or of leisure from the cares of business in another, or else on the couch of sickness and at the approach of death, the result became apparent. A Catholic priest was secretly summoned, and the soul reconciled to God and the Church before leaving this world. It was, no doubt, easier to make converts then, even in the midst of fierce persecution and the temporal miseries in store for those who embraced the ancient faith, than now, when, comparatively speaking, few and light are the trials which attend such an act. Persons were not then indifferent about religion. They did not admit that two opposite beliefs could both be true. Heaven and hell were looked upon as great realities, and the way of arriving at the one, and avoiding the other, a matter of no slight importance. Times are changed. Such a desperate controversialist as Luisa would not now be thrown into Newgate, but would be considered so great a nuisance that every door would be shut against her. She would not be tolerated in society. It may, however, be questioned whether Catholics in our days do not carry too far a system of absolute silence on religious subjects—whether for the sake of quiet and agreeable intercourse with Protestants, and free-thinking friends and relatives, they do not maintain too complete a reserve on the momentous questions which divide them ; whether there would not be a true and holy courage in braving looks of surprise and displeasure, and cold bitter words, for the sake of uttering a word which, perhaps, once in a hundred times might produce, sooner or later, an effect which a well-bred silence does not obtain. It is a difficult question, a hard one to resolve, but so important, that few, perhaps, should be more carefully weighed in the secret tribunal of conscience, and committed with more earnest prayer to the guidance of the Holy Spirit.

It was on account of the opportunities London afforded of intercourse with Protestants, that Luisa chose it as her residence. In smaller places it was difficult, she said, to get into conversation with people ; a brief salutation was exchanged, and there the acquaintance ended. To live in London her biographer considers to have been an act of heroic virtue, equal to any other she performed. He gives the following description of the capital of England.

It is a miserable place (*lugaraço*), very expensive, and the climate so dreadful, that there is scarcely a day in the year when one might not fancy oneself in winter. The air is so thick and heavy, that it produces many ailments. Besides the one great plague of heresy, it has others as numerous as those of Egypt. A pestilence, which they call *the* plague, continually recurs. It raged more or less during the first six years that Doña Luisa spent in England. When it is severe, it carries off almost one half of the population. The most zealous among the Puritans say that it is a great blessing to die of the plague, and a particular token of God's favour ; and if any one asks them—' Of what did your relative or friend die ?' they answer in a solemn manner, ' Of the Lord's token.' They take no precautions against contagion, because, say they, if a man is fated to die of that disease, there is no use in trying to get out of the way of it. Every one goes to the funeral ; afterwards the house is shut up, with all who are in it, and they feed them at their own expense for a month. An old wretch is posted at the door by way of guarding it, but he lets any one go out who will give him as much as a piece of bread. They sell the clothes and the bedding on the very day of a person's death, and there are always plenty of purchasers. The folly of this people and of their Government is incredible. It is a wonder they do not all die. And with all that they tell you that London is an earthly Paradise !

Little as Luisa could concur in that last view of London, as exaggerated in its way, no doubt, as the gloomy picture drawn by Luis Munoz, she enjoyed there a happiness greater than any earth can give, for sometimes, after many tears and prayers, and patient perseverance, she succeeded in bringing back to the

Church persons who but for her would never have known the truth about Catholicism. She writes thus to her cousin, the Marquesa de Caracena—

Sometimes my poor soul clámours to God for children— *da mihi liberos;* but generally speaking, I am satisfied to do all I can to please Him Who gives me these strong desires, and to leave all to Him. I am greatly rejoiced at the conversion of a married man, because, at any rate, this leads to his wife's conversion also, and insures a Catholic education for his children. The most impregnable stronghold of this people's obduracy is their incredible attachment to a quiet life and temporal prosperity. Even after one has worked hard to convince them of the truth of Catholicism, and that they admit that they are convinced, the fear of displeasing the heretics is of itself enough, without any other reason, to prevent them from renouncing heresy. I very often tell them that this sort of devil can only be cast out by prayer and fasting ; and in both those respects I am the poorest creature imaginable. If I fast, it is only because I have a loathing for food which scarcely ever leaves me. My health is very bad. I have had this winter severe illnesses and a great deal of pain.

Ill as she was, her energy did not flag. It seemed as if the strength of her soul increased in proportion to the weakness of her body. When she had once acquired a command of the English language, she astonished her hearers by her powers of argument and her natural gifts of eloquence. There was a fire of love and a holy impetuosity in her advocacy of the ancient faith, 'quite foreign to the laws of England,' Luis Munoz sarcastically remarks. Protestants used to say that they did not wonder at the Government thinking of banishing her, for that her skill in disputation, and the influence she gained over the minds of those she conversed with, was enough to win over the most determined anti-Papist.

Luisa never lost a single occasion of making a convert. At Highgate, where she went for change of air at the time of the plague, she met a painter, employed by Don Pedro, who had formerly been in Spain. In one of her letters she says—

I explain to him the points of our faith which he does not believe in. He understands Spanish perfectly, and speaks it also, which gives him great facility in learning. May it please our Lord to bring to my recollection all the most urgent and powerful arguments I have read and heard! I take one or two of my companions with me, and we find him alone. The poor man seems to like me very much. He has great quickness at understanding, so that it is a pleasure to talk to him about religion : he so readily catches the meaning of what one says. When I press him closely he looks aghast, and stares at me as if he was going to have a fit, till, suddenly recollecting himself, he casts down his eyes.

In another letter, alluding to the same person, she mentions that the painter is gone to London, and that she must return there, in order to renew their conversations at her home or at his studio, for that he had invited her to come and see his pictures.

Writing to the Viceroy of Valencia, she expresses her resolution never to leave England, and in reference to that subject she says—

This, my settled purpose, was mentioned the other day by a lady who lives in this street to her brother, who is a Councillor of State, and his wife. She is a great invalid, and can never go out to pay visits. They found me sitting with her, and in the course of conversation they asked me when I meant to go back to Spain. Before I could answer, the invalid said, 'I do not think she means to go back. England is the place she will be buried in ;' and certainly, señor, I think that there was that day some reason to fear that in that house I might have been on the road to my grave, for some of the members of that family are terrible heretics. I had been shown into a dark room, and no one was admitted there but her brother and her sister-in-law. My companion was taken into the garden by some of the servants. I could see that they were anxious and uneasy, and my companion downstairs had the same thought as I upstairs. This lady shows me great affection. I do not know if it is with the view of drawing me into the darkness of her errors, but I am glad of it, as I thus have the opportunity of drawing her into the light of my Catholic faith. I make her presents of . little things from Spain (*cosas de España*), which do not cost much and are thought a great deal of here ; and I take care not to let her know whether I am poor or rich. If I was to say I was rich, it would not be true, and if I said I was poor, she would take a dislike to me, for they do not at all understand here about poverty. I tell her, however, that I am a pilgrim, and she enjoys spending hours alone with me, talking about religion. I never begin on that subject, but I lead her to do so herself, which they always prefer. She is convinced as to the principal points of faith, but it is very hard work to bring her to the point. She is surrounded with brothers, children, and friends, who are violent Protestants, and determinately bent on their own opinions. I shall now push matters forward in my visits, and give and take boldly on this matter, even at the peril of my life. It would be a great happiness to win her and others.

Those who think it wrong to endeavour to persuade others to do that which we firmly believe will secure their happiness in this world and eternal bliss in the next, a judgment which condemns all missionary efforts— for if it is blameable to try to convert Protestants, under which name Unitarians and Deists are included, it must be blameable also to convert Jews, Turks, and Buddhists— will necessarily condemn Luisa as the most arch-proselytizer that ever tampered with the souls of English people. She would have had no idea of disclaiming the title, or have understood how Catholics can ever boast as of a merit that they do not try to induce others to abandon error for truth. If we are to believe her biographer, she effected a great number of conversions and reconciliations and returns to the Catholic Church, loved and believed in still by so many in secret and only disowned from worldly motives. A man with *one* idea is always powerful, some one has said. The one idea in her mind, the sole passion of her heart, was this work of winning back to God souls sunk or estranged in heresy. She lived for nothing else. She studied every means to that end, and devoted to it her time, her talents, her learning ; the Holy Scriptures, the writings of the Fathers, she had, to speak familiarly, at her fingers ends. She could adduce, if required, text against text, quotation against quotation, rectify false assertions, discern quibbles, and face every objection. To the poor and simple, from the depths of her heart she spake of the consolations, the hopes, the blessings, the sacraments, and the divinity of the Catholic Church ; made their hearts burn within them as they listened, and raised their eyes from a world where suffering and toil are their portion, to the one, where, as she teaches, every tear and every pang offered up here below is crowned with proportionate joy. She was ingenious in her devices, unwearied in her perseverance. In season and out of season, striving on God's side in the conflict waged between conscience pointing to a heroic sacrifice and nature pleading for a reprieve. And when in the home of the rich, or the hovel of the poor, one of those she had watched with prayers and tears during a time of doubt and darkness hearkened at last to the Voice which says, 'Follow Me!' her attenuated and fragile form was seen gliding in the dark evenings side by side with the new child of the Church, or the returning prodigal, to one of the secret hiding-places where a priest lately escaped from the torturers and on the next day perhaps to be again consigned to a dungeon on his way to Tyburn, was waiting to speak pardon in his Lord's name and reconcile to God and to the Church the weeping one at his feet.

Some of her converts seem to have caught her spirit of generous boldness. One young man, heir to a large fortune which he renounced to become a Catholic, and gifted with considerable talents, went about after his conversion preaching the Faith at the risk of his life. A student who had been through her exertions received into the Church, was not so bold. He had a friend whom he very much wished to convert, but he had not courage to let him know what he had done. However, he one day told him that there was a Spanish lady in London, the most extraordinary woman in the world. She knew the whole of the Bible by heart, and was more learned than the most learned divines. He gave such wonderful accounts of this foreigner that at last his friend's curiosity was excited and he expressed a wish to make her acquaintance. The first visit he paid her made so great an impression upon him that he returned again and again, and, struck with the truths she placed before him, he made up his mind after awhile to be received into the Church, but confided to her how much he dreaded his friend discovering it. Luisa contrived that they should meet at her house, and to their inexpressible joy the secret both had so carefully kept was soon disclosed. Many and many a young man called the servant of God mother and teacher. She helped them in every way she could, often furnishing them with money to go abroad, and giving them letters of introduction to foreign Colleges, whence several of them returned to England as priests, and became active missionaries. One of her principal converts was a Calvinist minister, a man of great learning and much esteemed by his sect. Father Michael Walpole asked him some time after his conversion how he came to be convinced by the arguments of a woman, he who had so often conferred with ecclesiastics aud eminent controversialists without any result. He answered that these persons had often given him the strength of conclusive reasons as to the truth of their religion, that he admitted their arguments, yet never felt impressed by them ; whereas Luisa said things which touched and converted his heart. Soon after his abjuration he was arrested and thrown into prison.

His good mother, as he always called her, did not fail to visit and to comfort him. Through her efforts his release was obtained, and she gave him the means of escaping to Flanders, from whence he went on to Spain, and became a priest and a Benedictine monk. A layman well skilled in controversy, and endowed with great gifts of speaking, which he had used on the side of Protestantism, was also by Luisa's influence won over to the Church. Some of the Puritans, whom his conversion changed from admirers and friends into bitter enemies, denounced him as a Papist. He was committed to the custody of the Protestant Bishop of London, who asked him why he had not fled to the Continent after he had changed his religion. He answered, like a true disciple of Luisa, that it was a merit to suffer for one's faith. Upon which the bishop assured him that if he did not speedily recant, ample opportunities of meriting would be afforded him. He was thrown into prison, loaded with irons, locked up with malefactors, and threats held out that if he persevered in his contumacy an example would be made of him. He contrived, however, to escape, and succeeded in reaching Luisa's house, where she kept him concealed till he could embark for Flanders. On his way to the ship he was again nearly arrested, but, thanks

o

to her presence of mind, the pursuivants were baffled and his departure accomplished.

Luisa's prayers seem to have sometimes obtained conversions that seemed, humanly speaking, hopeless, and in which she had no direct share. A priest had returned to England for the express purpose of persuading his mother to become a Catholic. She was violently opposed to Catholicism, and could not endure to hear the subject mentioned. After two months of fruitless effort, he came one day, quite disheartened, to Luisa. She comforted him, and said—' Reverend Father, do not lose hope. I think our Lord will have pity upon your sorrow, and that you will see your mother a Catholic.' Cheered by this answer, he exclaimed—' Oh, if you will take the matter up, I feel as if the work was done!' He went home, and in a short time afterwards came again to see Luisa, and to tell her that his mother had not only been received into the Church, but was a most fervent Catholic.

There was a poor woman in a village near London who was, or, at any rate was supposed to be, possessed. She was advised to have recourse to a Catholic priest, for that they had the power of exorcising evil spirits. Having heard of Luisa, she went to her, and begged her assistance. The latter availed herself of the opportunity of instructing her in the Catholic religion, and made her a good Christian. It did not please God to deliver her from her sufferings, whatever might be their origin, but she learnt to look upon them as evils which had been overruled by His mercy into the means of her conversion. Luisa kept her for some time in her house, at the cost of much trouble and anxiety of mind, and did not lose sight of her afterwards.

Sometimes, as she passed persons in the streets, a sudden desire came into her heart to pray for their conversion. If it was possible to find a pretext for accosting them, she did so. If rebuffed, she held her peace, and waited for another opportunity. If none occurred, she betook herself to prayer, and besought our Lord to inspire them Himself with the wish to seek her. One summer, at Highgate, she heard of an old woman in that neighbourhood who was between eighty and ninety years of age. Ever since Queen Elizabeth's accession to the throne, she had conformed to the times, and attended the Protestant service. Luisa's interest was instantly awakened for this poor creature, who had been born a Catholic, and she tried in every way she could think of to make her acquaintance; but the old woman, who suspected that she wanted to talk to her about religion, repulsed all her advances. Then Luisa pleaded for her at the throne of grace with many prayers and tears. Hour after hour she spent beseeching God not to let this soul die out of the Church, and for many days together reiterated these supplications. At last, of her own accord, the old woman made her appearance one morning at her house, curtseying and smiling, but without any particular object, as far as it seemed. Luisa told her it was high time to think of her salvation, and to prepare for the next world. Upon which she said that she had seen in a dream a radiant youth, who had warned her that if she wished to save her soul, she must be reconciled to the Church; that she had alleged in reply, that as she was situated, it was not in her power to do so; and that he had then charged her, in the name of our Lord, to go to the Spanish lady who lived near Don Pedro's house, and that she would help her.

The woman looked so feeble, that Luisa saw there was no time to be lost. She sent at once for a priest, who reconciled her to the Church. Her mind was quite

clear, and her memory unimpaired. She made a confession extending over forty or fifty years, with marks of
sincere contrition. During all that time she had been,
apparently, a Protestant, but devotion to our Blessed
Lady had always maintained its hold on her heart, and
she had never ceased to commend herself to her protection. Luisa took her into her house, and during the two
months she was there, she did nothing but pray from
morning to night, and kept constantly repeating—'My
Saviour, take me from this world before my lady goes
away and leaves me with heretics.' Her wish was
granted. Some days before Luisa left Highgate, she
and her companions knelt round the bed where this poor
old woman breathed her last, making to the end fervent
acts of faith, hope, and charity.

From Highgate, that year, Luisa wrote to her
brother—

We were staying all the winter out of London on account
of the plague, which threatens to be more violent than ever.
Though the inhabitants of this place are most determined
heretics, several persons have been already converted, and
there are many opportunities for work of that sort.

In a letter to Father Creswell, of the Society of Jesus,
she says—

I am working hard to attract as many souls as possible
from heresy into the Church. I feel no abatement of zeal in
this cause. On the contrary, an ardour that increases every
day. I manage to speak English tolerably well, without
having had the assistance of a master, solely by the work of
my own brain, for I have never been able to obtain any help
in it from my companions. No one seems inclined to take
the trouble to teach me.

One of the ways in which Luisa employed the sums
that her pious friends placed in her hands for the

promotion of Catholicism in England, was the purchase
of a number of books of controversy and devotion,
which she lent to those who were under instruction, or
whom she directed in the spiritual life. These books
were very expensive, for those who sold them charged in
proportion to the risk they incurred. Another constant
outlet for her charity, was the support of priests and
other Catholics in the prisons, who, if they could not
afford to pay for their board and lodging, were thrust
into the company of the vilest criminals. She was
continually engaged in these acts of charity, and whether
by her own personal efforts, or those of the Spanish
Ambassador, whose interest she commanded, innumerable services were rendered to persecuted Catholics
of every rank. With regard to this subject, her
biographer complains somewhat bitterly of the English
Catholic nobility, many of whom, he states, were
possessed of considerable wealth, notwithstanding the
fines and exactions they were subjected to, but which
did not oppress them in the same way as the gentry.
He thinks it very strange that it never occurred to them
to assist Luisa, who spent all she had on their countrymen, and was often reduced herself to the greatest
straits. They took it as a matter of course, he goes on
to say, that Spain should furnish large sums for the
relief of English Catholics, but that she might many
a time have starved if she had looked to them for aid.
Only twice during her residence of nine years in London
did any English people give her anything; and those who
did so were a lady who had lived twenty years in Spain,
and an English merchant at Seville.

These exceptions indicate clearly enough the reason of
this apparent churlishness. Luisa's life of voluntary
poverty was probably not in the least understood in
England. She seems to have felt herself the coldness

and indifference with which Catholics in some instances
behaved to her. This is expressed in a letter to the
Marquis of Caracena—

The hearts of the good, as well as of the bad, seem in
some sort closed against me. As far as I can judge, they
would not take the trouble to pick me out of the mud before
their doors, or offer me a corner of their houses as a shelter.
I cannot help admiring the clever way in which they defend
their neglect of me, calling it prudence and wisdom, for they
are in other respects, and to one another, exceedingly charitable. Still, what with His Divine Majesty touching the
hearts of now one and then another person in Spain, and
bringing us to their remembrance, and all your Excellency
does for me, and the pension our Ambassador transmits to
me from the King, we get on, and help others. The constancy with which good Catholics here persevere in their
faith makes up for all the miseries of this otherwise detest-
able country.

Whilst we allow for the feelings of Luisa and her
biographer, and can easily conceive how the stiff reserve
of English manners must have often pained her heart, it
is, on the other hand, just to call to mind that the
English Catholics must have had a not unreasonable
fear of her ardent, and—in spite of Luis Munoz's
assurances that it was prudent—we are forced to believe
not always discreet, zeal. One who thought it the
most desirable of all blessings to ascend the scaffold as
a martyr, who speaks of the *incredible* dread the
Catholics had of losing their property, who measured
happiness on earth according to the amount of pain and
suffering a generous heart can offer up for the conversion
of souls, may have been an object of great admiration
to good Catholics; but, if they were not her equals in
heroism, an alarming guest or even a perilous acquaintance. And unfamiliar as they probably were with

instances of secular persons despoiling themselves of their fortunes as she had done, and casting in their lot with that of the poorest of their fellow creatures, they could have had no idea of her position. It could hardly have entered their heads that Doña Luisa de Carvajal y Mendoza, the niece of a Cardinal, the relative of some of the chief grandees in Spain, and, moreover, one who gave large sums for all sorts of holy purposes—who, whenever a need occurred more pressing than usual, produced plenty of gold ducats and doubloons—could be often herself on the brink of destitution. They thought, perhaps, that to offer her an alms would have been a dire insult. Inviting her to their houses would indeed have been more to the point, but in some instances this might have compromised them very seriously, and occasioned a visit from the pursuivants.

Amongst the objects which Luisa had particularly at heart was the baptism of infants by Catholic priests. She knew, of course, that baptism if properly administered by persons out of the Church is valid; but, greatly distrusting the manner in which the Protestant clergy conferred that sacrament, she was always on the watch to secure to newborn children the benefit of an undoubted admission into God's Church. The fees required by the parochial ministers often caused delays in the baptisms of the children of poor persons. She used to obtain for them the gratuitous services of Catholic priests; and not only in London did she devote herself to this work, but she used to go into the neighbouring villages and persuade the poor people to let their children be baptized by a priest. The country was full of persons who had ceased to be Catholic, but had neither faith in, nor attachment to, the new religion by law established, and they were quite ready to accept the offer when the rite could be performed secretly and no danger incurred.

The Catholics, of course, gladly availed themselves of her good offices for this purpose.

Another of her good works was to take converts and other Catholics who wished to approach the sacraments into the prisons, and introduce them into the cells of the incarcerated priests. Strange enough, this was often the safest way in which their object could be attained. If once the gaoler's connivance was secured, there was then no danger of interruption. He could sometimes be bribed, or if, as frequently was the case, he was not a sincere Protestant, his inclination led him to assist in this manner those whose example he had not courage to follow.

She sent to foreign Colleges and Seminaries boys likely to have religious vocations, and received into her house, which resembled a monastery of the strictest observance, young women of all ranks who wished to become nuns. If after a time they seemed really called to that life, she procured for them admission into convents abroad, and paid for their journeys. She had often priests staying in her house ; it was always open to those who wished to see and confer with them, and food was provided for those who came from a distance. We must not omit one very important service she rendered to the cause of the English Catholics. The English Government of that epoch was striving to the utmost, precisely as the Prussian Government of this day is doing, to make it appear that they were not persecuted on account of their religion ; that the oppression under which they laboured, and the tyrannical treatment to which they were subjected, was simply owing to their disaffection and treasonable disposition towards the State. The priests especially were accused of conduct disgraceful to their sacred calling, and every sort of calumny heaped upon them to hide the truth that they were put to death because of their fidelity to the ancient Church. These false statements had gained some credence in foreign countries, and the sympathy and help which had been shown to the English Catholics had in consequence diminished, to their inexpressible discouragement and grief. It was of all injuries the direst that their enemies could do them, and one of those injustices that depress the bravest hearts. In our days, thank God, such untruths can never be long maintained ; and though the powers of the world can oppress and persecute, they cannot deceive the good, or rob their victims of the admiration and compassion of those who value faith and courage. But in the times we are speaking of, when the communications between different countries were slow and uncertain, it was difficult to the oppressed to raise up their voices in their own defence. Governments could tell their own story, and their statements remained sometimes uncontradicted. Under these circumstances the testimony of a person as well known as Doña Luisa de Carvajal—one acquainted from her childhood with the Sovereigns of Spain and of Flanders, and who had correspondents in France and Italy as well as in her own country—carried great weight with it. The Ambassadors from Catholic countries no doubt bore witness to the truth, but they lived in the sunshine of the Court to which they were accredited. They joined in its pleasures, made friends with its statesmen, had little intercourse with their persecuted co-religionists ; and though their faith and their hearts no doubt revolted against the unjust treatment of Catholics, the political interests of Europe and diplomatic prudence probably softened their impressions and their reports of these horrors. When a priest of noted holiness, such as Father Campion or Father Southwell, was dragged to the scaffold and quartered alive, they doubtless wrote letters of burning

indignation to their respective Sovereigns, and sympathized with their persecuted brethren ; but the daily,
hourly miseries of their harassed lives did not probably
come much under their notice.   Whereas, she who knelt
by the condemned priest in his dungeon ; she who often
listened to the lamentations of ruined families and the
sighs of bereaved children ; who witnessed the anguish
of Catholic homes invaded and despoiled—she could
write of what her ears had heard and her eyes had seen;
and with all the gifts God had given her of mind and
talent, of command of the pen, and influence over
others, she could vindicate the slandered Catholics and
denounce the cruel hypocrisy of their enemies.

   This was her constant aim and effort, and her labours
were not in vain. She established the fact of a relentless
religious persecution carried on against the English
children of the Church, and fostered in their behalf the
sympathy of their fellow Christians abroad. If she had
done no other good in coming to England, it would have
been in itself sufficient to compensate for the weary
years of her banishment.

CHAPTER VII.

Work in the London prisons.

THE chief and the crowning work of charity which marked Luisa's life in London, was her devotion to the Catholic prisoners in the London gaols, and especially the priests. It would be superfluous to dwell at length on the labours and sufferings of the Jesuit, the Benedictine, the Franciscan missionaries, and a number of secular priests, who risked their lives in the service of the faithful children of the Church. Banishment, imprisonment, and martyrdom, were always at hand for them, but as often as they were banished they returned, and few that did so escaped the penalty of death. Their patient courage kept the ancient faith alive in many an old ancestral home, secluded village, or secret haunt in the great cities of England. For three centuries the sacred deposit has been handed down, and what was then sown in tears we now reap with joy. Recently published works afford graphic details of the hair-breadth escapes, indomitable perseverance, courage under torture, and heroic acceptance of death, of these men of whom the world was not worthy. We shall speak only of those particularly mentioned in connection with the Life we are writing. Luis Munoz tells us, in his quaint style, that Luisa was not better acquainted with the number of of fingers on her hands, than with that of the priests immured in the London prisons. She knew their real, and their feigned names, the dates of their arrests, the charges alleged against them, and their various necessities and wants. She visited, consoled, and assisted them, each in turn, cheering their captivity, and animating their courage by every means in her power, and making them feel that they had a friend near at hand always ready to serve them. These charitable ministrations were only once intermitted, and that for a short time. Notice was privately given to her confessor that a warrant had been issued for her apprehension, and that the next time she was found in any of the prisons she would be arrested. In consequence of this warning, he forbade her for awhile to frequent them. It was suspected, and truly enough, that she powerfully dissuaded all Catholics from taking the oath of allegiance, which had been framed for the express purpose of ensnaring their consciences, and the more violent Protestants were urging that she should be at once expelled from the kingdom. During that time of banishment, as she called it, from the prisons, her letters, which she bribed the gaolers to transmit, supplied the place of her visits, and she kept up in this way a constant intercourse with her captive friends. As soon as the immediate danger subsided the prohibition was withdrawn, and she began again to go in and out without molestation.

Those who are familiar with Challoner's *Memoirs of Missionary Priests*, no doubt remember the names of Father Roberts, a Benedictine monk, and Thomas Somers (*alias* Wilson), a secular priest, who suffered at Tyburn, on the 10th of December, 1610. The first was, according to a contemporary writer, 'a man of admirable zeal, courage, and constancy, who, during his ten years labours in the mission, was four times apprehended and committed to prison, and as often sent into banishment, but still returned again to do his Master's work. His extraordinary charity had shown itself during the time of the Great Plague in London, where he assisted a great number of the infected and was instrumental in the conversion of many souls. He was apprehended for the fifth time, at Mass, on the first Sunday of Advent, 1610, hurried away in his vestments, thrust into a dark dungeon, and soon after condemned to die, simply for his priestly character. As to Mr. Somers, who went by the name of Wilson, his residence was also chiefly in London, and his labours chiefly dedicated to the poorer sort of Catholics there, whom he served with such extraordinary diligence and zeal as to be commonly known by the name of "Parochus Londinensis"—the parish priest of London. . . . When the bloody sentence was pronounced against him, it drew tears from the eyes of many, and created pity and compassion in most of the standers-by. He heard it himself with such calmness and compassion as affected the whole court with astonishment.'

These were the two men with whom Luisa had the happiness of spending the last evening of their lives. An exact translation of this portion of the original narrative will do more justice to the subject than any words of our own.

'With great consolation of heart, she (Doña Luisa) visited some hours before their deaths the holy martyrs, Father John Roberts, a Benedictine monk, and Thomas Somers (Samir in the Spanish text), a secular priest. She had often been with them on the preceding days, and had sent them some pear tarts made in the Spanish fashion. They were confined in a dismal cell without air or light. During an imprisonment of eight or ten months the blessed Father Roberts had been preparing for death with an increasing devotion and tranquillity of soul. He had often been in prison before, but not under sentence of death. Some days before he was brought to trial, some of his fellow prisoners made an opening in the wall, through which they escaped, but he would not take advantage of the opportunity, being of opinion that the shepherd should give the flock an example of courage and resignation. He showed the deepest humility and spirituality during the time he was in captivity. After appearing in court for his trial he was taken back to the prison, and found Luisa there waiting for him. When they came to fetch him, that he might hear his sentence read, he was so weak and exhausted from recent illness that a trembling came over him. His hands shook so much that he could hardly button his coat and tie the strings of his cloak. "See how I tremble," he said to Luisa. She bade him remember how the great Captain Himself trembled when arming for the fight, and said that his flesh was afraid of his heart. The holy man smiled, and bowed his head in thanks to her for these words.

'When he was removed from the tribunal they took him to the portion of the building occupied by thieves and felons. In order that he might not be left alone at a moment which is a hard one even to the bravest hearts, his faithful friend bribed the gaolers, and obtained access to him. Not satisfied with this, she increased the bribe until they consented to transfer him, by a secret passage, into the part of the prison where the rest of the Catholics were confined. His entrance was greeted with exclamations of joy from all those assembled in that place, many of them friends and acquaintances of Luisa, who had come to take leave of him. When it was announced that they (he and Mr. Somers) were to die for their faith, Luisa fell at their feet, kissed them with the greatest fervour, wishing them joy, and expressing her envy of their happiness. "I wished to show," she said, writing to a friend, "though by a worthless and ill-chosen representative, the just and high esteem in which the Spanish nation holds the martyr's name and state, and to excite to the utmost the courage of those heroic souls so free from the least taint of presumption and vainglory, and even from the horror which would naturally be felt at such a death as their sentence described."

'They then sat down to supper—twenty prisoners for conscience' sake—twenty confessors of the Faith— Luisa presiding at the head of the table. On no other occasion would she have accepted that post of honour, but she was invited to sit between the two martyrs, and for the sake of that privilege consented to occupy it. The meal was a devout and a joyful one—heavenly the refreshments ministered to the guests, great the fervour and spiritual delight which our Lord bestowed on His valiant soldiers, giving them that peace which passeth all understanding. Scarcely any one thought of eating. Some were shedding tears of joy at the hope which, in our Lord, they had of sitting down in a few hours at a divine banquet, where God ministers Himself to His elect. The others were gazing at them with eyes full of holy envy, wishing that it had been given to them to share their happiness. As to Luisa, her heart was lifted up far above even this touching scene. Rapt in contemplation, she saw in spirit our Lord at the Last Supper, and it seemed at moments as if she only remained in appearance on earth, so tender, so devout, was the expression of her countenance, and her words so full of holy fire and sweetness. It affected every one present to hear her imploring the blessing of the martyrs, and entreating them to obtain for her an end like their own. This was her constant prayer to all those whom she saw about to die in the same manner. The two holy priests kept also recommending themselves to her prayers, and charging her to plead for them during their last moments.

'In the course of the evening Father Roberts said to her, "Do not you think I may be causing disedification by my great glee? Would it not be better to retire into a corner and give myself up to prayer?" "No; certainly not," Luisa answered. "You cannot be better employed than in letting them all see with what cheerful courage you are about to die for Christ." The two martyrs suffered death on the following day with admirable constancy. They were executed with sixteen thieves (that kingdom swarms with such persons) and eight other miscreants. Their heads, like those of other martyrs, were placed on London Bridge.'

The supernatural joy and intense fervour which enabled Luisa, not only to endure the thought of the deaths of those holy martyrs, but to exult in it, could not always remain at the same pitch, and her heart would sometimes sink within her at sight of the miseries of the English Catholics. The follow extract from her letter to her cousin, the wife of the Viceroy of Valencia, express this feeling—

I do not know how I shall ever be able to go on drinking this bitter chalice. There is no relief from the constant suffering, of witnessing suffering, and of seeing the abomination of desolation reigning insolently in all the once holy and consecrated places of this land. And so I suppose it will be until I die. My soul is sometimes drowned in a sea of tribulations in this country, and needs all the support and strength our heavenly Master can give. His divine mercy sends various consolations, especially that of thinking how great must be the merit and value of the pains and trials endured in this persecution.

And again—

Things are getting every day worse for the Catholics Misfortune upon misfortune assails them. Horrors which elsewhere would make people shudder, and over which they would weep for a year at the least, are here our daily bread, and are looked at calmly and with dry eyes, simply because the multitude and excess of woes of soul and of body exhaust in some sense the faculty of grieving. My heart is continually encircled, as it were, with sharp thorns of pain at what I see and hear and expect; but I do hope in the goodness of God, that He will not abandon His people, but will make His mercies follow upon these great and fiery proofs of His anger, as has been so often experienced by the children of Adam when they have turned to Him with humble and contrite hearts. What we now ask of His Divine Majesty I am sure He will grant; that is, that at the cost of so many precious lives and the destruction of so many fortunes, the sacred ark of the true Faith may be preserved in this country.

The continual recurrence of searches in the houses of recusants particularly elicited Luisa's indignation. She writes on that subject—

Every hour of the day, or of the night, the houses of Catholics are liable to be suddenly invaded by men whom they call pursuivants, who come to search for priests, armed with warrants to arrest them. They can neither close their doors, or defend themselves against this outrage, so that they never have a moment of peace and security, or hear a noise at the door without a beating of the heart, especially if they have a priest residing with them. Numbers of people answer me when I speak to them of religion, 'We have not the least doubt that the Catholic religion is the true one, but how is it possible to exist in such continual fear and trembling; not to be able, whether in bed or at meals, in the house or out of it, to enjoy the least tranquillity?' And thus, driven to despair, they risk, or rather forfeit, their hopes of salvation. It is evident that nothing short of a supernatural grace can enable them to be patient under such treatment. One is continually reminded here of the words of the Gospel, ' Like lambs amongst ravening wolves.'

After describing the horrible manner in which the martyrs were hung, cut down whilst still alive, drawn

P

and quartered, their hearts plucked out by the hands of the executioner and exhibited to the mob, with the cry of 'Long live the King of England!' Luis Munoz quotes the following passage from one of the letters in which his countrywoman poured out the sorrows of her heart to one she tenderly loved, the daughter of that uncle who had been a father to her—

Yesterday [she writes] a lady of high rank came to see me. I could not help asking her what she thought of the dreadful crimes committed in this city, in putting to death men ordained by a holy unction and consecrated to God. Oh! if the incense of their fragrant and acceptable holocaust did not temper the foulness of this great sin which cries aloud to heaven for vengeance, we might expect to see this town falling around us in ruins. Sometimes when I am in the country and when I gaze upon it from a height, my heart is seized with an intense grief, and I feel how well those words of Christ apply to it, 'Jerusalem, Jerusalem, who killest the prophets who are sent to thee!' We can hardly go out to walk without seeing the heads and the limbs of some of our dear and holy ones stuck up on the gates that divide the streets, and the birds of the air often perching upon them, which makes me think of the verse in the Psalms, 'They have given the dead bodies of Thy servants to be meat for the fowls of the air, the flesh of Thy saints to the beasts of the earth.' We are indeed continually furnished with subjects of sorrowful meditation, and have ever before our eyes what we read in the Bible—'You will see the abomination of desolation standing in the holy places.'

When, after her first imprisonment, one of the chaplains of Don Pedro was urging her strongly to leave London, she had made him this answer—'It is fourteen years now since our Lord inspired me with a desire to come to England, and I used every means to ascertain His will on that point. When I made up my mind on the subject in Spain, the peace was not concluded. On my arrival in England, I found it signed. This deprived

me of one of the expectations I had cherished, and I
could not hope that a weak and ignorant woman like
myself would succeed in converting those whom so
many holy and learned priests had failed to convince.
But there is one thing which no one can prevent me
from doing, one only use I can be of, and that is, with
the help of God, to sympathize intensely with each one
of the unhappy Catholics and to suffer a continual heart-
ache with and for them; if I am to be a hundred
times banished, taken to Flanders, or embarked for
Spain, so many times shall I return to live and die in
England, were it to be on a dunghill. Not for any love
I bear to it, for my heart is thoroughly Spanish, and
there is nothing pleasing to me in London, but because I
am persuaded that such is God's will.'

Another trial befell her about this time, that is, in
1610, which, though of a different and less grievous
sort, nevertheless sensibly affected her. This was the
departure of her excellent friend, Don Pedro de Zuniga,
Marquis of Flores de Avila, who for four years had been
her constant protector and benefactor. It deprived her
also of many of the spiritual resources which his house
had afforded her and her friends. Luis Munoz says of
this Ambassador—'Don Pedro's departure was lamented,
not only by the Catholics, but by the English Protestants.
He had made so many friends, that he was equally
regretted by all parties. He was good and kind to every
one, but had the spirit of a lion when the interests of
religion or the honour of Spain were in question. By
his singular prudence, he raised the reputation of his
nation in England. He was a devout and zealous
Catholic. His manners were mild and courteous, his
mode of living generous and hospitable. People said
that he was the model of a perfect Ambassador.' This
account goes far to justify the predilection of Anne of

Denmark and her ladies for Don Pedro, and to throw doubt on Miss Strickland's assertion that he was a coxcomb of the first water, even though he did give embroidered gloves to the maids of honour. He used to ascribe the success which had attended his mission to England to the friendship and prayers of his holy countrywoman, and those most intimately acquainted with him ascribed in a great measure to her influence and example the edifying conduct of the members of the Embassy, and of his own household, who, during the whole time he was in England, never gave the least occasion for scandal.

Soon after this painful separation, Luisa experienced a still greater loss. Her confessor (probably Father Michael Walpole) fell into the hands of the pursuivants, and after a long imprisonment, was banished from the kingdom. She writes on this occasion—

I could have felt nothing more acutely, falling into sin only excepted, than the loss of my spiritual guide, and the medium of God's mercies to me, which he was, and took pleasure in being. To walk in a barren desert, void of good and full of evils, without this guide, no doubt causes me dismay. As regards my spiritual condition, no greater misfortune could have befallen me than the fact of his being taken and carried away prisoner, seeing that it is not easy, nay, very difficult here, to find another such as him whom I lose. Our Lord has willed all this to happen, but He spared me the excess of grief I should have felt had he been arrested in a house where my own eyes would have witnessed it.

But soon afterwards her courage revived, and she adds—

I wish to have lived only to please God, and to be united to Him in the closest manner possible, whatever it may cost me, and with or without help. If I have it, well; but if I have to do without it, this union will then be founded on nothing earthly, but on what is heavenly, and that rock of which it is said, 'And that rock is Christ.'

Another trial beset her in the shape of letters which continually urged her to return to Spain. Human prudence kept alleging reasons against what she felt to be her vocation. Even good people and pious priests often wrote to her in that sense. One of the holiest religious in Spain told her that she should accept as a martyrdom the sensation which her return would produce. She could only reply that her self-love would have very little to suffer, and would soon get over that mortification. Others said that it was an indiscreet devotion which kept her in England, and that it was to please herself she persisted in it. The Infanta, Doña Isabel, was requested to use her influence with Luisa, and insist on her coming home. That Princess wrote, in consequence, a pressing letter to her on the subject, but without effect. All these solicitations could not shake her conviction, though they often painfully affected her. In 1612 she wrote as follows to a great servant of God—

My friends have been fighting lately against my vocation, but I do not see that I have it in my power to give it up, nor to turn away one step from it. I do not know if it will always be the will of God that I should remain here. I have nothing to do with the future, but simply to adhere firmly and constantly to what at present I feel certain is His will. If I thought to-morrow it would please Him more that I should go to Japan or the Coast of Guinea, I would set off the next day. And surely this is not wonderful, seeing that I live here in the midst of a perfect sea of afflictions and miseries. Wise people write to me from Spain to come back, and accept as a martyrdom the humiliation of that return. They are wise and holy men who thus admonish me, but they do not know what the suffering is of living in England, or they would not think that I stay on here out of vanity.

And in a letter to her brother, Don Alonzo de Carvajal, she says—

I do not know a heart less fitted for the agitations and miseries of this country than mine, and can you imagine that I stay here to please myself, and out of a devotion which I am obstinately bent on carrying out? This is one of the ways in which I may suffer in reputation, and I hope in our Lord that it will not be the only one. But of this you may be certain : the moment I can see that it is God's will I should return to Spain, as I now believe it to be that I should remain here, I shall set off without an hour's delay, and with a far greater inclination to go back than I had to come to England. Self-love, and my imperfect longings for peace and rest, drawing me there, and not here.

Don Alonzo having accompanied to Brussels the Marquis of Siete Iglesias came over to London to see his sister and with the full purpose of taking her back with him to Spain. Those who knew her firmness of character doubted the result. The only effect of his visit was to afflict him with the sight of that beloved sister in what seemed to him so miserable a position. He wrote to her soon afterwards, and said that it had required a special grace from God to enable him to leave her in this state. She wrote in answer—

You say that you cannot understand how I can endure to live amongst people who may any day drive me out of this house and leave me without shelter or help. I see that you do not understand what God has done for me, sinner as I am, and this throws everything into the shade. Do you think any difficulties or sufferings I experience here will weary me of accomplishing what I believe to be His will, when I have been enabled to tread under foot all natural feelings as to honour and public estimation, the most precious of earthly possessions to a human creature, and I say the same of the love of relatives and friends abandoned for the sake of coming to this country? Do you suppose that I left Spain in my own strength, that I forgot to consider the difficulties and dangers of such a step, or that Satan refrained from placing them before me in the most vivid colours? You seem to think that I act in this matter without light from above, not with a sense of what is God's will and good pleasure, but out of self-will and a fanciful devotion subject to change and sudden impulses. Believe me, brother mine, when I say, that if my poor weak heart had leant on so feeble a foundation I should have died or returned to Spain the very first year I came here. Unless I should ever be so unhappy as to be blind to the knowledge of what God deserves at our hands, do not expect that I can think I do much in suffering for His sake, or that any power can avail to draw me an inch from it. Here am I, a woman, weak in health, as delicate or more so perhaps than many others, one subject to acute fears and nervous apprehensions, and by nature most desirous of esteem and affection, in a desert full of raging wolves, in a house poor and obscure, with companions whom I have to support in the midst of the dearness of everything, and by means of what others choose to do for us, and liable to the withdrawal of such assistance at the moment I least expect it ; and yet you would hardly imagine what is the peace and tranquillity of my heart, how ready I feel to resign everything as well as to have it, and to go into the streets and beg our bread from door to door in a place where most of the houses are inhabited by the enemies of our Faith. And how can you think that this is not the result of a supernatural strength from God, and that in the same strength I can shrink from meeting the greatest trials and going on doing His will? For what other purpose do I exist?

And now I must thank you for the tenderness with which you say that it was only through a special grace that you were able to endure to see me as I am. And indeed it was not the worst that you did see. Neither you or I had time to enjoy any consolation. In heaven I trust we shall both enjoy it. But much is required, brother mine, to secure this. It is not sufficient to lead a moral life, with a plausible semblance of loving God ; that love must be real and supreme in order to obtain salvation, and all we do must be directed to His glory. Love Him, brother mine, in order to accomplish the highest work of justice that is or that can ever be owing, on account of His infinite deserts to Whom it is due, of His being what He is, and furthermore, because God, as St. John says, has first loved you. Love Him out of gratitude for your creation, for your redemption, to accomplish which He gave His life, a life no less important than that of God made Man. He assumed that life in order to lose it for you and His other children, raising them who were servants to the dignity of sons. Love Him in acknowledgment of that capacity of loving Him which He gave you for that purpose, and not that you should spend it on creatures beyond loving them in Him and for His sake, and within careful limits so as not to abuse that power.

With this courage she remained at her post, in this spirit persevered to the end, and her letters all conclude with some such words as these—'Our Lord, brother mine, has not made my continuing here a matter of choice, for I find myself bound to England and supernaturally attached to it.'

CHAPTER VIII.

Fresh persecutions and fresh labours.

REPORTS of Luisa's devotion to the Catholic prisoners, and of the sympathy she showed to those condemned to death for their faith, in particular the details of the scene in Newgate on the eve of the martyrdom of Father Roberts and Mr. Somers, reached the ears of Archbishop Abbot. He could not contain his anger at the Spanish woman's audacity, and gave to the King's Council an indignant account of her proceedings. He declared that she laboured incessantly for the Catholic religion, that she did more harm than twenty priests put together, and had perverted a number of Protestants. She was constantly going into the prisons, and encouraged the Papists to refuse to take the oath of allegiance, and gave them abundance of presents and alms. She kissed the feet of the priests, sent them tarts (which he said were excellent, Luis Munoz adds), and she wrote letters to Spain which made that Court and people believe that the Catholics were persecuted on account of their religion, and not because they were traitors.

The indictment of the Protestant archbishop cannot be said to have been false. Luisa would have pleaded guilty to every charge contained in it, from the perversion of Protestants down to the excellent pear tarts. It was decided by the Council that she should be banished from the kingdom. More violent measures were precluded on account of her rank, her connections, and the esteem in which she was held by the late, as well as the present, Spanish Ambassador. Orders were given that the moment she entered a prison, notice should be sent to the archbishop, and means taken to arrest her. She was quite ignorant of this circumstance, but an illness, which providentially confined her to her bed just at that time, prevented her from going as usual to visit the Catholics in Newgate, near which she then lived. In the meantime the prisoners heard of the mandate which had been issued, and sent her word not to come.

After some days, the archbishop grew impatient at the failure of his plan, and despatched a constable to Luisa's abode, with a message to the effect that he wished to speak to her, and that she was to come to his palace. She was living, at that time, in a very small house adjoining the residence of Don Alonzo de Velasco, Conde de la Rivilla, at that time Spanish Ambassador in London. This order was against all law, for the archbishop had no jurisdiction over foreigners. Luisa would not have been at all sorry, as she wrote to one of her friends, to have had an opportunity of seeing the false archbishop, as she calls him, and telling him in plain words what she thought of him and his religion. But she knew the result of the interview would be a short imprisonment, and then a forced embarcation to Spain, so she refused to go, or to open the door to the messenger. Don Alonzo, hearing what had occurred, sent her word to excuse herself with courteous words from complying with the order. She always spoke courteously, her biographer remarks, and carefully abstained from any expressions reflecting on the King and his Council; and in this spirit she said to the constables, through a chink in the door, that there must be some mistake, that she did not think that message could be meant for her, and, in any case, that she was too ill to leave the house. They were obliged to content themselves with this answer, for, on account of the proximity to the Spanish Embassy, they did not dare to make a great noise and knock violently at the door. They rang, however, several times, the bell which; as Luis Munoz remarks, is affixed to most of the London houses.

The archbishop was very much provoked that she did not appear. He procured that evening a description of her features and person, and had it drawn up in writing. For two years attempts were made to arrest the Spanish lady, constables went about provided with warrants, and with a description of her person. Yet she went about as usual, as openly as her enemies were secretly plotting against her. Some one said that it reminded him of the words of the Gospel—'Every day I was with you in the Temple, and you did not take Me.'

At every new danger or difficulty which arose, fresh efforts were not wanting to induce her to leave London. It was the old story over and over again. The Spaniards could not endure the idea of one of their countrywomen, a highborn lady bearing one of the first names in Spain, being insulted by English mobs or English judges. She looked upon her position in the light of the Gospel precepts, and was in love with the folly of the Cross. They could not, therefore, agree. She used, however, a reasonable amount of prudence. Till the times bettered a little, she did not go into the prisons, nor into the streets save when there was an important reason for it ; but though some of her accustomed works of charity were suspended, not a day or an hour did she lose or fail to employ in the service of God.

We have already spoken of her devotion to the martyrs during their lives ; we have now to describe the honour which she paid to their remains. Whenever she walked through the streets along which they passed on their way to execution, tears ran down her face, and she exclaimed—'O holy and blessed pathway, sanctified by the footsteps of saints on their road to heaven!' When her eyes rested on their heads or their limbs, exposed on the gateways, or on London Bridge, she reverently bowed her head, and said—'Oh, how unseemly a place for such holy relics! God forgive this deluded people, who commit so great a sacrilege in the eyes of His Divine Majesty.' She preserved as many of these relics as she could, in order to preserve them with due care and reverence. She had chests full of their letters, their breviaries, their linen. She purchased and kept their clothes, and the smallest things which had belonged to them, as precious treasures. She took care to affix to each portion of their remains an inscription written by her own hand—'This is the hand, or the foot, or the arm, of such and such a martyr, placed in this chest by his unworthy servant, Luisa de Carvajal.' She distributed these relics amongst her pious friends, as the most valuable present she could make to them.

It was vouchsafed to her, in the course of the years she spent in London, to receive into her house the bodies of five martyrs. On the day of the death of John Roberts, a Benedictine Father, and Thomas Somers, a secular priest, with whom she had supped on the eve of their execution, Father Scott, also a Benedictine Father, begged her to suffer their bodies to be carried into her house. She was only too happy to afford them shelter. There was not another corner in London where they could have ventured to deposit these holy remains. A coach had been provided for the purpose, and the transit was successfully effected, although in a scuffle with the constables at the moment of removal, the leg of one of the martyrs and a part of the body of the other fell to the ground and were lost. Some priests who had heard, though not from herself, of what had been arranged, called on Luisa and tried to frighten her about the Council. She only seemed very much wearied by their cautions, and said that not for all the world would she have refused the offer of so great a happiness. She provided not only one but two sets of sheets for the holy remains, as she relates in a letter to the Marquesa de Caracena.

As I know that your Excellency will sympathize in my happiness, I will not put off telling you that yesterday I deserved, or rather that without deserving it, I had the honour of providing, for the second time, winding-sheets (it made me think of our Lord's) for our two last martyrs. The first had been so soiled with the preparations for embalming bodies that it became necessary to change them. They have not therefore had a single thread upon them from any one but me, since the hour when they gloriously delivered themselves up to God. My unworthy hands consigned them to their shroud, and sowed the linen, which the English call holland when it is not of a coarse texture. I wish it had been of cloth of gold, though in the eyes of the Divine Mercy, what is offered to Him or to His own for His sake has the value of the finest gold, which in His own good time He will repay with eternal rewards. The owners of that sacred deposit have carried it away, leaving me portions of the relics, in acknowledgment of the hospitality afforded them.

Not long after Father Scott had claimed that hospitality for the remains of his brothers in religion, Father Roberts and his companion, it was his turn to be received with the same honour under Luisa's roof. He and a secular priest, called Richard Newport, suffered martyrdom on the eve of Pentecost, in the year 1611. At that time, Don Alonzo de Velasco, of the Order of Santiago, and captain of a regiment of horse in Flanders, was staying in London with his father, the Conde de la Rivilla, who was then the Spanish Ambassador in England. Three days after they had been buried, Luisa proposed to him and to the gentlemen of his household to recover the bodies of the two martyrs, which had been thrown into the bottom of a deep pit, under those of the malefactors who had been executed at the same time, and for the express purpose, the executioner declared, of preventing the Papists from getting hold of them. The task was an arduous and difficult one, and the time for it short.

At that season of the year it does not get dark till near ten, and the light begins to dawn by two o'clock in the morning. But, out of affection for Luisa, and animated by her devotion, the servants of the Embassy volunteered to accompany Don Alonzo. As soon as it was quite dark the little party, numbering ten or twelve, set out on their pious errand, armed with pistols and swords, in case the guard attacked them. As soon as they reached the place, they set to work with desperate courage. It was a nauseous, horrible, and repulsive labour, but these brave men underwent it without skrinking, and after lifting up the decaying corpses of sixteen malefactors, they found the mangled remains of the two saints, and bore them away in silent joy and triumph. They wrapt them in sheets sent for that purpose by Luisa, and after many delays and difficulties, and with great risk of being discovered, they succeeded at last in bringing the sacred burthen to her house.

She had been watching for them with intense anxiety, and when the noise of the carriage stopping at the door announced their arrival, she went in devout procession with her companions to meet them. Twelve of them wearing white veils, and carrying lighted tapers in their hands, stood at the entrance of the house to greet the holy relics and the brave men who had recovered them. The passage from the door to the oratory was strewed with an abundance of roses and other sweet smelling flowers, and the walls ornamented with green branches. Tenderly, and with a mingled feeling of joy and sorrow, they deposited them on a couch before the altar of the little oratory, covered them over with a piece of new red silk, scattered flowers upon it, and then knelt around for a time in silent prayer. The whole of the following day, 'as if the devil had contrived it,' Luis Munoz says, heretics of their acquaintance kept calling and paying them visits. They were obliged to keep the oratory locked up, and to appear as if nothing was on their minds. The ensuing night was occupied in cleansing and embalming the sacred remains, which were then deposited in a leaden coffin, filled with aromatic herbs. The only rewards which the count's gentlemen would accept were portions of the honoured relics.

Moderate as Luisa was, and more than. moderate in her expenditure, she was careless of expense on such occasions as these. She says in one of her letters, with regard to a similar circumstance, the details of which are not given—'I spent last Christmas seventeen pounds, each of which is worth forty reals, for the recovery and preservation of the last martyr. The labour of this undertaking and the danger attending it were great.'

The bodies of these heroic martyrs, Father Scott and Richard Newport, were conveyed to Spain. At the date of the Life we are transcribing, that is, in 1832, they were venerated in the chapel of the Count of Gondomar, in the town of that name. Luisa sent to many of her friends reliquaries, containing particles of their remains; one in particular to the Duchess de Rioseco, mother of the Admiral of Castile, who valued it both out of devotion

to the holy martyrs and affection for Luisa. The following
circumstance is stated by Luis Munoz, who appears to
have been an eye-witness—

When that dreadful fire which we saw break out in the
duchess' house near Santa Maria, and which threw all the
Court into consternation, destroyed everything in her apartments, the reliquary was found safe and uninjured in the
midst of the ashes. The flames respected it whilst they
devoured the furniture of the room where it was kept. This
was considered as a miracle.

In the year 1610, Father Persons died. His loss
sensibly affected Luisa. The serious emotions and
fatigues of her life told sensibly on her health, and in
the course of that year she fell dangerously ill. Her
sufferings were so intense that those who witnessed them
were convinced that she was going through the pains of
martyrdom, which she had so often coveted. Her
strength was completely prostrated, and for months
together she scarcely ever closed her eyes in sleep.
To speak was an immense effort. When she went to
confession her voice was scarcely audible, and it was
difficult to distinguish if she spoke English or Spanish.
She would murmur in broken accents, 'O señor, with
what pain and anguish I have made this confession,' and
then offered up all her sufferings in a spirit of reparation
for the offences committed against God. She afterwards
said that in the midst of all these bodily torments and
mental afflictions, there was in the superior part of her
soul joy at the thought that it was granted to her to
expiate her sins in this world. Once the agony she was
in became so violent that she could hardly breathe, and
seemed likely to die every moment. She turned to her
confessor and said, 'I have been for eight hours in the
state you see.' He answered, 'It may be God's will that
you should suffer this torment during as many hours as

our Lord spent in the agony of His Passion from Gethsemani to Calvary.' These words gave her courage, but even the power of thinking seemed at times to fail her. Moreover, the habits which she had acquired by constant practice of making acts of conformity to the will of God enabled her, almost unconsciously, to form them then.

Once when the pain reached its greatest height she cried to God with deep groans, and implored Him to have mercy upon her. An interior voice seemed to whisper, 'If this is My will, dost thou wish anything else?' Strengthened in her weakness, she inwardly replied, 'I must not and do not wish aught else.' Then the devil tempted her with the suggestion, 'But if it was God's will that it should last to all eternity, would you wish it to be so?' A strange anguish came upon her at this thought. It seemed to her, in the confusion of mind which her extreme weakness produced, as if by accepting this possibility she was dooming herself to it, and her courage failed her. But reason and faith overcame the temptation, and with a strong effort she made an act of acceptation of God's will even in that extreme case, still not with the complete adherence of her will which she desired. However, grace and light increased as the struggle went on, and at last she resigned herself entirely to God without repugnance or reserve, and speaking to herself she said, 'God will give thee strength. Go to Him with a fervent will and let what pleases Him please thee for all eternity.'

This victorious strife raised her soul above the pains of the body. From that moment she gave herself up to a quiet acquiescence in suffering, now and again repeating softly the words, *O Cristo soverano; O eterno Dios*—'O Sovereign Christ; O Eternal God,' with a simple memory of what that name had ever been

Q

to her, but without sensible devotion or relief. From ten o'clock in the morning to one o'clock of the ensuing night these tortures lasted. When they subsided her weakness was extreme, but she would take nothing, in order not to lose her Communion the next day. This was often the case with her. She could eat nothing whilst the paroxysms of pain lasted, and if they did not cease before midnight, she remained fasting till she had received Him Whom she called, 'the only real Comforter of her soul.' It sometimes happened that during Mass her sufferings were so great she could not restrain her moans, but at the moment of communion our Lord gave her strength to conquer pain and suppress every sign of it. She speaks thus of this illness to a friend—

My recent sickness was more severe than the one I had at Valladolid, and far more dangerous. I am inclined to think there was something supernatural in it, and that God ordained I should in somewise experience the pains of martyrdom which I have so often petitioned for. Such violent suffering does not generally last beyond a few days, and this continued for five weeks. This attack was also complicated by various other ailments.

So great was the prostration of strength Luisa experienced after this illness, that it was months before she could move about. The physicians declared that they could not answer for her life unless she had change of air and left the close and confined house in which she resided at that time. It was much against her will that she complied with their orders; she was afraid that a change of abode would attract notice and cause her to be arrested and sent out of London, her sole and constant fear. However, she was forced at last to submit, and a convenient house was taken for her in a suburb of the city, called Espetil (Spitalfields), where the air was healthy and the view extensive. It was situated on the ascent of the hill, in the midst of a garden, and separated on all sides from the neighbouring houses. The distance from the Spanish Ambassador's residence was a drawback, but it happened fortunately to be close to the Venetian Embassy. Luisa called it her 'Oran,' and set about fortifying it as a castle about to be besieged. Double doors were placed at the entrance; the first was never opened till the second was locked. A fierce mastiff guarded the approach, and it would have required an armed force to break into the house. She lived there in great retirement, giving no offence to the Government, and now that she was at a mile's distance from the Spanish Ambassador she relied more implicitly than ever on the divine protection. Writing to a religious in 1611, she says—

My companions and myself are in special need of your prayers. We are no longer under the shadow of Spain, and we seem to be offering battle to the enemy from this height. Our house, which is on the ascent from London, stands alone apart from all the others, so that if they have a mind to besiege us there is full scope for their operations.

Though Luisa was not herself a religious in the strict sense of the term, she seems to have had a singular gift for training souls to that life. Several of her companions in Spain became nuns remarkable for the sanctity of their lives and the work they did for God. Her beloved friends, Ines de la Ascencion, Prioress of Villa Franca, and Mother Isabel de la Cruz, in the royal Convent of the Incarnation at Madrid, were both nuns of the Augustinian Reform and eminently holy. They had been with their pious mistress since their earliest youth, and attributed their vocations and the ardent desire of perfection which possessed their hearts, to her example and direction. She was not less successful in this respect

Q 2

in England. During the nine years she was there, a
number of Catholic girls eagerly availed themselves of
the opportunity of leading under her guidance a life
similar to that of a convent of the strictest observance,
with the one exception that they were not cloistered.
Many young and ardent souls who had longed to devote
themselves entirely to God, found in this way what had
seemed absolutely out of their reach, except by going
abroad, and that resource demanded means and opportunities not always within their power. Their devotion
and fidelity to her were remarkable ; and she looked
upon this work as one of the most important she could
perform. In a letter to the Marquesa de Caracena, she
says—

I am anxious that, notwithstanding my defects and
miseries, and the very imperfect example I give to these
young girls who live with me, our little home may be to our
Lord a peaceful and sweet garden in the midst of a wilderness of howling wolves. They are very pure souls, ready to
go through any amount of work and suffering for the glory
of God. They do not at all wish to leave England, but to
perfect themselves here, which is exactly what I so much
aim at and wish. The foul exhalations which arise from
this land, where such horrible sins are committed against
religion, and not only religion, but also against every one
of God's holy commandments, should be tempered by the
fragrant incense of lives entirely devoted to Him. Any
one here who wishes to be a nun, as a matter of course,
goes abroad. There is no exception to this rule ; but these
girls, struck by the simple fact of my having given up Spain
to live in England, have been moved, as it appears, by a
strong devotion to oppose a life of poverty, mortification,
and perfection to the surrounding might of Satan's legions.
I hope the number of them will increase, and unless they
are deficient in the spirit necessary for this vocation, I do
not think I can ever close the doors against any who wish to
enter, though they be as poor as those I now have with me.
The other day I was a little distressed, because I could not

dispose, except at a great loss, of the only work they can do well—that is, the embroidery, which they have quickly learnt from me, and execute with skill—the false gold being sent in great quantities from France at a low price, but I comforted myself and them with our Lord's words—' Seek ye first the kingdom of God and His justice, and all these things shall be added unto you.' Our business is to correspond with His grace, to spend our time well, and not to be remiss in working with our hands and in all the duties of our state ; and it is that of our very merciful God to provide for our sustenance, and the support of our existence in any way it may please Him; and may He give me courage to overcome the faint-heartedness which I sometimes feel at the prospect of having to beg in England, that country being what it is, and what at a distance no one can picture to himself !

Elsewhere she writes—

I always make it a point to live near one of the Embassies, where there is a chapel and Mass is said, and I go there every day with some of my companions to hear it, and receive Holy Communion. Then we come back to our little solitary corner, and all the hours are devoted in turn to our religious exercises and to the work of our hands, just as if, blessed be God, we were living in a convent. Our house, lady mine, is like a castle erected in the midst of the enemies of Holy Church, and defying all approach. We have our good watch-dog, and none could enter without a great noise. I have hiding-places for the things which it would be necessary to conceal. We are not afraid for ourselves. We have, fortunately, the reputation of being very poor, and this is a protection against robbers, and, indeed, against the heretics, for their love of money is marvellous.

In another letter she mentions the remarkable manner in which they had been spared calumnies and attacks against their character—

God be infinitely praised, that as far as regards our reputation, it has never been attacked in London, where there is no lack of ill-natured tongues, and hearts to match them, for not even does the Queen of Spain or the Infanta Isabella escape the most odious imputations, and as to nuns, they seem to think that as a matter of course they must be wicked. Hitherto, I have been happier in that respect than their own Queen, for, far from giving me any annoyance on that subject, they only reproach me and all my household for leading too retired a life.

Not only did this indefatigable servant of God maintain and train in her house many of these devout young persons, but she placed others in Catholic families, where they educated the children and exercised a most beneficial influence. She kept up a continued correspondence with them, directing and counselling them as if they had been her children. They all looked up to her with the greatest respect and affection, and called her their mother and their mistress. Luis Munoz relates how Anna, who seems to have been the most energetic of the little band, treated a man who had ventured to attack Doña Luisa. She was coming out, one day, of the house of Don Pedro de Zuniga, and, forgetting she was in London, and not in Madrid, walked into the street with her rosary in her hand ; some one who caught sight of it tried to snatch it from her. Anna flew at this person, gave him great thumps, and said, 'You wicked man—what do you want a rosary for?' Quite abashed, he ran away. These disciples of Luisa turned out most of them singularly good and pious. Most of them persevered, after her death, in the holy mode of life they had led with her. They were much sought for as governesses, and transmitted to those under their care the principles and spirit of ardent faith and contempt of worldly advantages which they had learnt in the spiritual home of their younger days.

From this work of a stranger, carried on for a few years in England, and leaving behind it such beneficial results, could not a hint be taken, useful in our days? Would it not be a great blessing if a special religious education were given to those who are to undertake the training of children in Catholic families; and if some of the teaching orders had a third order of subjects who could undertake, in the religious spirit and as a religious work, that hard, laborious, ungrateful, but sacred duty, so seldom well fulfilled, and, if well fulfilled, seldom well requited? A religious home to look back to and to look forward to; community of heart with absent friends devoted to the same objects; a yearly retreat specially directed to the special duties of those who instruct the young, and who are exposed at once to the dangers of the world and those of solitude—would not these be powerful aids and strong safeguards against the temptations of a life, bearable only in the light of faith and through the grace of vocation? Would that, years after the fervent heart of our Luisa has ceased to beat on earth, that passage in her life could suggest to some kindred soul the thought of such a work!

In the Appendix to this volume will be found the rule of life observed by the little community at Espetil (Spitalfields); but we will close this chapter with the beautiful instructions she gave at the outset to her spiritual children on the general principles of the religious life.

It is evident that she contemplated the foundation of an institute adapted specially to the needs of England, under the peculiar circumstances of the persecution; and we cannot help regretting that her death prevented the continuance of a society which, whilst it lasted, sanctified so many devoted souls.

Seeing, my dear Sisters, that God our Lord has, I think, drawn you to join me in this society with the object of giving yourself entirely to Him in the most religious manner of life that you possibly can, through His divine assistance, which will, I hope, supply my defects, I have resolved to give you a method of life and distribution of time that you will strive to observe with the greatest punctuality and exactitude that is compatible with our small number, the size of our house, and other difficulties, which you see are great. Go on in spite of all opposition, with hearty goodwill and abandonment of soul to God, night and day calling on Him, with ardent supplications, to give you His divine love and efficacious grace, so that your life and death may be a pure and acceptable offering to His greater glory and the salvation of souls in your native land, which needs spiritual aid to the degree you know. Would to God we might end our course by a violent and happy death in defence of the holy Catholic faith ! I begin by exhorting you to a close bond of charity and love by which I desire to see you united together, so that there may be only one heart amongst you, and, from the first, everything banished from the community which might tend to a diminution of this and of all other heroic virtues. Bear in mind that golden age of which it is said—'And the multitude of them that believed were of one heart and one mind.' From this source arises a remarkable beauty in all our exterior actions. ' How good and joyful a thing it is for brethren to dwell together in unity.' And as the Catholics of England find themselves in the same position as those of the primitive Church with regard to persecution, let them emulate their sacred examples, their mutual charity, and extreme peacefulness in the midst of the immense troubles and difficulties which went on increasing and exalting the holy Catholic Church.

And as it would be difficult to preserve this union of souls and this great perfection without a head and a government, to which the wills of all the rest submit, so that the most minute of your actions may be guided and amended, it is necessary that in the name and place of our Sovereign Lady the most Blessed Virgin Mary, who will be your sweet and especial Superioress and Mother of Mercy, you should always have one of your Sisters appointed, whose approved virtue, prudence and age, are suitable for the purpose, and whom you will love, respect, and obey in everything, and rest assured that the invisible direction of the Blessed Virgin

Mary will guide the visible direction, so that it may always lead to the greater glory of God.

As soon as the Superioress is chosen, the first thing to which she shall attend will be the appointment of a confessor and spiritual Father for herself and for you—a permanent one, if you have not already a suitable one—to whom you will entrust a particular care of your conscience and spirit with all sincerity and fulness, respecting and obeying him, not as a man, but as one whom God has appointed as His representative. You already know the importance of this, and the evil and danger the soul incurs who neglects it.

Your poor congregation is adorned by a name no less blessed and glorious than that of the Society of the Sovereign Virgin Mary our Lady, which name and title it will always preserve. Her image will occupy an eminent place on the altar of the oratory, and over the seat of the Superioress, who, in all that relates to her position, will always leave the first place vacant, in token of the supreme reverence and respect due to that celestial Lady.

Your dress must be very plain and religious; at present it is necessary to modify it, because you are obliged to go out of the house, and to be seen by so many enemies of whatever bears a religious aspect. But unite to this prudence a spirit which will induce you to give a holy example, and carefully and entirely avoid the least thing tending to vanity or fancifulness.

The difficulty of establishing our mode of life on a steady foundation in the midst of so turbulent and inconstant a sea as the present state of England, had made me doubt a little as to the vows of obedience, poverty, and chastity. But I came at last to the conclusion that it would not be well to deprive you of the great merit that arises from them. Nor do I think that you would ever be at peace without them; or that it would be possible to accommodate so many different wills to the practice of a perfect life by less efficacious means than the strict vow of obedience. To purity of soul and body you have showed yourselves inclined with supreme esteem and love, and as to holy poverty, the Evangelist St. Luke has already invited you to what I have appointed, so that I can see no difference between what he describes and our rule. He says—'And the multitude of believers had but one heart and one soul; neither did any one say that aught of the things which he possessed were his own, but all things were common unto them.' And likewise, in a preceding chapter—'And all they that believed were together, and had all things in common. Their possessions and goods they sold, and divided them all, according as any one had need.' And remember that many of these first Christians were subject to the yoke of matrimony, and to great persecutions for the faith, and that they animated themselves to perseverance by the Evangelical counsels, in which it has pleased Christ our Lord to let us know that He takes pleasure.

On this presupposition, therefore, without fear, and with great confidence in the majesty of God our Lord, you will make the three vows of strict obedience, poverty, and chastity, adding a fourth vow of very special obedience and reverence, beyond even what is the duty of every faithful Catholic, to His Holiness the Roman Pontiff, Paul V., and all his successors canonically elected to the Apostolical See of St. Peter. It is well to make a greater effort and resistance against the heretics of our time on that very point at which they most violently strive to beat down the walls of the holy Catholic Church.

Your life is to be in common, and no one may have anything of her own, only the use of what is necessary to her, with the permission of the Superioress, who has to decide what is actually necessary in each case, after having listened with great kindness to what is said to her on the subject, and who will also take care to provide everything required for the health and well being of the rest. Do not look upon it as a hardship to lead this community life, and one of great poverty, in a house not constituted like the religious houses of Catholic countries. Abandon yourself to the arms of Divine Providence. If you really love God, Who became poor out of love for you, and condescended to the lowest degree of need and humiliation, you will, on the contrary, be eager to tread in His footsteps. The courage and valour of those who have gone before you will condemn any remissness on your part, and give you an insufferable fear of deserving the reprehension addressed by Moses to the people of Israel, when he called them 'a perverse

generation, and unfruitful sons.' Take the advice of the
Apostle St. Peter, when he says—'Christ also suffered for us,
leaving you an example that you should follow His steps.'
Arm yourself with this thought against every disloyalty to
God, and watch over this point with a hundred eyes, so that
nothing of that sort shall ever enter or proceed from your
heart, even if it should cost you the sacrifice of your happiness, or even of your life. Nothing given up for God is ever
lost. It is only exchanged for something better.

You will take the greatest possible care to keep yourself as
far as you can always in the presence of our Lord, as it is
a means of infinite good, and be assured that in proportion
as you make progress in this practice your spiritual riches
will increase. You will delight in spending moments in
solitary prayer besides the hours which your rule prescribes;
not however at the expense of the least point of obedience
or of charity towards your Sisters, or of anything whatever
you have to do in the house in which you can help, or
that is intrusted to you. You will employ well all the
time given to prayer, though it may cost you trouble and
a hard fight against wandering thoughts which draw away
like leeches all the substance and strength that the soul
derives from this holy exercise, and leave it dried up and
enfeebled.

Do not make much account of sweetness in prayer and
devotion that is not solid, but when sensible devotion fails,
supply its place by faith and perseverance. Place before
your eyes the example of Christ in the crib or dying on the
Cross, and show this heavenly Physician the wounds in your
soul which trouble you most and seem most incurable, and
with faith and humility intreat Him to cure them and to give
you light and efficacious love to do always what is most
perfect, and transform you entirely to His likeness. You
will never forget a single day to pray to His sovereign
mercy for the necessities and the increase of Holy Church,
and to ask for the conversion of all the souls that do not
belong to it in the whole world. You will pray for the
suffering souls in Purgatory, for the salvation of your
relatives and friends, and for those who by spiritual or
temporal benefits, or by their prayers, have a claim on
your gratitude. God loves not those who are ungrateful

or cold in fraternal charity, and this sort of intercession can be made with much fruit.

Let your words be few and your love ardent. Guard against illusions in time of prayer and at other times also. You will give an exact account of all you experience in these matters to your confessor and your Superioress. This will deliver you from many perils, and deceptions of the Evil One, and secure you much consolation and peace of heart, if you do it in all truthfulness and sincerity of soul, and with great humility.

You will be very exact in keeping silence, exchanging conversation with your Sisters for converse with God. Whilst you are with friends, listen to the Voice of the Spouse of your souls. Ask Him to make you hear His Voice, that Eternal Word which speaks to us through all the things He has created and in ourselves with sovereign greatness and beauty. Do not dissipate your minds with a multitude of vain and imperfect thoughts, for a silence of that kind would offer to God bitter or tasteless fruit.

With the greatest care avoid idleness, which St. Jerome justly calls the mother of all vices. Consider that God has chosen that generally speaking the preservation of human life should depend on food obtained, as He said to Adam, through the sweat of the brow, through occupation and incessant labour. A merciful contrivance to deliver the world from that dangerous beast—idleness. If people who are obliged to work from morning to night to earn their food and raiment are wicked, how much worse would be their pride and vices without this constant check.

I charge you very earnestly that you spend usefully all the time allotted to manual labour. Do not think you are absolved from the blame of idleness by the fact that you do labour at something or other with your hands, if you do it lazily and with great negligence, for you thus contribute little or nothing to the necessities of the house or the relief of the Superioress who has to provide for its sustenance and support. To such can well be applied the name of drones, which St. Francis gives to the idle and useless friars who like to be supported by the work of their brethren.

My Sisters, we are in truth only what we are in the sight of God, and no more. We can deceive men and we can deceive ourselves, but we cannot possibly deceive God our Lord. Great and profitable are the virtues practised in the various convents and religious orders in other countries, but I assure you that it will be very pleasing to the Divine Majesty, if you truly seek to live with the utmost possible perfection here in England, in order that the acceptable perfume of your fervent prayers and holy actions may ascend to heaven and plead for mercy in the midst of so many fearful heresies and other sins committed every day which provoke the anger of God.

CHAPTER IX.

Luisa's second arrest and imprisonment.

WHEN Luisa left Spain to come to England she had entirely made up her mind that, if necessary, she would beg her bread from door to door; but God was satisfied with the offering of her will, and never left her unprovided with the means of supporting herself and her companions. The Spanish Ambassadors and her friends at home always gave her enough for that purpose. They thought no alms could be more conducive to the glory of God than those bestowed on that great servant of His. But her poverty of spirit, her detachment from every earthly possession, never altered in the least degree. The Jesuit Fathers at Louvain, hearing of her necessities, entreated her to accept at any rate a part of her income which she had so generously settled upon that house. Writing to the one who had made this proposal, she admitted that everything was very dear in England, and her means, such as they were, nearly exhausted. But she adds—

But with all that, our Blessed Lord gives me a great gladness and liberty of spirit in the midst of my poverty, and if your Reverence does not wish to vex and exceedingly to displease me, do not offer to me money which belongs to great servants of God far more poor than myself, for it is quite intolerable to me to be spoken to on that subject. If

any one where you are is disposed for the love of God to
send me an alms it will be a real and great charity, and you
can forward it by Father Baldwin. ·

Being pressed another time on the same subject, she
wrote—

By a mercy far greater than my deserts and solely through
the exceeding goodness of my very dear Lord, I resolved to
follow His steps in poverty, humiliation, and suffering, and if
it had been a wealthy kingdom instead of a little miserable
sum of money that I had it in my power to give, I am certain
that the Divine Majesty knows for sure that this poor heart
of mine would have made its offering with equal or rather
with greater pleasure, and this increases every day, sq that
there is nothing further from my imagination than to complain of my poverty, and still less to relieve it by taking
back what I sacrificed with so much joy, and gave to the
Mighty and Sovereign God in the practice and accomplishment of His Divine Word and most holy counsel, from
which I see no reason to swerve or to draw back my hand,
seeing that it is an efficacious means of raising one's heart
to Him and placing one's only hope in His boundless goodness. If I had anything to complain of it would be that
His Divine Majesty has made me go through but little of
the sufferings of poverty, for no sooner do I begin to have a
taste of its sharpness than His merciful providence immediately relieves my wants, and in a manner which so clearly
marks it to be His doing, that one cannot help recognizing
and adoring in it the result of His blessed promise which
never fails of fulfilment. Don Pedro de Zuniga is so liberal
a medium and so careful an executor of that providential
liberality, that had it been evinced by no other means it
would be sufficient to melt the heart with love towards our
great Lord. Experiencing as I have done and continually
do that generous mercy shown to me with so much greatness
and majesty, I feel often obliged to cry out in the words
of the Psalmist, ' He has spread a table for me in the
wilderness.' I think my case is one of the strongest
encouragements to trust in Providence. And before I
dismiss this subject, tell me yourself, for the love of God,

whether, supposing I asked your advice, you would counsel me to take back from the poor in Christ whåt I freely gave them, even if they were not as they are in the greatest need of it? Knowing what is your spirit, I am sure you would not do so, especially as our Lord has given me such a freedom of heart in this matter, that I really cannot tell which is greatest, my trust that He will never forsake me or His care to let me want for nothing ; and this His Divine Majesty effects in so tender and delicate a manner as if He took especial pains to mark it as His own doing towards one whose health and strength have been long since failing and are now as much shattered as possible in consequence of the climate, the loneliness, and privations of this country.

Luisa gave a great proof of her spirit of poverty by refusing a gift which was offered at a moment when she was in urgent want of money. The Marquis of Hinojosa, one of the Spanish Ambassadors during her residence in England, hearing that the sister of the Marquis of Almaçan was living in poverty in London, sent her at once an offering of five hundred pieces of gold. She thanked him very much, but said she could not accept what was meant for the daughter of her father's house, and not for the poor servant of Christ, and would not keep a single real of that sum. This answer, we are told, touched and edified to the utmost the nobleman who had proffered the gift. Luis Munoz, in commenting on this characteristic trait, says—

Her ideas on the subject of poverty are illustrated by an instance of a different kind. Father Lorenzo de Aponte one day spoke of Doña Luisa's needs to a rich lady in Spain who possessed countless wealth. She would not give him a single penny for her. It is not (he observes) every one's money God uses. He then had recourse to Doña Maria de Vergara, a friend of Doña Luisa's, who instantly sent him five hundred ducats, which was almost her whole year's income. Luisa did not hesitate to accept this offering, she knew in what spirit it was made, to Whom it was given, and Who would repay it with interest. Her dress, as has been already said, was most humble : a mixture of the Spanish and the Flemish attire, made of black and coarse material and often full of holes. Her food as sparing as possible. Fasting she called her delight, and maintained that she had a natural repugnance to eating. In her frequent illnesses she was obliged to take delicate nourishment. 'We cannot expect miracles,' she used to say, 'and are compelled to use human means where prudence requires it.' But the moment it was possible she abstained from every indulgence. A little beef or lamb, the ordinary meats of that country, was her usual sustenance.

During all the years she was in London she dined only once at the Spanish Embassy, though all the successive Ambassadors were her friends, and would have gladly welcomed on every occasion their holy countrywoman. Her love of penance was ever on the watch for occasions of mortification, and she was as anxious to avail herself of every opportunity of the sort as at the outset of her spiritual life. Whenever an interval between her sicknesses permitted of it, she resumed her wonted austerities. Her bed, during the last years of her life, was nothing but a straw mattress. By dint of importunity she obtained this permission from her confessor, who, for a long time, had refused it. She was delighted when at last he gave way to her wishes ; and as she stretched her weary limbs on that hard couch, used to thank God for His goodness, and to say, 'Blessed be our Lord Jesus Christ, Who has allowed me before I die to enjoy a bed so much to my taste. To think that I have been so many years in England and could never arrive at it till now !' Many whole nights she passed in prayer, and, when it was possible, before the Blessed Sacrament—her heart inflamed with an ardent desire to become more holy, and to do something for God. What she had done always seemed to her less than nothing. Her

R

letters evince her deep humility. The following to the Reverend Mother Maria Ana de San Joseph, Prioress of the Convent of the Incarnation, may be taken as a specimen—

How could I, lady of my heart (*señora de mi alma*), make you understand the bad account I have to give of all which our great and Blessed Master has placed in my hands? I find myself full of and surrounded with faults and imperfections which proceed from my heart, and in what appears sound in my actions, like the sacrifice of Spain, and all which leaving it I left behind, I now see great reason to say, and not with half the sorrow I ought, *Putruerunt et corruptæ sunt cicatrices meæ a facie insipientiæ meæ*—'My folly has renewed a thousand times these sad and lamentable wounds.'

To Mother Ines of the Assumption, she writes—

Sometimes when I consider my vocation, and knowing myself to be what I am, I feel ashamed of going to Communion, and as if all present must know it also, and I should like to go alone, or at any rate less publicly. Each time I try to hope in my dear Saviour that that day will be the last of my great sinfulness and His great patience, and I pray ardently that it may be so, yet without compassing it, and so my grief increases. If I think of punishing myself by going sometimes without the Bread of Heaven, the privation is so terrible, so intolerable, that a predominating feeling prevents me from so doing. Then as my last resort I place myself in the hands of my spiritual guide. He says, 'Go,' and, Ines, I go. Open the door of your heart to the pity I want you to feel for me, help me with all your might, and get as many prayers as you can for me from your holy companions.

She used to meditate much on what the Archbishop of Santiago, a very holy prelate, had once said in a letter to her—'Count up your debts to our Divine Lord, in order to pay them. But, no; do not attempt it. Their number is too great; you cannot count them.'

Referring to that sentence, she writes to the Mother Prioress—

They seem very easy words, but I assure your reverence that I am often absorbed in the consideration of that saying, ' Do not attempt it, you cannot count them,' and turning to examine my poor soul, I find it so full of meanness and all sorts of imperfections and disloyal thoughts, that I should wish to cry out like the Apostle, ' I am the greatest of sinners.' In the midst of it all, love, indeed, makes efforts, but it can scarcely relieve the soul, because it is speedily consumed and swallowed up in the immense fire of the divine love, like a drop of water falling into a furnace. I am so poor in love ! I would fain beg it of all creatures, and call with a loud voice that would resound through the world on all sensible and insensible objects, to love their Creator ! In heaven alone, señora, this thirst will be satisfied. There alone will love be perfect, without impediments or clouds, our lips applied for ever to the inexhaustible stream of eternal happiness.

She was so detached from purely human feelings of attachment, and indifferent to the worldly advancement of her relatives, that they never could prevail upon her to use her influence in forwarding any views of that nature. We find her writing to her brother, Don Alonzo de Carvajal, who had asked her for letters of recommendation to statesmen who were her friends—

The Reverend Mother Aña, with her usual charity, has asked me to write letters in your favour to certain persons, and scolds me because I will not do so. Do not those, who would wish to do me a kindness, know very well that I should naturally be very glad of anything they did for you that was just, and not against the will of God? But what would be more unworthy of my vocation than to be made an instrument for the temporal advancement of my brother and my relatives? It would be very well if it was anything that concerned your salvation, or that would increase your love of God. Do you feel sure that our Lord is pleased with these projects, and that He will prosper you by such means?

R 2

And to another person she writes—

You tell me that my brother wishes to be an Ambassador, and you seriously urge me to bring it about, I who am dead to all that sort of thing, and who hate having much to do with my relatives, except when I can give them useful advice.

In summing up the virtues which Luisa practised during the last years of her life in London, her biographer mentions the strongest proof of the perfection to which her soul had attained by long and diligent correspondence with grace. The vow she had made years before, always to do what she believed to be most pleasing to God, never proved a burthen to her, and was faithfully observed to the last. One of her religious friends, writing to her from Spain, inquired if she did not find it irksome and an occasion of scruple. 'On the contrary,' she answered, 'it had been a strength and support, and, through the mercy of our Lord, she did not remember having had anything to accuse herself of in confession regarding that vow.'

Two years had elapsed since the little community had established themselves in the lonely house in Spitalfields as in a fortress—the garrison, Luis Munoz says, 'being composed of most virtuous and courageous young ladies, fully prepared to encounter the trials which were ever threatening the faithful Catholics of those days. In the hours of recreation after dinner and on festival days, they were in the habit of talking over future possibilities of persecution, and of discussing the manner of acting when subjected to it, familiarizing their minds with the thought of chains, prisons, tortures, and death. Luisa gave them frequent instructions, and especially warned them to be very silent as to their mode of life, for nothing of the sort, if once discovered, would be allowed to exist. Their poverty helped to preserve them from notice ;

and for awhile they were left in great peace and quiet.'

Don Diego Sarmiento de Acuna, Conde de Gondomar, was at that time Spanish Ambassador in London. He had as great a regard and as profound an esteem for Luisa as Don Pedro de Zuniga, and often regretted that she lived so far away from the Embassy. He feared the dangers to which she might be exposed, and his apprehensions were well founded.

The Archbishop of Canterbury always had his eye upon her. She had left off going to the prisons; but he was aware of the good she did in other ways amongst the Catholics, and he was bent on getting hold of her. As she now seldom went out, he took offence at her retired mode of life, and began to say that her house was an inclosed convent, and that the inmates kept a religious rule. Before proceeding to extremities, he tried to get somebody into the house who might report what went on there. His plan was to send some constables or spies, disguised as porters, under pretence of an order from the magistrates, which gave them a right to enter into all private houses for any purpose of public utility, such as searching for saltpetre to make gunpowder. But neither this or any other pretext availed against Luisa's vigilance. She was never taken by surprise, and strong in the protection of the Catholic Ambassadors, and specially, of course, of the Spanish one, she always referred to them the question, and said that without their consent she could not venture to open her doors.

At last Dr. Abbot lost patience. He saw that nothing but force would effect his end, and ashamed of being baffled by a woman shut up within four walls, he insisted upon it, that the house was a regular convent, that the inmates made vows and led the lives of Spanish nuns. He spoke to the King and to the Council, and urged that so great an evil ought to be checked at the outset, or that there was danger that it would extend, and religious houses be founded all over the country, to the great peril and disadvantage of the Protestant Church. He dwelt on the way in which the house was closely shut up ; he described the vain attempts which his constables had made to obtain entrance. No convent could be more strictly guarded ; and in order to arrive at the truth, it was necessary, he said, that an armed force should be placed at his disposal.

The King was at that moment very much irritated by a book written by the famous theologian, Suarez, which the King of Spain had found means of introducing into England. The moment was therefore favourable to the Archbishop's views, and full powers were granted him to proceed in the matter in any way he thought fit. We give the account of this her second arrest in the exact words of the original Life—'On the 28th of October of the year 1613, before daybreak, two of the principal magistrates of the Court, called the Recorder and the Sheriff of London, came, accompanied by sixty men armed with halberts (many wolves against a few poor lambs), and many other persons on foot and on horseback, to surround Doña Luisa's abode. By means of ladders, some of them speedily scaled the walls and got into the garden, whilst others broke open the front door and forced their way into the house. This demonstration was in accordance with the urgent orders contained in the warrant. So sudden was the irruption, that she had only just time to throw her black mantle over her tunic, which sufficed for decency, but not for protection against the cold. The magistrates and the officials seemed struck with astonishment at the evangelical poverty which met their eyes, for with the Catholic Church it has vanished from England. They found no costly furniture, as they seemed to expect. Shabby, worn-out clothes, beds consisting of straw mattresses and common rugs for blankets, plain wooden tables, the chairs in such a state that it was difficult to find any on which the magistrates could sit down. The provisions matched the furniture; a few coals, which they call there sea coal, and which is used by poor people, two great jars full of water (that was not much to their taste), and nothing of the slightest value. Disappointed at the result of their first investigation, they did not carry it on further, and the oratory escaped their notice. It was beautifully arranged, adorned with pictures, and contained everything necessary for saying Mass. It was only for purposes of that sort that she ever purchased costly things.

'The rumour of this event quickly spread in the neighbourhood, and brought together a great crowd of people. Amongst others the Flemish Ambassador, who lived in that part of the town, heard of it, and hastened in great anxiety to console and encourage Luisa by his Christian and kind words. She answered very cheerfully, and whispered to him in Spanish, that she did not at all mind being arrested; it was what she always expected, and in some sense desired; but that she was anxious about a religious of the Society, who had come there that morning before daylight to hear the confessions of some ladies who could not visit him anywhere else, and that if he was discovered, his life would be in danger. Her anxiety was visible in her countenance. The prudent and clever Ambassador turned to the Jesuit Father, and said to him in the hearing of the officers, "I had before now ordered that none of my servants should come to this house. What are you doing here? Come along, I have a message for you to take," and making a sign to him to follow, they went away together without any one saying a word to them. The relief to Luisa was so great, that she could hardly hide her joy.

'At that moment the Conde de Gondomar entered and said, " Señora Doña Luisa, God be praised ! your desires are accomplished ; these are the festivals and the joys He gives to His elect. Courage—this may lead to the end you have long sighed for." Both the Count and the Flemish Ambassador made request that Luisa should be delivered up to their keeping and suffered to remain in her house. They offered to be answerable for her appearance when the King and the Council ordained it. The bailiffs declared it was impossible not to remove the prisoner ; and when the Count renewed his importunities, they showed him the King's order in writing, in which it was said, that even if the Spanish Ambassador should interfere himself in person to prevent her arrest, they were to carry her away, and that was the reason why they had come with so strong a force. When the Count saw the measures which had been taken, he was obliged to content himself with insisting that she should be taken to prison in his coach, escorted by his servants and those of the Flemish Ambassador.

'There were five young persons with her at that time, all virtuous and holy maidens. One of them was in bed, suffering from an attack of fever and a cold, which the doctors said had nothing dangerous in it ; but the shock and pain of seeing her beloved lady arrested brought on a sudden bursting of a bloodvessel, which proved fatal to her life. She thought something terrible would happen to Luisa. Her pure soul was surrendered to God on the following day ; and as it was religious persecution which caused her death, it may be hoped that she swells the ranks of the virgin martyrs in heaven. Another, who was in the kitchen, found means to escape. Three accompanied their lady to the prison. They were conveyed with a great escort of mounted constables, and bailiffs on foot surrounding the carriage, with halberts in their hands. The people as they passed looked on with astonishment. This procession traversed almost the whole of London, from Spitalfields to Lambeth. When they arrived at the Archbishop's house, he examined his prisoner. He asked her at what o'clock she got up in the morning; what prayers she said; how many nuns she had in her convent; what rule they followed; and other stupidities of that sort. Luisa looked at him sternly, and with great courage and composure told him he was not her judge.

'He left off questioning her, but kept ejaculating— "Has such a strange woman ever been seen in this world! To have dared to set up a convent in the very teeth of the State! In the very sight of the King and the Council!" He ordered her to be taken to the public prison. It was divided into two parts, in one of which there were many religious, priests, and other Catholics imprisoned for the faith. He particularly desired that she should not be with these, fearing that her courage and firmness, and the fervour of her words, should animate them to perseverance. For the same reason, he separated her from her former companions. They were placed amongst the Catholics, and the venerable Luisa amongst heretics and malefactors.

'Simon de Arizar, chaplain of the Conde de Gondomar, was one of the first to hasten to the prison, to see and offer his services to Luisa. She received him with a calm and serene countenance, and said that the only thing she wanted was, that he should bring her the Blessed Sacrament, in order that she might go to communion. Her affection and devotion did not take into consideration the evident perils and inconveniences which would attend the accomplishment of that act of piety. She pressed her request very urgently, and he again pointed out the risk she would run, surrounded as she was by the officials of the prison ; but he could not persuade her to forego her desire, and she seemed so afflicted that he would not afford her this consolation, that at last he was obliged to promise he would go for It, and left her with that hope. It proved, however, impossible to keep his word, on account of the obstacles and presence of the officials. But she communicated all the other days that she remained in prison.

'As soon as Doña Constançia de Acuna, Countess of Gondomar, heard what had happened, she ordered her carriage, and drove off instantly to the prison, to keep company to Luisa, quite resolved not to leave her side until she was set at liberty. She sent a message to the King, to say that till he gave orders for the release of the Lady Luisa, she was determined to be a prisoner also. She did as she had announced, and during all the time of her imprisonment, remained in her cell, comforting and cheering her in every possible manner. This act excited both surprise and admiration at Court, and drew attention to the character of that poor oppressed prisoner who inspired such strong feelings of esteem and affection. This Condesa de Gondomar was worthy of being Luisa's friend. During the whole time of her husband's Embassy, she was a mother to the English Catholics, relieving their wants and ministering to their needs with unwearied zeal till her death, which was a most holy one, removed her to a better world. The wife of the Flemish Ambassador was also constant in her visits to the saintly prisoner, who did not lose her time during the days of her incarceration. She very nearly succeeded in converting the gaoler and his wife. They were so struck by what she said on the Catholic doctrine regarding the Blessed Sacrament, that both declared that they had never had the least idea of what the Church teaches on that subject, and of the strong arguments in its favour.

'Meanwhile, the Conde de Gondomar was not remiss in his efforts to procure the release of his holy country-woman. He sent a message to the King, to say that the manner in which she had been treated was a clear proof of the little value he set on his own presence in England, and that if Luisa was not immediately set at liberty, he should be forced to cease his attendance at Court. The King was moved by this remonstrance, and at hearing that the Ambassador's wife did not leave the prison even for the night, and had her meals brought to her there. The discussion was carried on with vivacity; the Conde feeling that the insult to Luisa touched his own honour.

'A Council of State was held, in which no less than twenty members spoke on the subject. The chief charges against the prisoner were, that she had founded convents in England, that she tried to persuade every one to abandon their religion and become Catholics, and had already perverted many, and brought them over to her faith. These were her crimes, and the conclusion was, that she ought to be expelled from the kingdom, and sent back to Spain. The Conde spoke with great force and strength. He declared that the accusations did not warrant such a decision, and that even if they did, the facts were assumed, not proved. He was referred to a privy councillor of the name of Cottington, who was empowered to treat on the subject. They broke several lances concerning it, but the discussions always ended with the demand that she should leave England.

'After four days of earnest arguing on both sides, the King cut the matter short, and gave orders that Luisa should be given up to the Spanish Ambassador. He

and several of his colleagues and other Catholic gentlé-
men, stood at the door to receive her. The Condesa's
carriage was in waiting, and she and Luisa drove in it to
the Embassy, with eight or nine other coaches following ;
they passed through all the principal streets of London
in state, and before the royal palace. The Conde making
it a point, both as a Christian and a knight, to pay
honour to his religion in the person of a Catholic lady
persecuted for her faith. He lodged her in a part of his
house adjoining the chapel, and she henceforward used
the one where she had been arrested only when there
were persons to be reconciled to the Church, as this
could not be done at the Embassy, on account of the
spies, who were constantly on the watch to discover who
went in and out.

‘ Luisa's presence of mind, her courage, and tender care
of her companions, were generally admired, and every
one commended Don Diego's spirited and firm resistance both at the council table and in the private
discussions with Cottington. The release had been
granted on condition that the Conde should keep Luisa
in his house pending the decision of the Council, whose
intention it evidently was to order her out of the
kingdom. Meanwhile, the Count studied the means of
defeating this intent, and liberating her companions.’

CHAPTER X.

Luisa's Illness and Death.

PERHAPS one of the greatest trials which Luisa underwent was the demonstration in her favour at the door of the prison. To be carried as it were in triumph along those streets through which she had so often longed to pass with other Catholics as a condemned criminal on her way to execution, was a severe ordeal to that humble and ardent soul. 'How gladly,' her biographer exclaims, 'would she have exchanged the gilded coach with its armorial bearings for the real triumphal car, the ignominious cart in which the victors conduct their victims to martyrdom.' On no other occasion did she find it so difficult to make an act of perfect conformity to the will of God. This is expressed in a letter written a few days after her release to the Prioress of the Discalced Carmelites at Brussels.[1]

At last, señora mia, the poor man who was hunting for me in every corner, not being able to find me in the streets, caught me finely, and for four days I was in his power. Not longer, for the Señor Don Diego, who is naturally very determined, exerted himself valiantly to withdraw me from his clutches. This was not for my own part what I would have wished, unless my release was more for the glory of God

[1] This was the Venerable Anne of Jesus, the friend of St. Teresa, and the foundress of the Carmelite Reform in France and Belgium.

than my imprisonment. I am staying in the small house adjoining Don Diego's waiting for the moment when it will please God to send me my dear companions, which I am given to understand will be soon. It was impossible to bring them away with me. We were not in the same part of the prison. It has been all very wonderful and God's hand so visible in it, that those who carried it on are ashamed of themselves as so many monkeys.[2] They are striving against our Lord to banish me from this savage desert. Will this be, señora? This I do know, that those who leave this country are banished from many occasions of suffering.

When the Council found that they could not prevail on the Conde to embark Luisa for Spain, the King ordered his Ambassador at Madrid to beg His Majesty Philip III. to command her to leave England, and to bid Don Diego to see the order carried out. The servant of God being informed of this, felt afraid of being constrained by the Spanish King's commands to depart before she had time to submit to His Majesty her reasons against it, and she resolved to forestall the order by writing to the Duque de Lerma and intreating him to speak to the King in her behalf. He was in great favour with Philip III., and had a profound esteem for Luisa. Her letter is as follows—

Your Excellency sees how vain I am become now that I have twice had the opportunity of confessing the name of Christ in the prisons of His enemies and bearing witness to the Catholic faith, since I venture to write to your Excellency, and what confidence I have in your piety, since I cannot let pass this opportunity of begging you to rejoice with me and to glorify God very much for His great mercies. The particular circumstances of my being a Spaniard, a very devoted servant of yours and one who esteems and loves you much, enhance I know your regard for me. The spirit and determination of Don Diego have robbed me of a glorious crown which seemed within my reach, and I have a great

---

[2] A Spanish expression.

hope that they will seize on some time or opportunity when Don Diego will not know of it, and wait perhaps till he is no longer here. I can assure your Excellency that the vocation to devote myself to England, which I have had since childhood, is agreeable to the doctrine of the Catholic Church, has been well examined and found to be a true vocation from God. Events have tended from day to day to confirm it, for without especial assistance it would have been impossible that I could have escaped as I have done the dangers of this country. And I therefore implore your Excellency never to accede to the desires of those who seek through your means to procure my departure, but to leave it to those who by human violence will bring it about if our Lord permits it. The pretended Archbishop of Canterbury accused me at the council table of two crimes in the presence of Don Diego. They give here to piety the name of impiety. One was that I had founded convents of nuns, and the other that I had converted many Protestants to my religion. Though they have at their command the tongues of thousands, they could not bring forward the slightest proof of anything relating to either of these charges, nor in their blind ramblings hit upon what would have indeed made them indignant and driven them quite beside themselves. If your Excellency had seen the way in which Divine Providence directed this affair, you would have been in great admiration, for the enemies of God and mine did not say or do a single thing otherwise than I could have wished. Moral and peaceable persons, not violent in their heresy, show me affection. Some of them wept when I was arrested, and came to visit me in prison. A great number of Protestants of high or moderately good character, join with the Catholics in blaming this act of the Government, and speak of it as foolish and disgraceful. On the other hand, it has done great credit to Don Diego, and displayed his zeal for religion and the honour of Spain, which certainly is great and has given much satisfaction. It seems, señor, as if I was forgetting who I am writing to, by my venturing to do so at such length. Forgive me, I beseech you, and I humbly entreat the King our master, as I have entreated your Excellency, to let God dispose of this matter as He pleases. May He have you in His holy keeping according

to your needs and my supplications. Amen. May He bless
your Excellency in every way and enrich you with a great
increase of His most holy love.

Your Excellency's servant,

LUISA DE CARVAJAL.

London, November 20, 1613.

She wrote to the same effect to the Marquis de Siete
Iglesias, and inclosed to him her letter to the Duque de
Lerma.   But the English Ambassador had been beforehand with her, and insisted on the fulfilment of the
article in the recent treaty, which stipulated that in
neither kingdom should there be any interference in
matters of religion.   He succeeded in carrying his point,
and Philip III. desired Don Diego to arrange Luisa's
departure for Flanders, where she would be joyfully
received by his sister, the Infanta, Doña Isabel, and free
from all the dangers of England, might end her life in
peace and quiet.   This was the greatest difficulty she
had yet encountered, but even then her resolution was
not shaken.   She said to those who had been told to
execute the King's directions, that she had made a vow
not to withdraw herself from the perils and sufferings of
England ; that she would never go of her own accord to
Flanders, and unless they used force, and bound her to
the mast of the vessel, she should not embark.

It is, probable, however, that she would have been
obliged to give way, had it not been that the time was
come when God, in His merciful goodness, was preparing to call her from the land of banishment to her
home in heaven.   The end of her toils, the accomplishment of her desires, the reward of her sufferings, was at
hand.   She was saved from the anguish of abandoning
the scene of her labours, of forsaking the spiritual
children whom she had converted and trained, and
instead of the earthly repose, which would have been a

pain to her ardent soul, she was about to attain the rest of those who lay their weary heads on Jesus' bosom. The dying words of St. Teresa express what she, too, must have felt when, in that hour of perplexity, death came to her as a friend—'O Lord, the hour is come at last that I have looked for through all these long long years. Yes! it is time I should come to Thee. It is time, my Lord and my Love, that I should depart hence. The end of this weary exile is come at last, and my soul rejoices in Thee, Whom it has desired so ardently and so long!'

For years Luisa's frail existence had hung on a thread, the supernatural energy of her soul had supported her weak extenuated frame in an almost miraculous manner, but the last shock which it had experienced, when her house was invaded at night by a band of armed men, her cruel fears for the life of the priest whom she had invited to it, the intense cold she endured in her transfer to the prison, the bad air and closeness of her cell during the four days she spent there, the news of the death of the young companion—whom she had last seen only slightly indisposed, and who expired the following day—and when removed to the Ambassador's house, the absence of her other companions, about whom she was keenly anxious, and who were tender nurses to her in illness, and finally, the order to leave the scene of so much sorrow, where she knew it was God's will she should live and die, all combined to snap the feeble cord which bound her to life. She seemed tolerably well after leaving the prison till the 20th of November, on which day she was suddenly seized with a violent pain in the chest, corresponding with one in the shoulder, which almost took away the power of breathing. This proved the beginning of a terrible attack of colic, which caused her for several days agonizing pain. Two eminent

s

Catholic doctors attended her, and Don Diego summoned also one of the King's physicians. She bore her sufferings with the most perfect patience, went to confession and communion every day. Mass was said daily in her room, the English priests having the privilege, in the times of persecution, of saying it in any place they chose. In the midst of sufferings so excruciating that, alluding to her well known desire of martyrdom, the doctors declared that those endured by martyrs could hardly exceed them, the serenity of her countenance never varied. The expression of her face corresponded with the inward peace she enjoyed. Joy predominated over every other feeling. She had no fear of death. Some days before she had told her confessor that she felt convinced it would not be long before God called her out of this world, in which every other source of consolation seemed closed to her.

She obeyed implicitly all the orders of her spiritual and her medical advisers, even when the latter prescribed for her remedies which experience and her knowledge of her own constitution gave her reason to think would do her no good, or objected to remedies which in former illnesses she had found useful. She often thanked our Lord, Who was obedient Himself unto death, for these opportunities of practising that virtue, and often said that she could not have wished a greater happiness than to die obeying.

Her perfect conformity with God's will and her interior peace were so great, that she was herself almost astonished at it. She had never ventured to hope it would have been so entire in her last moments, or that she would be able to die without the slightest repugnance. This perfect tranquillity of soul was a clear proof that the fruit which our Lord was about to gather into His garner had attained its full maturity. In her previous illnesses, she had always felt some anxiety, some kind of depression at the thought of dying before she had carried out her designs, and the devil had always .availed himself of the very intensity of her desires for God's glory, to disturb her with those regrets. But now it seemed as if the victory was over, every enemy subdued, the divine will accomplished, and everything prepared for the approaching triumph.

She received with fervent devotion the Blessed Sacrament in Viaticum and Extreme Unction, which was administered to her by Fray Don Diego de la Fuente, a Dominican Father, the Ambassador's confessor. She was in the perfect possession of her senses, making all the responses, and answering all the questions addressed to her. To the last instant of her life she retained the full use of her understanding, and found strength, notwithstanding the oppression in her breathing and her great weakness, to make a solemn declaration that she died a true daughter of the Roman Catholic Church, professing its faith, and practising its religion, and she called on all present, and especially on her Spanish countrymen, to bear witness to the same. One of the things she most desired in her illness was to see her companions again before her death, and our Lord gave her this consolation. Through the strenuous exertions of Don Diego, they were set at liberty and brought to her. Her face lighted up with joy at the sight of her spiritual children. She spoke to them words of consolation, encouraged them to persevere unflinchingly in the Catholic faith, the practices of a perfect and interior life, and then committed them to the care of her confessor, with whom she had previously arranged everything relating to their safe disposal.

A great many persons visited her on her death-bed, and not a few Protestants among the number. They

S 2

were apparently much impressed with the sight of her
happiness in the midst of intense sufferings and the way
in which to the last she testified her ardent desires for
their conversion.   The hearts of some of them were
deeply touched by the words of burning zeal and tender
love which proceeded from her lips, even when the hues
of death were gathering on her brow.   Shortly before
her end, she had such a violent bleeding of the nose,
that it seemed as if she was losing in this way all her
remaining blood.   Father Michael Walpole asked her if
she was wishing that it had been on the scaffold it had
thus copiously flowed.   She answered, 'Father, I long
ago offered my life and my blood to God to deal with
them in whatever way might be for His greater glory,
and most according to His divine will.   As it is His
will that I should die thus, I no longer care that it
should be otherwise.   He has chosen what pleased Him
best, and it matters not to me if the sacrifice is offered
up in public or in private.'

When Luisa felt the near approach of death, of which
the increasing coldness of her hands and feet forewarned
her, she requested to be dressed in the garment in which
she would be buried ; and when her confessor came into
her room after this had been done, she said to him quite
joyfully, 'Here I am, Father, attired for death, and when
I am dead there will be nothing more to do than to put
me on the habit which I brought from Spain and which
has been kept for this purpose, and I have asked my
companions and the Ambassador, and I now beg of
you, Father, not to allow my body to be meddled with
after my death.   I have also prayed to our Lord to
prevent it, should any one wish to do so.'   She apprehended that, as was often the case with persons of high
rank, her body would be cut open and embalmed before
removing it to Spain.

Around her bed were kneeling her companions, Fray Diego de Fuente, Father Michael Walpole, her confessor,[3] and another Jesuit Father, the chaplain of the Conde de Gondomar, and other pious persons. They read aloud to her from time to time the Passion of our Lord, commenting on the most moving passages. Her breath was gradually failing, and everything about her as calm and religious as if she had been in the cell of a convent. Now and then the silence was interrupted by the sobs of her faithful old servant, Diego, a Frenchman by birth, who often cried out, 'My dear lady, when you are in heaven, remember poor Diego Lemeteliel!' He made as sure of her going straight to heaven, Luis Munoz says, as though it had been an article' of faith.

During the last hours of her life she kept frequently ejaculating, with the most affectionate devotion, 'Señor mio' (my Lord)! and 'Señora mia' (my Lady)! She spoke as if they were present and she was personally addressing them. Some thought they must have appeared to their dying servant, so tenderly and earnestly did she repeat their names. Sometimes she said, 'O my Lord, what do I not owe you?' and 'O my Lady, how indebted I am to you for your numberless benefits and favours! How can I be ever grateful enough for so many mercies?' and then again she softly murmured, 'Señor mio! Señora mia!'

She seemed in her last agony, and had apparently lost all consciousness, when a sharp spasm of pain ran through her frame, and with an appearance of strength she clasped her hands and pressed them together. Father Michael Walpole asked her if there was anything that troubled her mind. 'No, nothing at all,' she replied, 'her soul was perfectly tranquil.' Bodily pain

---

[3] Father Michael Walpole was several times banished, but as often returned to resume his apostolical labours in England.

alone had been the cause of that gesture. Then, in
the words of the Spanish writer, 'she quieted herself,
and in perfect recollection, with a countenance unalter-
ably serene and peaceful, invoking our Lord and our
Lady, in the interval between a fervent act of love and
thanksgiving and of an ardent desire to see God, amidst
the sweet tears, not only of her own people, but of the
very strangers present, and the fervent prayers of the
religious who surrounded her death-bed, that happy soul
put off the pure clothing of her mortal body, worn out
with austerities and sanctified, by penance, and went to
receive from her Lord the welcome promised to all who,
passing through much tribulation, have washed their
robes in the Blood of the Lamb.'   In a silent corner of
the proud, busy, restless city, where she had worked and
suffered for nine long years, that heart ceased to beat
which no human passion had ever stirred, but which
had throbbed with a vehement love of our Divine Lord
and a passionate desire to win souls to God.   Some may
deem that desire to have been excessive; that 'not
wisely but too well,' she had cared for the salvation of
others ; that the persecution which hurried her to an
untimely grave had been wantonly provoked, if not
desired.   Like the people amongst whom she came
to labour, they may have her in derision, esteem her
life a madness, and her name a byeword of reproach;
but those who stood around her death-bed, 'knowing
she was at peace,' felt, and all to whom it is given to
know the mysteries of the kingdom of God, feel that
'she now is numbered with the children of God, that
her lot is among the saints,' and, in the words of a poet
of her own days, that—

> 'Tis not so poor a thing to be
> Servants to heaven, dear Lord, and Thee,
> As this fond world believes !

CHAPTER XI.

Sequel to Doña Luisa's life.

IT was on the 2nd of January, 1614, her forty-sixth birthday, that Doña Luisa de Carvajal breathed her last. Her sorrowing companions, according to her desire, rendered her the last duties, and no one else touched her after death. They clothed her in the religious habit she had brought from Spain, and carried her into the Ambassador's chapel, where she reposed amidst lights and flowers. No one doubted that she was enjoying the presence of God, and the Conde' de Gondomar said that what would have been doing honour to a princely lady, that is, the embalming of her earthly remains, would be desecrating the body of one whom they looked upon as a saint. Whilst the body remained in the chapel of the Embassy, numbers of Catholics came to visit it and to pray by its side. They carried away portions of her clothes as relics. Those who could not come sent earnest requests for some memorials of the departed, who can be truly said to have died in odour of sanctity. Many of the Protestants in the neighbourhood who had known her felt her death very much. They complained of the way in which she had been treated, and commented severely on the conduct of the Archbishop, who had persecuted her and hurried her end. They were heard saying, 'Would he had never seen or heard of this lady! We might have had her for years living amongst us.'

Her obsequies were performed with as much state as if they had taken place in a public church in Spain. All the foreign Ambassadors and their families, and numbers of Catholics of high rank, crowded to the Ambassador's chapel. Don Diego de Fuente preached an eloquent funeral oration in which he expressed his conviction of the sanctity of Doña Luisa. Rare flowers, scarce as they must have been at that time of the year, were thrown on her coffin, which was deposited in a recess near the altar until it could be removed to Spain.

It was given to her to achieve in death a conversion which she had in vain laboured for in life. A Protestant carpenter named Richard Ingles was employed to make her coffin. Doña Luisa had known him for a long time, he had often been employed by her in making alterations in her house, and whilst he worked at the wooden materials of his trade, she worked on his heart by constant efforts to persuade him to be a Catholic. He was well inclined to it, but his worldly interest and his love for his wife and children kept him back, and though he gladly listened to Doña Luisa's exhortations, he never could make up his mind to act up to his convictions. However, when he looked upon her after death, when the memory of all her goodness and sweetness came back into his mind and the urgent words with which she had so often set before him the importance of a choice in which salvation is concerned; when he saw the wonderful calm beauty of her face, the silent lips preached more eloquently than the living voice had done, he exclaimed that he wished to live and die in the religion of the departed lady, and hastened to Father Michael Walpole, who instructed him and reconciled him to the Church. He afterwards went to Spain, where he exercised for many years his trade, and was known by the name of Ricardo Ingles (which probably meant English Richard).

As soon as the news of Doña Luisa's death reached Spain, solemn requiem services were celebrated for her in several of the principal cities of that country. The Seminaries of Valladolid and Seville, looking upon her as the friend and benefactress of English Catholics, and especially so as foundress of the Jesuit Noviceship at Louvain, vied in paying respect to her memory and offering up suffrages for her departed soul, according to the practice of the Catholic Church, which never allows the reputed sanctity of her children, or the pious belief that they have reached their heavenly home, to interfere with the humble supplications she puts up for them before the throne of God, Who alone knows if they are necessary. Churches were richly adorned, splendid functions took place, eloquent panegyrics were delivered in honour of the humble and during life often despised servant of God. Her biographer tells us that—

A few days after those ceremonies, at which her brother, Don Alonzo de Carvajal, assisted, he was taken dangerously ill. This was in March, about two months after his sister's death. The illness made rapid progress, he received the last sacraments, and shortly afterwards, so violent a paroxysm of the malady took place, that he was supposed to be dead. However, at three o'clock of the morning he recovered his senses, and his countenance gave the impression that he was looking at something that gave him pleasure. Turning to the rector of the English College, who was praying by his bedside, he said that he wished to make a general confession. When he had finished, he said to the Father, who was addressing to him some pious exhortations—' Your Reverence need not take this trouble, for my sister is with me, helping and consoling me. She tells me not to be afraid, for she is watching over me.' This accorded with what she said to Doña Beatrice de Sotomayor, the wife of Don Alonzo, the last time she had seen her ; that is, that though in life she was of no use to her brother, in death she would befriend him. It seems as if she was returning in this way the visit he had made to her in England, when he vainly sought to induce her to return to Spain.

In summing up the evidences of his holy country-woman's sanctity, the writer of her Life quotes the opinions on that point of those amongst her contempo-raries whose judgment, he considers, will carry most weight with it. The list begins with His Holiness Pope Paul V., who, as we have already seen, took a great interest in her residence in England, and held her in high regard. Philip III., King of Spain, and his pious consort, looked on the humble saint as a friend, and befriended her on all occasions. When informations were taken with a view to her eventual canonization, the Infanta Doña Margarita, who had abandoned the luxuries of a Court and taken the habit of St. Francis in the royal Convent of the Incarnation, testified to the belief which herself and all her imperial relatives held as to the sanctity of Doña Luisa de Carvajal. Her uncle, the Marquis of Almaçan, who had watched her day by day from childhood upward, proved his own conviction on the subject not merely by words but by the exceptional training to which he subjected that beloved niece, in whom he saw so rare a promise of future holiness.

In his quaint style, Luis Munoz tells us of her first interview with that excellent, prudent, wise, and expe-rienced Conde de Miranda, President of Castille, who made little account of virtues which show themselves off in drawing-rooms, but who held in the highest esteem characters such as Doña Luisa's. The first time she went to speak to him about her lawsuit, so great was his delight at hearing that she had asked to see him that, hat in hand, he went to meet her with all sorts of demonstrations of respect and reverence, and when they had finished their conversation he entreated her to come into his wife's apartments, to be introduced to her and his daughter, Doña Aldonça. He threw open the door with great exultation, exclaiming that he was bringing in Doña Luisa, and that they were to welcome and caress her exceedingly; and over and over again he repeated (much, we may conceive, to her discomfort), 'Look at her; she is a great saint.' The strictest friendship sprung up from that day between the holy visitor and that pious family, and amongst them and by their means she did an incredible amount of good.

Don Francisco de Contreros, who exercised some of the highest offices of the magistrature in Spain, and was judge in her lawsuits, likewise gave his evidence as to her singular holiness, which he had possessed ample opportunities of observing, and all that the Conde de Gondomar had related to him concerning her residence in England. The Cardinal of Trejo drew up a paper, which summed up the evidence collected on the subject, and ended by the expression of his own conviction that she had practised every virtue in an heroic degree, that her life deserved to be known and kept in remembrance, and her name inscribed amongst those of saints and martyrs.

But of all others, the Jesuit Fathers were most capable of bearing witness to the merits of one who had been trained by them, and always directed by members of the Society. When Mother de la Ascencion wrote to Father Luis de la Puente to announce to him the death of her dear friend, and to recommend her to his prayers, he answered, 'that by her works of supererogation many would be enriched.' Father Gaspar de Pedroça, who was for some time her confessor, declared her to be *unica en el mundo*, and that, much as her holiness had been spoken of, it was nothing in comparison to what was hidden in her breast. Fathet Hernando de Espinosa, and many other learned theologians, were in the habit of submitting to her their spiritual writings, so strong was their belief that divine lights were communicated to her in prayer. Padre Francisco de Salzedo was of the same opinion. Father Lorenzo de Aponte, of the Order of Clerks Minors, said her life was that of an angel more than a human creature. Father Gracian and Father Mareos de Guadölajara y Xavier, of the Order of our Lady of Mount Carmel, Father Miguel Salva, of the Order of St. Augustine, Father Antonio Sobrino, of the Order of the Discalced Franciscans, use the same language with regard to her. In the words of Father Juan de Pineda, S.J., in the sermon he preached on her death, they considered her as ' in strength of soul more than a woman ; in fortitude and courage superhuman ; in holiness and purity of life an angel ; in zeal for the faith an apostle ; in teaching, exhorting, and counselling, a doctor of the Church ; in defending the faith and bearing witness to it a martyr, not only in death but in life, by the continual desire of suffering.'

The Fathers of the English Seminary at Seville, in a book called *Las honras de Doña Luisa*, appear to have dwelt at length on her merits and her virtues.

The English Catholics [Luis Munoz goes on to say] look upon her with veneration, and many of them with the feelings due to a spiritual mother and teacher. The Catholic gentlemen who came to Spain with the Prince of Wales published the praises of our Doña Luisa. They state that she converted a number of persons by her example, her arguments, and her exhortations, that they had themselves seen her uphold and defend the Catholic faith in the city of London, and that she had conferred great benefits upon it with regard to religion. They added that if it did turn out that our Infanta became Queen of England, it ought to be stipulated that she should bring back to that country the body of Doña Luisa, that they and all the English Catholics would look upon her as their patroness and advocate in heaven, and many of the Protestants, they said, had great confidence in, and affection for, our saint, her charity to all having been well known, and exerted to the utmost of her power, so that her memory was borne in grateful remembrance. There was a great desire amongst the English Catholics that this holy lady should be canonized, especially amongst those whom she had persuaded to embrace the faith. If her body had not been removed with so great secrecy that few were acquainted with the fact, no doubt, they declared, that the Catholics would have made every effort to retain it, to keep it, and to hide it. They loved her in life for all the good she had done, and lamented that in death she was removed from them.

It had been the intention of Don Diego Sarmiento to keep the body of Doña Luisa in his chapel as long as he remained in England, and at the· termination of his Embassy to carry it back with him to Spain. Her devout friends could not endure this long delay, and they earnestly petitioned His Catholic Majesty to desire his Ambassador to send her remains to her native land as soon as possible. The order was given, and in such positive terms that the order could not be evaded, though many difficulties arose. The Fathers of the Society of Jesus at Louvain declared that they belonged by right to the Novitiate she had founded, and wrote very soon and very pressingly to the Ambassador on the subject. The King's commands, however, were imperative, and silenced every other claim.

On the 4th of August, 1615, the Licenciado Simon de Ariza, chaplain of Don Diego, took charge of the coffin containing the holy remains, and, accompanied by the Frenchman who had been many years in Doña Luisa's service and some other Spaniards, embarked on an

English vessel called the *Maria Luisa of London*. When almost in sight of Spain so violent a tempest arose that they were driven back towards the coasts of England. It seemed almost as if Doña Luisa's inanimate remains refused, as she had so often done, to leave that island. They neared the coast of France ; but the wind abated in time to permit of their pursuing their course towards Spain, where, on the 30th of August, they landed at last in the midst of a large concourse of people assembled on the mole of St. Sebastian to witness their disembarkation, and to carry the coffin in procession, to the principal church of the town, where it remained some days. Rodrigo Calderon, Marquis de Siete Iglesias, had been most active in forwarding the return to Spain of those precious relics. His wife, Ines de Vargas, was Doña Luisa's first cousin, and had held a constant correspondence with her during the whole time she had been in England. He considered that they had an indubitable claim to the possession of her remains, and desired to enrich with this treasure the Convent of Portaceli, which they had founded in Valladolid. Powerful personages easily find means of compassing their ends ; and though the Catholic King had expressed his will that the body should be brought to the Convent of the Incarnation at Madrid, the marquis sent orders that it should be consigned to the Correo Major of Irun, who seized the opportunity of the journey to the frontier of the Queens of Spain and France to convey it to Portaceli, where a place had been prepared for it by the side of Don Alonzo de Carvajal, lately deceased. But when the King heard that the body had been taken to Valladolid he was greatly displeased, and commanded that it should be instantly brought to Madrid. The marquis was anxious to secure some portion of the remains as relics, and for that purpose opened the coffin, but, finding that the sea water had got into it and exhaled a bad smell, he shut it up quickly, and said, ' Let it go as it is.'

The religious of the Incarnation received with inexpressible joy and consolation the body of one whom they had long loved and deeply venerated. They, too, opened the coffin, and, though the sea water had filled it and produced an intolerable stench, the body itself was in a perfect state of preservation, neither discoloured nor stained, flexible, and free from the least disfigurement. The features they had known and loved in life were before the eyes of these devoted friends—hallowed by the sacred associations of death in its holiest and loveliest form. They enshrined her in their beautiful chapel, and her memory lived amongst them. The prioress of the Convent of the Incarnation was that Mother Mariana of St. Joseph, who re-established in its primitive perfection the Augustinian Observance, and founded so many reformed convents of that order; and amongst her nuns was Isabel de la Cruz, who for eight years had been the constant companion of Doña Luisa, and witnessed all the details of her life; and likewise Mother Ines de la Assuncion, who had never left her side during the thirteen years which elapsed between the time she left the Marquis of Almaçan's house and her departure for England. None knew so well what her virtues had been; none could value more highly the treasure committed to their care. Their depositions before the Committee of Inquiry relative to her sanctity bear witness to their profound conviction that it had been of the highest order, and that the reputation she enjoyed fell below, rather than exceeded, her merits. Ines de la Assuncion testified that, during all the years she spent with Luisa, she did not remember to have seen her commit the slightest venial sin. She believed her to have received great favours in prayer; and that more than once our Blessed Lord and His Mother had appeared to their faithful servant. Nor were miracles wanting to support the high idea of her sanctity conceived by all those who had been acquainted with her. God often-times permitted that even during her life persons who recommended themselves to her prayers should be miraculously cured.

Whilst she was in England, a servant of the Conde de la Ribilla, in a quarrel with one of his companions, struck him with a knife, and wounded him so severely that he fell down to all appearance dead. The unhappy man, terrified at what he had done, rushed in despair to Luisa's house and told her what had happened. She answered very quietly that the wounded person was not dead, and would not die of that wound; that he would be up and about the next day; and that, for his part, what he had to do was to grieve over the sin he had committed and seek God's forgiveness. Not believing what she said, and afraid of returning to the Embassy, the man fled to Dover, where news reached him the following day that his fellow-servant was alive and getting better. This result was generally ascribed to the fervour of Luisa's prayers, who could only have known through a divine inspiration that the case was as she stated.

After her death our Lord worked many cures by her relics, and those who petitioned Him to grant them favours through her intercession obtained great graces. Mother Maria de San Joseph affirmed that, when her sufferings from spasms became so intolerable that it seemed as if they must end her existence, she had frequently obtained relief by laying on her heart a relic of her departed friend. Another nun of the same convent was suddenly cured by the same means of an ulcer in the arm, which had afflicted her for many years. So great, so frequent, and so well known were the wonders wrought by the application of the reliquary containing Doña Luisa's finger, which had been severed from her body when the coffin was opened on its arrival at the convent, that it came to be looked upon as an habitual instrument of God's mercy in relieving pain and restoring health.

The King of Spain and his brothers and sisters often knelt down and prayed before the altar where reposed the remains of the saintly companion of their childhood. They united together to petition the Holy See to proclaim her sanctity to the Christian world, and to authorize the public veneration in which her memory was held. The depositions relative to the heroic degree to which she had practised all the Christian virtues, and the attestations of those who witnessed or had been the subjects of the miracles wrought in favour of those who invoked her, were sent to Rome and submitted to the Sacred Tribunal, where the cause of her beatification was actively pursued for awhile, but as time went on and zeal slackened it became neglected and sank into oblivion. It requires great labour and perseverance, and no little expence, to carry to a successful issue a cause of this kind. Of the two countries most naturally interested in the posthumous honour of Doña Luisa, England could do nothing as long as her Catholic children were barely able to maintain their faith in obscurity and persecution, and Spain, once at the head of the Catholic world in power as well as in devotion, has for a full century and more been in a stage of decadence in both respects, though the ancestral faith of her people remains indelible even under all the adverse influences which have combined to ruin it.

We would gladly hope that it may be granted to English Catholics, the descendants of those whom she so

T

devotedly served, to revive the holy memory of Luisa de Carvajal, and to see her one day placed on the altars of the Church in company with our martyrs, with whom she had so ardently desired to suffer and to die. But, as the day of the triumph of Catholicism amongst us may yet be far distant, and as the interval which must elapse before it may dawn upon us may not improbably be marked by alternatives of prosperity and persecution, quiet and anxiety, we may well learn from the example of this holy sojourner in our country, not only to practise those lessons of personal holiness as to which she is our teacher, in common with all the saints of God the records of whose lives are preserved to us, but also to aim at the acquirement of those special virtues which seem to belong most naturally to a period of suffering. The public and private exercise of the Catholic religion is no longer proscribed, the prisons of London are not now crowded with priests charged with treason for saying Mass or reconciling converts to the Church, nor are our homes liable at any moment to be outraged by the violence of pursuivants in search of traces of the holy sacrifice and of the worship of God. We are free ourselves, and we are free also to instruct and assist others without legal, though not without social, persecution. And yet, if we consider the rights of God and the interests of souls, it may be questioned whether these were more fatally and generally disregarded in the days of James I. than in our own. For one form of error which then prevailed, ten prevail now ; sectarian bigotry has been more than replaced by the indifference of infidelity and the open propaganda of materialism, and souls are swept to destruction in ever increasing numbers, as the leaves before the autumn wind. The calumnies heaped upon Catholicism are as many and as wicked as of old. The laws press less heavily on religion, but the world and society are more hostile to it than ever, and their seductions avail with many souls which might have stood unquailing before the rack and the gibbet. The subtlety of the enemies of God is ever shifting its method of attack, and has never a better hope of success than when its tactics of assault are disguised and undetected. But the weapons of Christian defence are always the same : the simple earnest faith, the pure conscience, the strict practice of lofty virtue, the fearless contempt of the world, the disregard of human respect, the burning zeal for souls, the absolute confidence in God, and the love of the Cross of Jesus Christ, of which we have seen so many beautiful examples in the life of Luisa de Carvajal.

APPENDIX.

I.—*Doña Luisa's will.*

JESUS. MARY.

I, DONA LUISA DE CARVAJAL, being in the full possession
of the understanding which our Lord has been pleased to
give me, make this my will in the name of God our Lord,
believing and confessing the holy Roman Catholic faith.
And to begin with, I place my soul in the hands of its
Creator and Lord, and I invoke the intercession of our
sovereign Lady the Blessed Virgin and of all the saints,
especially those for whom I have a particular devotion,
and I humbly pray the Superiors of the Society of Jesus
and the Præpositus of the professed house, as a favour,
to grant me some little place in their church where my
body may be buried, in consideration of the devotion I
have ever entertained for their holy religious order; to
which order, in the manner that I have thought would
be most to the glory of God, I offer with the greatest
affection, a gift which, though but small, is all that I
have.   And if a burial-place be refused me in that
church, my executors will obtain for me a resting-place
in some other church of the Society; and if they are
unable to obtain this, let me be buried in some monastery in which, for the love of God, they may be willing
to give burial to a poor person like myself, and let my
funeral be conducted in accordance with this my poverty.
As executors I name Father Richard Walpole, the Vice-
Prefect of the English Mission, and the Confessor of the
English College in this city (Valladolid), or their successors.   After them (I have named them first from respect to
their priestly dignity), I name the Countess de la Meranda,

Doña Maria de Zuniga, and Doña Maria Gasca, and Don Francisco de Contreras, and Senor Melchor de Molina, and Don Luis de Toledo, Count of Caraçena. First of all I declare, that many years ago when I was with my uncle, I made a vow to dedicate all my property to the glory and greatest service of God. Then His Divine Majesty gave me large desires and a vehement attraction to devote myself, above all things, to the preservation and advancement of the English Fathers of the Society of Jesus, who sustain that kingdom like strong columns, defend it from an otherwise inevitable ruin, and supply efficacious means of salvation for thousands and thousands of souls. Wherefore I offer all my goods to the most holy Virgin our Lady. I place them under her protection, and I name and leave her universal heir of all my property. And I give possession of it henceforward to that most glorious Virgin, and in her name and place to Father Robert Persons, or failing him, to the Father who shall succeed him as Superior of the Mission, but with this condition and obligation, that such goods shall be applied to the founding of a Novitiate of English religious of the Society of Jesus, in whatever kingdom or part of the world shall seem to Father Persons to be for the greater glory of God; but in the event that England shall be brought back to the faith and obedience of the Roman Church, my will is, that the said revenue be transferred into that kingdom, for the foundation of a Novitiate of the Society there, unless it should seem better to Father Persons, for reasons concerning the Catholic religion, to leave the Novitiate beyond the kingdom. If the foundation of the Novitiate is delayed on account of the insufficiency of the sum in question, it is to be put out to interest, which said interest will be allowed to accumulate until it suffices for the purpose in view. If in the meantime, however, some pressing need in connection with the mission and conversion of England should occur, part of that interest may be employed for that end, provided that the ultimate object is never lost sight of. All the poor furniture of my house, its images and its books, I leave to the English Novitiate. I wish the holy crucifix I have, which belonged to my uncle, to be placed in the said Novitiate with particular veneration, as well as the particle of the wood of the true Cross which I carry about with me, and for that purpose it will be put into a cross, or little reliquary of gold, the same that the Emperor Henry III. carried about with him, and which was given to me by the Marquis of Almaçan, Don Francisco Hurtado de Mendoza.

To Ines of the Assumption, nun of the Order of St. Augustine, my much loved companion and friend, is to be paid all that I have promised to give for her dowry as a nun in the Convent of the Incarnátion; and if on account of her health, or for any other reason, she changed her mind and entered some other religious house, the same sum shall be paid for her as would have been paid to the one where she is now had she remained there. And if she should not become a nun at all, the sum of two reals a day is to be paid to her as long as she lives. As a token of my affection, I bequeath to her the marble crucifix which is in a box with a key in the drawer of my oratory. To Isabel of the Cross, in the same convent, I leave the image of our Lady of the People which is in the same box; and I humbly beg them to remember me in their prayers, and I beg the same of all the Fathers and Brothers of the Society, and the students in the English College. And I implore my brother to believe and understand that if I do not remember him in the disposal of my fortune, it is from no want of love for him, but from a strict obligation of conscience, which leaves me no option on the subject; and that if he acquiesces and takes pleasure in the fact that our Lord has chosen me to be entirely His, he will share in the reward, and find that spiritual blessings are not to be less esteemed than temporal ones. I hope our Lord will show him and his children great mercies. I beg His Divine Majesty to bestow upon them abundant blessings.

I ask my heirs, with the permission of the Superior, whom I humbly and earnestly ask to grant it, that an image of our Lady with her Divine Son in her arms may be placed above the principal altar in the future Novitiate, and a devout Mass with music celebrated there on each of her new feasts.

In case of any objections or obstacles against the rights of my said heirs, I endeavour beforehand to obviate them by adding, that I desire everything to be interpreted in their favour, and I beg that all my directions may be fulfilled as quickly as possible.

II.—The rule of life observed in Doña Luisa's house in London by herself and her Companions.

The first thing we have to do in the morning on awaking is to lift up our hearts to God our Lord with the tenderest affection, gratitude, and love we are capable of.

When up and dressed we must instantly prostrate ourselves in the Divine Presence, and offer up our hearts to Him with the supreme desire that each day may be more entirely devoted to Him than any of the foregoing ones. And add a thanksgiving for having passed the night without sin.

The time spent in these acts of devotion, in dressing, and making our beds, must not exceed half an hour.

From Easter to Michaelmas Day we are to get up at five, and from Michaelmas Day to Easter at six.

We are to make an hour of mental prayer in the oratory with great attention and recollection, helping ourselves with some good book if we find it necessary.

On Mondays and the three following days we are to meditate on the four last things—death, judgment, hell, and heaven, and always strive to advance in the knowledge of ourselves. On Fridays and Saturdays on the Passion, death, and burial of Christ, and on Sundays on the Resurrection. When a change in this order is desired, let permission be asked.

Our hearts should be watchful and attentive during our prayer in order to draw from the various flowers presented to us the dew of divine love in its purity, hatred of self, and distaste and weariness of all that is not good.

Let there be no weakness or carelessness in resisting and banishing unseemly thoughts, ill-suited to so holy an occupation. The evil of bad and sinful ones is of course evident.

If it is better for any one to be alone during her time of prayer, the Superioress, if she thinks so, can grant her that permission.

After mental prayer, Prime is said, and in summer, Terce and Sext.

In reciting the Psalms and Divine Office much care must be taken to offer up harmonious music to the heavenly King of our souls, and not to wound the divine ears by the dissonance of tepid affections, and failure in that humility and profound reverence we ought to feel, or even by the slight distractions of mind that occur.

After the Sisters have come out from saying Office they shall go to their needlework or manual labour, and in these let them employ themselves sedulously, but no task shall be set to them, and let them not think that the fact of being thus employed excuses them if they are idle in their way of doing it.

The work is to be carried on apart or in common according to the decision of the Superioress, who judges of what is most expedient and desirable on that point at different times and for different persons.

We must endeavour to preserve in our lives the devotion and recollection which we have in our prayers. If health requires it, we may during part of the time assigned to work take some exercise in the garden or other quiet places belonging to the house, in the same spirit of devout recollection.

Silence is to be kept from the time of rising till after Mass, which is said in our oratory at eight when we get up at five, and at nine when we get up at six.

When there is a sermon it is to be, if possible, after Mass, unless the Superioress should name some other more convenient hour in the morning or afternoon.

After Mass and the sermon, if there is one, None is said in the winter, in summer, Terce and Sext, and None at ten o'clock. In Lent, Vespers are said at ten o'clock.

After None, and from that time till the particular examen, the time is spent in work, and conversation may be held on spiritual and edifying subjects, great care being taken not to mix up with them objectionable or even unprofitable remarks.

At a quarter to eleven, examination of conscience, and if any time remains after it before the hour is ended each may spend it as she likes, provided it is in a pious manner.

When the signal is given for some community exercise, they must all go to the room nearest to the place of meeting, and enter together in good order.

At eleven, dinner. Before sitting down to it a short Psalm is recited and every one stands up and raises her heart to God whilst the Superioress says a short *Benedicite.* Then each takes her place according to the order in which they entered.

No one is to speak without necessity, and then only to do it in a low voice. The reader for the week reads aloud during all the time of the meal unless the Superioress makes a sign to her to stop.

No more time is to be spent at meals than befits the religious life.

After dinner, the hour glass is turned down and there is an hour of recreation and cheerful conversation tempered by religious modesty.

The recreation ended, each has to betake herself to her work according to the office allotted to her for the week, beginning by the Superioress, who must as much as possible give the example of humility, in imitation of the unspeakable humility of Christ, signified by those words—'I am in the midst of you as one that serves.' In this spirit she will go to the work appointed to her like the rest.

From one to three o'clock strict silence has to be observed, except that from two to three on certain days, and never less than once a week, the Superioress will give to all the others an instruction in the work room or else she will see and speak to each one of them in private according as she sees any occasion for counsel or reproof.

At that time also on Fridays, all will meet in the oratory, and on their knees salute the most holy Virgin our Lady, reciting the *Ave Regina cælorum,* and then, having seated themselves, each in her turn, beginning with the oldest, has to come forward and kneel before the Superioress, and remain in that position till she desires her to rise. Standing up, she then has to accuse herself of the faults she has discerned in herself, always taking care not to mention what might shock or disedify the others. This done, the zelatrice steps forward, and if there is occasion for it, bowing low to the Superioress, she says—'With your permission, I will mention what she has forgotten, or what she has not discovered in herself.' The Superioress having answered, 'Say on ;' simply, without comment or exaggeration, and in a charitable and kindly spirit, she mentions the faults she has observed in the speaker. When all have gone through this exercise, the Superioress having said a few words to them on the importance of a diligent care of their souls, according to the perfection they aim at, it finishes by the recital of the *Miserere* and prayer.

On the days not occupied in these ways, the said hour will be spent in reading aloud to those who work the lives and histories of the saints, or some other book combining edification and entertainment.

At three, Vespers are said. Those who do not recite them, attend and listen, unless their occupations, or the orders of the Superioress, detain them elsewhere. After Vespers, the Litany of the Life and Death of our Lord is said, in which are found many sweet stations of His love, and a real treasure from which spiritual instruction may be derived. Afterwards, a part of the rosary (five of the mysteries) is recited. In Lent, the same litany and rosary is said at three.

Silence is observed till four, and in Lent till six, and each attends to her occupations if any time remains before Compline. The same rule applies to it which has been given for that which precedes None and follows particular examination.

This time appears the most convenient for receiving the visits of seculars who come by permission to see any of us. These interviews are not to last more than an hour, unless under exceptional circumstances, which the Superioress takes into consideration; and in ordinary visits, where no formalities are necessary, can be limited to half an hour, or even a quarter of an hour. No one is to receive a visitor alone, not even women and relatives.

Compline is to be said in summer at half past five, and in winter at half past six, and afterwards there is to be a half hour of mental prayer, ending with the Litany of our Lady which is sung at Loreto, and the *Sub tuum præsidium.*

If time remains before supper, it is to be employed in the same way as that which remains before eleven o'clock in the morning.

Supper is at seven in the summer, and at eight in the winter, and everything goes on in the same way as at dinner, till the end of the hour's recreation.

In summer, Matins are said at half past eight, and in winter at half past nine. Matins are followed by a brief examination of conscience, and on Mondays, Wednesdays, and Fridays, all take the discipline, retiring for that purpose alone to their rooms. This they do every day in Lent, except on Sundays and great festivals. The other days a short lecture is read on the meditation for the following morning. That ended, every one retires to rest.

The hair-shirt is worn once a week, and three times a week during Lent.

III.—*The Cross in Cheapside.*

Extract from the Memoirs of the Mission in England of the Capuchin Friars from the year 1630 *to* 1699, *by Father Cyprian of Gamache, one of the Capuchins belonging to the household of Queen Henrietta Maria, wife of Charles I.*

'Although she (Queen Elizabeth) manifested so rancorous and so strange a hatred against the Catholic religion, she never suffered the beautiful cross in Jaipsaide (Cheapside) to be touched; on the contrary, she had some of the gilding repaired, which the course of several centuries had effaced, so that this rich monument of the very fervent and commendable piety of the ancient English was not merely suffered to stand, but was embellished, during the reign of that barbarous Queen.

Her cruelty was not great enough to demolish and ruin it ; for that, the raging fury of a regicide Parliament was required.'

Father Cyprian goes on to speak of Luisa, and her act of public homage to this holy cross in Jaipsaide, as he calls it, but makes a mistake in stating her to have been a widow. 'It (the regicide Parliament) would not suffer what the Queen had tolerated in a good Spanish lady, a marchioness, a widow, and wealthy. Having heard of the sanguinary persecutions to which the Catholics were exposed in England, animated with a holy zeal, she went thither, in the genuine spirit of Christianity, to relieve the poor with the riches God had bestowed on her, and to suffer with the persecuted. Her alms to the needy were very extensive ; and to draw upon herself every kind of contempt, confusion, and insult by a virtuous act of religion, she did honour publicly to the great cross of Jaipsaide, prostrating herself before an innumerable concourse of people, who loaded her with abuse, pelted her with mud and stones, hustled, and struck her. The generous marchioness took pleasure in this ignominious and dangerous treatment, and by so holy an example she animated the Catholics to endure suffering. . . . To prevent similar circumstances, and to abolish in England all Catholic marks of religion, the rebel Parliament ordered that noble cross to be pulled down, demolished, and laid level, with the statues of the twelve Apostles which were around it. The Puritans, triumphing in this accursed decree, carried it immediately into execution. The report of this proceeding spread throughout the whole city of London. People thronged to the spot from all quarters, drums and trumpets were sent for, ladders were raised against the cross.

The first whom fury urged to mount, drew upon himself a just punishment for his sacrilegious outrage by a fall upon the iron spikes surrounding the statues of the Apostles, which pierced the body of the wretched man, and put an end to his life. This fatal example, which ought to have made the others tremble, rendered them neither more timid nor less furious. They mounted the ladder, put ropes around the cross and the necks of

the Apostles, which were pulled down by a number of
men. . . . These outrages to the images of the servants
were transferred to those of the Master, from the figures
of the Apostles to the cross of Jesus Christ. Trans-
ported with rage, those men pulled down that beautiful
and ancient cross. They sapped it to the foot, and
demolished and razed it so completely, that not a vestige
of it was left.[1]

The above narrative is corroborated by the account
given of the same Cheapside cross in a recent number of
Old and New London. It states, 'That it was built in
1290 by Master Michael, a mason, of Canterbury.
From an old painting at Cowdray, in Sussex, repre-
senting the procession of Edward VI. from the Tower
to Westminster, we gather that the cross was both
stately and graceful. It consisted of three octangular
compartments, each supported by eight slender columns.
The basement story was probably twenty feet high ; the
second, ten ; the third, six. In the first niche stood
the effigy of probably a contemporaneous Pope ; round
the base of the second were four Apostles, each with a
nimbus round his head ; and above them sat the Virgin,
with the Infant Jesus in her arms. The highest niche
was occupied by four standing figures, while, crowning
all, rose a cross, surmounted by the emblematic dove.
The whole was rich with highly finished ornament.'
The cross, which was rebuilt in 1441, escaped the
fury of the Reformation, but in 1581 the Puritans made
an attack upon it, and mutilated the statues. 'The
Virgin was robbed of her Son, and the arms broken
by which she stayed Him on her knees, her whole body
also haled by ropes, and left ready to fall.' Queen
Elizabeth caused the statue to be repaired, but soon
after the rioters (perhaps the Church Association of that
day) again removed our Lady, and substituted the
goddess Diana. Elizabeth, who had no sympathy with
the Iconoclasts, caused the Blessed Virgin to be restored,
and again the statue was mutilated. In 1600 the cross
was again rebuilt, and it was referred to the Universities
whether the crucifix on the summit should be restored,

[1] *The Court and Times of Charles I.*, p. 385.

and they both sanctioned it. In 1641 the cross was again defaced; and tracts were written with a view to excite the people to its utter destruction. In 1643, during the Great Rebellion, the Parliament ordered Robert Harley, with a troop of horse and two companies of foot, to pull down the cross. With characteristic malignity, they chose the Feast of the Invention of the Cross as the most appropriate day on which to accomplish their profane deed. As the cross fell drums beat, trumpets blew, and caps were thrown into the air, to mark the fiendish joy of the mob. A curious tract was published on the day the cross was destroyed, entitled, *The Downfall of Dagon; or, the Taking down of the Cheapside Crosse,* &c. The cross, in this tract, makes a will, from which we extract the following curious prophecy, which is being fulfilled now before our eyes: ' I give my body and stones to those masons that cannot telle how to frame the like againe, to keepe by them for a pattern ; *for in time there will be more crosses in London than ever there was yet.'*

IV.—*Extracts from Luis Munoz's letter to the Rev. Mother Mariana, of the royal Convent of the Incarnation.*

' It was my good fortune to behold the face of Doña Luisa de Carvajal y Mendoza when she was about thirty years of age, and it has remained imprinted in my memory. I remember well, that having gone to Valladolid to visit my father, Nicholas Munoz, who at that time was carrying on his business there, he called me to see and to speak to her. I was a mere child then, and hardly knew in whose company I was. I always heard a good deal of her virtues and of her journey to England from my dear mother, who knew, and visited, and greatly esteemed her. The praises of Doña Luisa were continually in her mouth. They used to meet for many years at the church of the Jesuits. I kept by me for some time a short record of her life, printed in Seville, to which was added a description of the funeral honours that were paid to her throughout Spain, and I preserved a great affection for her memory. Since last year, I have had it always in my mind to write her panegyric, and my wishes at first extended no further. I wrote to a person who had been much devoted to her, to procure for me the narrative published at Seville, and though he did not succeed in finding it, his researches did not turn out fruitless, for he gave me notice that her life was written by a religious of the Society of Jesus. This increased my curiosity, and I made many inquiries amongst the members of the Society, and in other quarters also. They wrote to me from Seville that I should find what I wanted at the royal Convent of the Incarnation at Madrid. Soon afterwards your reverence's charity enriched me with the chapters of the Life of Doña Luisa, written by her confessor, the English Jesuit, Father Michael Walpole, a man of so great virtue and learning, that he was in his country an eminent labourer in the cause of the Catholic religion ; on which account he was a prisoner in the dungeons of London. His merit and his wisdom were such, that Doña Luisa chose him for her spiritual guide. Together with his manuscript were thirty-seven depositions, made upon oath by the desire of His Majesty and the authority of the ordinary, with a view to her canonization.

'I made myself acquainted with the contents of these papers, and it seemed to me that it had not been without a special design of Providence that they had come into my hands, and that, by means of the information they contained, I could write, not merely an eulogium, but a history of the pious lady in question. I felt strongly my own incapacity for this undertaking, and the difficulty of accomplishing it in the midst of my overwhelming occupations. But your reverence's wishes and the help of your prayers, and of those of your holy daughters, which I knew I could rely on, encouraged me to attempt, I do not know whether I ought to call it this additional labour, or rather, this diversion from the heavy duties of my position.

'In the last chapter of Father Walpole's manuscript, speaking of the great secrecy Doña Luisa observed with regard to the things that concerned her soul, he says,

"That her confessors gave her an obedience to write certain details on this subject, for the better guidance and enlightenment of those who directed her, and also that she might, from time to time, compare these records of her spiritual condition, and be thus excited to acknowledge the mercies God had shown her. She never allowed any one but her confessors to see these papers, and always kept them under lock and key. When in England, without any expectation of returning to Spain, she collected them all, tied up and sealed them, and wrote upon the parcel, 'I beg and desire my companions, if I die, to keep these papers locked up, without breaking any of the seals; if my confessor is in England to deliver them up to him as they are; otherwise, to see them burnt in their presence.'" This was written in Spanish and in English, and the following words were added in English, 'These manuscripts are not on any account to be read, because they are things that have to do with conscience.' It pleased our Lord that her confessor should return to England in time to secure the possession of these writings from whence many of the materials of her spiritual history have been drawn.

'I should not have considered that I had fulfilled the duty of a faithful historian if I had not endeavoured to see these papers. I found out that they were at Seville, in the hands of the Rev. Henry Pollard, Father Walpole's companion, who took charge of them when our Lord withdrew His friend from this world. He was most careful of these writings, valuing them highly as remains of Doña Luisa. After long and earnest efforts, I succeeded in obtaining them from Father Norton, another English Jesuit, who took a great interest in my undertaking. Your reverence has seen and recognized them. Some were separate pages, others bound together. They contain details as to the writer's early years, her interior life, and the mercies our Lord vouchsafed to her. They are not arranged in any particular order, and bear the impress of having been written at the spur of the moment. I compared them carefully with Father Walpole's manuscript, and found that, word for word, they corresponded. The arrangement of these materials was no small labour, and I had, in addition, to collate them with Doña Luisa's letters, in which she gives an account of the various events which took place during her residence in England. I can candidly declare that I consider Father Walpole as the real author of this work, or indeed, I can say, that it is from Doña Luisa herself, that I derive authority for all I have written. The facts I have related I have seen stated in her handwriting. I affirm, for I consider this a most important point, that every word I have written is exactly there. No human respect has moved me to use the least flattery or exaggeration in so grave a matter, on the contrary, I have rather fallen short than gone beyond what Doña Luisa deserves. I am sure that what I have said of her virtues does not come up to what I know to be your reverence's opinion of her sanctity. I return to you, reverend mother, the flowers you have given me, made up into a nosegay. God grant my unworthy hands may not have injured them. In any case, I have only furnished the string that binds them together, and the green leaves which encircle them.'

V.—*Doña Luisa's poetry.*

The following specimen of Luisa de Carvajal's poetry may please those who are acquainted with the beautiful Spanish language.

Romance Espiritual.

En una graciosa isleta	In a lovely islet
Que un claro rio ceñia,	Girdled by a clear river
No lexos de Nazareth,	Not far from Nazareth,
La de engrandecida dicha,	Unutterably blest,
Estava el Verbo encarnado	Was the Word Incarnate
A solas, sin compania,	Alone, and unattended,
Sentado en un verde assiento,	Sitting on a verdant seat
Que la misma terra hazia.	Which the earth itself was furnishing Him,
De fresca yerva adornado,	With the green grass adorned,
Junto a un olmo, do se arrima,	Close to an elm-tree; thereon He leaned,
Pensativo, y cuidadoso,	Thoughtful and anxious,
Al tiempo que se ponia.	At the time of the setting
El sol, quedando sin el,	Of the sun; without it (the sun) being
Apazible a maravilla,	Wondrously peaceful,
Aquel venturoso puesto,	That blessed spot
Que occupava el de justicia.	Which the Sun of Justice occupied.

U

Desde do se, señorea,
La clara agua cristalina,
Que contenta y placentera,
En las orillas batia,
Muy claramente, mostrando,
Que a su Hacedor conocia ;
Y el bello moço divino,
Que a la belleza excedia,
Las garzos ojos serenos,
En sus criaturas ponia,
Con cuya vista de gloria,
Y lindez la vestia.
Y aquellos campos amenos,
De varias flores matiça,
Las avezillas cantando,
Con acordada armonia.
Solenizan su ventura,
Que la conocen y estiman,
El cielo quedò dorado,
Al tiempo que a el se bolvian,
Los cristalinos espejos,
En que los cielos se miran,
Y aviendo estado suspenso,
Que el amor le embevezia.
Mil amorosas querellas,
De sus labias despedia,
Y como orientales perlas,
Gruessas lagrimas vertia.
Diendo, Como desechas,
(Ay dulce enemiga mia),
Tal amante, y tal esposo,
Que por ti pena e suspira?
Dulce enemiga a te llamo,
Q'eres dulce, aunq' enemiga.

Y Jengo por proprios daños,

Los con que à ti te lastimas,
Buscas tu mal, y el bien huyes,

Mas aunque yo dè la vida.
Con ella he de rescatarte,
Que te me tienen cantiva,
Yo te obligarè a que me ames,
Dexandote tan herida.
De mi amor, que non descanses,
Ni un punto sin mi, alma mia,

Y si enemiga mi fuiste,
Dulce, quanto mas amiga !

Then controlled itself
The clear crystal water,
Which calmly and pleasantly
Beat upon the shores,
Most distinctly showing
That it knew its Maker.
And the beautiful Boy divine
Surpassing all beauty,
His blue eyes serene
Upon His creatures rested,
Whose gaze with glory
And with beauty clad,
And the pleasant plains
With diverse flowers embellished,
The little birds singing
With regulated harmony
Keep the feast of their bliss,
Which they acknowledge and esteem.
The sky was golden
When up to it were turned
The crystal mirrors
Wherein the heavens are seen.
And being entranced,
For love made Him beside Himself.
A thousand loving complaints
With His lips He uttered.
And like pearls of the orient,
Great drops of tears He shed,
Saying : Why undervalue
(O sweet enemy of mine)
Such a Lover, such a Bridegroom,
Who for thee is in pain and sighs.
Dear enemy I call thee,
For thou art sweet, though an enemy,
And I regard as wrongs done to Myself
Those which thou art bewailing.
Thou seekest after evil, and fleest from good.
But though I give My life,
With that I have to ransom thee,
For I am thy captive.
I will force thee to love Me,
Wounding thee so with My love,
That thou shalt have no rest.
No, not for a moment, without me, thy sweet life.
And if as an enemy thou hast been
Dear to me, how much more as a friend !

A Select Catalogue of Books

PUBLISHED BY

BURNS, OATES, & CO.,

17 & 18, PORTMAN STREET,

63, PATERNOSTER ROW.

BOOKS LATELY PUBLISHED

BY MESSRS,

BURNS, OATES, & CO.,

17 & 18, Portman Street, and 63, Paternoster Row.

———◦◇◦———

Memorials of those who Suffered for the
Faith in Ireland in the Sixteenth, Seventeenth,
and Eighteenth Centuries. Collected from Authentic and Original Documents by MYLES
O'REILLY, B.A., LL.D. 8vo, 7s. 6d.

"A very valuable compendium of the martyrology of Ireland
during the three, or rather two, centuries of active Protestant persecution. The language of many of these original records, written
often by a friend or relative of the martyr, is inexpressibly touching,
often quite heroic in its tone."—*Dublin Review.*

"Very interesting memories."—*Month.*

———

Life of St. Thomas of Canterbury. By
Mrs. HOPE, Author of "The Early Martyrs."
Cloth extra, 4s. 6d.

A valuable addition to the collection of historical
books · for Catholic readers. It contains a large
collection of interesting facts, gleaned with great

BURNS, OATES, & CO, 17, PORTMAN STREET, W.

industry from the various existing Lives of St. Thomas, and other documents.

"Compiled with great care from the best authors."—*Month.*

"The rich covers of this splendidly-bound volume do not, as is often the case, envelop matter unworthy of its fair exterior. This is a volume which will be found useful as a present, whether in the college or school, for either sex."—*Weekly Register.*

"An agreeable and useful volume."—*Nation.*

"A more complete collection of incidents and anecdotes, combined with events of greater weight, could not be compressed into so compact, yet perfectly roomy, a space."—*Tablet.*

By the same Author.

Life of St. Philip Neri. New Edition.
2s. 6d.; cheap edition, 2s.

NARRATIVE OF MISSIONS.

The Corean Martyrs. By Canon SHORT-
LAND. Cloth, 2s.

A narrative of Missions and Martyrdoms too little known in this country.

"This is a notice of the martyrs who have fallen in this most interesting mission, and of the history of its rise and progress up to the present day."—*Tablet.*

"No one can read this interesting volume without the most genuine admiration of, and sympathy with, such zeal and constancy."—*Literary Churchman.*

MISSIONARY BIOGRAPHY.

1. *Life of Henri Dorié, Martyr.* Trans-
lated by Lady HERBERT. 1s. 6d.; cloth, 2s.

"The circulation of such lives as this of Henry Dorie will do much to promote a spirit of zeal, and to move hearts hitherto stagnant because they have not been stirred to the generous deeds which characterise Catholic virtues."—*Tablet.*

2. *Théophane Vénard, Martyr in Tonquin.*
Edited by the Same.   2s. ; cloth elegant, 3s.

"The life of this martyr is not so much a biography as a series of letters translated by Lady Herbert, in which the life of Théophane Vénard unfolds itself by degrees, and in the most natural and interesting way. His disposition was affectionate, and formed for ardent friendship ; hence, his correspondence is full of warmth and tenderness, and his love of his sister in particular is exemplary and striking. During ten years he laboured under Mgr. Retord, in the western district of Tonquin, and his efforts for the conversion of souls were crowned with singular success.   During the episcopate of his Bishop no less than 40,000 souls were added to the flock of Christ, and Vénard was peculiarly instrumental in gathering in this harvest." —*Northern Press.*

"We cannot take leave of this little volume without an acknowledgment to Lady Herbert for the excellent English dress in which she has presented it to the British public ; certainly, no lives are more calculated to inspire vocation to the noble work of the apostolic life than those of Dorie and Vénard."—*Tablet.*

3. *Life of Bishop Bruté.* Edited by the Same.

The Martyrdom of St. Cecilia: a Drama.
By ALBANY J. CHRISTIE, S.J. With a Frontispiece after Molitor.   Elegant cloth, 5s.

"Well-known and beautiful drama."—*Tablet.*

"The receipt of the fourth edition of this beautiful play assures us that our own opinion of its merits has been shared by a wide circle of the Catholic public.   The binding is exquisite, and the picture of St. Cecilia is a work of art."—*Weekly Register*

BURNS, OATES, & CO., 17, *PORTMAN STREET, W.*

The Life of M. Olier, Founder of the Seminary of St. Sulpice; with Notices of his most Eminent Contemporaries. By EDWARD HEALY THOMPSON, M.A. Cloth, 4s.

This Biography has received the special approbation of the Abbé Faillon, Author of "La Vie de M. Olier;" and of the Very Reverend Paul Dubreul, D.D., Superior of the Seminary of St. Sulpice, Baltimore, U.S.

Edited by the Same.

The Life of St. Charles Borromeo. Cloth, 3s. 6d.

Also, lately published, by Mr. THOMPSON.

The Hidden Life of Jesus: a Lesson and Model to Christians. Translated from the French of BOUDON. Cloth, 3s.

"This profound and valuable work has been very carefully and ably translated by Mr. Thompson. We shall be glad to receive more of that gentleman's publications, for good translation, whether from the French or any other language, is not too common amongst us. The publication is got up with the taste always displayed by the firm of Burns, Oates, and Co."—*Register.*

"The more we have of such works as 'The Hidden Life of Jesus,' the better."—*Westminster Gazette.*

"A book of searching power."—*Church Review.*

"We have often regretted that this writer's works are not better known."—*Universe.*

"We earnestly recommend its study and practice to all readers."—*Tablet.*

"We have to thank Mr. Thompson for this translation of a valuable work which has long been popular, in France."—*Dublin Review.*

"A good translation."—*Month.*

BURNS, OATES, & CO., 63, PATERNOSTER ROW, E.C.

Devotion to the Nine Choirs of Holy Angels,
and especially to the Angel Guardians. Translated from the Same.   3s.

"We congratulate Mr. Thompson on the way in which he has accomplished his task, and we earnestly hope that an increasea devotion to the Holy Angels may be the reward of his labour of love."—*Tablet.*

"A beautiful translation."—*The Month.*

"The translation is extremely well done."—*Weekly Register.*

Library of Religious Biography.   Edited by
EDWARD HEALY THOMPSON.

Vol. 1.   THE LIFE OF ST. ALOYSIUS GONZAGA, S.J.   5s.

"We gladly hail the first instalment of Mr. Healy Thompson's Library of Religious Biography.   The life before us brings out strongly a characteristic of the Saint which is, perhaps, little appreciated by many who have been attracted to him chiefly by the purity and early holiness which have made him the chosen patron of the young.   This characteristic is his intense energy of will, which reminds us of another Saint, of a very different vocation and destiny, whom he is said to have resembled also in personal appearance—the great St. Charles Borromeo."—*Dublin Review.*

"The book before us contains numberless traces of a thoughtful and tender devotion to the Saint.   It shows a loving penetration into his spirit, and an appreciation of the secret motives of his action, which can only be the result of a deeply affectionate study of his life and character."—*Month.*

Vol. 2.   THE LIFE OF MARIE EUSTELLE HARPAIN;
or, the Angel of the Eucharist.   5s.

"The life of Marie Eustelle Harpain possesses a special value and interest apart from its extraordinary natural and supernatural beauty, from the fact that to her example and to the effect of her writings is attributed in great measure the wonderful revival of devotion to the Blessed Sacrament in France, and consequently throughout Western Christendom."—*Dublin Review.*

"A more complete instance of that life of purity and close union with God in the world of which we have just been speaking is to be found in the history of Marie Eustelle Harpain, the sempstress of Saint-Pallais. The writer of the present volume has had the advantage of very copious materials in the French works on which his own work is founded, and Mr. Thompson has discharged his office as editor with his usual diligence and accuracy."—*The Month*.

Vol. 3. THE LIFE OF ST. STANISLAS KOSTKA. 5s.

"We strongly recommend this biography to our readers, earnestly hoping that the writer's object may thereby be attained in an increase of affectionate veneration for one of whom Urban VIII. exclaimed that, although 'a little youth,' he was indeed 'a great saint.'"—*Tablet*.

"There has been no adequate biography of St. Stanislas. In rectifying this want, Mr. Thompson has earned a title to the gratitude of English-speaking Catholics. The engaging Saint of Poland will now be better known among us, and we need not fear that, better known, he will not be better loved."—*Weekly Register*.

The Life of S. Teresa, written by herself: a new Translation from the last Spanish Edition. To which is added for the first time in English THE RELATIONS, or the Manifestations of her Spiritual State which the Saint submitted to her Confessors. Translated by DAVID LEWIS. In a handsome volume, 8vo, cloth, 10s. 6d.

"The work is incomparable; and Mr. Lewis's rare faithfulness and felicity as a translator are known so well, that no word of ours can be necessary to make the volume eagerly looked for."— *Dublin Review*.

"We have in this grand book perhaps the most copious spiritual autobiography of a Saint, and of a highly-favoured Saint, that exists."—*Month*.

The Life of Margaret Mary Alacoque. By the Rev. F. TICKELL, S.J. 8vo, cloth, 7s. 6d.

"It is long since we have had such a pleasure as the reading of Father Tickell's book has afforded us. No incident of her holy life from birth to death seems to be wanting, and the volume appropriately closes with an account of her beatification."—*Weekly Register*.

"It is one of those high-class spiritual biographies which will be best appreciated in religious communities." — *Westminster Gazette*.

"Of Father Tickell's labours we can say with pleasure that he has given us a real biography, in which the Saint is everything, and the biographer keeps in the background."—*Dublin Review*.

"We can only hope that the life may carry on, as it is worthy of doing, the apostolate begun in our country by one who our Lord desires should be ' as a brother to His servant, sharing equally in these spiritual goods, united with her to His own Heart for ever.' "—*Tablet*.

"The work could hardly have been done in a more unpretending, and at the same time more satisfactory, manner than in the volume now before us."—*Month*.

The Day Hours of the Church. Latin and English. Cloth, 1s.

Also, separately,

THE OFFICES OF PRIME AND COMPLINE. 8d.

THE OFFICES OF TIERCE, SEXT, AND NONE. 3d.

"Prime and Compline are the morning and evening prayers which the Church has drawn up for her children; and, for our part, we can wish for nothing better. We know not where an improvement could be suggested, and therefore we see not why anything should have been substituted for them. . . . Why should not their use be restored? Why should they not become the standard devotions of all Catholics, whether alone or in their families? Why may we not hope to have them more solemnly performed—chanted even every day in all religious communities; or, where there is a sufficient number of persons, even in family' chapels?"—*Cardinal Wiseman*.

"These beautiful little books, which have received the imprimatur of his Grace the Archbishop, are a zealous priest's answers to the most eminent Cardinal's questions—such answers as would have gladdened his heart could they have been given when first demanded. But the Cardinal lives in his successors

BURNS, OATES, & CO., 17, PORTMAN STREET, W.

and what he so greatly desired should be done is in progress of full performance."—*Tablet.*

" The publication of these Offices is another proof of what we have before alluded to, viz., the increased liturgical taste of the present day."—*Catholic Opinion*

POPULAR DEVOTION.

Now ready.

Devotions for the Ecclesiastical Seasons,
consisting of Psalms, Hymns, Prayers, &c., suited for Evening Services, and arranged for Singing. Cloth, 1s. Also in separate Nos. at 2d. each, for distribution, as follows :—

1. Advent and Christmas.	4. Whitsuntide.
2. Septuagesima to Easter.	5. Sundays after Pentecost.
3. Paschal Time.	6. Feasts of our Lady.

7. Saints' Days.

Music for the whole, 1s. 6d.

" A valuable addition to our stock of popular devotions."—*Dublin Review.*

Church Music and Church Choirs: 1. The Music to be Sung; 2. The proper Singers; 3. The Place for the Choir. 2s.

" The special value of this pamphlet, and the seasonableness of its circulation, lie in this : that it attempts to solve—and, we believe, does really solve—several important points as to the proper kinds of music to be used in our public Offices, and more especially at High Mass."—*Tablet.*

" We earnestly recommend all who can do so to procure and study this pamphlet."—*Weekly Register.*

" Masterly and exhaustive articles."—*Catholic Opinion.*

BURNS, OATES, & CO, 63, PATERNOSTER ROW, E.C.

Liturgical Directions for Organists, Singers,
and Composers.   Contains the Instructions of the
Holy See on the proper kind of Music for the
Church, from the Council of Trent to the present
time ; and thus furnishes choirs with a guide for
selection.   Fcp. 8vo, 6d.

New Meditations for each Day in the Year
on the Life of our Lord Jesus Christ.   By a
Father of the Society of Jesus.   ith the imprimatur of his Grace the Archbishop of   est-
minster.   Second Edition.   Vols. I. and II.,
price 4s. 6d. each ; or complete in two vols., 9s.

"We can heartily recommend this book for its style and sub-
stance ; it bears with it several strong recommendations. . . .
It is solid and practical without being dreary or commonplace."
Westminster Gazette.

"A work of great practical utility, and we give it our earnest
recommendation."—*Weekly Register.*

The Day Sanctified : being Meditations and
Spiritual Readings for Daily Use.   Selected from
the Works of Saints and approved writers of the
Catholic Church.   Fcp., cloth, 3s. 6d. ; red
edges, 4s.

".Of the many volumes of meditation on sacred subjects which
have appeared in the last few years, none has seemed to us so well
adapted to its object as the one before us."—*Tablet.*

"Deserves to be specially mentioned."—*Month.*

"Admirable in every sense."—*Church Times.*

"Many of the Meditations are of great beauty. . . . They
form, in fact, excellent little sermons, and we have no doubt will
be largely used as such."—*Literary Churchman.*

BURNS, OATES, & CO., 17, *PORTMAN STREET, W.*

Our Father: Popular Discourses on the Lord's Prayer. By Dr. EMANUEL VEITH, Preacher in Ordinary in the Cathedral of Vienna. (Dr. V. is one of the most eminent preachers on the Continent.) Cloth, 3s. 6d.

"We can heartily recommend these as accurate, devotional, and practical."—*Westminster Gazette.*

"We are happy to receive and look over once more this beautiful work on the Lord's Prayer—most profitable reading."—*Weekly Register.*

"Most excellent manual."—*Church Review.*

Little Book of the Love of God. By Count STOLBERG. With Life of the Author. Cloth, 2s.

"An admirable little treatise, perfectly adapted to our language and modes of thought."—*Bishop of Birmingham.*

NEW BOOK FOR HOLY COMMUNION.

Reflections and Prayers for Holy Communion. Translated from the French. Uniform with "Imitation of the Sacred Heart." With Preface by Archbishop MANNING. Fcp. 8vo, cloth, 4s. 6d.; bound, red edges, 5s.; calf, 8s. 6d.; morocco, 9s. 6d.

"The Archbishop has marked his approval of the work by writing a preface for it, and describes it as 'a valuable addition to our books of devotion.' We may mention that it contains 'two very beautiful methods of hearing Mass,' to use the words of the Archbishop in the Preface."—*Register.*

"A book rich with the choicest and most profound Catholic devotions."—*Church Review.*

BURNS, OATES, & CO., 63, PATERNOSTER ROW, E.C.

Holy Confidence. By Father ROGACCI, of the
Society of Jesus. One vol. 18mo, cloth, 2s.

" As an attack on the great enemy, despair, no work could be
more effective ; while it adds another to a stock of books of devotion which is likely to be much prized."—*Weekly Register*.

."This little book, addressed to those ' who strive to draw
nearer to God and to unite themselves more closely with Him,'
is one of the most useful and comforting that we have read for a
long time. We earnestly commend this little book to all
troubled souls, feeling sure that they will find in it abundant
cause for joy and consolation."—*Tablet*.

The Invitation Heeded: Reasons for a
Return to Catholic Unity. By JAMES KENT
STONE, late President of Kenyon College, Gambier,
Ohio, and of Hobart College. Cloth, 5s. 6d.

" A very important contribution to our polemical literature,
which can hardly fail to be a standard work on the Anglican controversy."—*Dr. Brownson in the New York Tablet*.

. Of this able work 3000 have already been sold in America.

The New Testament Narrative, in the
Words of the Sacred Writers. With Notes,
Chronological Tables, and Maps. A book for
those who, as a matter of education or of devotion,
wish to be thoroughly well acquainted with the
Life of our Lord. What is narrated by each of
His Evangelists is woven into a continuous and
chronological narrative. Thus the study of the
Gospels is complete and yet easy. Cloth, 2s.

" The compilers deserve great praise for the manner in which
they have performed their task. We commend this little volume
as well and carefully printed, and as furnishing its readers, more-

BURNS, OATES, & CO., 17, PORTMAN STREET, W.

over, with a great amount of useful information in the tables inserted at the end."—*Month.*

" It is at once clear, complete, and beautiful."—*Catholic Opinion*

Balmez : Protestantism and Catholicism
compared in their Effects upon European Civilisa-
tion. Cloth, 7s. 6d.

    ⁎⁎ A new edition of this far-famed Treatise.

The See of St. Peter. By T. W. ALLIES.
A new and improved edition, with Preface on
the present State of the Controversy. 4s. 6d.

Lallemant's Doctrine of the Spiritual Life.
Edited by Dr. FABER. New Edition. Cloth,
4s. 6d.

" This excellent work has a twofold value, being both a biography and a volume of meditations. Father Lallemant's life
does not abound with events, but its interest lies chiefly in the
fact that his world and his warfare were within. His ' Spiritual
Doctrine' contains an elaborate analysis of the wants, dangers,
trials, and aspirations of the inner man, and supplies to the
thoughtful and devout reader the most valuable instructions for
the attainment of heavenly wisdom, grace, and strength."—
Catholic Times.

" A treatise of the very highest value."—*Month.*

" The treatise is preceded by a short account of the writer's
life, and has had the wonderful advantage of being edited by the
late Father Faber."—*Weekly Register.*

" One of the very best of Messrs. Burns and Co.'s publications
is this new edition of F. Lallemant's ' Spiritual Doctrine.'"—
Westminster Gazette.

The Rivers of Damascus and Jordan : a
    Causerie. By a Tertiary of the Order of St.
    Dominick. 4s.

"Good solid reading."—*Month.*

"Well done, and in a truly charitable spirit."—*Catholic Opinion.*

"It treats the subject in so novel and forcible a light, that we
are fascinated in spite of ourselves, and irresistibly led on to follow
its arguments and rejoice at its conclusions."—*Tablet.*

Eudoxia : a Tale of the Fifth Century.
    From the German of IDA, COUNTESS HAHN-
    HAHN. Cloth elegant, 4s.

"This charming tale may be classed among such instructive as
well as entertaining works as 'Fabiola' and 'Callista.' It adds
another laurel to the brow of the fair Countess."—*Weekly Register.*

"Instructive and interesting book."—*Northern Press.*

Tales for the Many. By CYRIL AUSTIN.
    In Five Numbers, at 2d. each; also, cloth, 1s.;
    gilt edges, 1s. 6d.

"Calculated to do good in our lending-libraries."—*Tablet.*

"We wish the volume all the success it deserves, and shall
always welcome with pleasure any effort from the same quarter."
—*Weekly Register.*

"One of the most delightful books which Messrs. Burns and
Oates have brought out to charm children at this festive season."
—*Catholic Opinion.*

In the Snow ; or, Tales of Mount St.
    Bernard. By the Rev Dr. ANDERDON. Cloth
    neat, 3s. 6d.

"A collection of pretty stories."—*Star.*

"An excellent book for a present."—*Universe.*

BURNS, OATES, & CO., 17, PORTMAN STREET, W.

"A capital book of stories."—*Catholic Opinion.*
"An agreeable book."—*Church Review.*
"An admirable fireside companion."—*Nation.*
"A very interesting volume of tales."—*Freeman.*
"Several successive stories are related by different people assembled together, and thus a greater scope is given for variety, not only of the matter, but also the tone of each story, according to the temper and position of the narrators. Beautifully printed, tastefully bound, and reflects great credit on the publishers."
"A pleasing contribution."—*Month.*
"A charming volume. We congratulate Catholic parents and children on the appearance of a book which may be given by the former with advantage, and read by the latter with pleasure and edification."—*Dublin Review.*

By the same Author.

The Seven Ages of Clarewell : A History of a Spot of Ground. Cloth, 3s.

"We have an attractive work from the pen of an author who knows how to combine a pleasing and lively style with the promotion of the highest principles and the loftiest aims. The volume before us is beautifully bound, in a similar way to 'In the Snow,' by the same author, and is therefore very suitable for a present."—*Westminster Gazette.*
"A pleasing novelty in the style and character of the book, which is well and clearly sustained in the manner it is carried out."—*Northern Press.*
"Each stage furnishes the material for a dramatic scene; are very well hit off, and the whole makes up a graphic picture."—*Month.*
"'Clarewell' will give not only an hour of pleasant reading, but will, from the nature of the subject, be eminently suggestive of deep and important truths."—*Tablet.*

WORKS BY LADY GEORGIANA FULLERTON.

Life of Mary Fitzgerald, a Child of the Sacred Heart. Price 1s.; cloth extra, 2s.

BURNS, OATES, & CO., 63, PATERNOSTER ROW, E.C.

WORKS BY LADY GEORGIANA FULLERTON (continued).

Rose Leblanc. A Tale of great interest. Cloth, 3s.

Grantley Manor. (The well-known and favourite Novel). Cloth, 3s.; cheap edition, 2s. 6d.

Life of St. Frances of Rome. Neat cloth, 2s. 6d.; cheap edition, 1s. 8d.

Edited by the Same.

Our Lady's Little Books. Neat cloth, 2s.; separate Numbers, 4d. each.

Life of the Honourable E. Dormer, late of the 60th Rifles. 1s.; cloth extra, 2s.

Helpers of the Holy Souls. 6d.

Tales from the Diary of a Sister of Mercy. By C. M. BRAME.

CONTENTS : The Double Marriage—The Cross and the Crown—The Novice—The Fatal Accident—The Priest's Death—The Gambler's Wife—The Apostate —The Besetting Sin.

Beautifully bound in bevelled cloth, 3s. 6d.

"Written in a chaste, simple, and touching style."—*Tablet.*
"This book is a casket; and those who open it will find the gem within."—*Register.*
"Calculated to promote the spread of virtue, and to check that of vice; and cannot fail to have a good effect upon all—young and old—into whose hands it may fall."—*Nation.*
"A neat volume, composed of agreeable and instructive tales.

BURNS, OATES, & CO., 17, *PORTMAN STREET, W.*

Each of its tales concludes with a moral, which supplies food for reflection."—*Westminster Gazette.*

"They are well and cleverly told, and the volume is neatly got up."—*Month.*

"Very well told; all full of religious allusions and expressions."—*Star.*

"Very well written, and life-like—many very pathetic."—*Catholic Opinion.*

"An excellent work; reminds us forcibly of Father Price's 'Sick Calls.' "—*Universe.*

"A very interesting series of tales."—*Sun.*

By the Same.

Angels' Visits : A Series of Tales. With Frontispiece and Vignette. 3s. 6d.

"The tone of the book is excellent, and it will certainly make itself a great favourite with the young."—*Month.*

"Beautiful collection of Angel Stories. All who may wish to give any dear children a book which speaks in tones suited to the sweet simplicity of their innocent young hearts about holy things cannot do better than send for 'Angels' Visits.' "—*Weekly Register.*

"One of the prettiest books for children we have seen."—*Tablet.*

"A book which excites more than ordinary praise. We have great satisfaction in recommending to parents and all who have the charge of children this charming volume."—*Northern Press.*

"A good present for children. An improvement on the 'Diary of a Sister of Mercy.' "—*Universe.*

"Touchingly written, and evidently the emanation of a refined and pious mind."—*Church Times.*

"A charming little book, full of beautiful stories of the family of angels."—*Church Opinion.*

"A nicely-written volume."—*Bookseller.*

"Gracefully-written stories."—*Star.*

Just out, ornamental cloth, 5s.

Legends of Our Lady and the Saints: or, Our Children's Book of Stories in Verse. Written

for the Recitations of the Pupils of the Schools of the Holy Child Jesus, St. Leonards-on-Sea. Cheap Edition, 2s. 6d.

"It is a beautiful religious idea that is realised in the 'Legends of Our Lady and the Saints.' We are bound to add that it has been successfully carried out by the good nuns of St. Leonards. The children of their Schools are unusually favoured in having so much genius and taste exerted for their instruction and delight. The book is very daintily decorated and bound, and forms a charming present for pious children."—*Tablet.*

"The 'Legends' are so beautiful, that they ought to be read by all lovers of poetry."—*Bookseller.*

"Graceful poems."—*Month.*

Edith Sydney: a Tale of the Catholic Movement. By Miss OXENHAM. 5s.

"A novel for the novel-reader, and at the same time it is a guide to the convert and a help to their instructors."—*Universe.*

"Miss Oxenham shows herself to be a fair writer of a controversial tale, as well as a clever delineator of character."—*Tablet.*

"A charming romance. We introduce 'Edith Sydney' to our readers, confident that she will be a safe and welcome visitor in many a domestic circle, and will attain high favour with the Catholic reading public."—*Nation.*

"Miss Oxenham seems to possess considerable powers for the delineation of character and incident."—*Month.*

Not Yet: a Tale of the Present Time. By Miss OXENHAM. 5s.

"The lighter order of Catholic literature receives a very welcome addition in this story, which is original and very striking. The author is mistress of a style which is light and pleasant. The work is one to which we can give our heartiest commendation."—*Cork Examiner.*

"We are indebted to Miss Oxenham for one of the most interesting sensational Catholic tales yet published." — *Catholic Opinion*.

"Wholesome and pleasant reading, evincing a refined and cultivated understanding."—*Union Review*.

"Miss Oxenham's work would rank well even among Mudie's novels, although its one-volume form is likely to be unfavourable in the eyes of ordinary novel-readers; but, in nine cases out of ten, a novelette is more effective than a regular novel, and any more padding would have merely diluted the vivid and unflagging interest which the authoress of 'Not Yet' has imparted to her elegantly-bound volume. The plot is as original as a plot can be; it is well laid and careful'y and ably worked out."—*Westminster Gazette*.

Nellie Netterville: a Tale of Ireland in the Time of Cromwell. By CECILIA CADDELL, Author of "Wild Times." 5s.; cheap edition, 3s. 6d.

"A very interesting story. The author's style is pleasing, picturesque, and good, and we recommend our readers to obtain the book for themselves."—*Church News*.

"A tale well told and of great interest."—*Catholic Opinion*.

"Pretty pathetic story—well told."—*Star*.

"Pretty book-history of cruelties inflicted by Protestant domination in the sister country—full of stirring and affecting passages."—*Church Review*.

"Tale is well told, and many of the incidents, especially the burning of the chapel with the priest and congregation by the Cromwellian soldiers, are intensely interesting."—*Universe*.

"By a writer well known, whose reputation will certainly not suffer by her new production."—*Month*.

Marie; or, the Workwoman of Liège. By CECILIA CADDELL. Cloth, 3s. 6d.

"This is another of those valuable works like that of 'Marie Eustelle Harpain.' Time would fail us were we to enumerate either her marvellous acts of charity, or the heroic sufferings she endured for the sake of others, or the wonderful revelations with which her faith and charity were rewarded."—*Tablet.*

"The author of 'Wild Times,' and other favourite works, is to be congratulated on the issue of a volume which is of more service than any book of fiction, however stirring. It is a beautiful work—beautiful in its theme and in its execution."—*Weekly Register.*

"Miss Caddell has given us a very interesting biography of 'Marie Sellier, the Workwoman of Liège,' known in the 17th century as 'Sœur Marie Albert.' Examples such as that so gracefully set forth in this volume are much needed among us."—*Month.*

The Countess of Glosswood: a Tale of the Times of the Stuarts. From the French. 3s. 6d.

"The tale is well written, and the translation seems cleverly done."—*Month.*

"This volume is prettily got up, and we can strongly recommend it to all as an excellent and instructive little book to place in the hands of the young."—*Westminster Gazette.*

"An excellent translation, and a very pretty tale, well told."—*Catholic Opinion.*

"This is a pretty tale of a Puritan conversion in the time of Charles II., prettily got up, and a pleasing addition to our lending-libraries."—*Tablet.*

"This tale belongs to a class of which we have had to thank Messrs. Burns for many beautiful specimens. Such books, while they are delightful reading to us who are happily Catholics, have another important merit—they set forth the claims of Catholicism, and must do a vast deal of good among Protestants who casually meet with and peruse them. The book before us is beautifully got up, and would be an ornament to any table."—*Weekly Register.*

BURNS, OATES, & CO., 17, PORTMAN STREET, W.